WILD
WOOD

POSIE GRAEME-EVANS

WILD WOOD

**SIMON &
SCHUSTER**

London · New York · Sydney · Toronto · New Delhi

A CBS COMPANY

First published in the USA by Simon & Schuster, Inc., 2015
First published in Great Britain by Simon & Schuster UK Ltd, 2015
A CBS COMPANY

1 3 5 7 9 10 8 6 4 2

Simon & Schuster UK Ltd
1st Floor
222 Gray's Inn Road
London WC1X 8HB

www.simonandschuster.co.uk

Simon & Schuster Australia, Sydney
Simon & Schuster India, New Delhi

A CIP catalogue record for this book
is available from the British Library

Paperback ISBN: 978-1-4711-4989-4
eBook ISBN: 978-1-4711-4990-0

To Frank Graeme-Evans
My father

You always loved history, Dad,
and maybe fascination with the past is in the
DNA you handed down to me.
And though you're not around to see this book published,
I hope you're smiling.

WILD WOOD

THE BORDERLANDS, NOVEMBER 1068

I HEAR THEM." The child huddles at the Mother's feet. She claps her hands twice, imploring attention. But the shining face does not change. Why had she believed it would? Stone is not flesh.

The little girl has watched men on horses, many men, ride into the valley all day. Small as ants from this height, they boil among the trees, shouting to each other. *What are they doing?* The child wears a cape of rabbit fur and shoes of skin, but she shivers. They come from the direction of her village, and smoke is rising beside the river.

She must have faith. She's been sent by her grandmother to offer holly berries at the pool outside the Red Door. She was proud to be chosen, but now she is frightened.

Below! A woman. Screaming.

Panicked, the child scrambles to the fissure that guards the entrance to the cave.

Outside is terror. Men swarm on the narrow path.

They will find the pool! The child is shocked. Only women come here.

She hesitates, half in light.

1

A shout. A man in armor points and spurs his horse to the pool.

"Arrête!" The animal is rammed through the troops, and men leap away. They might not understand the language, but they know the look.

The hard-faced rider has seen the child. He turns in his saddle. "The treasure is here?" The knight speaks the bastard Norman-Norse of all Duke William's followers.

His captain, following behind, is tempted to shrug. But does not. "So they said in the village." Night is close. They must make camp soon. The men are restless; there were women in the last village, and like dogs the men scent the captives.

A grunt, and the Norman jumps from his horse. A path clears to the fissure in the cliff face. They have all seen him fight, and he knows they call him the Wolf, or the Devil.

He tears cobwebs with his sword but must bend to find a way through the opening. It's dark inside the cliff, but there's something shining and . . .

He stops with a jerk.

And laughs out loud at his fear.

Perhaps, for a breath, he had thought a woman stood there. A silver woman. But it's a statue, a tall, pagan idol, among pillars of the same glittering rock.

The Norman strides closer. The idol, unseemly in its naked-ness, does look like a woman—arms, hips, breasts—though the face has holes for eyes and a mouth. She holds a child in one arm and seems to stare at him. Closer, and he sees she too was once a limestone pillar until someone released her shape from the stone.

"A treasure?" The Norman snorts. The peasants here must have the minds of children.

He stares around the cave. He cannot see the child, if child there was. The light was dropping outside. And where could she hide? This place is empty.

He turns to go and finds something curious. A thicket of red handprints is pressed on the rock around the entrance. More pagan rubbish. Another reason to despise the hardly human creatures who live in the forest here. The priests will sort them out—save their souls. If they have souls.

"Did you find it?" The captain holds the stirrup for his leader.

"Treasure? No. They lied to you. That was foolish, as they will understand."

"And the child?"

"There was no child." The commander swings a leg over the saddle and has a first clear sight of the crag above, crowned with great oaks. "What do you see?"

His captain follows the Norman's finger.

"There is the real treasure." The commander waves at the stream falling from the pool to the river below. "Water. And a place to build my keep. And timber. Very good timber." The Norman smiles. He actually smiles.

His captain does not know if this is good or bad.

The child hears the men ride away. She has been hiding, in a place that only women know.

The cave is dark now, but the Mother shines. She always shines. A light in the shadows of their lives.

And the little girl kneels. And claps her hands. The Mother will hear her. And she will help. She always helps.

1

LONDON, JUNE 1981

JESSE MARLEY adopts a smile like it's an orphan. Looked at from the outside, there's confidence in that long stride as she pushes on through waves and flurries of strangers, anonymous in that happy crush.

In six weeks Prince Charles and Lady Diana will marry, and London is already full and swelling as tides of people glut the streets, the hotels, the theaters, and the pubs. Jesse might be one of them—just another tourist waiting for the wedding, loving all the excitement. But she's not.

She's dressed carefully today. There's the skirt—summery, cut on the bias, floral—and a voile shirt with a Peter Pan collar. A cute denim jacket is slung over the top, and flat pink shoes tone with the skirt. Respectable. Feminine. A nice change, some would say, but are they good enough, are her clothes right?

Nerves.

And, yes, she's overthinking again, but Jesse can't escape the feeling that *they* might be looking for her, just as she's looking for them. She's tried not to think that thought ever since she arrived in this sweaty city three days ago; the idea that the two people she wants to meet most in all the world could be in London, could, actually, be among those on this footpath today, is glorious. And strange.

Would it really be so weird to meet by chance? Everything else in these last weeks has been on the far side of odd—why not this too?

Play the game. Just pretend.

So Jesse stops, and the mass of hurrying people divides around her, as if she's an island in a river. Eyes half closed, she filters faces looking for clues.

That tall woman in the blazer with the shoulder pads? She's got a good face and the age is right. The man striding beside her is well dressed too. If she's her, maybe that's him.

A surge of people sweeps the couple past. They stare at Jesse because she's smiling at them, but there's no flicker of recognition—she's just a face in this place of far too many faces.

Jesse's disappointed, but she isn't crushed. There'd be recognition on both sides, so they can't be the ones.

Ah, London. Too many cars, too many people—scrums marching in lockstep push her to the curb too often—*and* there's the smog. She'd thought Sydney was bad, but this? The air has substance.

Jesse doesn't have a handkerchief, so she wipes sweat from her face with one hand as a woman pushes past. She gets it when the stranger looks through her. She's been judged. It's not just what she wears or how she walks; so often it's as soon as she opens her mouth and they hear the accent.

"Hah!" She hadn't meant to shout.

Pin-striped, bowler-hatted, a man stares.

A bowler? Things like that belong in black-and-white movies. But Jesse so longs to stop him and say, "It's okay. I don't bite. I'm lost, you see, and . . ." Lost? In many more ways than one.

Jesse clutches the strap of her shoulder bag as if it's a rope thrown to the drowning, something that can save her from herself. Maybe that's the literal truth, because inside the bag is the envelope. She wants to open it, but to think she soon will makes her heart fill her chest.

Washed by fear, strafed by yearning, Jesse ignores the traffic; she just wants to get to the other side of the road.

Bad idea.

Good, though, that the guy on the Norton was just idling past. Well, almost good, because that instant the motorcycle sweeps her away doesn't actually hurt. Not then.

Heads swivel. Someone screams. Three strangers, two men, one girl, rush to help. Even the guy who's knocked her down gets up and limps over, leaving all that vintage machinery splayed on the road without a glance.

This is all surreal.

Swatting kind hands away, Jesse levers to her knees, stands, and wobbles as she smooths her skirt,

"No, I'm fine. Really. This?" Her pretty blouse is a bit ripped at the front. Well, a lot ripped. She pulls the jacket closed, but moving her right arm hurts. "No, really, it's nothing. Thanks. Truthfully, all's well. I just didn't see."

The bag! Panicked, she tries to find it. Gutter. Footpath. "My shoulder bag? Has anyone seen my—"

The guy who took her down looks even more embarrassed. He almost points, but clears his throat instead.

There it is, still on the *other* shoulder. "I just need to be—that is . . ." *Somewhere*, anywhere, out of this.

Jesse takes the piece of paper he offers. The guy's scribbled an address and his name on the back of, what? A butcher's bill.

"George, is it? Thanks. I mean, that is, you're very kind. It was my fault." She can feel her face hitch up in a grin.

That confuses the poor man, but Jesse doesn't offer him her name. And she doesn't have an address; just the hostel, and she's only staying there for one more night.

"That's my bus." It isn't, but it's stopping and at least she knows the name on the front: Smithfield. Jesse half runs, to the extent she can. And lurches up the steps as the front door sighs open.

"Ticket?"

"What?"

"Where's your ticket, love?" The black driver is a patient man but it's lunchtime.

Her right shoulder hurts now, as well as her arm, so Jesse scrabbles with her left hand in the bag. "It's here somewhere." She's so close to crying when she hands it over.

The man clips her pass, and Jesse stumbles along the deck as the bus takes off. There's an empty seat by the back door and, wincing, she swings herself into it, left hand on the pole.

Where is she going, really?

Away. That's all. Away from this place to another one.

But the old bus bumps over a broken road near Smithfield Market, more pothole and rut than street, and Jesse pings the bell. Enough!

She stands alone among another crowd as the bus growls away from the curb.

And starts to walk. There's a hospital around here; maybe she should get her arm checked. Or, not so much her arm but her shoulder, though it'll cost money she doesn't have.

No. Can't be done.

There's a secret in this busy street, and Jesse finds it though she doesn't know she's looking. Maybe the entrance is deliberately hard to spot and that's why she almost walks past. Almost. But she stops when she sees the sign to St. Bartholomew the Great. A garden is on the other side of an open, ancient door, a place of green leaves and soft light. And there's an empty bench to sit on. Maybe she'll just catch her breath, only for a moment.

Nearly a thousand years old, this church: that's what the sign says. That's around how old Jesse feels. Her head's aching and her right shoulder—well, it doesn't feel much like a shoulder. It feels like a thing that's all about misery.

Like an old woman, she walks the path between the graves, makes it to the seat, and sits. She's not Zen enough to ignore her shoulder; it hit the ground first and the throb in the joint is a half-heard drum.

Can she will the pain away? She tries.

No.

Face it.

Ah. Of course. The inner voice.

But Jesse doesn't want to *face* whatever is brewing between her ears. Too much facing of things lately. Way too much.

She shrugs. And almost screams. In that giddy moment, vomit fills her mouth.

Breathe deep! Deeper. Head down. Go on.

As the trees, at last, regain their proper places in the sky, Jesse sighs. Sun is coming from somewhere.

But she can't allow herself to rest.

Very, very carefully, she opens her bag with the good arm and finds it. She stares at the thing in her hand. It doesn't look like a bomb. It looks innocent. Public-service beige, her name on the front: Jesse Marley. It's the one she's used to. Maybe that's good.

Is it hard to open an envelope? Sometimes. Today it's impossible.

Jesse puts it back in the bag.

Wedged into a corner of the cloisters is a café. The Brits would call it a tearoom, wouldn't they? So, yes, let there be . . .

"Tea?" The girl behind the counter has a pleasant face. Not especially pretty—in fact, not pretty at all—but her skin is beautiful, clear, bright, and soft. Only the English or the Irish seem to win the skin lottery. All that water in the air? Must be.

But another asset surrounds that plain face: tawny hair that swings in a mass when the girl moves her head.

"Can you make an espresso?" Jesse smiles without hope.

Those sincerely apologetic eyes. "I'm so awfully sorry, we only do instant."

What is this place? Does no one know how to make coffee in London? It's 1981! Jesse doesn't let it show; she shakes her head politely. "Tea's fine. Really." She doesn't ask what it is. There's no point. Tea's tea in England.

"Help yourself to a table. Would you like something to eat?" She has a name badge, this gracious waitress: ALICIA.

Not wanting to stare, Jesse looks away.

Alicia. So English. Such an educated voice too. A class marker, that voice. This girl might be working in a café, but she comes from somewhere, went to a "good" school. Plainly.

"Is that an Eccles cake?"

Don't buy it.

But Alicia provides permission—encouragement, even. "I'll bring it with the tea. Everyone needs a little treat." Her smile matches the skin. Flawless teeth decorate her mouth, and her eyes twinkle nicely. Very un-English.

Jesse warms to Alicia. She might be all class, but she's also endearing. Does endearing get you further than good legs? Probably not. Maybe. But you'd have to work harder.

Jesse sighs. Once, she'd been so sure of herself, so gregarious. Confident, even. Now all she wants is a table on her own. And she'd like to be invisible while she licks her wounds—the psychic ones—and reads the letter.

A table at the far end of the café has a view of the garden. Jesse sits with great care, her back to the few customers, but it's hard to take the bag off her shoulder. Somehow she eases out of the jacket too. She's feeling hot.

Alicia follows her. She puts a small china teapot on the table, a matching cup and saucer, and what might possibly be a silver jug of milk—and even a strainer in its own little bowl. Last, the plate with the treat. Tea and cakes. The British gift to civilization. "It looks very nice."

The girl seems pleased. "Let me know if I can get you anything else. It's no trouble." One quick glance from the waitress as she goes back to the counter lets Jesse know her disheveled appearance has been noted. Noted, but perhaps not judged. Not that kind of a girl, Alicia, not toffee-nosed; in fact, she looks kind, full stop.

Jesse stares down at her cup. She sips. Fragrant and really hot. Really delicious as well. And the Eccles cake. As promised, sensational. Currants, sugar, butter. Comprehensive sin. But God is just beyond the cloister, so that's all right.

Jesse closes her eyes to savor the tastes.

So, feeling better?

Jesse jumps. "Sorry?"

The waitress is beside her. "Pardon?" She's mopping crumbs that somehow leapt off the plate.

"Did you say something?" Jesse's confused.

The girl smiles. "No. Would you like anything else?" She nods at the empty plate.

"A new life would be good." Jesse would grin, but her face is hurting. And her head.

"You've come to the right place, then." A final swipe and that lovely smile.

"What?" Jesse stares.

Alicia nods. "I'd talk to Rahere. He's a very good listener." The girl tilts her head toward the entrance to the church.

Jesse smiles uncertainly. "Oh. Well, might go and introduce myself."

"He's always there, day and night. You'll find him by the altar."

"Rahere. Is that a first name?"

"Yes. Well, first and last together." The waitress picks up the tray. "Finished?"

As Jesse's fingers dance on the tabletop—nerves—she mentally counts through the meager stock of coins and notes in her wallet. She's still got to pay for the hostel, cheap as it is, and if she's going north, she'll use up what's left; maybe she'll get a temp job somewhere to cover costs. Absolutely, definitely, she shouldn't have had the cake. "How much do I owe you?"

"One pound and seventy-five pence."

Jesse scrapes back her chair and goes to the counter. "Is Rahere the pastor here—the, um, vicar?"

Alicia seems less plain with each smile. "No. He's the founder of the church. And the hospital."

Awkwardly, Jesse counts the coins with her left hand. "The founder?" She picks up a brochure on the counter. "But the church is over nine hundred years old, right?"

"It's his tomb you want." Alicia makes little shooing motions.

Jesse doesn't even blink. *Advice from the dead, recommended by a stranger.* That fits.

The great church is empty. A tiered rack for votive candles is in a side chapel. It might be blasphemous if you no longer believe, but Jesse puts ten pence in the tin and lights a taper anyway.

The rap of her heels disturbs the hush as she looks for Rahere's tomb. It lies in a wall niche, and the face and hands of his effigy are glazed a tanned pink while his head rests on a red pillow with gold tassels. His robe, so crisply carved, is shiny black. He has company too—a crowned angel holds up a heraldic shield at his feet.

Favoring her damaged shoulder, Jesse sits in a chair across from the tomb and scans the brochure. *It says here you were known to be cheerful, Rahere. That you liked helping people.* She stares at the effigy. *So, can I ask you for that—just to be cheerful while I sort this mess out? I don't want to be bitter. I don't want to be angry. I just want to know.*

Jesse's eyes fill. She sniffs; manages to rub one eye and then the other. As if she's got something stuck.

She's avoided grief for some time now, pushed it down, closed the lid on that box and locked it up. Now, like an idiot, she's allowed misery to jump out and sock her right in the eye.

There's only one thing to do; she knows it. Reaching into her bag, she takes the envelope out, rips the top, and unfolds the birth certificate.

The details.

Child: female. Name: Jesse Mary. Date of Birth: 1st August 1956.

She stares at Rahere. *Does this feel like betrayal to you? It does to me.* Her birthday's always been celebrated on October 3.

Jesse keeps reading. *Place of Birth: Jedburgh, Berwickshire.*

Mother's Name: Eva Green.

Date of Birth: 13th March 1940.

Occupation: blank.

Father: unknown.

Something hits in Jesse's chest, hard as a fist.

No father?

In that moment she's certain she will choke. But. She doesn't.

There's a word, *Informant*, with a signature beside it.

Jesse makes herself look at it. Anything to avoid the other information. Peering, she can see a woman's name—it's hard to read—and there's an abbreviation at the front of it: *Sr.* Her finger traces the name. *Mary Joseph.* And beside the last name—*Magdalene?*—there's a cross inscribed.

At least the address is clear: *Holly House, Priorsgate, Jedburgh, Berwickshire, Scotland.*

Jesse stares. She's Scottish? She's been told she was born in Durham.

Date of registration: 23rd October 1956.

In Sydney, when she went to apply for her passport, that registration date was the first clue that something was wrong. She'd handed over what she thought was her birth certificate, the one she'd found in her mother's—no, her *adoptive* mother's—desk in their house in Crows Nest, and they'd queried the date her birth had been registered; turned out, October 1956 was months after she'd actually been born, according to British records. That happened, sometimes, in cases of informal adoption between family members. It was a way of fudging the actual date of birth.

Conclusion? She'd handed over a falsified birth certificate.

The irony was, Jesse was getting her first adult passport as a surprise for her parents. A nice one. She'd saved for two years after university earning crap money and working two jobs—typing for a solicitor during the day, cleaning at night—because she so, *so* wanted to go to England in the summer and see the place she was born for real. And then Charles and Di got engaged.

Her friends all laughed, but Jesse didn't care. She just wanted to stand on a London street and see them pass by. Be a part of living history, part of their fairy tale—the prince and his virgin bride.

Her parents had never been keen on Jesse's traveling by herself, and she thought she'd understood the reason—a girl, all alone, out in the big world. So she'd meant to get her passport and say to Janet and Malcolm, "Come with me! Let's all go home together and be there for the wedding. My treat."

But there'd been no ticket for her mum and dad. Because they weren't her mum and dad.

In Sydney, the woman Jesse called Mum had slammed her bedroom door and cried all day behind it when Jesse even tried to ask that loaded question: *Who am I?*

Malcolm, her father, shook his head when she trapped him in the kitchen. "I knew this day would come. I warned your mother so."

And he'd walked out of the house. Jesse knew he'd gone to the pub; a nearly silent man, he always went there when her mum asked too much of him. Which was often, in his terms.

When she was past teenage sulking, Jesse had wondered sometimes if her parents' marriage was actually happy. They organized their lives in the length of the pauses between the careful words they spoke to each other, and in what was *not* said in Jesse's hearing. After she was about nine years old, Jesse knew that something was being managed between the two—between all three of them—in that quiet house. And she'd not understood what it was.

Now she does.

And here it is. Her real birth certificate, picked up fresh today on this far side of the world. The actual object. The thing that proves who she is. A bastard child. Jesse stares at the paper in her hand. It feels as if she can see right through to the other side, as if her eyes were scalpels slicing truth to strips of nothing.

She touches the letters on the page.

This is her mother's name. Her actual mother. Eva Green.

Why did you give me away, Mum?

That does it. Tears drip, and when Jesse bends her head, they're a torrent she can't stop.

She tries to stifle the sound but she can't bear this. The pain. All kinds of pain.

It's a while before she wipes her face one-handed. *Stand up. Come on. Sitting here will solve nothing.*

Cruel, but fair. "You're right."

Holding to the back of the chair in front, Jesse stands. She's done sniveling, she's done feeling sorry for herself, and she'll ignore the shoulder too. But she chews her bottom lip. That's a habit when she worries.

Is it something you do, Mum?

Maybe she'll skip the hospital, go to a pharmacist and get a painkiller. Then she'll go back to the hostel and sleep; tomorrow will be better. She'll *make* it better because she'll find a library and scour what they have about Jedburgh. And libraries have telephone books. She can look up everyone called Green in Scotland. And she'll ring them all.

That's a decision. And a plan. "There you are."

Jesse has her hand on the door to the outer porch of St. Bartholomew.

"You left this?" The waitress holds out Jesse's jacket. "Too

pretty to lose, but I didn't want to disturb you in the church."
Alicia smiles warmly.

"Thanks." Half turned away, Jesse's hiding her face. But she
fumbles the handover and her bag drops to the floor. Out spill far
too many things, including the birth certificate.

"Let me." The waitress bobs down. Jesse drops too, just as
Alicia stands. Their skulls connect.

Jesse's knocked back on her shoulder as she falls. She can't
breathe and the vault reels above her head.

"What a day you're having." The other girl reaches out a hand.

Sobbing a breath, Jesse takes it. But she can't control her face,
and she can't stand.

"Up you come." Alicia, this surprising girl, helps Jesse to her
feet. Alicia's touch is gentle but her arms are strong. "I think you
need to rest for a while."

"I couldn't, really. I have to—that is . . ."

There's a door marked STAFF ONLY, and it's easily opened.
Beyond is a room filled with mismatched furniture, but there's a
couch. Alicia fluffs a cushion, places it invitingly. "It's quite comfortable. Why not sleep for a little while?"

Jesse stutters, "N-no. That is, I do need to go. You've been
so kind and . . ." But she sits anyway. She can't fall down again.
Three times in one morning? Too much.

"Put your feet up." Alicia tucks an old picnic rug around Jesse's
legs.

Jesse wants to reply, wants to say thank you, but the rug does
it. She just can't speak.

Pressing a box of tissues into the girl's hand, Alicia opens the
door soundlessly as she leaves.

Jesse's alone. She cries until her eyes swell shut, head ringing
like a bell.

Jesse shifts in her sleep, twitches and sighs. Her eyes open. She struggles to sit up. Pain bites her shoulder like a dog. She screams out, "Christ!" Shaking, she tries to look at the watch on her right wrist. Past one o'clock!

Jesse fumbles the rug off. She stands. Too fast. Feeling sick, she grasps at a table as Alicia opens the door.

"Got it." The waitress catches the lamp before it hits the floor. Somewhere, through the open door, people sing Gregorian plainchant. Calm as a distant sea.

Jesse mutters, "What are you, patron saint of people who fall over?" She's trying to keep it light.

"That would be the social worker. Comes Mondays and Wednesdays." Alicia picks up the rug and shakes it out, folds it in three. And again. A neat shape. "I heard you stir."

Where "stirring" is blasphemy. In a church. "Sorry to have been a nuisance." Jesse picks up her jacket as she tries to flex her shoulder. Gasps.

"Sore?"

Sweating, Jesse sort of nods. Her head doesn't want to help. It's blazing in there; red, black, white—pain of many colors given form.

"Um, a friend of mine sings in the choir here." Alicia gestures through the door. "They practice at lunchtime. He's a doctor at Barts and . . ."

"Please don't think me rude, Alicia, but I do really have to go. I feel much better. Honestly." Jesse tries not to flinch as she picks up her bag. "Must do this again sometime." She makes it to the door. Forgetting, she pushes it open. Her right hand.

Did someone just remove a hunk of bone? Pain explodes and Jesse cannons into the doorjamb, slides to the floor. Four, today. A record.

"Alicia?" A man's voice. Legs in the doorway, knees level with Jesse's nose. A startled pause. "Hello. No. Stay put. Don't try to get up."

She knows she can't move, not now, but Jesse seems to see the voice that comes out of the man's face as it looms closer to hers. The sound distorts, slows down, as her eyes drift closed because she's very, very tired.

"Who is she?"

"I don't know."

A rustle. Jesse hears breathing close by. A large hand covers her forehead completely. Feels cool.

"Can you tell me your name?" The male voice, speaking each word really, really slowly.

She manages, "Jesse." It's thick-sounding. What's her mouth doing?

"I think you might be concussed, Jesse."

She winches her eyes open—who knew eyelids weighed so much?—and murmurs, "Okay."

He's smiling at her. Faint, but genuine. So's Alicia.

Jesse tries to sit up. That doesn't go well.

"We need to get you to the hospital." He's kneeling beside her. Quite close. Red hair. No. Chestnut. Pale eyes—water-green, water-blue. That English skin. Looks good, even on a man.

A deep breath. If she talks on the *out*, the pain isn't as bad. "Don't have insurance." She'd shrug if she could. Her eyelids droop.

Jesse hears two voices. Him. Her. Him again. Then another rustle as Alicia squats down.

Jesse knows Alicia's smell now. Soap from a morning bath— wouldn't be a shower—and clean hair.

"Jesse, you don't have to pay."

Then him. "You'll be admitted into emergency. I think you need to be."

Magic words, *You don't have to pay.*

Jesse surrenders to the dark.

2

M AUGRIS GAVE me the signal, a hand swept across the throat. *Death.*

I turned in the saddle, repeated my brother's gesture. Rauf nodded, passed the message to Tamas and John and the others massed behind.

It was the dark of the moon before dawn, and there was nothing to show that we lay so close to our enemies. Maugris, my brother, was a careful leader; he had ordered mud rubbed on each cuirass, so that no surface shone.

Our family knew the worth of fighting men and always had. These past weeks had been blood-soaked as we did what was asked of us, but Rauf and the others understood we would not waste even a single life—not theirs and not ours. The core of our band had survived three years in the service of our overlords, the Percys, and their overlord, Edward, the king in London. But Scotland was a flint-hard country then, and while Robert Bruce had beaten Edward Plantagenet seven years ago at Bannockburn, the Scots were foolish to think us crushed. Their contempt was our best weapon.

Snorting, a horse flung up its head. Maugris glared at the rider. Sound travels at night.

19

I kneed Helios close to my brother's roan and pointed at the breach in the high wall. It was hard to see, but it was there—I had found it scouting ahead of the others. The earth ramparts of the fort were not well maintained. Perhaps that spoke of few men and fewer supplies, or poor leaders; perhaps it spoke of arrogance. This place lay far inside Scottish lands. And if the brigands there thought themselves safe, that only friends would approach these walls, they were wrong.

Maugris nodded. Helios had the strength to charge the slope and jump the gap in the wall. The others? We would find out. But we had cut our way into such places before and would not linger. The reivers of the Scots borders used this fort as a base for raids into our English lands. We would destroy it, and them, and run.

I beckoned Rauf, a veteran of the wars of the East March, and the man nudged his horse forward. I made the sign of a bow being drawn and held up two fingers. He nodded and scanned the men. Tamas and John, one young, one old, both steady, had bows slung across their chests; Rauf waved them close. Two to ride, two to cover.

I trusted our lieutenant. Rauf was good with a sword, better with a dirk. And pitiless.

Maugris offered his sword to me and I touched it with my own, blade to blade; *Dame Fortune be our friend.* All soldiers are superstitious. We were no different.

Do not think.

I pulled the reins short, spurred Helios, and set him running at the breach. I heard Rauf behind, only a pace away, and I could not falter or his horse would run us down.

It was the day of the solstice, and yet the air was bitter; it numbed my face as the stallion sprang the gap. But Fortune kept us safe. Mist had settled inside the walls, a covering as we ran for the gate.

At full gallop, a heavy horse will shake the earth. Perhaps this woke the sentry to his death. The man startled awake as Rauf's knife slashed a mouth in his throat; he made no sound as he dropped. I flung from the stallion's back and we heaved aside the bar that held the gate.

And so it began.

Arrows skinned the air, and Maugris, howling, our men behind him, charged the shelters of heather and stone that hid the raiders. Half naked, half armed, they boiled from the doorways, still warm from their last mortal sleep. Faces, open mouths, and women in the shadows, screaming as blood flew from the swords that bit and sliced; we had the force of surprise and would soon be gone.

"Burn the huts!" Slashing forward, cutting down, I slung the words away. A misplaced slice and a man's hand fountained through the air—it still held a sword—as I booted Helios through the heaving, howling melee to Rauf's side; at its center, he cut as neatly as a tailor, eyes no brighter than his blade.

A panicked woman screamed; she had a baby in her arms. I saw a man run to the girl. He stood above her, and his blade dealt death in a red and silver wheel. He fought well for her life, for the child; some men's faces, in battle, are not easily forgotten.

"None to live!" My brother had a voice that was always heard. He scythed men like barley as flame bloomed and jumped from thatch to thatch and light flared across bodies, piled in heaps.

Flank beside flank, Rauf and I slashed on, pushing the few defenders away from the open gate, away from freedom. Our horses were scarlet to the hocks, but we, and they, were used to that.

A bellow from Maugris—"Fall back. Back!"—and the band, man by man, obeyed.

I was the last away. Inside the ring fort, there was no movement, and the only sound was the spit and crack of fire. The man and the girl and the child were nowhere I could see.

"Bayard!" Rauf lingered by the gate to see I was safe away.

And then we fled to the east, toward the rising light.

Fog moved over the face of the Pentland Hills, a shawl of rags flung across bracken and moor; it slowed us as we rode. But if it hid the track, there was this advantage: sound is trapped by mist. And snow. Though that was yet to come.

I nudged Helios to a trot and rode up beside Maugris. "Nothing moved as we left."

My brother grunted. It was my role to search for survivors and dispatch them.

This raid had always been a gamble—a foray to stanch a running wound. Yet Maugris led us and we followed, for his orders came from Henry Percy. And if they were never easy commands and some of the Scots raiders in the fort had lived to pursue us, what was different in that? The Scots believed they had won their country back from the English, yet these small wars still swung across the border, out of England into Scotland, and back again. Territory was bought by death, theirs and ours, as it had always been.

And our own troop? They were accustomed to this work, but their hearts had likely shriveled since the morning. Some will deny it, but to kill a child stays with you. Women also. Those faces, those fragile bodies, were too much like their own babies, their own wives.

It was dangerous to think too much. I hunched deeper in my riding cloak and allowed Helios to fall back until I was in my proper place at the rear of the column.

For some time we rode at a league-eating amble until, ahead, Maugris threw up an arm and stopped. "Rauf!"

Our lieutenant cantered up the line, and I, along with the others, watched as the two conferred. We all respected my brother's instincts.

Rauf touched a hand to his helmet. We saw him ride into the

mist behind us, saw it swallow him whole. Soon, there was nothing to hear, not even his horse, though the track was wet.

Maugris held up one hand, palm out. *Wait.*

Time passed—long or short I am not sure. Should I speak to him? His face held no expression, though he inspected the mist as if quartering ground. And he had drawn his sword.

When I caught his eye, he nodded.

I signaled, *Weapons, draw!* And wrenched Helios around, facing him back to where we had come. Now I commanded the front of our troop. Behind, I heard the men. I did not look back. They would be massed in lines, four wide—swords to the front, archers at the rear.

Maugris called out, "Nock!"

A stretching creak as the bows were bent.

Standing in my stirrups, I heard a single horse. Running too fast, a half-seen shape cannoned from the fog. Rauf. "They come!"

Maugris bellowed, "Now!"

I spurred Helios as Rauf wheeled his horse and the men at our backs screamed the challenge.

It was answered.

Fury tore the fog to rags, for as we charged and arrows striped the air, we saw them. Men in filthy plaid on horses half the height of ours. They came at us like wolves, teeth bared to tear our throats out.

But I did not doubt my stallion. Strength and speed and heart would scatter the reivers after the arrows, falling as knives, did their work.

Man, horse, sword, ax—as the mist cleared we saw the truth. The Scots rabble had pursued us too fast, for we were more than they, and better trained; all they had to throw upon the field were their lives and their fury. Neither would be enough.

Snow had begun to fall—snow on this first day of summer— and sight became uncertain. But Maugris cut the sinews of a pony as its rider lunged for me, and therefore I did not die; I took the man's face off from the side. Perhaps he was their chieftain, for seeing him fall, the clansmen scattered. As last blood flew from the blades, the snow, as it settled, turned pink. That startled me. In the pleasance at Hundredfield, my mother had roses of the same delicate hue.

Distracted, I did not see the man with the ax. He came up behind and got a slash away, low and wide.

I twisted, too slow, and we saw each other clear as the face of Christ. This was the man from the fort; bristles sprouted in a circle where hair had been scraped away at the top of his skull.

A monk had tried to kill me.

"Hah!" Maugris. His sword came down between the priest and me. A chance blow, it should have killed him, but it sank into the pony's neck.

The animal screamed and fell, and snow hid the monk as he ran.

"Bayard?" Maugris circled his horse. "Rauf! Over here."

Slumped over the pommel, I raised a hand. "No need."

Rauf waved. He was busy, though few Scots still stood.

Breathing against the pain, I heard the last of the reivers scream.

I did not think I was wounded for the mail I wore was of good quality, and the blow to my ribs seemed more a bruise than a cut. But as Maugris and Rauf gathered our men from the field, the leather under the rings become wet as blood seeped from my chest into my breeches and boots.

I did not tell Maugris.

Soon enough, the blizzard turned corpses to lumps on the ground as we rode to find shelter. But I was weak and, riding behind the men, fell from the stallion's back.

Maugris found me, and that was a strange thing. Too weak to save myself, I had dropped into a drift as the dark busied itself in weaving me a thick, white shroud. . . .

3

THE SOUNDS come first. Rhythmic. Hush in, hush out.
I can't breathe!

But she can. Something is breathing for her.

"Jesse, it's okay." That hand on her arm. She feels it. If she tries really hard, she *can* open her eyes. But the world has become an odd place. As if she's under the sea, air thick as water. *What does that mean?*

Jesse tries to ask the question. Nothing. No sound at all.

He swims into her sight, the man with the chestnut hair.

"There's a tube down your throat, Jesse. It's taking air and oxygen straight into your lungs and bypassing your vocal cords. That's why you can't talk." He pats something out of her line of vision. "It's attached to this. And if you feel strange, we're administering a sedative while you're on the ventilator. You had a seizure as your head wound was being cleaned. Now we want you to rest, and . . ."

Head wound? Seizure? *Ventilator?*

"Nurse?" He can see Jesse's panic.

Someone else wades closer.

"Good to see you looking so much better, Miss Marley." She's sympathetic too. They do a nice line in that here. "When you're a bit stronger, I'll give you a pad to write on. You can ask questions." A bright smile, almost a flourish.

Now. Give it to me now! But when Jesse tries to move her writing hand, it all goes to shit. Pain mauls her shoulder. She wants to scream. She really, really wants to scream.

The shape of the woman wavers, but Jesse hears voices. His and hers. That strange effect again. As if she can see the words. Something about getting a sling for the arm and . . .

Awake?

Eyes open by themselves. Tube still there. Surrounding situation normal—where normal means machines and beds and unconscious people.

Jesse still feels like she's under the sea, and the drip is dredging odd stuff from somewhere deep. Even now, there's . . . something not quite gone. A woman. Just her face, and not all of that.

Eyes. And veiling around the head—like a nun.

Jesse turns her head from that stare. Not easy. Intense. Direct. Words like that. But, what? Kind too. The nuns at her school were tough. *Kind* was never the word.

Pain sweeps the nun away as a thumping, red stutter settles in behind her temples. Jesse snaps her eyes closed, screws them tight. After a time—minutes, hours, seconds—who can tell, not her—she opens up to the light again and there, as promised, is a notepad and a pen. She tries to grab them, but a sling is in the way and something like a cattle prod belts her right hand when she tries to move it.

That leaves the left.

It's just stupidly difficult to reach across her own body as the wash of pain recedes, but Jesse perseveres. Time stretches out, and writing *No machine* seems like the work of hours. At last she has enough actual letters on the page, but . . .

It's depressing. They wobble everywhere; even she can't understand what they say.

"You're awake. Excellent." He's back, the doctor, shining and healthy and fit.

Jesse bumps her left hand against the notepad.

"Oh. Let me see." He picks the pad up. Tries not to look confused.

She can't point properly, but it's an indication. The machine. Tries to mime cutting her throat.

Those benign eyes snap focus. "Jesse, we can certainly help if you're feeling depressed." He pats the machine like a friend. "Everyone finds it hard to adapt at the beginning. We hope you feel you can persevere. It's easier if you just let go."

Hah! You try.

Jesse tries to breathe deep, but the machine won't let her, counting out each ration of air, doling out oxygen like she should be grateful.

The doctor nods encouragement. "Mr. Bynge is your specialist. He'll see you on his rounds today. If everything settles down"—the doctor doesn't quite look at her—"we could start weaning you off the ventilator in a day or so. We need to be sure you can support your own breathing without undue stress."

Wean? Settle down? What?

The nurse arrives. A big smile. And one offered to the doctor too. Bigger. "Hello, Jesse."

What happened to Miss Marley? Jesse feels weirdly aggrieved.

"Nurse, would you page me when Mr. Bynge arrives?"

"Certainly, Doctor."

That's a breathy giggle.

The nurse sneaks a glance as the doctor walks away. Turning back to the ventilator, she even stifles a sigh.

Jesse would laugh if she could. Not unkindly. Just from . . . what?

"Temperature time." Default-bright, the nurse slides a thermometer into Jesse's armpit, an unasked-for intimacy. "Blood pressure next." She picks up a cuff. She's got a lot of observations to get through. "This is all perfectly standard, by the way. Good obs and we're so much closer to getting you out of the ICU." She takes out the thermometer, makes a note, picks up the left arm.

Jesse stares at the ceiling. It's not interesting. Her eyelids droop.

What if the machine stops? Her eyes jerk open.

The nurse looks up sharply as the air deflates from the cuff. "All done." Another note, and the clipboard is dropped on the end rail of the bed. "You can trust your ventilator, Jesse. Utterly. It will never fail you. It's stronger than your own heart, and my charts say yours is excellent. What good fortune."

Now that is a genuine smile.

Jesse watches the nurse as she goes to the next bed. When Jesse thinks about it, she is more than lucky.

George might have killed her. But he didn't. She's here for a reason. Must be.

She closes her eyes. That nun's there again.

Jesse sighs. It's not a problem, she's not doing any harm. . . .

"Your progress is excellent, Miss Marley. A model patient in every respect." Thus says the specialist from central casting. Black hair, discreetly gray at the temples, tanned skin. Expensive suit.

Glad I'm not paying for that, thinks Jesse. But she's sitting up and feeling better.

"Wouldn't you agree, Dr., er, Brandon?" The specialist is vague with the neurological registrar's name.

"I would, Mr. Bynge. Excellent. The very word."

So that's his name! Jesse watches the younger doctor smile. Everyone else around the bed is smiling too: specialist, two nurses, the ward sister, and all the students clustered in a neat fan around the great man. Concentrated benevolence, and all aimed at her like the beam of a flashlight.

Jesse narrows her eyes. Four days in this place and she's had enough. She pulls the pad over and, though it hurts, forces her hand to write, *Machine?* Even she can read what she's written; that's something.

"I'd say we can start weaning you off it from today." A charming smile—well, crinkles around the eyes—and off goes Mr. Bynge.

Jesse's not quick enough to ask another question. The mob breaks up and throngs after the surgeon, fluttering down around the next bed like birds in from the sea. She'd sigh if she could, but not in a resigned way. It's hard staying alert, hard fighting the sedative in the drip. Off guard for even a moment and hazy dreams well up behind her eyes.

"Back again." Dr. Brandon stands at the end of the bed.

Jesse picks up the pen and manages, *Machine go?*

"Much better!" Dr. Brandon beams. He points at the pad. "Your writing."

To grind her teeth right now would be satisfying. But like a cart horse trying to clear a fence, Jesse struggles for liftoff. What is it? What . . .

The thought appears, fully formed. *I do feel better.* She smiles.

"Now that really is good. We like it when you smile." His own grin is charming.

Jesse's not for distracting today. She labors with the pen, and Dr. Brandon watches with interest. He peers at the page when she's finished and reads out loud, " 'ICU. Why?' "

She nods. He's professionally kind, but there's something else in those eyes as well. Detachment. That's it. In the end, the patient is just an amateur operative in this world; he's the professional, the keeper of the keys of knowledge.

"Do you mind?" He waves at the chair beside the bed.

Jesse waves back. *Knock yourself out.* Unintended interior pun.

He taps his skull above one ear. "So, your fracture was a minor one. Do you remember I told you that?"

Jesse nods. His expression is neutral. She distrusts neutral.

"The treatment for a simple fracture is not complicated: clean the wound, apply cold compresses, control the swelling with medication if required, and observe the patient for a day or so." He pauses. "And if we diagnose concussion also, strict observation, two hourly, is mandatory. We check really, really thoroughly that we haven't missed anything: fragments of bone driven into the lining of the brain as a result of the accident, for instance." He leans forward slightly. "Was it an accident, by the way?"

Jesse's left hand moves. She's surprised to see it write *Yes*.

"However, there was a complication I didn't tell you about, er, the last time." He clears his throat. "After you had the seizure, you blacked out. That's when the bleed was found."

Jesse writes, *?*

"The seizure only happened once and your condition has improved greatly in the last few days." He hesitates.

The left hand scribbles, *And?*

He sits back. "Well, we eliminated the need for further surgery—the bleed was only small, as I said, and further X-rays showed no evidence of a depressed fracture. However, Mr. Bynge, your surgeon, had you transferred to the ICU. He was concerned about the possible severity of the concussion and wanted you very closely monitored. We'll start some cognitive tests when you're off the machine, but there's a very good chance we'll find all's well." He pats the ventilator like a dog. "And *complete rest heals best.*" A faint smile. "Sorry. Drummed into us as students. So, just a day or so more in here, a few more days after that in the neurological ward, and then, with luck . . ." He mimes opening a door and waving good-bye.

She stares at him. *What are you not telling me?*

He stands. "So, I'll see you again tomorrow, Jesse. Rest well." That professional smile as he goes.

"He's a brilliant neurologist, Dr. Brandon. Cutting-edge." The ward nurse is back. She launches into tidying Jesse's bed, unconscious of the irony. "Yes, you're lucky to have him on your case."

By sleight of hand she turns and fluffs the pillows and straightens the blankets. "There, all nice and neat. I'll give you a sponge bath a bit later, and you can look forward to a real bath quite soon." A last twitch as she folds the top sheet down and tucks it in, tight as a drumhead.

Shower. I want a shower.

The nurse is about to go. "Has anyone let your parents know what's happened?"

Which ones? But Jesse labors *Australia* onto the page.

"They live in Australia? That's a long way." An encouraging smile.

Jesse's sick of smiling but she manages to write, *Doc says me OK. Not worry them.*

"If you're sure? It would be no trouble to drop them a line."

Nothing they can do. As the nurse walks away, Jesse puts the pen down and closes her eyes. Conversation over.

But it isn't. Not inside her head. Will she really recover? Heads are fragile things.

At a pool party for her best friend's fifteenth birthday, while flirting with the birthday girl's boyfriend—showing off on the diving board—Jesse overbalanced and fell in. They all shrieked and screamed, laughing, pointing. But she was drowning, and the BF worked it out. He jumped in and dragged her to the surface. Everything seemed fine at first—she fussed over, he praised as the Hero du Jour—and even the headache she suffered seemed like justified punishment to her, weirdly, for her wicked, wicked ways.

But Jesse didn't make it to school the next day. The headache got worse, and then there was fever, and vomiting, and her neck hurt so much she couldn't lie down, or stand, or sit. Alarmed, her mum and dad had taken her to the hospital a day later, and the lights were impossible to look at. They sliced her eyes like knives.

No one worked out what the symptoms meant, and after three days and three nights of agony, she'd nearly died. Jesse knew it was happening, she could feel the approaching dark, but just as in this place, she couldn't tell anyone, couldn't speak. But her mum sat beside her bed the whole time. Whenever Jesse opened her eyes, trying to scream, too weak to move or open her mouth, her mum had been there. Later, after the diagnosis of bacterial meningitis, and the antibiotics began to work, she was told her mum had broken all the hospital rules. She'd refused to leave Jesse alone for even a moment, ICU or no ICU. So they'd given in, gowned and gloved her, and let her go on holding her daughter's hand.

Only I wasn't, was I? Your daughter.

Slow tears. Jesse can feel them gather and slide down her face.

Mum. Oh, Mum, tell me I'll get better.

Which mum?

The one she knows. The woman in Sydney.

Hurt, misery. Yearning. And fury. Jesse wants to groan. Tries to. *I can't bear this.*

But she can. She has to.

"Nurse?" A whole day without the ventilator and it still feels novel to hear her own voice. Jesse presses the button on the cord that hangs near her hand.

The curtains flick back. "Yes, Miss Marley?" The ward sister peers through the gap. She doesn't look pleased.

Jesse remembers to smile. "Sorry, Sister. I'm sure you're busy. But do you think the television might be turned down?"

"I'll see what I can do." A swish and the curtains sway closed.

"Mrs. Darling, may we have the volume a little lower?"

Jesse tries not to listen. It seems rude, somehow; the lady in the next bed is deaf, and touchy.

"What did you say?"

"The television. Could you turn it down."

"It's not loud. I can't hardly hear it."

Jesse cringes.

The ward sister cracks, "Nurse! Would you take over, please."

Heels tap, tap away over the linoleum.

"Hello, Mrs. Darling. Can I help?"

Jesse breathes out. This is the nice nurse. Closing her eyes, she hears the morning show fade a notch or two. That's so good. Yes, the wedding's exciting, yes, she thinks it's all a fairy tale—just like everyone else—but really, *do* they have to go on about *the dress*?

"Sorry about that." The pretty nurse with the Scottish accent bobs in between the curtains.

"I hope Mrs. Darling's not too upset."

"Och, she'll be fine." The girl picks up Jesse's chart and studies the figures. "Have you had any more headaches, or . . . ?" She wriggles a hand beside her head.

"No. Nothing." Jesse wriggles her fingers obligingly. "My throat's still sore, though. And I'm really, really bored." Another day gone and she's nowhere closer to doing what she needs to do. And money. What's she going to do about money?

"Being bored's a good sign." The nurse pronounces it *gude*, which Jesse finds charming. "The sore throat will last a few more days, I'm afraid—it's from the tube. I can ask the doctor to prescribe something if it's bothering you." Moving closer, she murmurs, "Would you like a bit of good news?"

Hope lights up like a sparkler. Jesse says fervently, "Yes, please."

The nurse looks around. "I shouldn't be telling you, but if all goes well with your tests today, you might be back in the real world sooner than you think."

"Cross your heart and hope to die?"

A grin. "Yes. But, *only* if Dr. Brandon thinks you're well enough. There. Stuck my neck out."

"Hooray!" Jesse tries to throw her arms up. The sling gets in the way and she yelps as her elbow bumps the bedside table.

The commotion upsets the old lady in the next bed. "What's going on?"

"Won't be a moment, Mrs. Darling. Everything's fine." The nurse tries to make Jesse comfortable.

"It is not. The way this place is run, it's a disgrace!" The morning-TV presenters are back to shouting again.

Rolling her eyes, the girl helps Jesse move her right arm back across her body. "Oh. You must have dropped this." Scooping up the notepad Jesse had in ICU—it's open on the floor—the nurse goes to hand it back. And pauses. "Is this your drawing?"

Jesse, eyes closed, is slumped against the pillows. "Can't draw." She's drained and abject.

The girl says, "It's very good, though."

Jesse opens her eyes.

The nurse is holding the sketch so Jesse can see. "Amazing detail. Just like a photograph."

Jesse shifts uncomfortably. In the sketch, the massive walls of a castle rise tier after tier above a river that defines the base of a hill; above, a brutal tower dominates the site.

The nurse hands the pad to Jesse. "Try to rest." She grins. "I know that's hard. Would you like some earplugs?"

"Might as well get used to the real world."

Even louder, there's no avoiding the TV now. ". . . and a source at Buckingham Palace has a tip for us. The soon-to-be Princess of Wales has approved final designs for her wedding dress. Woven from silk thread spun by British silkworms."

"Silkworms? What's that?" Juggling the cord on the cumbersome remote, Mrs. Darling presses the volume button with impressive results.

". . . Lady Diana has been quoted as saying that she hopes this wonderful fabric will help restore the British . . ."

Mrs. Darling shouts over the booming presenter, "I can hear it now."

Jesse says nothing. She's staring at the sketch of the castle. Like a tooth that's loose, she can't stop worrying the stump of that anxiety one more time. She stares at the picture, really looks at it, as if each detail of the drawing can tell her more than the whole.

Turning the page over, Jesse clutches the pen in her left hand.

Eventually, indecision makes marks on the paper, but the lines are tentative and she screws up her face when she holds the image at a distance. She tries again, but none of her scrawls is anything like the drawing on the other side.

She mutters, "Useless."

"What?" Mrs. Darling leans over between the beds.

"Nothing. I didn't say anything." Jesse rips the page out and drops it in the rubbish bin beside the bed.

4

I REMEMBER MAUGRIS calling my name, though his voice was faint, and I had no breath to respond. How he took the ring mail from my body I cannot say, and though he bound my chest with his own shirt, the mouth of the wound was too wide to be closed and I could not ride. All I have left from that night is an image of Rauf trying to light a fire on the snow. I was told later of a litter made from pikes and that Maugris had it slung between Helios and another horse. He tied me in it and wrapped me in his own riding cloak. I do not know why he did not freeze to death.

With little food but snow, Maugris led our men over three days and nights, where two should have done before I was wounded. But Maugris got us back to Hundredfield. He did not lose one man, not even me, though they told him each day I was dying.

If I did not die, when I first opened my eyes there was no sound and no light, and it was hot. Terror stopped my breath. My many, many sins had found me out, since I could feel the fires of hell! But night broke like a bowl and I was surprised by the sun. Somewhere, in the dark, I had given up the thought of life, expecting never to feel Sol's heat on my face again.

I lay in a curtained bed, and there was Talbot, my coursing hound. He saw me open my eyes and scrambled to lick my face, whimpering. By this I understood I could not be dead; animals are not found in hell, or in heaven, since only men have souls.

Yet at the edge of sight, two figures stood. Against the sun it seemed they had no substance but light. I watched them for a little time. One, the shorter, leaned to the other as if listening, yet I heard no words. And I was again uncertain. Were these angels?

"Is this . . . ?" I swallowed. "Am I . . . ?" The words hurt my throat.

The taller figure moved and I saw it was a woman—flesh, not spirit. Sunlight dazzled the silver basin this lady held in her hands and I could not see her face, only that her head was veiled. The other was a girl, her face so pretty and young I almost wept to see such grace, for I had been a long time gone among destruction.

Turning, the girl touched her companion on the sleeve, and the lady came to the bed. Dressed in ruby velvet, the train of her gown held up in in one hand, she bent close and smiled at me. And I saw she outshone the girl as day obliterates night. Christ's own mother could not have been more beautiful.

I heard a voice. My oldest brother, Godefroi, appeared at the chamber door, and his expression was joyous. Many had called Godefroi de Dieudonné cold, and his hand was hard when I was a child, but today we seemed true kin.

"An honest welcome home at last, dear Bayard. The Lady Flore and I, and Maugris, of course"—I saw him there also—"despaired these many, many days that you might not live. The whole household has prayed for your recovery, and they shall be rewarded by this news. A mass of thanksgiving shall be sung in thanks, but you should know that it was my wife, the Lady Flore, who saved your life. She nursed you devotedly, and without her skill, well . . ." He picked up the red-clad woman's hand and kissed it. When she turned toward Godefroi, I saw the beginnings of a proud belly beneath her gown.

Maugris murmured, "We must wish Godefroi and his wife, the Lady Flore, much happiness in their marriage, Bayard."

It hurt my chest to force air into my mouth, but I said, "Yes. Blessings to you both." I hoped my face did not betray me, but I was bewildered. Why had our brother not sent for us to come to his wedding?

Godefroi leaned down to the pillow and murmured, "We have been married some few months only, and you should know, brother, that my wife does not speak. Or rather, she does not know our language. It was for that reason a small wedding seemed best. However, we understand each other well for the power of God is very great. I am blessed in my wife." Godefroi straightened and held out his hand. "Come with me, lady."

I turned my head on the pillow to watch the pair leave. The girl at the back of the chamber bowed as Flore gave her the bowl and, with returning sense, I saw that I knew her. She was Margaretta, the daughter of Edmund Swinson, Hundredfield's reeve. I remembered a brother also, Alois, but he had been sent to the brothers at the priory. Our father had sponsored him since the boy was considered clever.

At the door, Godefroi turned. "Bayard, my wife's servant will shave your face." He pointed at Margaretta. "Truly, you would frighten even the Scots with that beard." The Lady Flore nodded pleasantly as if she understood the joke.

The girl closed the door, and we three were left alone.

Godefroi's chamber was high in the keep, Hundredfield's great defensive tower, and a gust of wind nudged through the open window, sending smoke from the brazier through the room.

The girl tried not to cough. "Shall I heat the water, lord?" She nodded at the bowl, her expression timid. "It will not take long on the coals."

Maugris spoke for me. Often, this had seemed natural to me. "We must lift my brother first. He will be too weak to sit un-aided."

I began to protest, but Maugris, smiling, said, "Ignore Lord Bayard, girl. His wits desert him."

I let them help me—and was grateful, though I did not show it—and as the shaving water warmed in a firepot, I lay half upright against Godefroi's pillows, in Godefroi's bed, and stared around the room I no longer knew.

This had been our parents' bedchamber, washed with white lime. The only ornament in their time had been a plain crucifix over the prie-dieu my mother used each morning. The bed had never been curtained, and since so many people slept here each night—our parents, us children on pallets, my mother's waiting woman, and with at least one fighter outside, sleeping across the door—a brazier was little needed. Human breath kept the room warm.

Godefroi had used much coin to transform this room. Woven hangings of red, green, and white now covered the walls and rush mats lay on the floor—a luxury our mother had never been permitted. Glassed casements replaced shutters in several of the windows and new dressing coffers stood in a row near the door; some of the bright oak was inlaid with darker wood and patterned in ivory, and each was richly carved, most often with the Dieudonné arms. This was the same image that Maugris and I had on our shields, when we did not carry the Percy arms: blue wavy lines in parallel, for the river at the foot of the keep, surmounted by a tower. Above the tower was an arrowhead and a sword crossed with an ax.

The bed in which I lay was not the one where my brothers and I had been conceived and born. Godefroi's new bedstead was vast and filled near half the space; four men might sleep abreast there and still have room to turn in the night. Piled on it were mattresses of feathers and wool, with woven blankets, fine linen, and a cover-let of winter fox. But certainly, if a man has to die in his bed, goose down is better than straw.

"The water is hot, lord. May I fetch soap, and the knife?" Margaretta fixed her eyes on my brother's feet and her tone was humble. Someone had trained her well to the service of the Lady Flore.

"Knife?" Maugris did not mean to sound suspicious. Women made him nervous, and he had no talent for charm or light con-versation.

"It is Lord Godefroi's, sir. It is kept in the garderobe for the purpose, with the soap."

Maugris stepped back. "You may bring what is required."

Margaretta hurried to the door that led to the privy and we both watched her go.

Maugris found something of interest in the sky beyond the glass, and I closed my eyes with relief. Questions churned, and perhaps the girl could provide answers, but I would need to gather what strength remained to me.

When she returned, I asked, "Do you personally shave Lord Godefroi?" The words came a little easier, but my voice was thin.

"Yes." She held up the towel. "May I spread this across your shoulders, lord?"

"Of course." Her touch was deft, but I lay naked in the bed, and though I was used to servants, being tended by a girl one does not know well is intimate. The women of the town baths can be hired for service such as this, and other things as well, and where money is given embarrassment does not exist, for the rules are clear. Yet this was awkward, and I looked away as Margaretta rubbed curds of soap into my beard. Her fingers were gentle, and both her breath and person pleasant—unusual enough to be remembered.

"I shall use the knife now, lord."

A blade at the neck is a thing to worry a man if the edge is keen, but she held the steel with confidence. I began to relax. "Maugris, I—"

The blade stopped. "Lord, perhaps not to speak?"

I waved for Margaretta to continue and said nothing as she finished her work and then wiped my face with linen dipped in the last of the water.

"Would you like to see?" She held the silver bowl close to my face.

I had not seen myself reflected since I was a child; my mother had a hand mirror brought back from the Levant—rare and precious. Now, a gaunt man stared at me, eyes sunk in pits of dark flesh. I looked like my father.

Maugris guffawed. "Poor Bayard. Pretty boy all gone. They will be disappointed when they see you tonight."

"What do you mean?"

"There is to be a feast in your honor, and I am to escort you to the hall. Lean on me and you will not disgrace us, little brother."

"If I am to walk, *brother*, it will be without your arm."

Maugris was amused. "And if you cannot?"

"Believe me, I shall walk."

He chuckled. "A silver penny says you trip on the stairs."

"You have always been foolish with money, Maugris."

An annoyed look was my reward for his being embarrassed in front of the girl. Turning to Margaretta, I continued with some serenity, "You have a most generous mistress. It was kind of the Lady Flore to provide your service to me."

Her expression changed. "I am indeed fortunate in my mistress, sir. She *is* kind, and compassionate." The girl's face shone with sincerity.

"And yet, she cannot speak to give orders. Is that not confusing?" I was curious.

Color flamed in her cheeks. "My mistress has no need of words. We understand each other very well."

Godefroi had said something similar, and I swear there was

no evil intent when I asked Margaretta how Godefroi came to meet Flore.

Tidying up, she replied, "In the forest, lord."

"She was out hunting, the Lady Flore?"

Margaretta shook her head. "Your pardon, I must dispose of the water." A bob of a curtsey, and she hurried to the garderobe.

Maugris coughed, an elaborate performance.

I stared at him. "Met in the forest? What does that mean?"

He sauntered over to stand beside the bed. "He came upon her one day; the lady was cold and our gallant brother offered his cloak." Maugris peered at my face. "You look almost tolerable, Bayard. Less like a monster fit to frighten children."

I was impatient. "There is more. I can tell."

Maugris replied pleasantly, "Not according to our brother— though I have heard, from others, that Flore was naked when he met her. He gave her the cloak so that she would not freeze." An elegant movement of one shoulder, not quite a shrug.

My jaw dropped so fast I heard it click. "A *hedge*-girl?" Only the most destitute of prostitutes haunted common roads. "And he married her?"

Maugris had his tongue well controlled. "Our dear sister-in-law, the Lady Flore, now carries the heir to Hundredfield. Godefroi desires we pay her the respect her position demands."

Margaretta returned. "If this is all you need, lord, I must go to my son. He will need feeding."

"Of course." I waved dismissal.

As the door closed behind her, I waited a moment until her footsteps died away. "What son? She is little more than a child herself."

My brother leaned against the door. "It seems we have a nephew, Bayard. The boy is Godefroi's."

The words would not assemble properly. "His bastard?" I tipped my head to the door. "And she waits on his *wife*?"

"Yes."

"Does that not cause scandal?"

"More than that." Maugris's expression was grim. "The name of Dieudonné suffers by Godefroi's actions. We have been away too long, brother. Much has changed in two years, and not much that credits our family."

5

MAUGRIS WAS right, for I did nearly fall as I stepped down to the hall. Quivering, my thighs and calves had all the strength of a sixth-month child, but the keep's household was gathered and, once dressed, I could not allow weakness to be my master.

Godefroi waited with Flore on the landing outside the hall. "Hundredfield's household is impatient, brother. Maugris, escort Bayard. He will need your strong arm."

Maugris offered a broad grin with his hand. "Certainly, brother."

I did not like to lose, but just then Margaretta stepped from the shadows to pick up the train of Flore's dress; this too was of velvet but richer than the last, since it was sewn with pearls.

As he fell in at my side, Maugris murmured, "A very queen, apparently."

"And dressed in Madonna blue. Shameless. She wears clothes that would build a village." I spoke softly, but perhaps not low enough, for Margaretta glanced back. I could not tell what her expression meant.

Entering, I had never seen the hall look so fine. Hangings of green—a pattern of oak leaves picked out in gold thread—were stretched along three of the walls, and fresh rushes had been laid so that the appearance, at least, spoke of summer, even if the air did not. And though that great space was crammed with Godefroi's greater and lesser servants, and some of Hundredfield's tenants, I saw no guests from among our own friends. That seemed odd to me.

There was silence as we walked to our places at the high board past Swinson—the castle reeve sat among captains from Hundredfield's guard. Our own men too were ranged close, with Rauf in the place of honor sharing a bench with Godefroi's horse master. One or two of my childhood companions smiled as I passed—tenant farmers on the estate now—and I saw some barely familiar sycophants. Perhaps it was hard to know the first from the second after all this time.

With some ceremony, Godefroi led Flore to a backless stool at his right hand, and I, the cause of the celebration, was placed beside her. Maugris sat to our brother's left. Godefroi, as master, had an oak chair with lion heads at the end of the arms and a high back. I had never seen it before. Tall as a throne and massively carved with the Dieudonné arms, it would have dwarfed a lesser man. He did not immediately sit.

If it had been quiet as we entered the hall, the silence now was thick, as if smoke in the rafters hid thunder as Godefroi began to speak.

"My brother, the Sieur Bayard de Dieudonné, has returned to us from the borderlands of death. Those that are real, where murderers and thieves lurk—the men who almost killed his mortal body—and those where God alone rules. That fearful place to which, one day, we shall all go." He crossed his chest, as did we all.

I should say that *sieur* was a courtesy title, as was *lord*. I was the youngest legitimate child of this house, a soldier of little account, and that was known to all at Hundredfield. However, if I was suspicious of the flattery, the courtesy warmed me.

"Therefore, tonight we celebrate his living presence." Godefroi put a hand on my shoulder. "And for this, we give thanks and gratitude to our Father." Godefroi crossed himself again, a graceful sweep. Dutifully, all in the hall followed his example.

I was surprised that my brother spoke in English. Maugris and I used it with our men and in the garrison towns of the East March, but with our parents and among friends court French was always spoken. Godefroi said often that English was coarse, the language of peasants, and unfit for expressing thought, or poetry, or any of the finer sentiments. But that day he used it well, as I will freely admit, and proved himself wrong.

"Perhaps, however, the knowledge and tireless effort of my beloved wife, the Lady Flore"—he lifted the girl's hand and kissed it—"pleased God, for it seems to me that this hand was the means by which He permitted the Sieur Bayard to return to us. I know that later my dear brother"—Godefroi bowed to me—"will pay just tribute to the skill that has saved his life."

My attention was caught by a sound. Less than a sigh, not a wind; something like a soft groan passed among the people seated below us. It seemed to me that the men in the hall stared at Flore with hard eyes.

Were they offended that Godefroi had seated me next to his harlot? Perhaps. Yet I was alive when I should, it seemed, have died. Her hands, those same hands that lay like lilies on the cloth, had saved me, and this woman, whatever her past, was now my brother's wife. No help for that.

"Eat and drink well, therefore, in honor of this day." Godefroi nodded, and Father Matthias, our house priest in those times, stood up from his place beside Maugris. In a firm voice he began the prayer: "*In nomine Patris et Filii et Spiritus Sancti*, amen." But as the words continued, the man's tone altered—he seemed furtive, or uncertain in some way, and I wondered at the change, but as he finished the grace, food was immediately brought from the kitchens and set out on all the boards, starting with our own, and I wondered no more.

Placed between me and Flore was a dish of pike fritters with a green sauce of pounded walnuts and sorrel; then came a mighty raised pie of hare and leeks and hard-boiled eggs, which was set beside my salver alone. Salmon too, caught from our river, lay covered in a saffron sauce—an expensive delicacy. Deer, taken from the forests around the castle, had supplied venison pastries, and these were scented with cinnamon and stuffed with onions and almonds and currants from Spain among the meat. Ale flowed as if a fountain were hidden in the cellars, while jugs of Gascon wine were filled beyond overflowing, and no goblet on the boards was permitted to stand empty.

To cover the lack of conversation between us, and as courtesy demanded, I offered choice morsels of the feast to my sister-in-law and tried not to stare. I found her face distracting—it is hard to hate beauty, after all—and was annoyed by the weakness of my flesh. If I thought it strange she ate none of the food on her plate, I resisted the charm of the modest way she patted her belly to excuse herself.

As I looked at her with hostile eyes, I tried to convince myself that Flore was not alluring. Her mouth was certainly wide and full—not the rosebud of convention—and the bones of her cheeks seemed too strong for a woman's face. Her chin offended me also, and the dimples that came and went in her cheeks when she smiled. I could not see her hair, covered by a pointed headdress slung about with ropes of pearls, but it seemed unlikely to be blond, since her brows and lashes were dark.

I sniffed. *Black. Peasant coloring.*

But as Flore turned to look at her husband, I saw a truth I could not distort. Her eyes were a true sea topaz, clear and bright as water, while her pale skin had a clarity and quality that was well flattered by the sheen of blue velvet and rich fur in the neck of the gown.

Godefroi, on her other side, kept up a steady stream of information for his wife: this person, seated below, had nine children, all of them boys; that woman raised good pigs for the home farm (a delicate gesture to his nose, as if he could smell her, even at a distance); that man . . . Flore seemed to listen carefully, a lively expression on her face, touching his arm and laughing from time to time.

Not deaf, then, Flore. Just without speech.

Somehow that made me more aggrieved. A slut who cannot speak, after all, must have some advantages.

Godefroi tapped a knife against his goblet and the small wash of voices dwindled to nothing.

"Friends, we have all eaten, and very well, and I know that Sieur Bayard is anxious to speak." As a courteous salute, my brother drank a long swallow of the wine, his eyes fixed on mine.

Now, I had been ill for some time and my mind was weak, as was my body, but not so weak I could not see the truth. Nothing, really, had changed. Godefroi was a spider. He had spun this web carefully, and I had allowed myself to be caught in it. He wished me to speak in praise of Flore because she had few supporters at Hundredfield, at least among the men. But if the woman was as Maugris described her, sister-in-law or not, I would betray the honor of the Dieudonné in complimenting her. Yet, she had saved my life and she carried Godefroi's heir.

Offering to fill Flore's beaker—a gentle shake of the head—I slopped wine into my own and stood, with no certainty I would remain on my feet.

"Friends"—I turned away to belch discreetly—"we have known each other since"—I waved a hand, uncertain how many of those in the hall I really did know—"I was less than a pup."

My hound, who had followed us into the hall and lay under the table, barked.

I said gravely, "Very well spoken."

That got a laugh. I glanced at Flore for I felt her eyes on my face. *I am not a whore.*

It was hard not to stare. Flore had not spoken, but I had heard her.

Fearful of witchcraft, I crossed myself so fervently that, after a pause, the gesture was mimicked around the hall.

But Father Matthias was staring at me, and I began to sweat.

A hand touched my arm and I looked down. Flore smiled, and the kindness in those eyes brought such peace that the terror of even a breath ago seemed absurd.

"Forgive me, friends." I stumbled on the words. "I, a weak man, find myself dazzled by the renewed sweetness of life." I did not look at Flore. I did not have to. Some in the hall had seen my face, and the silence growled like a dog.

I wanted to shout, *Why do you hate her?* Instead, I raised my goblet and bent a stiff bow. "Gracious lady, I thank you. With God's help, you made whole what was broken. May this marriage be blessed even more than it already has been."

I sat because I could no longer stand and had Godefroi's expression as my reward. His glance was loving. This was the brother I had never had.

Maugris was staring at me also. His eyes were hard as pebbles. In honoring Flore, I had done what was expected, what he himself would have done if Godefroi had asked him. But only I saw the gesture he made with his right hand. Staring at Godefroi's wife, he made the sign of the evil eye.

6

JESSE HASN'T slept since dawn. She'd dreamed of the nun again. Just a feeling at first, a sense of consolation as the woman stroked her forehead. In the dream, Jesse opened her eyes and saw her smiling; it was as if she understood Jesse's sadness, as if she had come to offer comfort. And Jesse had woken on a pillow soaked with tears. Now she's sitting beside her bed, fully dressed.

"Hello, Miss"—the new day nurse pulls back the curtains and picks up the chart—"Marley. How are you feeling today?" Her teeth dazzle when she smiles.

"Good, thank you. Very good." Jesse can't resist the sound of the girl's accent. Bahamas? "I'm leaving today."

"You are?" The nurse looks worried.

"Yes, it's all arranged. My doctor, Dr. Brandon, the neurological registrar, he said it would be fine and—"

"I said *should*, not *would*. Thanks, Nurse. I'll take over." The man himself appears behind the black girl's shoulder.

The nurse puts the clipboard on its hook and maneuvers past in the limited space. "That's fine, Doctor. Call me when you're ready."

Dr. Brandon twitches the curtains closed.

Jesse keeps it cheerful. "So, what time's checkout?"

He points at the transverse shape across her chest under the cotton shirt. "That might be more comfortable on the outside? The sling, I mean."

"I dressed myself. Best I could do." She absolutely will not wince in front of him.

"Impressive." He takes in Jesse's pale face. "Is your shoulder painful this morning?"

Jesse lies valiantly, "Not at all."

"What about your head?"

"No. Not even a headache."

"Remarkable. World-record fracture recovery, I'd say. Must tell the *Lancet*." He pauses to smile. "But seriously. No pain at all?" Not to accuse, more to support.

Jesse unclenches that rigid smile. "Only a bit. Maybe."

"I prescribed some tablets yesterday. Would you like a couple?"

Jesse tries not to sound relieved. "That would be good. I think they're on the table." Getting dressed in her own clothes—her case sent to St. Barts from the hostel—has exhausted Jesse, especially pulling the jeans on. She'd not expected it to be so hard.

Dr. Brandon tracks around the bed to the opposite side. The top of the table is clear except for a water jug and a glass; no pills. "Shall I look in here?" He gestures at the top drawer.

"Go for your life." Jesse's deliberately cheery. She's absolutely, positively not giving in now, and this man is key to her getting out and getting on with her life.

The doctor smiles as he pulls out the drawer and pops the top off the pill bottle. He likes this girl's spirit. "Just what we need." Shaking a couple of tablets into his palm, he fills a glass with water. "We don't believe in pain around here."

You would say that, wouldn't you? But Jesse swallows the tablets obediently. Distracted by the ongoing protest from the broken clavicle, and the fizzing ache in her skull, her attention wanders and she doesn't see him glance back at the open drawer.

"Jesse?" Dr. Brandon has pages of the pad in each hand. He holds them up, side by side. The first is the drawing the nurse saw last night—he's picked it out of the wastebasket—while the second is a much closer view of the same place. In this, the tower broods over the castle and the lower levels of the hill. "I know this place."

It feels like he's just dropped something on her head. "What?"

Dr. Brandon stares at the second drawing. "It not like this now, of course. A lot of the structures are in ruins—but it's recognizable. Definitely." His finger traces the river below the walls. "And this too, of course, the Norman keep." He taps the paper. "Quite famous in the north, this keep."

"The north. Where in the north?"

He says absently, "It's an estate in the border country—top of England, bottom of Scotland."

Jesse takes that in, starts to say something, but then he asks, "Are these your drawings, by the way?"

She slides her eyes away. "I don't know."

Dr. Brandon says nothing.

Jesse swallows. Her throat is dry.

"Take your time. No rush." He holds the glass to her mouth and she sips from it, her hand over his. She's shaking and the surface of the water trembles as she gulps like a child.

"Enough?"

She nods, sits back with her eyes closed. "Looking forward to those drugs kicking in." The pain in her shoulder feels as if it's found a home for life. "Please, Dr. Brandon, just . . ." Jesse winces. She has absolutely no idea what she's asking for.

"Rory." He sits on the chair beside the bed, assessing his patient.

"Doctors don't sit."

A faint smile. "I'm different."

There's a pause, and Jesse holds out her left hand, staring at it.

"Look, I'm right-handed. I taught myself to write with this only because I had to, okay? But draw?" She shakes her head and there's a strange feeling, as if her skull's a balloon and might just float off her shoulders. "I tried to draw with my left hand last night, and I couldn't make it work. How can the sketches be mine?"

"It's my job to find an explanation for your symptoms. That's what I'm here for. Let's take this one step at a time." Rory offers Jesse the drawings just as the curtains part and the pretty nurse peers through.

Rory barks, "Not now." Her confused expression modifies his tone. "If you could see that we're not disturbed, Nurse, I'd appreciate that."

The girl nods hastily and backs away. "Certainly, Doctor." The curtain rings clatter as she leaves.

"So, you've seen this place before?" He points to the first picture.

"I live in Australia. We don't do castles." Jesse doesn't want to look, she really doesn't. If she tries to think about the *why* of the drawing, it's like being forced to stand on the edge of a cliff. A tall cliff. Heights nauseate her; in fact, they make her want to jump. A not-so-secret terror her mum has always known about.

"Magazine, then, or a book? TV?"

"I don't think so. No. I'm sure." She really is. "Why do you want to know?" The question frightens her. She'd take it back if she could.

He says patiently, "Because remembering is important. It speaks to brain functioning and what your mind has retained after the accident." He picks up the second drawing, the image of the keep. "There's more detail in this one. Would you agree?"

Jesse feels odd and tired and close to tears. She mumbles, "I suppose so."

Rory relents. He's pushed her too hard. "I'm sorry. How's the shoulder now?"

"Better." She sniffs, but something dark churns and coils at the edge of her sight. "The pills are making me weird, that's all. I can't think properly. Maybe I'm seeing things." Half serious.

He says gently, "If they take the pain away, that's no bad thing in the short term. Nurse?"

The curtains open cautiously. "Yes, Doctor?"

Rory stands. "Would you help Miss Marley back into bed, please? She'll need a fresh gown."

Jesse starts to protest.

Rory interrupts politely, "Jesse, I wouldn't suggest this if I didn't think it was a good idea. You're not ready to leave the hospital. In fact, I'd like to suggest we do a few more cognitive tests. As I said, what you can remember after head trauma is important. It can be an indicator of recovery." He doesn't have to name the opposite. "I'll visit again this afternoon. That's a promise."

Jesse starts to say, "I don't need more tests," but with a pleasant smile, Rory Brandon strides away.

The nurse, a tactful person, says kindly, "It won't take a minute to get you changed, Miss Marley. You'll feel more comfortable in bed." She opens the second drawer and picks up a clean gown. Shaking it out, something flutters to the floor.

Jesse's eyes follow the piece of paper.

The nurse stoops. "Here you are." She says pleasantly, "What an interesting face."

A man stares from the page. His face is gaunt, the planes strongly angled, and hair falls against a broad collar that seems to be made of fur. There's no escaping the eyes. Jesse looks away.

"That's some vest he's wearing." The nurse smiles.

Jesse says nothing. She doesn't protest as the nurse unbuttons the shirt, or when the hospital gown is eased over her shoulders and arranged around the sling. She even tolerates the moment when her jeans and knickers are pulled down, leaving her half naked.

There's nothing to say.

She doesn't remember drawing the man's face, just like all

the other stuff. Is someone else making these sketches and leaving them to be found, just to mess with her head? But who? She doesn't know anyone in London. And why would anyone bother?

Jesse stares at the drawing. The man's eyes are filled with suffering. Abruptly, she drops it in the drawer. Closes it with a snap. Nothing explains why she knows he's wearing a cuirass. *How*? And what's a cuirass anyway?

Maybe it's silly to complain about more tests. Maybe she needs them.

7

DAWN WAS rigid with frost, and morning crept over Hundredfield as if shamed to hold winter's hand.

Fulk, the Norman who had built the keep, would have been offended by such unseasonable weather. Long summers and brief winters were part of the unshakable luck that lasted all his life, and he took such things, and much else, as his due.

Following William the Bastard to England, our ancestor had cut his way to fame at the side of the duke. For as the country drowned in a tide of blood, Fulk swam high, and understanding he had a servant of some worth—a man as brutal, as pragmatic as himself—Duke William sent him north. He was to assist in the conquest of the borderlands by slaughtering the lowland Scots, and for this service, Fulk was licensed to carve an estate and build a castle in that disputed territory. To hold what he grasped, Fulk picked out a defensible site for his first keep—a high crag that overlooked the land for leagues uncounted.

This crag had a river at its feet and a grove of oaks on its summit. These great and ancient trees Fulk cut down to build the keep and its palisade.

And when the Saxon nobles rebelled—in horror at the desecration—he burned them from their homes and forced them to build his stronghold in the ashes of their own houses.

Throughout the north, and whatever their former station in life, those who survived the starvation of William's second winter were reduced to slaves. But at Hundredfield the misery of its former lords was not complete.

Below the oak grove was a holy pool, and Fulk's new captives were forced to dig it into a well, while the stream that fell from the lip was diverted into a moat for the castle he had begun to build. And when stone was quarried to replace those first oak walls, the Saxons built a tomb over their hopes. For the sacred wood was torn down again and burned under cooking pots and in braziers to warm the new stone keep.

In this way our house was founded—by blood and in misery and by the hand of God, for that is what our name, Dieudonné, means: "given of God."

Now, standing on the battlements above the gatehouse, I remembered other dawns like this at the hinge of the year. Hundredfield had been a bleak place as we grew up. I was taken from my mother at six, as Maugris had been before me, and from that time he and I slept on the floor of the hall with the castle servants and the fighting men. Maugris said he was glad because at least we could curl together like hounds for extra warmth.

My brother became my protector then, and it was good we had each other, for I was not permitted to speak to my mother in that first year—except when I waited at table, and then only formal words. This was supposed to make us strong.

My father was the example, for he had been treated in the same manner by his own parents, and he was a formidable man. Our mother, though she cried, did not oppose her husband's will, and perhaps he was right, for when we were sent away to the Percys at Alnwick, to learn the profession of arms and the behavior of gentlemen, I did not whimper. I was eight then, Maugris ten; later than was usual.

And if the hall of our keep had been cold so far from the fire, I thought I would die of frozen loneliness in that first winter at Alnwick, far, far away from all I knew.

Godefroi, as Hundredfield's heir, was sent south to the court in London. He entered the service of Edward, the Prince of Wales— the boy so hated by his father, that pitiless king who, for all his life, harried Scotland like a hound with a wounded fox. One day, this same son would lead the English at Bannockburn—and lose all that his father had grasped and held. And for this failure, our young king Edward, Godefroi's master and friend, would never again be trusted by those of us he tried to lead.

I was four when Godefroi left for the court at Westminster, and he was six years older. By his refurbished bedchamber and the luxuries of the hall, he made clear the royal court, and the royal prince too, had given him a taste for things he had never had at home. Restraint is not a virtue much found in London, or continence of any kind, but even at Hundredfield, out in the wilds of the borders, men talked of the vicious life of the new king and his court. Gossip about the great is a cruel wind—a thing you do not see but only hear as it torments dead leaves—but I would not be one of those leaves, wherever Godefroi's loyalties lay. For I had played at dice with Death and won, and this sharp dawn reminded me of that luck, for as I watched, shadows rose like curtains to display the sleeping earth. Soon the sun would find gems in the white grass, and the sky would blush and flare, helpless, in the end, against the sun's desire for a new day.

As a child, beauty haunted me, and this shining morning told me not to forget; glory, sometimes, is real before it dies.

"Bayard?" Maugris was wrapped to the eyes in a cloak as he joined me on the battlements over the great gate. Staring down at the houses on the far bank of the river, his expression changed. "Something is wrong in this place."

Did I want this conversation? "No one likes change."

My brother leaned out into the dizzy air. "The priest spent

God's own time dripping poison in my ear last night. He does not accept this marriage. He believes Flore is a succubus."

I laughed. "A succubus. And you agree? Matthias is jealous. Godefroi listens to her now."

Maugris hunched defensively. "While you were ill, I saw much. Now that woman carries his child—*if* it is his—she winds around Godefroi like ivy. She drains our brother, and the estate. The cost of her gowns—"

I spoke over Maugris. "The Lady Flore is a pretty woman and he is a fond husband. Why would he not wish to adorn such beauty?" *Bewitched.* I refused to hear the word in my head.

"Ah. The *Lady* Flore. What happened to *harlot*?"

I shook my head. "Has she spoken to you?"

"She cannot speak." His expression was puzzled.

I hesitated. In the sharp light, life seemed simpler, less clotted with unspoken meanings. As the glow from last night faded, perhaps it was harder to believe what I had heard. And felt. I leaned forward, pointing. "The houses need work."

"That is just what I was saying. Godefroi spends money on his wife's back as Hundredfield falls down."

Below, a boy yelled as a fight began. A woman ran from a cottage and hauled him from the melee of tumbling children. She cuffed one or two and dragged her child inside. The door slammed on his howling.

I turned to walk away, but Maugris called after me, "We must speak to Godefroi, Bayard. He cannot ignore what is happening. The peasants did not like his wife. And they like him less for marrying her and dressing her like the noblewoman she is not. Their sweat paid for those pretty clothes, and the bedstead, and all the folderols we see. Pushed too hard, they will kill us all one day if they can. Her too. And the heir."

I could not say he was wrong. I raised a hand and turned away.

"Where are you going?"

"The stables."

"If you want to ride, go beyond the village."

"Why?"

His tone was grim. "Because you need to."

Hundredfield's estate stretched wide on both sides of the river and away deep into the forest. Oak, ash, and beech—this was good chase country, and for more than two centuries our family had preserved the red deer for our family to hunt.

I did not seek the splendors of the forest that day. I had come to see our champion lands, the fertile meadows where Hundredfield's serfs grew barley and corn for the castle, and turnips and beets to feed the estate cattle; close by they had their own strips in the commons on which to grow food for their families. But as I rode the track past the straggled houses, I saw that many buildings were empty, the doors agape, the thatch of the roofs half gone. And people stood behind their shutters, watching as I passed.

I knew they were there; small sounds, little shifts of light, told me of their presence, but they did not show themselves. The place was quiet. Where were all the children? I had seen them this morning. They could not all have been hiding.

Beyond the village was a more shocking change. The common land was gone. Where the food gardens had been and the ancient rabbit warren—the wild chicken so prized in lean times—were fields divided by walls of gray stone. Sheep were grazing where before families had toiled to grow onions and cabbages, leeks and beans and apples.

I pulled Helios to a stop. A shepherd with two black dogs was driving his flock along the track beside the river. The bleating mass moved slowly and it was not hard to catch up.

"Good day to you." I knew the boy minding the sheep. He had been the smith's lad in the village. "Your name is John?"

The youth half bowed, but his eyes were anxious. "Yes,

lord." Perhaps, like the others, he thought I would like to be flattered.

I slowed Helios to the boy's pace. The stallion, not liking sheep around his hocks, snorted and danced.

"So"—I gestured at the walls that bordered the fields—"do you like being a shepherd, John?"

"Well enough." He did not look at me.

"Did I see you in the smithy when I was last here? That would have been a year or two ago."

The boy shouted at the dogs, "There! Bring them back. Back!"

Arrows of fur and bone, the dogs flew after the wanderers. Weighted with fleece, the ewes were no match for the hounds and returned to the flock at a panicked stumble, bleating loudly. "You were saying, lord?"

I dropped the reins to amble beside the boy. "Did you like working with the smith?"

"Oh, yes." John's tone was fervent, but he went quiet, throwing a stone at a lamb that had fallen behind.

"And?"

Reduced to an orderly tribe, the sheep filled the lane, calling out to one another. But now the boy had had time to think and he said carefully, "The smith moved away."

I thought about that remark. What smith moves from his home village?

"As you see, we have no need for plows anymore." The boy's voice was bitter. "Welyn thought that wrong, and he told the reeve."

"Swinson?"

The boy tipped his head toward the keep, looming high on its hill. "They took his cottage and his tools. Turned him out on the road with his family. Three little ones and a sick wife." The boy's face worked. "There's another smith, but he is at the castle now. He does not help the people of the village because he works for—" He gulped and swallowed. His eyes were terrified, for he had remembered who I was.

Why the people in the hall had been so sullen, and why the village houses stood like teeth broken in a mouth, was now clear.

The boy continued, half speaking to himself. "But I am lucky." He was staring at the flock. "My mother still eats, and my sisters. And we have a roof." His eyes were hopeless.

I dipped into a saddlebag and pulled out a piece of cheese and a hunk of bread. "Perhaps you will help me, John. I have been ill and am not hungry." That was true. My appetite had been sated at the feast last night.

When I offered the food, the boy took it, but only after a worried pause.

"I cannot take it back to the keep. The cook would think I do not like his bread."

John was thin, and the speed with which he ate, as if I might change my mind, spoke of real hunger.

Gathering the reins, I turned the stallion back toward the village. "My best to your mother." Spurring Helios, I called out, "This remains with us, John. Just you and me."

But I was angry.

Godefroi was driving our tenants away because sheep made Hundredfield more money than people.

"Men are beasts at heart, Bayard. And all beasts must have masters or the world descends to disorder." Godefroi waved a hand broadly. "Maugris, is that not so?"

Maugris cleared his throat and would have spoken, but I did not let him. "The people of Hundredfield are not beasts, Godefroi, unless we make them so. And turning them off their land—"

Godefroi's tone was severe. And cold. "It was never their land. It *is* Dieudonné land. And I do as I do so that our family, and you, my brothers, may continue to prosper."

Maugris said quietly, "But what will happen when the beasts return with other masters?"

"That will not be disorder, Godefroi. It will be war." Perhaps I was shouting.

"Lower your voice, Bayard." Godefroi was irritated. "It is necessary to control enemies of the king."

We were in the hall, he in his great chair, Maugris and I two steps below the dais. "Edward Plantagenet may be your friend, and you wish to please him, as do we also, but these people are not enemies—not his, and not ours. Be careful, Godefroi. By your actions you may make them so."

My brother lifted his brows. He said mildly, "Ah, righteous anger. It improves your color, Bayard. A relief to us all."

Perhaps I glowered, for he smiled and said, "Yes, I serve the king. But I turn out only those who oppose his will through me, their lord. We must all do better in Edward's service if the realm is to thrive. I certainly plan to." He threw me a scroll.

Maugris peered over my shoulder as I unrolled the parchment. "These are mason's drawings."

Godefroi leaned forward, his face animated. "There will be improved fortifications at Hundredfield, and I shall build a much larger outer ward. The inner ward will be extended too, as you see, and the gatehouse made stronger—prudence in the face of those who envy the good fortune of our family. But this is what royal favor brings, Bayard, and you should be grateful." He gestured. "There will be separate quarters as well."

So many new buildings were on the plans it was hard to understand them all. "For what purpose?" I stared at him.

"The family and the house servants will live here." He pointed to a large structure with many rooms at one end of the ground within the walls. "Even now, the keep is too small for Hundredfield's household. It will become garrison quarters for the men."

Maugris tapped the mason's drawings with some respect. "Impressive. But can the estate afford all that you plan?"

Godefroi leaned back. "Our wool is excellent quality; soon the river will drive fulling mills and there will be looms in all the cottages. Weavers from France, and dyers also, shall be our tenants, and there will be expert craftsmen for each stage of the cloth. Those sheep you despise so much will make us all very wealthy, Bayard. And the estate will need more than me to run it. Think on that when you are both sick of soldiering." Godefroi grinned and picked his teeth with the point of a knife.

I did not let him change the subject. "Give our people the chance to serve us in this new way, brother. Teach them, let them live in their homes. Winter is early again; we can all feel it. If you have no compassion, at least think of—"

My brother's eyes were alive with malice and, yes, a certain pity. "The world is changing, Bayard. You think me harsh, but what I do is necessary—for my children and for yours. One day they and you will be grateful that I saw what needed to be done and did it."

I thought of John's pinched face, of the roofless buildings in the village. "Your children. Do you mean your son, or the child carried by the hedge-girl? Is it even yours?"

Maugris put his hand on my arm, but I shook it off.

Godefroi half rose in his chair. "I must presume your mind is still weak."

I heard the hushing of skirts behind me and saw Godefroi's expression change. He held out his hand. "There you are."

I turned. Behind me, Flore was framed in the doorway, and as the girl walked to the dais, I saw tears in her eyes.

I was shamed and brushed past without grace.

"Brother!" Maugris called after me.

I ignored him. I ignored everything as I strode from the hall.

Bayard.

Flore called me by name. No voice, but still the word was in my head.

Fearful, I half turned.

She was standing beside Godefroi's chair. My brother held her hand as if she were a captive. And if he glared at me, her sorrowful gaze struck my heart.

"Come." Maugris was beside me.

And I let him lead me away.

8

S O MY aim for today is to work out your mental and physical state before the accident and compare it with your condition now. Apples with apples." Rory and Jesse are in a consulting room in the oldest part of St. Barts. Anonymous, white-walled, the space has a desk, Jesse's chair, and a pin board with fire-regulation notices. Deep-set windows and the low height of the door are the only hints of the history of the building.

"Most of what I'll do shortly will be familiar, but I'd like to ask some questions first."

"Okay." *Most*. What does that mean?

"I prefer to take notes as we go, if that's all right?"

Jesse nods.

Rory pulls a lined pad closer. "Right. Here we go. How would you describe yourself before the accident?"

"In what way?" That tight, cold feeling is back. Why does she feel so fearful?

"Well, your principal character traits. For instance, would you say you were a practical person?"

She considers. "That can mean anything. Give me a hint."

"Okay. Resourceful, decisive, good at making plans and carrying them out?"

"On that basis, I'd say I was practical." She smiles at him nicely.

Rory makes a note. "And did you think of yourself as physically competent—play tennis, climb ladders, drive a car? Actions that require mental and physical coordination?"

She nods again. "Hockey, not tennis, and I learned woodwork in high school. The only girl in the class, but I wasn't bad. I could even use a lathe." *True story, Dr. Brandon.*

"Good at math?"

"Better than words, that's for sure."

"And could you think your way through problems—life, not just equations?"

Jesse lifts her left shoulder into a half shrug. "I could always rely on logic to see me right."

He looks up from the notepad. "And what were you most proud of about yourself?"

Jesse says promptly, "That I faced my fears and did something about them."

He's working to keep up. "Good. Very good. Now, a change of tack. Would you have described yourself as imaginative or creative before the accident?"

"Not creative, I think. And maybe not especially imaginative, either." *Or anxious. How things change.*

"Could you sing?"

"Sing? No. They always stuck me in the back of the choir at school." A faint smile. Some of that stuff had been funny. A bit. When it wasn't humiliating.

Rory nods thoughtfully. He puts down his pen. "So, Jesse, play a little game with me. Just word association. Say the first thing that comes. Don't think about it."

"This is the other side of 'most,' is it?" She's trying not to be defensive.

Rory leans forward. "Just try. The results are often interesting."

In the end, she nods.

"Thank you. So. Fear?"

"Loathing."

"Love?"

"Landscape."

"Together?"

"Sometimes."

"Black?"

"Red. Look, is this helping? I'm not an ink blot."

Rory laughs. "Just mapping the boundaries, nothing sinister. Your word association is interesting, by the way. Tangential." He picks up the pad again. "And just to make a formal note for the record"—he holds up his pen—"in the ward yesterday, you told me you could not draw."

"Yes."

"Please consider your next answer, take your time. The pictures I saw of the castle. Do you think you drew them?"

She closes her eyes and the seconds tick by.

Rory says nothing.

"It might have been someone else." The eyes stay closed.

"Do you have any idea who?"

"No." A pause, then a false start. "I suppose, well, I have to think it might have been me. But I don't know how."

He makes another note. "I'm going to suggest we come back to that in a little while, Jesse, but meanwhile, have you ever heard of a person being referred to as left- or right-brained?"

She shakes her head.

"Medicine has made some strides into brain functioning and consciousness in the seventies, but the research that interests me is the broad biases that make up different kinds of functioning and personality—how they're created and how they interact. As you've described yourself before the accident, I'd say you stacked up as a classic left-brain person: organized, methodical, process driven. But listening to you today and having seen the sketches, it seems to me you exhibit an increased, or increasing, right-brain bias. The right-brained person, by the way, is broadly defined as creative, intuitive, good with language, an innovative thinker. And it's interesting too that you spoke of 'seeing words' just after the accident; that could be a description of synesthesia. That's where nerve impulses get scrambled in the brain: sounds can seem to have form, smells exhibit colors instead of scent. That sort of thing. That seems to have died away, but it could be a useful pointer to the other things you've been experiencing."

Jesse settles deeper into her seat. What's he *really* saying?

"It's striking, don't you think? There you were—rational, competent, no-nonsense, in your own estimation. And now. How would you describe yourself now, Jesse?"

She opens her mouth. And closes it. Twice.

"Does what I've said bother you?"

"There's so much I can't seem to control about myself anymore. Like someone else is driving." The words are a blurt.

"Ah, control. Who says that's real?"

"Hello? The concept of free will?" Jesse can hear herself—she sounds so vulnerable, and this man is an almost-stranger. She really, really hates that.

Rory responds patiently, "But that's just what it is. A concept. In my terms, that means a hypothesis that needs rigorous testing if we're to accept it as having merit. There's little hard science that favors the existence of free will, by the way; it's more a matter for philosophy."

She stares at him in confusion, and his gaze softens. "Philosophy of Science 101. Sorry. I'm here to listen. Literally." He holds up a stethoscope. "And that's a cue for the basics. Heart first."

"Haven't I done enough of this?"

He nods. "Yes. But it's consistent monitoring that counts. And I always feel happier checking patients myself."

Jesse hesitates, then gestures to the buttons of her shirt. "Shall I?"

"Just the first couple." Calm and professional, Rory holds the end of the stethoscope in his palm. "Shouldn't take long to warm this."

Jesse nods, but she watches his hands.

Rory says gently, "It's okay to be nervous. You've had a difficult time with the profession lately." His eyes are kind. "Ready?"

She nods, and he slips the head of the stethoscope inside her shirt on the upper left side. "So, deep breath, and hold it. . . . Good. And again." Eyes unfocused, he listens to her chest. "Excellent. Now, we'll do the same for your back to check lung function." He waits without fuss while she pulls up the back of her shirt and gives him a nod when she's ready. She rates him for that.

Rory taps Jesse's back in several places, efficient but not perfunctory. "Absolutely all clear. We worry about problems with lungs after prolonged bed rest. But you're young and fit and healthy. Excellent outcome. So, just temperature, pulse, and eyes to go. Not long, I promise." Rory holds up the thermometer encouragingly. She *is* a fit girl, and well put together—long legs, small waist, wide shoulders. Pretty, too, with an open face and striking eyes. Rory smiles faintly. A doctor can still be a man.

"Funny, am I?" Jesse wills herself to remain calm as he slides the little glass stick under her tongue and picks up her wrist.

"Me, I'm lousy at telling jokes. No sense of timing." Rory concentrates on her pulse.

They're so close, Jesse can feel him breathe, hear the sound as air moves in and out of his nostrils. It occurs to her that she's with a man she hardly knows, in a small room in a hospital where she's a name on top of a list of injuries and little else. Even her parents don't know where she is. If she disappeared, it might be days or weeks before— *Stop this!*

"Something wrong?" Rory looks up.

She forces herself to speak. "Imagination, that's all. It's a riot in here." She taps her skull.

"You don't have to be brave, Jesse. And it's okay to be vulnerable. We both want to get at the truth of what's happened to you."

She mutters, "*Happening*, you mean."

Rory nods. "Yes, happening, and it's making you anxious every time you think about it. Maybe too anxious to actually help yourself get well." He's watching her.

"What does *that* mean?"

"What if I said there was a way I could help you deal with all the worry?"

"Not more pills!" Jesse scrambles to sit up. "Because I've had enough of drugs and—"

He shakes his head, amused. "Not pills. Hypnosis. It can take you into a very deep state of relaxation. I'll be able to ask you challenging questions and you'll be able to answer without becoming upset."

Jesse looks at him pityingly. "I'm immune, trust me. I used to bite my nails, and Mum"—there's a self-conscious pause—"well, I had a couple of sessions. It was crap."

He smiles. "Most people think that. So what happened?"

"Oh. Well, I just stopped chewing them naturally. Growing up, I suppose." Jesse resists glancing at her nails; she likes them long these days. "I'm not suggestible. Truly."

He nods. "But you're not, what, fifteen anymore?"

She can't help it. She grins. The man is good.

"I wouldn't suggest hypnosis if I didn't have faith it would help. I think you're blocking things you can't explain, and that's driving fear you can't deal with or really acknowledge. Rational people can be like that, but it makes the unknown worse when that scaffolding gets kicked out from under."

"Right. And I never would have guessed." Jesse frets at her bottom lip. Does she want to do this? "Will you keep me in the hospital if I don't agree?"

Rory leans forward, his hands on his knees. "Jesse, you have the right to sign yourself out at any time. *But*, I have an absolute duty to help make you well; that is, to assist in your progress to the full extent of my training and knowledge. And that is what I intend to do if you will let me do it. Your situation is"—he searches for the word—"unusual. To treat you best I need more information than, perhaps, conventional diagnostics and treatment will provide. X-rays only give us so much. And I think you want to know what's happening to your mind as much as I do." He lets that sink in, and when she says nothing, he murmurs, "You're in pain, Jesse, and not just from broken bones. It's holding you back."

"What are you, Sherlock Holmes?" But the laugh is shaky, and she stares at her hands, willing herself not to sniff.

"Something neurologically profound has happened to you." Rory hesitates. "And we don't yet know if that's good or the opposite—but I do think it's important. And not just for you, but for other people who've experienced brain injury because yours is such an unusual case. At the very least you're displaying characteristics I've never seen before."

Jesse's alarmed. "But the fracture was minor, you said that, and the bleed was small too?" She's not sure if that's the term, but he nods. "You told me it wasn't serious."

"I still think those things. But there's nothing in the literature I've so far found that is able to explain the phenomena you've been experiencing. The sketching, for instance."

She stares at him unhelpfully.

He moves on quickly. "There could be an elegant and simple explanation for what's happened. You might, for instance, have a genetic tendency for being ambidextrous, and not being able to use your dominant right hand has flushed that out. The ability to draw might've been similarly latent; perhaps the bleed after the fracture put pressure on an area of the brain that allowed those talents to finally express themselves. And yet . . ."

"You don't believe it, do you? That the answer is as simple as that?"

"Simple is often right, I've seen that over and over again, but asking questions under hypnosis may tell us things you have never consciously known about yourself. That could be very useful in the search for answers."

She stares at him for a long minute. "It doesn't explain the castle, though, does it? The fact the pictures show things I've never seen before."

"Let's see what we find out, shall we?"

Jesse exhales, a long sigh. "So you think there is an explanation?"

"Of course. There's always an explanation."

"First, make yourself really comfortable."

Jesse burrows deeper into the armchair, tips her head against the high back.

"Good. Now, I want you to think of something pleasant. A place you like going to, or an enjoyable pastime—something that gives you pleasure. Soon I'll count from ten down to one, but right now, all you have to do is breathe deep, relax, and listen to the sound of my voice."

Relax? Huh.

"So, here we go. Ten, nine, eight, feeling happy, and peaceful, and quite safe. And very relaxed."

Safe? But Jesse's eyelids drift down.

". . . seven, six, five; you're in your favorite place now, you love being where you are."

Swimming in a warm sea . . . No. It's not the ocean. There are reeds: bending and dancing. Sun on the water . . .

". . . four, three, two . . ."

Like a mirror, the water, liquid silver . . .

". . . one. You're feeling peaceful, Jesse, so comfortable. Zero. Nothing worries you at all."

I'm swimming. . . . It's cool and clear and green and . . . What's that?! Jesse's eyes leap open and the flesh on her arm dimples.

Rory says soothingly, "Just remember, you're safe and calm and warm—mind awake, body asleep. And you're detached, just an observer, like someone watching a movie. Nothing bothers you, or frightens you . . ."

The sound of his voice has a rhythm like a chant and Jesse's eyes droop closed.

"Jesse?"

No reply.

"Can you hear me, Jesse?"

The girl moves her head in a slow nod, as if it's an effort, as if her head is heavy.

Rory scribbles a quick note. "So, we'll count down just like before. Peaceful thoughts, so comfortable, and with every breath you're more relaxed, even more deeply relaxed than before. Ten, sleepy now; nine, lovely thoughts, so happy; eight, look around at where you are, this is your favorite place, remember; seven, focus on one thing you're drawn to; six, go toward it."

Jesse's head lolls. She's smiling. Under the lids, her eyes move as if she's watching something.

"Mind awake, body asleep. Five, don't hurry; four, nearly there, all the time in the world." Jesse's feet twitch. "Three, so close you can almost touch." Her feet begin to move on the floor, as if she's walking. "Two. Stop." Jesse's feet are still. "You're there. One. Just take it all in, no stress, no rush. Nod if you can hear me."

Jesse does not respond.

"Jesse? Can you hear me?"

She sighs deeply. Nods.

"That's good. Very good."

Jesse has the slight flush of a sleeping child. Rory stares down at her. He feels the urge to touch her face. But he does not.

"Excellent. Now I'm going to ask you a number of questions. You'll find this an enjoyable process and you'll remember what I ask easily and happily."

"Don't want to."

Rory jumps. It's as if a statue has spoken. His expression clears. "Okay, then, let's play a game instead."

She nods. "I like games."

"That's good, Jesse, that's very good. So this is the question-and-answer game. Are you ready to play?"

Jesse frowns. "No. No questions."

Rory stares at the girl with intense interest. "Remember, this is just like a movie. You're watching what's happening and you're quite safe and happy and calm. I'm going to count from three to zero now, and when I say *zero*, you can tell me what you want to do. Okay, Jesse?"

The girl's face relaxes. "Yes."

"Here we go. Three, even more calm than you were. Two, no anxiety at all, you're enjoying this process. One, so happy, so positive, and getting ready to tell me what you want to do. Zero." He bends closer.

"I want to stay where I am."

"Describe what you see."

Jesse says softly, "The trees are all around me."

"How does that make you feel?"

The girl chafes her arms. "Cold. The leaves block the sun. But I am happy. I like the forest because of the birds. They fly for me." Jesse's left hand rises and sweeps through the air.

Rory says cautiously, "Why is that?"

"Because they like me." Her hand flutters to her lap, like a feather floating on the air. "They sing for me too." She purses her lips and whistles. At first the sound is soft, then it rises and expands, long, liquid-sounding trills.

"Good, very good. But you can stop now, Jesse."

The birdsong cuts, as if a tape has stopped.

"What song was that, Jesse?"

She turns her head toward him. "My friend the blackbird. He has a lovely voice." Her feet begin to move.

"What are you doing now?"

"I am walking." The feet move a little faster and Jesse's expression begins to change, as if a tide is rising. A tide of emotion.

"Remember how relaxed you are, Jesse. How warm and safe you feel."

But Jesse's face works, she's panting.

"Breathing deep, nice and slow, Jesse. No anxiety, no fear. You're safe and warm. Just watch the movie. Remember, you're not *in* the movie, you're a spectator and you can control what you see. You can tell me if you like."

"Dark." Her head turns from side to side. "So cold. Cannot feel my hands." Her jaw trembles.

Feet stop. Head stops turning. Breathing . . . stops.

"Jesse?"

The girl does not move.

"I'll click my fingers three times and you'll be fully awake. Ready? Here we go." A light sweat forms on Rory's brow as he clicks his fingers—once, twice, three times.

The girl's eyes remain closed, but her chest begins to rise. And fall. And rise again.

"Nice and relaxed, that's good. So calm, so happy to listen to my voice. I'm picking up your wrist now, Jesse, but that does not worry you at all. Can you hear me?"

A nod.

Fingers on the inside of one wrist, Rory checks Jesse's pulse. And swallows. The pulse beats evenly. "That's good. That's very good." He puts her arm back at her side. "So, I'm just going to open a drawer." He fumbles, pulls open a drawer in the desk. Nothing. Tries another. There's a box of tissues, and hastily he blots his face. "More relaxed than you've ever been. With each breath you take, you sink deeper, much deeper; mind awake, body asleep."

Jesse's head lolls on her shoulder.

"Where are you now?"

The girl says nothing.

"Can you describe this place?"

"No. I want to go now." Anger.

"Please describe what you see. Pretend I don't know. Like the game we played before."

"I want to leave."

"Leave where?" Rory speaks carefully.

"You are cruel. You are trying to make me stay. I do not like it here." She huddles in the chair, making herself small.

"Watch yourself from above, Jesse, like you're in a helicopter. You don't have to feel afraid; this is interesting. You're curious."

Jesse turns her head. Sightless eyes, blank as marble, stare at him. "I do not understand you."

That gaze is eerie. Rory stumbles as he says, "Just remember, Jesse. This is a game. What do you think I mean?"

Her expression turns stubborn. "I do not know. You say things that seem strange."

Rory shifts in his seat. "We're just playing, Jesse. This is fun, and you're very happy. And relaxed." He speaks soothingly.

"Why do you call me that name? And I am not happy. I will not listen to you anymore." Her left hand flies to her ear.

Rory watches Jesse's right hand move as well, fighting the sling. "Well then, I'll count back from three, and when I say *zero*, you'll feel much, much better. So content, so pleased to be playing our game. Three, two, one, zero."

Jesse's left hand floats down to her chest. Her face relaxes.

Rory clears his throat. "So, what name should I call you by?"

"I have no name." Jesse shakes her head. "They said you would ask me."

"Who is 'they'?"

"If you do not know, I cannot tell you."

"Why can't you tell me?"

Jesse sits up. Open-eyed, she points at him. "Because you have no right to know."

The moment freezes.

His face is tense, but Rory says softly, "You are sleepy. Very, very sleepy. The chair is so comfortable. And warm. So soft. Much, much nicer than a bed . . ."

Jesse's eyelids flutter and close. She leans back, sinks deeper as Rory says, "Now, I'm going to count down from five this time, and when I snap my fingers twice, you'll be awake, fully awake, and you will feel happy and refreshed. Are you ready?"

Jesse nods, her face expressionless.

"Very good. Five, starting to wake, gently and happily. Four, closer to waking and you've just had a pleasant dream. Three, getting ready to stretch and open your eyes." Jesse stirs but her face stays serene. "Two, sleep is almost gone." Jesse's eyelids twitch. "One, you can see the light. It's lovely to be almost awake. Zero!" Rory snaps his fingers twice. "Fully awake."

Jesse stretches luxuriously.

"Feel good?" Rory smiles at his patient.

"Yes. I really do. Did you find it useful?"

"Very." He holds up the notes.

"Any answers about the . . ." She mimes sketching.

"Not as such. I'm not expecting the anxiety you've experienced will go away instantly, by the way, though this is a very good start." He pauses. "Do you remember much of what you said?"

"Not really. It's a jumble. I know there was water and"— she waves her hand vaguely—"there seemed to be someone else around. I could hear her talking, but it was my voice." She hesitates. "That sounds a bit nuts, doesn't it?"

Rory pauses before he makes a careful note. Then he leans forward and touches Jesse's good shoulder. "Confusion often happens ahead of a breakthrough. Therapy takes the time it takes, but consistent effort, just chipping away, asking questions, is important. The good news is I haven't picked up any cognition impairment."

"Such big words." Some kind of smile. "But what if I don't *have* any time? Or money, either. I can't stay here forever. My life's on hold."

He says carefully, "Your treatment as a result of the emergency is, of course, without charge."

"There's a *but* somewhere in there."

A half nod of acknowledgment. "Rehabilitation is a separate issue."

"And this is rehabilitation?"

Rory puts the cap back on his old-fashioned cartridge pen. "How about I do some work on what I've observed and we can talk later about your concerns."

"Back in the ward." Her expression is gloomy.

Rory manages a grin. "Don't want to exhaust you."

"I know, I know, 'rest is best.'"

"Exactly." Rory picks up the phone on the desk, dials a number, and murmurs into the mouthpiece, "Yes, ready now. . . . That would be good."

Jesse makes a disappointed sound that is neither yes nor no, but she gets into the wheelchair without protest when the nurse appears. "Thanks, Dr. Brandon." Somehow, she doesn't want to call him by his first name. "I'm sorry to be such a difficult patient."

"Not difficult—not compared with some." His grin stays in place until the door closes, but he stares down at his notes as if the words make no sense. Finally he writes, *Rehab* and *Where?*

Distracted as he thinks, he doodles and a shape begins to emerge on the page.

He stares at what he's drawn.

9

AT THE end of a cart road that wandered away from the village, a house stood by itself. Every man on the estate knew what this house was for and who lived there, hidden behind the holly fence. It was called the House of Women because whores had always lived there. The wives and daughters of the village spat as they walked past, and stones were thrown at the shuttered windows, but the whores never came outside to challenge the women. They knew how frightened the good wives were of losing their men.

Mary, the bawd at the House of Women, called herself an ale wife, because that was all she sold since her looks had faded. Perhaps her mother had been a pious woman or perhaps she had been hopeful. Some in the village said it was a disgrace for Christ's mother's name to be dishonored by such as she; as a child, I did not know what they meant. But the first day Maugris took me to the House of Women, when I was fifteen, I understood; Mary had me out of my clothes and into her daughter's bed in less time than it took to skin a rabbit.

Mary did not know how old the daughter was—she reckoned by seasons because she could not count. Perhaps Rosa had seen a summer or so more than me, but a boy will often seem younger than a girl of the same age. Yet in all the time since that first day, there had never been a child from Rosa's body, so far as I knew. Not mine, nor anyone else's. Rumor said the ale wife knew how to enchant babies away so they never grew in her daughter's belly. Others told another story. The old bawd kept a bucket by the bed, and each time Rosa gave birth, Mary drowned the child and buried it under the holly hedge. That was why it grew so fast.

But these were the slanders of the village women. Truth was, I thought, if Rosa began lying with men as a very young girl, she might not be capable of children. A useful thing in a whore, though sad perhaps.

However, the things Rosa had learned to do with her body were pleasurable, and since I was a Dieudonné, I might have been treated better than the villagers. I paid well for her services and for a time was even persuaded, and perhaps Rosa was too, that some special sweetness lived between us, especially at the beginning.

Today I tied my horse behind the hut so it could not be seen from the track. Angry though I was, I looked forward to being with Rosa again for many reasons. My dreams last night had been potent, and though my body was still weak, it was good to feel the sap rise. Also, being with this girl always left me cheerful, and I could speak to her as few others in my life since she was shrewd in her way; beds, after all, are the place for conversation as well as other things.

Thinking to surprise her, I crept through the only door the hut possessed. Perhaps that is not wise in the house of a whore, but I found Rosa throwing peat on the fire and coughing at the smoke.

I was shocked. It had been two years since I had last seen her, but she seemed older; the bloom gone from her skin, and her hair, once so thick, was a straggle of wisps around her face. The worst of it was she was no longer buxom, but far too close to thin. Soon Rosa would look like her mother. Would ale feed them when men no longer came for either the daughter or the mother?

"A welcome for a stranger?"

"Bayard!" Rosa ran at me and jumped. I caught her easily, and she wrapped her legs around my waist, her lips at my ear. "So handsome," she breathed. "So fine. Brawny Cock Robin returned to his nest." She leaned back to look at my face, and the muscles I was left with worked hard to hold her weight.

A clever girl, she uncoupled herself and slid down my body, pressing herself against me. "I heard you nearly died, wasting away in your bed." Her eyes were innocent but the hand that eased under my jerkin and down my breeches was not. She grinned. "Don't feel like that to me. And I have a bed too. Deep and soft and hot and open, all open, for you, sweet cockerel."

It was not unpleasant being with her again, and with the promise of what was to come, my temper improved. Also, she was chewing an herb, new mint from the pot by the door perhaps, and she smelled fresh. My mother had taught all her sons to be fastidious, and I had encouraged Rosa to wash when I was with her, though Mary had not liked such things; I was pleased she had kept the habit. But I knew last year's harvest had been a bad one after a wet summer, and it was easy to see the coin Rosa made between her thighs had grown scarce, for the house was comfortless, and peat, not wood, was stacked beside the hearth; poorly dried, it filled the room with smoke.

Perhaps I did not hide dismay well enough for Rosa said, in a humid whisper, "I can promise you delight, my lusty knight; a good ride and no quarter until the battle's done. When has Rosa ever let you from the saddle with less?"

An open shutter threw light on her face. There were lines around her eyes and beside her mouth, and she'd lost a tooth or two. It made me sad for what was gone, but I let her take my hand and lead me behind the wattle screen and to the bed she shared with her mother at other times.

She cupped my face in her hands. "I had thought our time together was done, my love. And that distressed me because I could not tell how many times we had lain here on this bed. But now you are here again, and you can count. Tell me how many times we have coupled, so that I may remember each when you are gone again."

I unlaced the strings that held the bodice of her kirtle together. "The stars in the sky are not more numerous. How may we count the stars?" The linen beneath was clean enough, and I pulled it aside to find her breasts. She laughed as I took them in my hands and, eyes half closed, guided my fingers to her nipples. I felt them, hard as blackberries, and when I put my mouth there and teased them with my tongue, she gasped. "Ah, you do not forget. You never forget." She knew her trade, Rosa, that I will say.

Turning in my arms, she took my jerkin off and slid her hands over my back and my arms. Raking the skin with her nails until it puckered, she said, "Come, beloved, and you shall see more of me. All that you wish." She paused before she slipped from the top part of her clothes, turning into and out of what light there was, so that her body was revealed for my pleasure. Then, both of us naked to the waist, she pushed me back over the side of the bed. There she straddled me, pulling up her skirts with one hand, pressing me deep into the mattress with the other. She was just a shape in the half dark, her head higher than my own, but as she unlaced the points of my breeches and her fingers grew busy between our bellies, I forgot to think her old. When, at last, she teased me no longer and, with a quick shift of her hips, had me between her legs, it was all I could do to hold the tide for even a little while. Then I stopped trying.

The little death is a pleasant thing after the itch is sated, and this was often the time when Rosa and I dallied the day away talking. Today, lying on the bed with no covering but Rosa's body, I half woke as the air struck cold.

The girl was not asleep, though she pretended to be; having

known her so long, I could tell. If I was not to meet another of her clients—arriving as I had, unexpected—I must dress and leave.

Rolling the girl off my chest, I yawned and sat up. The creak of the ropes under the palliasse was familiar. The bed was old, and too well used.

Rosa murmured, "So soon, my love. Would you not stay with me a little while?"

I felt her arms around my belly and put a hand over hers. "If I do not return soon, they will look for me." It was the truth. I did not want another argument with Godefroi.

She murmured, "But the night is a long time away." For a pause I said nothing. Rosa, a sensible girl, wriggled off the bed. She turned away slightly, but I watched her skirts drop to the floor and cover her legs. These were sturdy with round calves. I had been surprised the first time I saw them since her upper body was delicate, yet the contrast was erotic. I had come to appreciate those legs and Rosa's wide hips, for both seemed made to bear a man's weight as he worked up a sweat.

Rosa knew I was looking at her as she went to the settle. Returning with my clothes, she swayed her hips, thinking to provoke me. When I did not respond, she stood back with a swallowed sigh and watched as I dressed. "You are too thin, Bayard."

I did not say the same to her, though I thought it. Perhaps she saw it in my eyes, and did not look at me as her finger traced the scar on my chest. "Is it true you died, and she brought you back?"

I had the shirt half over my head, and Rosa did not think I saw her sign the evil eye. "I was not dead. Just"—what had I been?—"just close. There is nothing strange in a man recovering from his wounds. I was well nursed." I hurried to tie off the points of my breeches. This was not a conversation I wanted to have.

"Well nursed?" Rosa swatted my hands away and continued what I had begun. "Some say your *nurse* is a sorceress. That when she flies from the keep on nights without a moon, she curses the children so they die in their cradles. There have been many deaths in the village."

Outside, rising wind rattled the latch, and Rosa quickly turned. Wide-eyed, she stared at the door as if expecting Flore herself. "They say too that she does not eat and neither does she drink. Can that be true?"

I took the girl's chin in my hand. "And are 'they' the other men who lie in your bed?" She dropped her eyes and would not look at me. "The woman is pregnant. Food turns her stomach. It is common enough."

"And how do you know? You a chaste, unmarried knight." The glimmer of a naughty grin. And then a frown. "Bayard, be careful. Promise me. I mean it." Her voice was earnest. "She has enchanted the Lord Godefroi and all the bad things in this year have been . . ." She did not finish the thought. Perhaps she remembered whose brother I was and where my loyalty must lie.

"Who says such things? The men who come here?" I was dressed again. A man who, only moments since, had thought himself the equal of gods and angels. That is what a woman does with what lies between her legs.

She sniffed. "Not the women. They do not talk to us. But I know what I know."

"This is foolish. The Lady Flore—"

Rosa spat on the dirt floor. This time she made the sign and did not try to hide it.

I continued calmly, "The Lady Flore is"—I was not sure what word was best—"is not a witch."

"No?" Rosa stood on her toes and grasped my shoulders, forcing me to look down into her face. "Ah. I see. You too have been bewitched." She dropped her hands and stood away from me. "I say she is a whore *and* a witch. And I should know."

"Which?"

She stared at me. "Do not think me stupid because of what I do, Bayard." Her face, in the half-light, was less old than ancient.

I tried to kiss her, but Rosa turned her face away. Perhaps she did not want to see me leave.

"Put it back."

I looked over my shoulder as I pulled the saddle off Helios. "What?"

"Boy!"

Dikon, the stableboy, ran as Maugris called out, "Help Lord Bayard."

"I can do it myself." I heaved the saddle to its place again. Helios was sweating from the ride, and he was not pleased when Dikon tried to drag his head from the manger to put the bridle on again.

"I shall need armor." It was not a question. The look on my brother's face was grim, and he was suited in a steel hauberk.

"You will if we ride after them."

"After who?"

Maugris did not reply, but as we left the stables, he called out to the boy, "Keep the horse ready."

Enoch, the castle farrier, was working at the entrance to the stables shoeing a line of horses. The air was acrid—scorched hooves and hot iron.

I raised a hand in greeting. He had been kind to us as boys when we hid in the stables to avoid our father.

Smiling, Enoch waved back but Maugris ignored the man and hurried on. The farrier's expression soured as he crouched to pick up the next hoof.

"That was not well done."

Maugris ignored me as he ducked through a low door that led into the chain of cellars where the tenants' rent of grain, fruit, and roots was stored.

We heard voices. Godefroi. And the lighter tones of a woman.

Without speaking, Maugris pushed on a door.

Head bowed, Margaretta knelt in front of Godefroi. He was staring at her. "You must have known."

"No, lord." The girl did not look up. Her voice shook.

Godefroi wheeled. "Reeve!"

Swinson stood in the far shadows of the cellar, behind his daughter. Flambeaux picked out lines of sweat on his face. None of the three had seen us.

"You are right to be afraid, Swinson. No servant of mine can be allowed to lie."

"My daughter is an honest woman, lord."

Margaretta's eyes were tragic. "Father, let me."

Godefroi held up a hand. "He shall speak for himself." And pointed. "Kneel."

Swinson's body was rigid as he knelt, but he spoke with dignity. "Me and mine have always obeyed you, lord. And your family. We are loyal. In your father's day—"

Godefroi slapped the man across the face. An explosive blow. "This is not my father's day."

Watching, I could not remain impassive. Ignoring Maugris, I pushed the door wide and strode through.

Godefroi flicked a glance from me to the reeve. "Answer what I asked. You knew he did this, both of you. Confess it."

Edmund Swinson raised his head. Blood joined sweat on the side of his face. He seemed sincerely puzzled. "But he is a monk, lord. Your own father sponsored him to the monastery. It cannot have been my son." The man was pleading.

Godefroi pulled the reeve to his feet and dragged him to where a body, dressed in Hundredfield livery, lay on the floor. "Excellent work for a man of God." The face was covered but both hands had been cut off.

Swinson turned his head away.

"Look!" Godefroi ripped the covering away. The eyes had been gouged out. "Nothing to say? Your son the traitor was seen, reeve, and his men. He took the eyes with his own knife." Godefroi kicked Swinson in the back. The reeve fell beside the corpse, his head knocking on stone.

"Father!" Margaretta tried to reach Swinson, but Maugris stopped her, held her as she struggled.

Godefroi shouted, "If Alois thinks to send us a message, one shall be returned." He wheeled, glaring at me. "You! Take this girl to my wife; she will not speak of this to anyone if she loves her father."

"No!" Margaretta tried to claw Maugris's face as he dragged her forward.

Pushing her at me, he said, "For your sake and hers, obey him, Bayard. This cannot be ignored."

A girl when she will not be held, even so slight and young, is never easy to manage. In the end I picked Margaretta up and slung her across my shoulder.

"Maugris!" Godefroi had his sword at the reeve's throat as the man tried to stand.

"Go." Maugris pushed me through the door and closed it in my face.

The wood muffled my brother's voice, but it did not disguise the screams of Edmund Swinson.

10

I've been thinking."

Staring out the window at the sprawl of London, Jesse is in the patients' day room. She jumps when Rory strolls up behind her.

"Sorry. May I?" He points at one of the chairs, smiles nicely.

"You won't like it."

"Uncomfortable?"

Jesse nods with feeling.

Rory drags an austere 1950s armchair to where she's sitting. "That's the National Health Service for you: no pampering. At least it's free."

"A free prolapsed chair. Don't tell. Everyone will want one." Jesse's staring at the springs; they bulge out as he sits. She makes an effort. "So, thinking. Excellent. What about?"

"Rehab. Yours. The where and when."

Jesse takes a deep breath. "Dr. Brandon, please don't think I'm not grateful for the extra time you give me, but I need to move on. I was going to tell you a bit later today." The early-morning bustle outside the Smithfield Market is suddenly fascinating.

He murmurs, "Rory. Please." He shifts in his seat. "Do you mind if I ask you something?"

"Depends what it is." Said pleasantly, but Jesse's wary.

"What's more urgent than getting better?"

"I'll take it easy. Doctor's orders." Not much of a joke.

Rory sits back. He's happy to wait.

"You must be busy. Don't let me hold you up." Jesse tries not to squirm. *Take the hint. Go!*

He glances at his watch. "You're not. Plenty of time."

She looks away. The noise she makes might be a sniff. "Look, I found out only recently that I'm adopted. I'm in England to find my birth parents. If I can." Jesse feels her eyes filling. She blinks rapidly, tries not to sniff the tears away.

A pause. Rory leans forward. He's offering his handkerchief. When she takes it, he says gently, "Do you have somewhere to start?"

Jesse blows her nose. "I know I was born in Jedburgh. That's where I want to go. As soon as I can." Should she give him back the handkerchief?

"Keep it."

Jesse nods. She feels like a pane of cracked glass.

"I've got a suggestion—something for you to consider. Especially since you were born in Jedburgh." Rory hesitates. "What if I told you . . ." A pause. He starts again. "Do you remember the girl in the café?"

"Café?" Jesse's puzzled.

"Alicia. The waitress. At St. Bartholomew the Great."

Jesse frowns. She says uncertainly, "That day's all a bit of a bus-smash in my head, but she was kind when she didn't have to be. She found you too, didn't she? And the rest"—Jesse waves her hand, a vague sweep—"is history."

Rory says abruptly, "She and I know each other. Quite well, actually; I got her the job in the café. And the odd thing is . . ."

The pause stretches. That gets Jesse's attention. "What's odd?"

"The castle." He mimes sketching.

"My castle?"

He nods. "It's always been owned by Alicia's family. They built it."

Jesse's almost too startled to speak. "A *waitress* owns a castle?"

"She does now. Her parents died not long back. The thing is, I think you should see it. See Hundredfield, I mean. That's what it's called."

"Why?"

"Because it might help unlock things for you. The sketches didn't draw themselves."

Jesse won't meet his eyes.

"And I'm off there tomorrow. I spend time at Hundredfield every summer." He takes a breath. "You could come with me, Jesse. I could continue what we've started. Rehab, I mean. No charge." Rory shifts position. With his back to the light, it's hard to see his expression.

Jesse opens her mouth, closes it again.

Rory speaks before she can. "The offer's real. Hundredfield is an extraordinary place, by the way, and it's only rarely open to the public. Alicia's ancestors built up the estate over hundreds of years until it became one of the greatest landholdings between Carlisle and Berwick, and that includes Alnwick. That's the seat of the Percys, of course."

Jesse murmurs, "Oh, of course." She has no idea what he's talking about.

"It was begun by conquest and—"

"Conquest? As in William the . . ."

He nods. "Fulk, the founder of Alicia's family, was a Norman warlord, basically. The English-Scottish border changed many, many times over hundreds of years—and always in a welter of blood—but that was profitable for some people. Including the lords of Hundredfield. That's where it got the name—from all the land they took."

"But if she's so grand, why does she work in a café in London?"

"Everyone needs a job from time to time. Even Alicia."

"But that makes no sense. If I had a castle I'd—"

Rory interrupts, "Find it hard to pay for, actually. History can be a burden."

"And what's it got to do with rehab?"

"Coming-clean time." Rory shifts uncomfortably. "I told you I knew the castle in the sketch, that I'd been there." Rory pauses. "Actually, I lived on the estate in a tied cottage. With my mum."

Jesse just stares at him.

"I didn't know how to tell you, not after I'd seen the sketches."

She says feelingly, "This is . . . I don't know *what* this is."

"No." Rory mulls. "But what it *could* be is interesting." He leans farther forward, his eyes locked to hers. "Jesse, I think it's important for you, and for me, that you see Hundredfield. I wouldn't suggest this otherwise."

"Oh. Right. Important for you. How long did you live there?"

"I was born on the estate."

Jesse's mouth drops open. After a false start she says, "You do know this is a ridiculous conversation."

He says urgently, "You need time to recover, you need proper cognitive therapy and ongoing assessment. And your body has to heal. I can help you with all those things if you'll let me. And you can help me also. Yes, the coincidences are odd, but your case is . . ." He shakes his head. "I'd say it's unique, so far as current science understands the results of head trauma."

"Rehabilitation at Hundredfield, in return for cooperating in your research?" He nods. An uncomfortable pause. "Is that usual? I mean . . ."

"No. Not usual. But if you agree, I'll inform my supervisors in the specialist program of my intentions, and offer an overview of what I would like to achieve with your help. They will approve or not, as the case may be. They may also wish to interview you before making their decision. If you agree." His voice is neutral, his expression polite and nothing more.

Jesse considers what he's said. "Where's Hundredfield again?"

"About an hour from Jedburgh." Now he permits himself a smile. And stands. "Thank you for considering what I'm suggesting, Jesse."

She shoots back, "Who says I am?"

"I need to do the morning rounds, but I'll be back after that. Meantime, why don't I get one of the ward ladies to bring you a cup of coffee?"

"Don't you dare!"

"Tea, then. And something to eat. Doctor's orders. Real ones." At the door, Rory turns back. "Think about what I've said?" He doesn't wait for an answer.

Jesse watches him go. Is the man arrogant, or just sure of himself?

Standing on the curb outside St. Barts, Jesse looks at her watch. The place is busy as buses disgorge passengers and taxis pull up.

She's beginning to hope. Is that good, or is it bad? The guidebook helped; Frommer's is quite informative about Jedburgh. Apparently it's an ancient town on one of the main routes between London and Edinburgh, and Mary Stuart, Queen of Scots, stayed there for a while (at the end of the love affair with Bothwell; not good). There's an abbey and a castle, and it's about six hours from London in a fast car. She's found Priorsgate on the foldout map of the town. She hadn't expected that. Can it really be this easy?

The honk of a horn and she swings around. Rory Brandon's waving from a NO STANDING zone. Jesse hefts her shoulder bag, careful to carry it on the left.

"All set?" He leans over to unlock the door. "Sorry to be late." She says impulsively, "I'm glad your supervisors agreed, Dr.

Brandon. And I just wanted to say thank you." Her mood has lifted. She means it.

Mock severe, he says, "Rory. Go on. Repeat after me . . ."

A duck of the head. "Rory. There." But she doesn't quite look at him.

"Seat belt." He points.

But it's not easy pulling the belt across her body with the left hand and negotiating around the sling.

Rory reaches over. "Let me."

Jesse leans back against the seat, trying not to get in the way.

"There you go. Done."

But it feels unexpectedly intimate. Jesse says hastily, "Should you be parking here?" A parking cop is working his way along the curb. "I don't want to get you into trouble."

Rory waves at the cop—who, surprisingly, waves back. "They know me here. Off we go." The Saab slips away from the hospital like a fish joining a greater shoal as he turns the car to the north. "I prefer the indirect route, by the way. The drive's longer but it's worth it—you see the countryside a bit more. We'll head for Durham first—that'll be about half the day with traffic—then on to Newton Prior. It's about an hour inland from the coast, just where the country rolls up toward the border with Scotland."

"Newton Prior?"

"It's a pretty little market town on the English side." He flicks her a glance. "D'you mind if I speed up a bit? It's quite a distance."

She holds up the guidebook. "Frommer's says it's around six hours in here—to Jedburgh, at least. Speed away."

"Only if there's no roadworks. My advice is, try to sleep."

"No thank you. Banked enough zeds to last for a bit." Jesse smiles at sunny London flowing past. Hypnosis. Who'd have thought it? No more odd dreams, or drawings either, and even the pain of knitting bones is less with each passing day. Weeks of weirdness and now this: a moment that feels as if she's breathing champagne, and the beginning, the true beginning, of the search.

How could she have turned him down?

Everything has a reason, Jesse. The girl hears her mum's voice as clearly as if Janet Marley's sitting in the backseat.

Jesse finds she's smiling. She's actually feeling quite light-hearted. She can't remember the last time.

In the morning light, London glitters and flirts as it rushes past, and whenever he can, Rory pushes the revs as he weaves across town toward the ring road and the motorway north.

Jesse shouts over Roxy Music on the tape deck, "You're a lead-foot!"

"No one's ever called me that before." But Rory's grinning as they slip onto the motorway and dodge into the fast lane. Sixty, seventy, seventy-five . . .

Jesse eyes the needle. It's nudging red. "Not concerned about the cops, then."

"Never had a ticket."

"What, true?"

"I'm invisible when I want to be." The grin is wider.

"Me too. But I was six last time it worked."

"O ye of little faith." He shifts down until the engine whines, then drops back into top gear as the car divides the air like an arrow. Settled in front of the flow again, he flips a glance at his passenger. "Relax. Really. I know this road."

"*Relax.* Now there's a word." Jesse wriggles deeper into the seat. Her eyes drift closed as she wills her breathing to slow. She's better at that than she used to be. With each mile that passes, she gets closer to her past, her true past.

And her real mother.

If there's any certainty in this world, Jesse knows she'll find her. She absolutely will.

11

DECEMBER 1321

THAT COLD summer bled into a wet autumn and, with the sun hidden behind clouds, the harvest failed again in the border country. By October, a murrain appeared among the cows and the sheep began to founder, their feet rotting in mire that never dried. As the year turned dark just before the blood month, nights became cold too early and famine stalked the people, for they had no stores of food.

The year saw other kinds of pestilence also—winds that brought down forests, hail that beat through roofs, and a constant rain that reduced the folk to misery and the trackways to bogs. And then came death. Children died first of a sweating sickness, followed soon enough by their starving parents. When wind blew from the north, the land reeked of rotting flesh, and the crows had never been fatter.

Perhaps we were luckier than most. With so much of the countryside famine-struck, the reivers in the border country had been less active. Though our troop was expected to live off the land—a task that could not be pursued with compassion—we carried some provisions, meager though they were.

"They will not take so many beasts this year. Unless they wish to kill their own with the pest." After eating, Maugris had emptied his bladder beyond the light of our fire. My brother was fastidious. He said it kept him sane when all we did was ride and fight and sleep on freezing ground.

"Have you seen cows worth taking around here? I have not." I made room for him beside the hearth of the ruined house.

"Anything on four feet is worth eating these days. I expect that will be their downfall." Maugris wiped his eyes as the wind changed, blowing smoke over us both. "Mary's milk, I'm getting too old for this life. We should have taken them by now."

I sucked marrow from the shank bone I'd cracked. There was nothing to say. We had followed a band of raiders for days through the glens and forests—Scots or English, we could not tell—but this morning they had outrun us back over the border toward Jedburgh, so confirming who they were. Our men and our horses were exhausted, and there were not enough of us to challenge the raiders on their own ground, as we had earlier in the year. Tomorrow, we would turn back toward Alnwick to report on the engagements we had fought. I brooded on what that would mean; pursuing men who turned to mist would be no excuse when we spoke with Henry Percy.

"Brother." Maugris pointed at the grease running down my chin. He thought we should set an example, but this was the first fresh meat we'd had in a week and I did not care.

I threw the shank into the coals. There was nothing to burn but the bone. "Do not reproach yourself. They had the advantage today, that is all."

Maugris found a place on the log we'd dragged to the fire. "Is there any more meat?"

I pointed with my knife. The ewe's carcass had been dismembered on the hearthstones when it was cooked. The men had been patient as the food was distributed, but all they had left was a puddle of fat and the feet. At least tonight we were more warm than cold.

Maugris sighed. "Ah, well. At least we found this place. That was luck." He waved toward the stars above our head. "It's even got a roof, if you don't count the holes."

I rolled on my back. Maugris was right: enough of the roof remained to make it worthy of the name, though the slates were not well held to the rafters. The hearth and the fire had cheered us, though, along with the poor old ewe. We had heard her bleating, her voice still strong for one so close to death, and that had drawn us to this place as dark fell. A chestnut tree had fallen in a storm and broken one of her legs, but the ending of that pain-filled life was worthy, for she saved ours. Maybe she understood our gratitude as I slit her throat.

I waved toward the roof timbers. "This would have been a good house once. Defensible." Unruined, the building must have stood two or three stories tall, though all the floors were missing.

"Do you really care?" Maugris yawned.

"Someone has to. Too many abandoned homesteads in the marches."

Maugris said testily, "If you are still angry at Godefroi after all these months, then you are a fool."

"Lower your voice." I tipped my head toward the men on the other side of the blaze. Some were asleep, but others were not.

"He will not change, Bayard. He does what he thinks is best for Hundredfield. For us all."

"So it is *best* he nearly killed the reeve who served our family for longer than our own lives? It was not Swinson's fault Alois did what he did."

My brother's face was hard. "Tell me this, Bayard. If it had been you, what would you have done? A man died, one of our own."

There was no resolving this argument. He thought me soft, I thought him blind. I gestured toward our men. "Why do they fight for us?"

Each year greater levies of men were commanded by the wardens of the march to counter the Scots who hurled over the border into English lands, and to contain the English raiding families who pillaged the other side from vengeance. Sometimes the English and the Scots worked together against us. We were surprised by nothing in those days.

Maugris did not look at me. "We feed them, and our work protects their families. And we take them home when their service is done."

"Feed them? Take them home?" I shook my head. "Do you know why none deserted for the harvest this year?" My brother was silent. "Because there was no harvest."

"This bitter weather is everywhere, Bayard."

I spoke over him. "No. Sheep graze on Hundredfield's common and on the flats beside the river. And some of our men have no homes to return to because Godefroi wills it so. It is no wonder the raiders fight as they do and take what they can. There is no justice in the border marches."

Maugris murmured, "We are justice, Bayard."

The old wound on my chest began to throb. I shook my head.

He said quietly, "Godefroi has a wife now, and soon a child. He wants to give them a better life than we had. Times change. A man has to fight if he is to hold what he has." Maugris wrapped his cloak tight and lay down by the fire with a sigh. "I will be glad to sleep in some kind of bed soon. Even straw would make me happy." When I did not answer, he nudged me with his boot. "Are you awake?"

"No."

His bark of laughter rolled out into the night.

"I hear nothing good from Hundredfield. Godefroi is too much in his bedroom, and the reivers encroach. They have a new captain. A renegade monk, I'm told."

I started, but Maugris said smoothly, "The Lady Flore, our brother's wife, is with child. If he is in her chamber, it is to offer comfort as a good husband should." Out of Henry Percy's sight, Maugris nudged me.

I said hastily, "Yes. Gossip spun from malice."

The baron ignored me. "There you are!" An impatient shout.

Lady Idonia Percy hurried out from the door to her husband's private closet. A pale girl, she had the worried face of a tame rabbit. "I am sorry, husband, but the baby frets with this fever and will not eat, and—"

"The boy will survive. We're late." Henry grasped his wife's hand and strode toward the chapel door, towing his lady as if she were a barge. We had to run to keep up, as did most of Alnwick's household. They had been waiting in the outer chamber also— knights, their wives, even the steward of the castle with all the upper servants. But none muttered in complaint. We were all used to Henry Percy.

The baron stopped suddenly. "Gossip, you said. From what source?" He stared from Maugris to me, sharp as a jackdaw. Behind, those closest strained to hear.

Maugris lowered his voice. "Our brother's marriage was, ah, unexpected. That may be the cause." He shrugged. "Envy, perhaps. The Lady Flore is very beautiful."

I tried not to stare. This was the first time Maugris had spoken well of our sister-in-law.

"Envy?" Henry Percy yelped a laugh. "Someone said your brother's wife was a hedge-girl once. But yes, very pretty. Too pretty for him." He poked Maugris in the chest. "You were looking in the wrong place all this time. The raiders have been in your forests, and among your sheep, driving them away. And that is *not* gossip. This new captain is growing powerful. Hundredfield must not be weakened." He crossed himself. "You will have to do better."

We both knew our overlord was right, and he had little tolerance for those who failed.

Maugris murmured, "This winter drives the peasants to find

food where they would not have dared before. I doubt they were reivers."

A fierce glance. "Oh, you *doubt* what I say?" Henry snorted, started up at a pace again, his wife barely clinging to his arm. "Do not cant to me of hard winters. This new man is a potent threat. That would never have happened in your father's time."

Maugris said, "Sir, when we left the keep some months ago, Godefroi had the matter in hand."

Another snort. "Not well enough."

At the chapel door, Henry Percy seized my brother's arm. They spoke in lowered voices, and then, dismissed, we stood together as the household flowed past. I ignored the sideways glances. "Well?"

Maugris sighed. "He is sending us home."

"Now?" Alnwick blazed with fire and light, and it was well known that pretty women flocked to the Christmas revels. I had been looking forward to that.

"Yes, now." Maugris was irritated too. And disappointed. No feather beds for us, then, not even straw. "Orders are to go back and right the situation."

"Clean up Godefroi's mess, you mean."

Before we had left Hundredfield the last time, Swinson had been dumped, barely alive, outside the gates of the castle. He was gone the next morning, and it was presumed he had died, his body taken by Alois. If what Henry Percy said was true, the reeve's son was making this fight personal.

And Margaretta? I wondered what had happened to the girl, and also to Godefroi's little son. I did not allow myself to think about Flore.

12

J ESSE, HELLO."

She feels the hand on her arm. It's confusing. She's deep in the sea at Bondi, wading through the waves and not getting wet.

"You slept, but we're here now." The Saab is parked in front of a building of weathered gray stone.

Jesse scrambles out and cranes to look up. Hard to take it all in. Four stories under a steep roof rear against the sky—gables and pepper-pot turrets and deep-set casement windows. A building from a fairy tale. She turns. It's there, that square, brutal tower. Of course it's there. "It's real, then." Has time and damage robbed it of power? *No.*

Rory dives into the trunk and pulls out Jesse's small case. "Don't be intimidated. It's just a pile of stone."

"I'm not. I'm just . . ." *What?*

He slams the lid. "Come on. You must be hungry."

"Rory, I don't know if—"

A dog barks as light floods from the house. The waitress from the café stands framed in the open door. "Hi, Rory. Good trip?"

"Yes, thanks. Great to see you, Alicia." Rory hurries forward as a frantic black Labrador hurtles out to the drive, his whole body wagging. "Good boy, Ollie. Good dog. Get down!" Pandemonium rules as the dog jumps and yips, scrabbling at Rory's legs.

"Oliver, behave. Sit!" Alicia's voice registers, and Ollie finally does as he's told, his tail fanning the gravel at Rory's feet. Until he sees Jesse and takes off.

Alicia calls out, "He won't bite. He's just a baby, really." She hurries over as the dog, a barking blur, tears around and around. "Oh. Hello there." The slightest uncertainty flickers across her face.

"I like dogs. Really. Especially friendly ones," Jesse burbles from embarrassment.

"He really is naughty. No manners at all." It's Rory Alicia's staring at. Her tone is light, but there's a cool edge.

Rory grabs Ollie's collar. "It's all my fault, boy."

A pleasant smile from Alicia. "But we're used to that." She takes the dog from her visitor. "It's the boot room for you, my lad, before you create any more havoc." As she tows the reluctant Ollie back to the house, she calls over her shoulder, "I was just going to have a drink. All welcome."

"Coming." Rory picks up the bags and starts off in Alicia's wake.

"You didn't tell her, did you?"

"Alicia's a lovely girl. You'll see."

"That's not what I asked, Rory."

Alicia calls from the front door, "What about that drink?"

He leans closer and murmurs, "It would be rude to refuse."

Jesse hesitates. Finally she says, "Just one." But she's not happy as she stalks past.

Somewhere distant, Ollie's barking. Alicia's smile is quite polite. "A delinquent, that animal." The three are standing just inside a vast hall, with a ceiling three stories above their heads. Alicia points to a door covered in green felt and studded with brass nails. "Kitchen's through there."

Jesse stares. "The green baize door. Seriously?"

Alicia's expression warms a bit. "Yes. It's the way to the servants' hall and the kitchens."

"What, as in *Upstairs, Downstairs*?"

Alicia grins. "We can't afford the 'downstairs' these days. Not even a handyman, or I'd have sent him for the bags." The face is smiling, the eyes are not, when Alicia turns to Rory. "Shall we?" She holds the door open. "Perhaps you'd show our guest the way, Rory?" The slightest of emphasis on *our*.

Rory shepherds Jesse like a cattle dog. "Mind your step. The stairs can be—"

"—dangerous," Alicia finishes.

Jesse peers at the stone treads winding down and out of sight.

"Second on the left at the bottom. You can't miss the door." Rory catches Alicia's eye. She makes an ironic bow: *After you*.

Clattering down the stairs, Jesse opens a door into a vaulted passage. She waits politely for Alicia to precede her.

"Just in here." Alicia twists an iron ring in a slab of iron-studded oak. "Watch out, the lintel's quite low."

Jesse ducks past, but her head just grazes the keystone of the arch. As she stands in the middle of the room on the other side, light from above sculpts Jesse's face into planes and shadows. Absorbing the size of the kitchen, she turns with contained grace. "Vast, but somehow cozy." She has a lovely smile. "Did you have short ancestors, by the way?" She points at the door.

"Not often *vast* gets paired with *cozy*, in my experience." Rory's trying not to stare at this shining Australian girl.

Alicia sees that. She says briskly, "Not all of them were short. There's a suit of armor upstairs—the man was huge." She strides to a big, old fridge lurking in one corner.

"Shall I bring the car around the back?"

"No need. Not expecting anyone this evening. Except you." Alicia bumps the door closed with her hip.

Jesse stares around the enormous space. If the kitchen's not half the size of the hall above, it's close. "Sixteenth century?" Her tone is hushed.

"Early fourteenth, most likely. The castle was 'restored' in Victorian times when my great-great-great-grandfather tried to turn it into Fantasy Gothic. Fortunately, he ran out of money." Alicia's tone might be warmer. Or not.

"This room is original? Really?"

"Oh, yes. Much of this wing is. Hundredfield has a way of resisting face-lifts."

Rory's propped against a porcelain sink on one wall. He's watching the exchange with interest.

"Hundredfield," Jesse echoes the name. A pause and she points at a window above Rory's head. "Is that ground level?"

"It is. We're mostly belowground in this range of rooms—which was good for storing food, of course, but pretty cold in winter." Alicia waves at the fireplace. "Not just for decoration. Would have been warm in here when they roasted an ox. It's different on the other side of the passage, though. The ground drops away outside, and in daylight you can see all the way down to the river and beyond."

"Oh. The river." It all comes back with a crash like a saucepan hitting the floor. This is the place in the drawing. "The buildings here—were they"—Jesse swallows—"were they bigger once?"

"Hope this is okay." Alicia's pulled a bottle out of the fridge and goes to a cupboard for glasses. "Yes. This was once one of the largest castles in the borders; state-of-the-art in terms of defenses too. Mind you, they needed that and more. The reivers were trouble."

"Reivers?"

Alicia inserts a corkscrew with professional ease. "Bandits, basically. Moss-troopers, raiders—they had lots of names; the border between England and Scotland was porous depending on who was winning. Not good news if you were caught in the middle. So we fought the Scots and the Scots fought us, but the reivers fought for themselves because the ordinary border families on both sides were treated badly by the English *and* the Scots."

The cork pops and Jesse jumps.

"Prosecco?" Alicia holds up a glass.

"Just one. Truly." A glance at Rory. "It sounds desperate."

Alicia hands a full glass to her guest. "The only loyalty the reivers had was to their own, and even that wore thin. Betrayal, blackmail, blood feuds that went on for hundreds and hundreds of years—and that was just the good times." A grim smile. "The Mafia has nothing on the reivers, believe me. Rory?"

Rory ambles over, but as he's given a glass, conversation dries up.

Jesse makes an effort. "So, this?" She points at the central point of the ceiling from which stone ribs spring out.

"You mean the Boss." Alicia sits at the kitchen table.

Jesse's intimidated. In this place, the compassionate waitress from the café is a different kind of being—sure of herself, detached. That initial hunch had been right—Alicia's posh. Definitely. And doesn't like being taken advantage of. "I suppose I do." Jesse cranes to look. "Is that a mermaid? She's very cheery." Long hair doesn't quite cover the mermaid's breasts, but a perky tail and a wide smile lend a certain charm to the naive little figure sitting above the lantern.

"Ah. Well. That's controversial. One school of thought has it that a mermaid is actually a symbol for a prostitute. Or it was in the fourteenth century."

"You never told me." Rory's surprised. "What's it doing in the kitchen?"

"Part A, you never asked. Part B, I don't know." Alicia leans forward to pour. "More? I'll put dinner on shortly."

Jesse says hastily, "Oh, Rory's taking me to the village. I'm staying the night," she improvises, "at the pub, and he booked me in for dinner as well." She stares at Rory, daring him to contradict.

Alicia inspects him too. "Oh? Which one?"

Rory eyes their hostess, as if lining up a shot. "Which village, or which pub?" A lob.

She returns it over the net. "Either. In both cases."

Jesse picks up her glass and says too loudly, "So, I'll just finish this and then we'll be off like a dirty shirt." Her smile concentrates on Rory.

He says carefully, "You know, I've been looking forward to this. Dinner with you, in Hundredfield's kitchen, is a lovely idea, Alicia. Jesse's just being polite. I've observed she has very good manners."

"I do agree. So much better than—" There's a crash, and a frenzy of barks. Alicia sighs. "Sorry about this. Ollie hates missing out." Alicia hurries from the room.

"There. You see? All fixed. Just one more?" Rory holds up the bottle.

Jesse stares at him balefully. "I hate playing games where I don't know the rules. Take me to the pub, Rory."

"Which one?"

Jesse clenches her jaw. "Don't start."

Rory surrenders. "Look, I tried, but I couldn't get hold of Alicia last night to tell her I was bringing you with me, and there's no time to talk now. What about in the morning, we—"

"I am not sleeping here! It's an imposition. You're her friend. I'm not."

The other girl returns with Ollie at her heels. "Basket!" Alicia points, and Ollie slinks to a battered old dog bed.

Rory stares at the Labrador. "What did you do, Oliver?"

The dog sinks his head on his paws.

"Chewed my new boots, that's what." Ollie closes his eyes. "Don't pretend you're invisible. I can see you, Ollie!"

A look from Jesse to Rory. "I suppose he does look rather guilty." She's trying not to smile.

"Written on his face, I'd say." Alicia's not letting anyone—dog or man—off the hook. "But really, there's no reason not to stay here. Plenty of room at Hundredfield. That's one thing we do have."

Jesse is trapped. "That's very kind, but—"

Rory chimes in, "So, how many bedrooms are there?" His expression is mischievous.

Alicia replies with dignity, "I've never been entirely sure. It seems to change. Come with me, Jesse. We'll take the back stairs."

"'Back stairs.' Isn't that another way of saying 'servants only'?"

"I suppose so. But I use them as a shortcut." On a landing partway up the tight spiral, Alicia opens a door. "Here we are." The pair step out into a stone-walled passage. "There are bedrooms on the floor above this one, and the one above that too; you're welcome to have a look. Mine's just down there." She points to the end of the corridor. "Place this size, it's nice to know someone else is sleeping close by, I always think."

Jesse swallows. "This really is so kind of you, Alicia. Just, right-out-of-the-park hospitable. I feel so embarrassed and—"

Alicia interrupts, "Oh, it's a pleasure to have company. Rory's right. He often is, though I don't tell him that."

There's something, some subtext to the words, that Jesse doesn't quite catch. She stares through one of the casement windows, says politely, "Such a lovely view." The river lies like a silver snake between the trees.

"Yes. It is." Alicia almost visibly shakes herself. "And even better in here." She turns a doorknob.

"Oh!" Jesse hurries to a window seat. "This is just—" There's a rent in the clouds, and last light, the color of honey, pours down over the crowns of the distant hills. Jesse's eyes fill with tears she doesn't understand.

"When I was small, I amused my mother by saying I thought this view was splendid. I was three at the time." Alicia joins Jesse. From on high, darkening countryside stretches away like the coverlet on a vast bed embroidered with trees.

"You see such a long way." Jesse puts her face against the glass. She doesn't want the picture to fade.

"Almost as far as Cumbria to the west and up north into Scotland too. Well, that's what I like to think."

Jesse says thoughtfully, "It's wild here. I've never thought of England as wild."

"Haven't you?" Alicia half closes her eyes. "The borders have always been fierce. As wild as you'd ever want them to be." She gets up. "So, there are four more bedrooms on this floor, and you're welcome to any one of them if you change your mind. There's just one bathroom, though, and you'll have to share that with me; it's next door. Sheets in the linen cupboard in the hall. I'll come up later and we'll make the bed together."

Jesse falls over herself. "I'm sure the others are just as lovely, but I'd be so happy to stay here. Thank you. And I'll do the sheets. Truly. It will be a pleasure." Jesse wanders to a worn Persian carpet. It lies at the foot of a high bed that is too wide for one person, but not—to her eyes—quite big enough for two.

"I'm glad you like it. Rory can bring your case up. Least he can do." That glimmer of a smile. "Towels are in the linen cupboard as well, if you feel like a bath before dinner." She stares around the room. "I think you'll sleep well here. I always have."

Jesse watches the door close. Why live in London and work as a waitress if you could live here? What's all that about? And Rory. Just how close is he to Alicia?

She shakes her head impatiently; none of this is her business. At the moment, the view is all she cares about. On the other side of the casements, gauzy apricot light has fused to the hills as the first stars make ice-white lace across the sky. Jesse lifts a latch on one of the windows. It's heavy, hasn't been opened in a while, but she pushes it wide and drinks a draft of the evening. She can smell—what?

"Honeysuckle!"

And it occurs to Jesse Marley that this scent has traveled to her from long, long ago. The scent of childhood? That makes her happy, and it makes her sad. Her childhood is a mystery now. So is Hundredfield.

This place. How can she have *drawn* it?

The fear she denied when she first saw the tower, standing alone at the top of the hill, seeps back.

What does it mean? What does any of this mean?

13

A COLD RIDE we had from Alnwick, Maugris and I, and
the silence of the wasteland matched our mood.

"I could sleep on twelve-month rushes so long as
my feet were turned to the fire." Maugris looked happy enough,
though the skin of his face was red from the cold, as mine must
have been also; twenty-eight at his next name day to my twenty-
six, yet sinew contained in bags of skin was all he and I had become.

I thought of Rosa and how all life withers. "Perhaps there will
be a feast for the prodigals when we return?"

"Only if Godefroi forgets your bad behavior."

"For a place by the fire I might forget his."

It was good to laugh. We were riding on frozen tracks as the
country began its climb. It would have been safer to stay at Alnwick for the twelve days and all the festivities of Christmas and
ride out after the New Year feast, but we had seen few abroad in
these dark days.

"Will the child have been born?"

Maugris shaded his eyes against the iron sky as if he could see
the keep already. "Perhaps."

The image of beauty fades. I could not recall the lines of Flore's face, though I remembered her eyes. The blue of pale, clear water.

"One more night, please, God. Just one." Maugris crossed himself, as I did. "And pray the freeze holds."

"Amen to that."

There was a moon to guide us as the day waned. Rising, she cast light across the hills and glens as we made camp below the fells in a valley we knew. A day's ride from Hundredfield, we had used this place before on our way home because there was a cave large enough to bring horses in for the night, and we could light a fire with no fear it would be seen. The cave was defensible too, since it looked over the valley below and was guarded by the sheer cliff above.

The garrison quartermaster at Alnwick had given us food for the journey, twice-baked bread and salt fish—one hard, the other dry—and skins of strong ale. After a time, the beer made the food taste better, and it brought sleep as we lay beside the fire.

I had taught myself long since not to dream, yet now, as I wrapped the riding cloak around my body and surrendered to the dark, such things came as, even now, it is difficult to speak of.

There was blood and I waded through it as if it were the water in a pool. But as I washed my body in some man's death, hands grasped my ankles and dragged me down.

I was plunged into a void that flickered with flame, and through it all a child cried out, high and desperate.

I could not breathe, I could not wake. If I tried to scream I knew none would hear me, and the taste of iron filled my mouth until, at last, I voided a tide of rust that would not stop and grew greater with each spasm. Trees grew up where the vomit fell, with branches that reached and clasped and folded me tight, as if bark were my winding cloth.

"Brother."

The world was shaking, the leaves, the tree.

"Bayard!"

Sweat ran into my eyes. I could not open them.

But I did. To see that I lay beside the fire among our fighters, and Maugris had his hand on my shoulder.

And if my brother had been a different kind of man, I would have clung to him as I once had, long ago, when as boys we slept in Alnwick's great hall for the first time. Alone.

Maugris pointed. "Tell me what you see."

I shaded my eyes. "There are no men."

We had ridden along the river track, and the bridge to the keep lay before us. Beyond, the great gate was shut, the drawbridge drawn up tight. I voiced what we both thought. "Why would there be no guards?"

Maugris shortened the reins on his horse as, nervous, it stepped this way and that. "What is Godefroi doing? It is broad day."

"Perhaps he is dead. Be careful." I pointed at his restless mount. "He thinks you want to jump the gap."

Maugris glared at me. "To speak of death tempts fate."

We were both tired so I did not reply. I pulled out the hunting horn in my saddlebag.

"Why did you bring that?" But my brother's expression lifted.

I tipped my head to the forest. "Hunting. Venison for Christmas." I held it up. "Shall I raise the guard?"

Maugris reined back, allowing Helios room as I kicked forward.

Putting the horn to my mouth, I blew. Out of practice; the first note was an embarrassing fart. Behind, trying not to laugh, the men snorted. I guffawed anyway and even Maugris smiled.

I tried again, and a keening whine blew clear.

Nothing stirred over the water.

"Again."

Twice more I blew the horn.

We watched, all of us. There was nothing to see.

"If we can get across the river, there's the postern."

Maugris was right, but we had no boat, and though a postern gate *was* in the outer wall of the gardens below the keep, it would be barred on the inside.

"Perhaps there is sickness in the keep?"

Maugris nodded. "The sweat, maybe."

Weakened by hunger, people died fast, and sickness spread from house to house faster than a man could walk; no one knew what caused it. Maugris turned his horse in a tight circle, staring back at the gate. "If they have the pestilence, Godefroi will certainly have ordered Hundredfield closed."

I said nothing. Selflessness was not Godefroi's strength. "So shall I ride to the village? They may know more."

Maugris's face must have mirrored my own disappointment. "Try once more."

And so I blew the horn a final time.

I waited until the echo died, then turned Helios.

We heard a shout.

A man's head topped the battlements; I saw his helmet gleam as he waved an arm. I did not know his face.

Maugris cupped his hands. "Drop the bridge."

Another head appeared, then the two disappeared.

The crash of chain as the drawbridge came down was never more welcome than on that day. And as the mouth to the castle yard dropped open, the gates drawn back inside, we saw the inner ward. It was empty of the usual bustle of men and women, dogs and horses.

Behind us, the men muttered.

I murmured, "Ride on?"

"Yes." But Maugris dropped the visor on his helmet and eased his sword from its scabbard.

I turned in my saddle. "Form up." Behind, Rauf gave the signal to draw steel.

Without haste the column rode under the great gate and into

the inner ward, Maugris at the head, me at the rear. The men who dropped the gate had vanished.

As Maugris called out the halt, I gave the signal to mass the horses.

"What do you think?" He spoke in a murmur.

"Secure the gate. Then the keep."

Maugris nodded. "Agreed. Gate or keep?"

A smile for the benefit of the men and I replied, "The keep. Perhaps I can make peace with Godefroi."

"Take half the troop, then. Use the horn if you need to."

Iron struck sparks as we rode across the cobbles in orderly array, but the stables and the kitchens, the barns and outbuildings, were as the village had been all those months before; eyes were behind those doors and shutters. I felt them, but we heard no calls of welcome, no voices happy at our return. Ahead, the tower of the keep seemed almost to lean down, like a tree beaten over in a storm. A trick of the light, but strange—as if the very building implored our help, and I will not deny I remembered the dream.

I held up an arm and the troop stopped. A wall and a narrow gate protected the way to the tower, and here was a difficult decision.

Beyond, the lowest part of the keep had arrow slits facing the way we were to ride, and above, the height of three men, were larger windows. Too high to reach without siege ladders.

Godefroi's chamber was higher still, two stories below the caphouse at the top of the tower. We had to first pass under the gate to where a path climbed to a flight of steps. Only then could we approach the door that was set into the wall, far above the ground.

Since the gate was narrow, a horseman could only ride through it alone, and if men lay in wait on the other side, or behind the arrow loops inside the tower, he faced a quick death. The defenses of the keep had been well planned; Fulk knew the business of war.

I beckoned Rauf forward. "What do you think?"

"Tamas and three of us could keep the loops busy." Wiry, and strong as bent yew, Tamas was the best archer we had.

I considered what Rauf had said. Only a steady archer could shoot directly into such a narrow target, but rapid fire might intimidate the men inside. Might.

"Where would you stand?" Beyond the gate there was no cover.

"Leave our horses, run through, and you follow. Strike first and keep shooting, cover your back and those who ride after you."

At least the light was behind us. Shooting into the sun from the keep would not be easy. I nodded. "Pick your men." I waited as two others were selected—Edwin, the youngest in our troop, and Walter, the survivor of more seasons of fighting than even Maugris had seen. Good choices.

I sketched a cross in the air as the archers dismounted. "Now!"

Screaming, the four ran forward as I both spurred Helios and held him hard, building power in his haunches, trusting the others to follow.

On the far side of the gate, arrows sliced past my head as I let Helios run. The stallion's strength and heart propelled me to the foot of the tower in two breaths—the longest breaths I had ever taken—and I flung from the saddle and up the stairs, the others at my heels. Hard against the walls, we were under the flight of the defenders' arrows, but the murder hole was above our heads and . . .

"Stop!" I shouted through the tumult of yelling men and milling, riderless horses.

The only arrows were ours. Nothing had come from the keep.

The silence, as it fell, was eerie.

I beckoned Rauf and the archers closer. They came forward with arrows nocked, but when I tried the door latch, I could not move it; inside, the bar was in the keeper.

"My ax." Three crosswise layers of oak were bound with iron and studded with great nails. To destroy the structure well enough to fire the wood would take time, and though the keep seemed deserted, I had no faith that was true.

Rauf found my ax and ran to place it in my hand, but before I could take a swing, someone called out, "Wait!"

Inside, the bar scraped back.

I ran back down the steps with the men and stood with the archers as they brought their bows to bear on the door as it opened. A man stood in the doorway, blinking. He was as pale as the walls behind and I did not know who he was.

"Hold!" A bellow to our men. "Your name!"

"Robert, sir. I am your brother's reeve."

"Are you ill, Robert?" I craned to peer for assailants behind him in the tower.

"No."

"Lord Godefroi and his wife?"

The man crossed himself. "The keep has no sickness." He hesitated. "But come out of the cold, sir. Lord Godefroi is in his chamber." Something crossed his face, too fast to understand what the expression meant.

"Rauf, take the men to the stables." But I waved an arm behind my back, and the men at my shoulder rushed the door, swords raised.

"Mercy!" Robert gulped.

I ran up the steps and gestured for the man to precede me. "Then lead us to my brother."

In its own narrow tower, the staircase scaled the height of the main keep. Supported by a stone pillar into which the treads locked, it was wide enough to swing a sword, but the advantage would always be with those coming down. Since Godefroi's chamber was three ranges of rooms above, we stepped cautiously behind the reeve. The only sound was our boots, and the wind—it haunted the stair tower always, a lonely voice from the hills.

"There." Robert pointed at Godefroi's door. I came up close behind, my sword nudging his back. "Brother?"

Breath silvering the air, we waited.

"Godefroi?" The door, a dumb slab of oak, had no story to tell. I stood close against the reeve, my eyes fixed on his. "Is there more to say?"

"Lord Godefroi has not come out of his chamber since . . ." The man swallowed and shook his head.

I took him by the shoulder and twisted my sword against the knuckles in his spine. He yelped. Perhaps I was cruel, though I would not have called it that then. "What has happened here?"

"Sir!" Rauf beckoned me to the door.

I shoved Robert toward Tamas and laid my head against the wood. Nothing. And then, something. A sound I did not recognize. I thought it an animal, whimpering.

Was the door barred? I did not know. Stepping back, I pivoted, dropped one shoulder, and charged. After two bruising attempts, the latch burst from the jamb, the impact so great I fell into the room.

On the great bed my brother sat. Like the Madonna cradling her dead son, Godefroi held his wife across his lap, her head resting against his shoulder.

Tears streaked his face as he sobbed. The woman's clothes were stiff with blood, and she was dead.

14

"**B**UT YOUR wife must be washed, brother." Maugris spoke gently to Godefroi. "She cannot be taken to the chapel until"—Maugris coughed—"until all is made decent." When there was no response, he looked at me.

I said, "It is true. It will be best if you allow your lady this service. She shall be afforded every honor."

Godefroi did not answer. He held Flore closer.

Maugris and I exchanged a glance. I had sent Rauf to find him, and in the minutes since he had arrived, I had tried to persuade Godefroi to surrender Flore's body; but he would not permit me to touch her and still would not speak.

Both of us stared at the corpse. Maugris's face worked with pity, and perhaps I was shocked also. Death among men is a normal thing; if there is blood and suffering, it is something that happens quickly under an open sky, and we were trained to it. But the secret death of women as a child is born strikes to the heart.

"Reeve." Maugris controlled his voice, but I knew why he struggled to speak.

We both remembered our mother. She had died birthing a

dead child. Our sister. We arrived too late to see her face or the baby before they were enclosed together in her coffin.

I said quietly, "Go, Robert. Bring help."

Godefroi would not look at us, nor did he speak. If we approached, he flinched.

Even when the servants crept out of hiding, it was no different. Three girls, hastily chosen by the reeve, had gathered outside Godefroi's chamber. They would not come inside, though we heard Robert arguing with them.

I beckoned him. "Why was Lady Flore left without help?" It was impossible to believe Godefroi would have been in the birthing chamber. He must have found her afterward.

The man's expression changed. "Margaretta was with her mistress. She was the only one. That was the choice of the Lady Flore."

Maugris glowered. "The girl is still at Hundredfield?"

The reeve looked helpless. "She is—was—the only servant the lady would allow. And Lord Godefroi—"

A disgusted mutter from my brother. "Lust. What a fool it makes of us all." He caught my eye.

Oh, I knew what Maugris would have done. After Swinson was beaten, he would have slit the girl's throat as an example and dumped her body outside the walls for Alois to find.

"Thank you, Robert." I nodded as if I understood what he was saying, though far too much was strange in this birth. "How long since . . ." I hesitated to say *she died*.

The man did not look at me. "It was at dawn."

"And the child?"

Robert's face cleared a little. He said with some relief, "The child is alive."

"Boy or girl?"

"Bayard!" Maugris called me to the bed, and I waved for Robert to wait outside.

Godefroi still stared at me as if I were a stranger, and as Maugris drew me aside, he whispered, "The body will be stiff very soon. She must be laid out or it will be too late."

I nodded and moved closer. "Godefroi, we have women outside to attend the Lady Flore."

"No!" Heaving the girl's corpse up from the bed, Godefroi stumbled as he tried to carry Flore away and—perhaps from weakness—the body began to slide from his grasp.

Maugris and I surged forward. Flore's flesh was cold when we caught her and that was a shock enough, though God knew we both understood what death was.

Godefroi gave up. His arms dropped and he stood back, his face as remote as hers, as we lifted Flore's body and placed it carefully on the bed.

Maugris cleared his throat. "The servants will do all that is suitable for the Lady Flore and dress her also." He flicked his eyes to the coffers. They had been pulled back along one wall to make room for two cradles, one large and elaborate, one a simple box on rockers.

But I understood. I opened the lid on the first coffer, but there were only bedcoverings and linen bath sheets inside. In the second were gowns as well as veils and folded cloaks. One of the dresses was especially fine. I showed the garment to Godefroi. "This will honor her."

Godefroi stared at what I held. The blue-black of deep night, the gown was brocaded damask, with sleeves and a bodice faced with cloth of silver. "She wore that for her marriage to me." His face turned gray.

"Bayard!"

Godefroi slumped into our arms. We propped him between us like a half-stuffed doll and carried him from the chamber, leaving the frightened girls, herded by Robert, to do their work. Then the reeve, like an anxious hound, shadowed us down the stairs.

Maugris and I took Godefroi to a small chamber that opened from the hall. One of the few private rooms in the keep, it had been used by our mother and her women when they sewed; now it would protect her eldest son from the gaze of all who lived in her home.

"Robert, Matthias must be told that the Lady Flore will lie in the chapel tonight. Then set trestles before the altar on which to place a bier. A coffin must be made also."

"I shall ask Father Matthias, but . . ." Robert faltered.

I was puzzled. "Order and decency must be restored. The priest will know what to do."

"Father Matthias is . . ." The man was sweating. "He does not like, that is, he . . ." Words ran out.

I grasped Robert's sleeve. "What is this?"

"Father Matthias will not speak with the Lady Flore. Or remain in the same room where she is." The words were gasps.

"The Lady Flore is dead. He must attend to his duty to our family or it shall not go well for him. Tell him that." I spoke the bald truth.

Robert bowed, but as he left I heard him mutter, "I'll have to find him first."

I watched him go with narrowed eyes.

"Bayard. Help me!"

I hurried to Maugris and slid an arm behind Godefroi's back, propping him up as my brother tried to help him swallow wine.

"God's teeth and balls." Maugris rarely swore, but a stream of red liquid trickled from Godefroi's mouth and stained his jerkin; Maugris the Grim was deeply fearful.

"Godefroi is not dying, Maugris."

"How would you know?"

"Because you and I have seen enough dead men. This is shock."

Maugris put the goblet down, and I thought he was leaving our brother to my care, but he wheeled suddenly and cracked an open hand across Godefroi's face. "Enough!"

Godefroi mumbled something, but his eyes opened. Perhaps

this was good; I could not tell, though. Shaking my head at Maugris, I pointed to the hall.

He spoke more quietly. "Bring a brazier. Go on!" As if all that had happened was my fault, he glared at me.

To argue with my brother, either of my brothers, was rarely successful. I hurried to the screens that hid the back stairs to the kitchens. That is where the servants would be gathered.

"Wait! The mass?" Maugris tipped his head at Godefroi; he did not want to use the word *funeral*.

"I have sent Robert to talk to the priest, but Godefroi must tell us what he wants." At least it was freezing weather. If the body was not to be buried for a day or so, all would still be well.

"Good. Have more wine brought, the best we have in the butts. They are to heat it with honey and raw eggs. Our brother's strength must be restored."

And so, I thought, must ours. We had eaten nothing since the cave last night, and that had been little enough. "I shall see our men have food, also. And the horses." Dikon, the stableboy, would most likely have hidden when the trouble began, but I trusted him to do what was needed when I found him.

Maugris was calmer. "You must find out where the child has been taken. The baby will comfort our brother. What sex is it?"

I glanced at Godefroi, who was staring at Maugris. "I have a daughter." Godefroi's voice, at least, sounded as it always had, though his face was pale as old dough.

"Do you hear that, Bayard? We have a fine niece."

But I knew Maugris, and I felt as he did. A girl. What was the use of a girl to our house?

"Lords?" Robert had returned.

"Well, did you find the priest?"

"No, Lord Bayard, but trestles will be set in the chapel for . . ." Feeling Godefroi's eyes on his face, Robert did not finish the sentence.

Maugris glowered. "This is unacceptable. Where has he gone?"

"My lord, I do not know."

Godefroi sat up straighter. "My daughter. Bring her." His voice was harsh.

Robert looked from face to face. And swallowed. "I shall find Margaretta." He backed hastily away before he could be stopped.

15

THE CHAPEL lay within the base of the keep. Without light it was dark as a cave, but morning and evening candles were lit, and oil lamps, as the household gathered for prayers. But even though the earth floor had been laid over with tiles as our family prospered, the place still seeped cold, even in summer. In winter, breath lay on the air like incense.

Generation by generation we, the Dieudonné, had adorned the chapel rather than the keep. Some said it was to atone for what Fulk had done; others said it was pride, for as we grew rich, the place became one of the wonders of the north.

In Fulk's son's time a rood screen had been made, the wood cut from our own oaks and gilded by Flemish craftsmen. Below this lay an altar faced with Purbeck marble, brought by sea at great expense. Other objects too had been given by our family to inspire the devotion of all who worshipped here. One of these was the great rood itself that hung on the screen. The body of the Savior was larger than that of a man and made from a single sheet of beaten silver with the crown of thorns cast from bronze and gilded. Garnets were set into that glimmering flesh as tokens of the blood from the holy wounds, and the eyes of the Christ were ivory and topaz.

And there was this.

The cross upon which the Savior hung was carved from timber brought back from the First Crusade to the Holy Land; it was said to be olive wood from the Garden of Gethsemane, the very place in which the Lord had been betrayed. Of all the glories in the chapel, this, truly, was thought to be the greatest.

But the people of Hundredfield thought differently, for in a covered niche beside the altar stood the Madonna of the River. This statue was shown only at the feast of the Annunciation and at Easter, and women prayed to Her with special devotion especially at the birth of a child, or its death. She stood on a plinth enameled in green—said to represent the reedy waters of our river—and each tenth year on Palm Sunday, She was clothed in new robes of white silk with a cloak of blue velvet cut and stitched by the women of our village.

Our Madonna had silver hands and a silver face with eyes similar to Her Son's; perhaps the craftsman who had made the Christ made these things also for His mother.

When, at each festival, the doors of Her shrine were opened and the hangings drawn back, it could be seen She gazed up at our Lord, Her Son, with particular devotion. For all the other days of the year, She was hidden. Not even the family was permitted to see Her face.

The chapel of the keep was served by a priest who, by tradition, came from the Benedictine priory some hours' ride from Hundredfield. This was a daughter house of the great abbey at Durham and had been endowed by the founder of our family as a chantry to pray for the souls of the Dieudonné for all time. Fulk's deeds in life must have required much praying, since this chantry was one of the most wealthy in the north.

Yet in all the time since the Frenchman had grasped Hundredfield as his and built this place, the chapel had never seen a day of this kind.

Matthias the Benedictine—our chaplain—stood now on the highest of the altar steps. Fleshless and hollow-faced, his mildness made him seem a kind man. But he was not. This priest was armored by passionless certainty, and it was the muscle of his spirit if not his body. Robed in black and a devout believer in his own humility, he thought himself a match for the will of any man. In this he was deluded.

"Lord Godefroi, I have prayed on your request, but the Lord's answer cannot be mistaken. The lady may not lie beside your mother, for this is a consecrated place and she was a Christian woman." Matthias bowed his head in what might have been profound sorrow and sketched a cross over the place our mother lay.

Maugris and I exchanged a glance. We had always disliked the man.

Godefroi stood in the chancel, leaning on his sword. He was dressed as if for war, and his face, though pale still, was hard. "It is not a request, Priest. Pray again. Keep praying until the answer changes."

Matthais raised his hands open-palmed, as if to bless the trestles waiting for Flore's bier. But that was not his intention. "It is not for you, Lord Godefroi, or for me, to bargain with God. His will is clear. He speaks, and I, His frail servant, must listen and tremble. And obey. So must all his subjects. For this is the house of the Lord, a place of peace"—the chaplain stared pointedly at Godefroi's naked sword—"and what you ask may not be done."

Rank sweat wove through the air. At least one of us was terrified.

"What I ask may not be done." Godefroi repeated the words as if speaking a response.

The priest thought he had won. "Ah, Lord Godefroi, let us ask for His blessing together and for His guidance too, at this sad time. In His grace He will provide us with an answer. He always does. Have faith." Matthias knelt, turning his back to the man who provided him with bread and salt and shelter. That was a mistake.

In the half-light, Godefroi seemed not to move, yet instantly he stood behind the priest; candle flame buttered the blade in his fingers.

"Brother!" I forced my body between them as Maugris grasped Godefroi's wrist, bending the sword away from the priest's throat.

"Think, Godefroi!" Maugris was panting.

The chaplain managed to stand. He did not flinch. "Yes, think, Lord Godefroi. To spill blood in this holy place, the blood of a servant of God, is to be damned. Even kings are punished for such blasphemy." From the monstrance at the back of the altar, Matthias brought out the disk of unleavened bread and, in silence, held it above Godefroi's head. Our brother, at last, bent to one knee. We followed.

"Lord, forgive, I pray, the actions of these men." The chaplain's hands shook as he raised the bread yet higher. "Grant me strength to drive Satan from the heart of your servant, Godefroi de Dieudonné. And just as you cast out demons and drove them into the Gadarene swine, let the spirit of evil depart from this house with the body of she who has bewitched this good man."

Godefroi shook Maugris's hand away. "Put the bread down, Priest. It does not belong to you." He spoke softly, but I swear if he had looked at me that way, I too would have trembled.

He pointed his sword at the trestles. "Tonight my wife will lie here, and I, in vigil, shall pray at her side with my brothers. Tomorrow, on the anniversary of the birth of our Lord, her grave will be dug under these stones beside our mother's resting place, and the Lady Flore will be buried according to the rites of the Church." He did not bow as he turned his back to the altar and the priest. At the chapel door he said, "My wife will be escorted from the bed in which she died by me and my brothers. You will not be here to receive her body. Do you understand me, Priest?"

Matthias found his voice. "This is God's house."

Godefroi stared at the man, his face dispassionate. "You are wrong. It is mine. Think on that."

Maugris caught my glance as he crossed himself and left the chapel with Godefroi.

This breach with the priest was troublesome. It was not just Flore's death, but fear of the future and of Alois's raiders that troubled the keep. And fear, like disease, is contagious; if Matthias left without burying Flore, its spread would be difficult to contain. I knew what I had to do.

"He loved her, Father. Grief has consumed his mind. I am certain you see that and will have compassion."

The priest did not answer at first, but holding the consecrated bread up to the cross, he bowed low and placed the body of our Lord back in its keeping place. Only then did he say, "I know that is so. That was her power as a sorceress. But that woman, if woman she was, is now in hell for all time." He turned to look at me. "I know you understand, Lord Bayard, that such as she may not be buried beside your mother in consecrated ground—and especially not on such a holy day as that of the Lord's birth." Staring at me, he crossed himself.

I sketched a response. "However, that is my brother's decision, Father, not ours, and—"

He interrupted, "I speak for God. Lord Godefroi will think on this matter again, I know, and he will see the sense in what I have told him. And that will be an end to the matter. He can bury the woman where he likes, but it shall not be here." The priest's face was closed. And smug.

I said patiently, "It is the view of my family that our sister-in-law was a woman like any other. She died as many women do, and now a motherless child must be thought of. However, I agree that my brother, in anguish, may not have meant all that he said."

The man laid one hand on the altar and pointed to my mother's grave with the other. "That must be so, for your lady mother, a noble Christian woman, would be disgraced and polluted by such a companion in her final resting place."

It was becoming harder to maintain a reasonable tone, but I

tried. "It seems we cannot agree on this matter, Father Matthias; therefore, regrettably, I shall ask Rauf to supply an escort of men to protect you on your journey to the priory."

He smiled calmly. "But I shall not go. I am needed in this house. Your own soul, Lord Bayard, is also in peril; you would not defend the pariah of whom we speak if that were not so."

If I had once thought Flore a witch, even for one moment, the pity of her death reproached such foolishness. "Enough!" My voice cracked the air.

From shock, the man's jaw unhinged as I thrust my face to his.

"I hunt and kill the enemies of our lord, the king; therefore, think on this: As the declared enemy of your master, my brother—whose authority comes from King Edward himself—you are the king's enemy now." I tried to control my anger, saying more softly, "The Lady Flore was Lord Godefroi's lawful wife. You married them at the door of this place."

Matthias turned his shaken gaze to the great rood, as if the Christ might fly down and protect him. "Yes, I administered the sacrament after Lord Godefroi vouched the woman had been baptized and was willing to marry him." He beat his chest. "But I was deceived. In marrying them, I sinned. Sinned grievously."

The humility did not last. Gathering himself, he pointed at me and almost spat, "Bury her here and the people will rise up against you and your family, and you will deserve your deaths as servants of the devil, for she was his minion."

I was bored with this man and had killed many better. "However, *Father*, you are still alive—though that may be a temporary condition. I had thought to reason with you, but I see my brother was right. I repeat his command therefore: You will not bury the Lady Flore tomorrow and you will leave this place now. Go back to the priory and send someone willing to perform the duty you have so foolishly vacated. My brother will not come for you there. Not immediately. But if he is not obeyed, in his rage he may turn you and the brothers out and seize the lands and buildings."

"In this weather?" The fool was appalled.

I shrugged. "Do not think that any of you will lie safe in your beds if you oppose the will of our family. Best you keep silent on what was seen in this place, for your sake and for theirs."

This was good advice. Truly, Godefroi, for pride's sake, would not let matters rest. I did not think he would risk excommunication by evicting the monks, but in the end he was Fulk's descendant, as I was, and he would do as he chose.

I left the man to his God. Perhaps He would protect our former chaplain, for this, most assuredly, was what Matthias now was. And we, the brothers Dieudonné, would do what needed to be done. There was no other choice.

16

ALICIA THOUGHT you might need this."

Jesse slews around.

Rory stands in the doorway with her case. "She won't mind if you put a light on." He grins.

"Oh. Sorry." Jesse fumbles to the bedside light and looks for the switch. "Um, how do you . . ."

"Ah, well, lots of ancient electrical devices in this house; approach with caution." Rory bends down, and she joins him, their heads close. "So, you *twist* the switch—and voilà." The bulb blinks on and rosy light blooms from a shade of ballerina pink.

A pause. And Rory steps back. "It's the same on the other side. Very fifties." He picks up the case. "Where would you like this?"

Jesse points. "Over there. Beside the—what *is* that?"

Rory strides to a shape hulking behind the door. "It's an armoire. Fancy French name for very large cupboard." He pulls the cabinet doors open. "You can live in it if you don't like the rest of the room. No trouble fitting this in." He waggles the bag.

Jesse tries not to grin as she snatches it back. "Don't be so rude."

"Not rude. Just penitent. Please accept my formal apologies,

Jesse. I know you were embarrassed down there. Don't be. Please. As you see, Alicia's pretty adaptable."

"Adaptable. Right. You've told her everything, then?"

"Certainly not. Doctor-patient—"

"—*confidentiality*. Would that be the word?" Jesse sits on the edge of the bed, her eyes on his face.

"Of course. I will never betray the trust you've placed in me."

Said with conviction. "So tell me about her. Why does she work as a waitress when she's got all this? That's what you call being adaptable, is it?"

"Do you mind?" Rory waves toward the window seat.

Jesse nods. "You don't have to ask."

He sits. "From the outside, Alicia looks like a girl who's drawn the one silver straw in the bunch. This estate still has a few thousand acres—"

"So, not big at all."

The sarcasm doesn't land. "Not in Australian terms, I suppose. But it's been poorly managed for generations, if not hundreds of years, and so much has gone." He shakes his head. "Actually, I got Alicia the job six months ago. She needed it. Quite a few nurses and doctors at the hospital sing in the choir of the church, and I heard it was going, so I let her know."

"I can't believe café wages would make a dent on this place."

"She just wanted to get away from here. For good reasons." Rory falls silent.

Jesse's curious, but she doesn't want to seem nosy. "So, did you grow up here?"

He nods. "For a while. My mum was a maid in this very building. Dad walked away not long after I was born, and Mum has never talked about him. I haven't met him, don't even know where he lives. He worked on the estate, though, and Mum said he looked after the livestock—sheep, principally. Hundredfield has always been famous for its wool."

Another fatherless child, but Jesse says nothing.

Rory runs his fingers through his hair. "Divorce was a pretty big thing in those days, but Alicia's parents stuck by Mum because her family had been in service here. She worked part-time until I was old enough to go to school, and then she took over as house-keeper. When I was about nine, she married again and we moved away to respectability and a new start." He grimaces.

Jesse's eyes soften. "It can't have been easy for you."

"Worse for her. She had to cope all on her own while we lived here." He points out the window. "We had one of the tied cottages on the other side of the river. The house belonged to the estate and it was free. That probably kept me out of the orphanage, because Mum had no family support. She always said we were lucky. I could never work out why."

"So, you and Alicia?"

Rory sighs. "When I was little, we played together—older sister, younger brother, that kind of thing. There were no other kids on the estate by that time—a lot of the cottages were empty and most of the workforce gone. Turns out her father thought I was bright, and when she was sent away to boarding school at nine, I went as well. I was seven."

"Pretty young."

He nods. "I thought I'd been sent to prison, that my mum didn't want me anymore." He's staring out into the night.

Jesse says nothing.

A moment later and Rory snaps into focus. "I survived. Lots had it worse than me."

"What happened then?"

"Maybe that's where luck really did come in. The Donnes, Alicia's parents, paid for my whole education even though we moved away from Hundredfield not that much later. I never understood why her old man did that, but I'm grateful. I got my own scholarship to university, though. Edinburgh. Best medical school in the world." A crooked smile. "So here I am. I owe them a lot, Alicia and her family, and I come back whenever I can because it still feels like home, especially in summer." He half closes his eyes. "Honeysuckle. What you first know as a child settles into your bones."

"But before she went to London, Alicia lived here alone?" Jesse's absorbing the honeysuckle statement.

He nods. "Yes. But now the house is shut up for most of the year." He sighs. "It's difficult. Hundredfield has always been hungry, and she's got hard choices to make. Alicia's an only child, and her father left things in a mess when he died. Lots more to tell, but . . ."

"We should go downstairs."

"So?" Alicia offers Rory a bowl of buttered new potatoes.

He laughs as he serves himself with a tarnished silver spoon. "Obvious, huh?"

She flashes a grin at Jesse. "Like a pane of glass, you. Tell me all."

Rory forks up a piece of poached salmon. "Very good, by the way. Hundredfield salmon?" He's smiling.

Alicia looks pleased. "Caught this morning."

He nods. "You always did have the touch. Under the bank below the bridge?"

She nods pleasantly. "And you can answer the question anytime you like, Rory."

"But it's really not about me." He catches Jesse's alarmed gaze. "Relax. This is normal." He smiles at her.

Alicia watches the byplay. "Oh, no, you don't. It's you on the hook, not Jesse. Stop wriggling."

"Hook?" His expression is so flagrantly innocent, both girls laugh.

"You and Ollie"—Alicia drops a morsel of salmon on the floor, snapped up by the Labrador—"opportunists from birth." Picking up her fork, she stares at Rory. Her eyes are no longer quite so benign.

"You know me too well, Licia."

"That I do."

"All right, yes. I've a favor to ask." He hesitates. "Thanks to you, I was handed this intriguing case after choir practice all those weeks ago." A reassuring smile at Jesse.

"You happened to be there, that's all. I could have asked someone else from Barts—that other doctor, the one who's a tenor." Alicia is polite. As if she's slightly bored.

"Henry? He's a pathologist. Wouldn't have known one end of Jesse from the other; they look at people as collections of cells." A grin. He's baiting her.

"Rory." There's an edge to that polite voice and Ollie growls.

He throws up his hands. "Oh, all right. I *was* very grateful, Alicia. Fate. 'The mills of God, they grind—'"

"'—slow. And exceeding small,'" she finishes the quote. "Yes, I know. So?"

Rory nods. "So, I've been studying the long-term effects of head trauma, as you know. Principally, I've been investigating how we should best manage post-traumatic care to maximize rehabilitation outcomes."

Alicia murmurs, "Goodness."

Rory flicks Jesse a glance. "And all I want to say about this particular case is that it offers some interesting information on how the brain can heal itself."

Alicia's eyebrows ascend. She says smilingly, "You were a willing research subject, Jesse?"

Rory doesn't let Jesse reply. "Just to finish what I was saying. Jesse made a good recovery and improved to the point where the next step was discharge from the hospital. I was down to take a couple of weeks off, and planning to spend it here—as you know—and I didn't want to leave her to the tender mercies of National Health rehab."

Alicia glances at her guest. "Hope you don't mind being talked about in the third person."

It has been annoying her, but Jesse shakes her head. "Rory

was very kind to me in the hospital, and when he offered me a lift, I was grateful because I was planning to visit Scotland anyway. Jedburgh, actually."

Rory jumps in. "Yes, I did do that, but that was after I got the idea of supervising Jesse's rehabilitation and advancing my research at the same time. Which she was good enough to agree to."

"Ah. So you thought you might do that here?" Alicia's expression is bland.

"Just for a couple of weeks." A contrite glance at Jesse. "I tried to ring you last night, Alicia, really, but . . . I hoped you wouldn't mind if we came up anyway."

Alicia catches Jesse's embarrassed expression. "He's always been like this. But why would you particularly want to go to Jedburgh?"

Jesse's brusque. "I was born there and given up for adoption. My adoptive parents took me to Australia." She moves the salmon around her plate. She feels like she's taking her clothes off in public. "They didn't tell me. I found out by accident."

Alicia puts her napkin down as the silence stretches. "You're welcome to stay, Jesse. Truly. Least I can do, considering." She flashes Rory a *You'll keep* glance. "It was always full house in summer at Hundredfield when I was little. Lots of parties. I miss that." Her eyes are wistful.

Rory leans across the table. "Come on, Jesse, what have you got to lose?"

The light beside the bed spills a line of pink under the door of the bedroom. Jesse sees it as she walks along the corridor. The glow is comforting somehow, a welcome of a kind. She pushes the door open and stares at the room. She hasn't said she *will* stay, but why does she feel so upset? Rory and Alicia have a complicated relationship, that's for sure, but it doesn't have to affect her. She's here for a purpose. Two purposes.

With a snort, Jesse marches over to the window to pull the curtains closed. And pauses.

There it is. The keep. Black and silver. Moonlight disguises the damage of centuries—it might have been built last week.

Jesse's heart bumps quickly in her chest. A wrench, and the curtains swing closed. She stamps to her case beside the armoire. Upset? There's no one word for what she's feeling, but it will do just fine till another comes along.

Snapping the catches on the bag, she stares at the clothes inside—all so neatly packed.

The other me did this. That girl who planned ahead, who didn't run off with doctors, who didn't draw buildings she'd never seen with her left hand. Underwear, pajamas, two skirts, two pairs of jeans, a jumper and one dressy cardigan, three shirts, two T-shirts, flat boots, one pair of heels and one of sneakers—plus her jacket. Obedient witnesses to the fact that that girl was real, the one who's currently gone missing.

On automatic, she starts to unpack and notices two shirts where there should be three. Of course. She'd told the first nurse to throw the damaged one away—once she could write. She's never been any use at sewing or mending. *Like you can't draw?*

All the clothes she owns in the world are now arranged in neat piles on the shelves of the armoire. Leaving Sydney, she only took things she'd bought for herself—nothing her parents had given her made it into the case. Slowly, she takes out her sponge bag and a pair of pajamas, then hesitates. Suddenly, she flips the lid down. Snapping the catches closed is satisfying; so is bundling the case in the cupboard where she doesn't have to see it.

Out there, somewhere in the dark, are her real parents. Her real mum and her real dad. And whatever Rory might want, whatever he thinks he can do to help her brain repair itself, what she *needs* is to find them. And she will.

A library and a phone book. In St. Bartholomew the Great all those weeks ago with Rahere as her witness, she'd promised herself she'd ring everyone called Green in Scotland. And she will. But she's weary now—so tired—and this whole experience from soup to nuts feels like some kind of hallucination.

Has the world gone mad, or is it just her?

She'll think about what that might mean in the morning.

17

CROSSING THE inner ward, wind sliced my face as I went to find Ambrose, the carpenter who served the keep. His father, a charcoal burner, had trained his son well, for the man was skilled at picking good timber to cut and work, and in splitting, sawing, and shaping logs into useful things for the castle.

A bier is assuredly a useful thing at the end of life, but there would be little time for its fashioning today, and Ambrose, a craftsman, must be convinced to hurry. He would not like that.

As the day faded, I passed three men I did not know. The woad-dyed hoods that all the Hundredfield serfs wore were pulled low over their faces, and they did not meet my glance or respond to a greeting. In the keep Godefroi never acknowledged our servants, but that was not my way; at another time, I would have stopped and spoken to them, found out their names and where they worked on the estate. As it was, I hurried on to the carpenter's hut. Sullen faces and silence seemed normal in Hundredfield now. That would have to change. *Godefroi* would have to change.

"Ambrose?" I pushed back the panel of wicker that served as

a door. The place was empty and shavings blew across the floor like leaves.

"Lord Bayard?" Robert was behind me. He held up a torch and the light hollowed his face to a mask.

"Where is he? There's a bier to be made." But the flare from the torch told the story. No tools remained in the hut.

Robert cleared his throat. "The man has gone, Lord Bayard. Three months ago." He did not meet my eyes.

"Gone where?"

"I do not know." The man was lying.

"I see strangers' faces in the keep, Robert. And Ambrose is missing. Why?"

The man muttered a few words I could not hear.

"Speak louder."

"The times are hard, lord. And when there is not enough to eat . . ." The reeve raised his eyes. I saw a man who was frightened, but brave enough to test if I was worth his trust.

"At Alnwick, we were told men had been seen in Hundred-field's forests. Strangers. Raiders, maybe." I watched Robert's face keenly. "Is this true?"

Robert hesitated—and nodded.

"And this is where Ambrose has gone?"

Another pause. "Yes."

"Alois, Swinson's son. Is it he they go to?"

The man's face shut down. That was my proof, but I said, "A bier must still be made. How shall we do that?"

"We could use a door, lord. That might serve, if we cover it with cloth."

"Do it."

When the man turned to go, I called out, "I thank you, Robert. My brother shall know of your service to our family."

The man's expression lifted a little as he bowed and strode away.

I lingered as the moon climbed the wild sky. One night past

full, the cold light searched out desolation and found it in the carpenter's empty hut. If there was fear and anger in this place, here was evidence. And voiceless reproach.

Maugris called out, "Where are you?"

"By the cistern." I was in the storeroom under the stables where the spare horse tack was kept, and though I was exhausted, the filth after the ride from Alnwick—and all that followed—was yet to be removed. I would not defile Flore's corpse with dirty hands.

As my brother clattered down the steps, I took the bucket from the well's windlass and tipped it over my head. The water near stopped my heart.

Maugris stared.

I pointed at the bucket. "Again." I was naked but for linen covering my privates, and resolve would soon shatter. "Hurry."

Maugris dropped the pail into the water and, grumbling, pulled it up. Then he threw the contents over my chest.

It seemed I could not breathe. Until I yelled.

Slipping on the wet stone, Maugris pulled a horse cloth from a peg. He rubbed my body hard and the flesh burned. "Fool. The kitchen would have heated water."

My jaw clattered like a leper's rattle. "There was no time." I snatched the blanket and pulled it around my shoulders.

"A sword in your hand would be more useful."

I knew that look. Maugris expected trouble. He said grudgingly, "Where are your clothes?"

On a ledge were piled my new doublet—black and amber silk with squirrel-fur tippets—and green hose, along with an undershirt of fine-spun and a mantle of black wool lined with squirrel. If we had stayed the twelve days at Alnwick I would have worn them at the feasts.

A snort from Maugris when he saw them. He thought fashionable clothes a waste of money and tossed the garments to me as if they were of no value.

After I pulled on the undershirt and tied the points of my hose, I dragged fingers through my hair. From months in the wild it was long and tangled, so a thong must suffice to hold it back. I could do nothing about the beard. "Wash your hands and face at least, brother. Godefroi will want us to put her on the bier."

"There is no time for such foolishness."

"No time to honor our house? They must see us in control and know that all continues here as it always has—that we do not change and all will yet be well."

My brother did not say he agreed, but he dropped the bucket down, and we both heard the distant splash. "In my saddlebag are clothes, though not as rich as yours. Hurry."

The face of the dead woman shone like a gilded saint as she was carried down on the shoulders of our fighters.

But the stairs from Godefroi's chamber to the chapel were steep, and Flore's body was bound to the door on which she lay. Seeing a corpse tied this way was eerie—as if she might yet struggle against the bonds. But in death, the grace of Godefroi's wife rivaled that of any living woman. Hair loose like a maiden's, she lay in the gown of blue and silver—the bride of the lord of Hundredfield still—and her pale fingers clasped snowdrops. These flowers, innocent symbols of new life, brought hope to even this—the last, dark night of her marriage.

Godefroi walked beside his wife's corpse, but the procession was led by Maugris; my position was at the back, behind the group. We three were armed as were our fighters, but the men were silent and did not look at the girl they carried. From all they must have heard since our return, I knew it would not have been their choice to bear Flore's body to the chapel.

Ill lit, the stairs commanded our attention, and there was no sound among us except for breath and the scrape of boots on stone. But when the wind began to rise, the night was given a voice, and it seemed such a howl of lamentation that the men faltered, even Rauf, and their grip on the bier slackened.

"Bear her up." It was my plea and not an order.

Rauf nodded. "With me now." And the fighters did as he asked.

Then Godefroi did an eerie thing. He picked up the snow-drops and, taking one of Flore's hands, said pleasantly, "Come, dear love, I am with you." It was as if they were setting out on a visit together, and his wife were a little shy of those she might not know.

Maugris held a torch above his head, flames guttering in the draft. Below, the stairs descended into dark. "Not far, friends." He stepped to one side so the bier could pass him by.

The fighters moved on and their shadows fled before us.

Holding the bier, the men paused before the chapel doors. They were closed and Godefroi nodded to Maugris, who stepped forward to turn the iron ring.

It did not move.

Maugris tried again and would have used more force, but Godefroi said, "Rauf, take the men to their posts. Vigil shall be kept tonight for my wife, and we are not to be disturbed."

Who else but the priest would have dared lock the chapel doors? This act of silent rebellion was the same as if the man had stood on the battlements and shouted that the Dieudonné were all damned, that Flore was a demon, and neither had rights to God's grace.

Perhaps muscles had cramped from the long and careful descent, but the bier was almost dropped when our men put it down, as if it were suddenly too heavy to hold.

As the fighters filed past, I put my hand on Rauf's arm. "This is a sorrowful time. We must all respect the dead. Gossip will not be helpful." But I saw that the cause was lost when he looked at me. He was as frightened as any of the others.

Maugris watched Godefroi place his wife's hand beside her body with great gentleness, as if to soothe a bird that might escape. Bemused, my brother shook his head and muttered, "Bayard, we need—"

I said abruptly, "I can see what is needed." I thought Godefroi's actions as strange as Maugris did.

I ran up the stairs from the chapel. A forcing bar would be in the smithy; perhaps we could lever it between the doors. If not, an ax must be used.

One floor above, voices came from the great hall, though the murmur was subdued. I did not wish to be seen and left the keep wrapped in my cloak, the hood over my face.

The wind chased me inside the smithy as I opened the door. It too was deserted but with enough light to see what was needed.

Behind the forge, a long bench stood against the wall. Whatever else he was, the new smith was an orderly man; his tools hung from pegs or were grouped in half casks close to the forge. I found a hammer with a massive head, a flat bar with a rounded point, and a new-made ax also. Damage to the chapel doors could not be hidden, and the sound of blows would echo up into the tower, but the blade was honed well and would quickly bite a hole if that is what we had to do.

Returning, I hurried down the last of the stairs past Godefroi. His eyes were fixed on Flore's face. He made no sign he had seen me.

I showed Maugris what I had. "There's an ax as well."

"We should try to force it first. There will be less noise."

"How much light remains?"

"Begin." Maugris was calm, but a glance at his torch was my answer. It was half burned away, though the second was less consumed.

The lock was fatally well made, and the doors sat tight against each other. With some effort I worked the point of the bar into what gap there was and stood back as Maugris hammered with the head of the ax, trying to break the tongue of metal that held them closed. All we did was splinter the wood and disturb the dark with the crash of the blows.

"The point must be driven down harder." We were both sweating as the first torch died. "Give me room." Maugris had the hammer poised. "One, two, *three*!" He struck, and we both felt the lock shatter. Under our weight, the doors burst apart.

No cross, no candle stands, no sacred ornaments remained. And there were no trestles. The tabernacle had been stripped.

Godefroi walked in behind us. "He has taken the monstrance. And the pyx also." Slowly, his face turned scarlet, swollen with fury.

Apart from Easter, Christmas Day was the most sacred feast of the year; tomorrow, also, the grave had to be dug and Flore laid in the earth. For that we had to have a priest, and the furnishings of the altar returned to their places. If the funeral mass was not held, the people of Hundredfield would believe we had truly been deserted by God. And most particularly, Flore would be all Matthias had claimed she was. For her sake, and for the honor of the Dieudonné, the malice of the man could not be permitted to prevail. We must do what was possible immediately and deal with the rest as it came.

First the bier was to be placed before the altar—three men to do the work that six had done before.

Maugris said, "Bayard, you take the foot and I the head. Godefroi—"

Our brother had gone.

We found him kneeling in the vestibule beside his wife. At first I thought the soft murmur was prayer for her soul, but closer, I heard what he said:

"We left you alone, my dearest child. God strike me for that unless you can forgive me." He stroked Flore's face tenderly, leaning close to the mouth of the corpse as if to kiss her.

Maugris cleared his throat. "All is well, brother." He knelt too. "Come. You and I and Bayard will carry your lady in together."

Godefroi stared into the chapel. "It is dark. She must have candles around her, many candles. Where have all the candles gone?"

Maugris measured Godefroi's expression, as I did. His face was confused as a child's. "First we shall prepare for tomorrow, brother. You and I will take vigil with the Lady Flore, and then she is to be buried. That is what you told Matthias."

Godefroi spat on the flags and held his wife's hand against his chest. "That man shall never upset you again. I swear this." He smoothed the hair from Flore's brow as if it had become disordered.

"I will ride to the priory and bring another priest. Will that please you?" I spoke to Godefroi, not the corpse.

"As you hear, lady. Do you find Bayard's offer acceptable?" Godefroi leaned down. Kissing her brow, he nodded to me. "The Lady Flore is well pleased." He stood, apparently calm. "It is time. We have her permission." His face was serene again and his tone sensible, if you discounted the words.

We bent, all three, to lift the makeshift bier. And as we approached the chancel, torchlight glimmering on the silver God above our heads, sadness grasped and held me so hard that in my heart I called out to Him, *Accept this woman, Lord. Love her. She has done nothing wrong.*

And it came to me that I was glad Flore would be buried beside my mother, for hers had been a kind and tender heart. Godefroi's wife had had too little kindness in this place. Our mother would understand that this girl would never hold her own daughter, never hear the child learn to speak, never see her a grown woman or give her to her husband as a bride; yes, our mother would understand such anguish.

We laid Flore on the tiles at the foot of the altar, but as Godefroi knelt beside her corpse, and Maugris and I held our sword hilts high above them—the warriors' cross—I saw something.

The air was thick with shadow, it is true, but it seemed to me that Flore's eyes moved beneath their lids. From shock, the sword dropped from my hand. My brothers turned at the clang of the blade on the floor, but they did not see what I had seen.

I bowed my head as if shamed, staring at the dead girl's face. And if I could, I would have asked, *Are you still alive? And if you are not . . .*

In the Lady Chapel next to the Madonna's shrine were candle stands that had been too large and too heavy for the priest to steal. Maugris and I set them around the bier on which Flore lay. Lit, they were a circle of stars, just as Godefroi had wanted.

"You must leave us now."

Maugris said, "Brother, allow one of us, at least, to—"

"You do not understand," Godefroi said gently. "This will be the last night I shall have with my wife on this earth. You would not grudge me that, Maugris?" Godefroi turned to look at me also. "Or you, Bayard? I wish to keep vigil alone."

What point was there in saying more?

My last sight was of Godefroi kneeling beside his wife, the pommel of his sword held up like a cross over her body. And Flore seemed happy.

If I could have run from the chapel, I would have.

18

THE PRINCE of Wales will today visit Brixton, the site of recent riots in London. Ahead of the visit he expressed the wish that his marriage to Lady Diana Spencer may provide an opportunity for the British people to—" The transistor radio clicks off as Jesse enters the kitchen.

"I don't mind. Truly. I got used to hearing the news in the hospital. It was on all the time."

Alicia puts a kettle on the Aga and says pleasantly, "Hardly news. The country's obsessed. You can't turn the radio on or pick up a newspaper or even talk to the butcher without being bombarded by 'the wedding.' Tea?"

Jesse hasn't slept well and she's woken up worried. "Let me help."

"Oh, I can just about manage." A friendly glance, though slightly cool. "Besides . . ." Alicia points at Jesse's sling. "So what about some toast? Or there are eggs and tomatoes."

Jesse says impulsively, "Toast. But only if you let me make it."

"And yet, here's some I prepared earlier." Alicia opens the warming oven with a flourish and lifts out a silver toast rack crammed with crustless triangles of brown toast as if she's Julia

Child. "Get the butter if you like, it's in the fridge. Jam's on the table." She puts the rack on a cork mat.

It's a first for Jesse to eat breakfast with napkins in silver rings and china with gilded crests. "You've gone to a lot of trouble."

"We all have to eat." Alicia carries the teapot to the table. Sturdy, brown earthenware. "Have you seen Rory?"

"Not so far." Jesse's got that uncomfortable feeling again. Alicia's manners are impeccable, but *there's something*.

"More trouble than he's worth, that man." Alicia offers the pot.

As Jesse holds up her cup, she says lightly, "Could be worth a bit, though, when he sets up in Harley Street one day. Maybe when he's really famous and really, really old, he'll die and leave everything to Hundredfield."

A grim little laugh. "That's years away. Or not, as the case might be. Lots of times I've positively yearned to murder Rory Brandon."

Is that a joke? Jessie's not completely sure. "Rory told me he was born here and that you played together as children. That must count for something. When the will is finally read, I mean."

Alicia hesitates. "True. But then his mother remarried and they moved away. Cancels out, I'd say."

And that's a world of loneliness, right there.

"Um . . ." Jesse hesitates. "I just wanted to ask, if you don't mind, that is . . ." Half formed, the words bubble from her mouth.

Politely, Alicia cuts the knot. "Could you pass the jam?"

"Oh. Yes. But, what I meant was, were you serious last night? The invitation? I really, really don't want to impose." Jesse's always been a blurter. She hates that.

"Of course. And you're not." Alicia chews placidly.

"It's just that, well . . ." Jesse hauls in air as if there's not much left in the world. "I was surprised, you see, and . . ." Alicia nods patiently. "I'm just more accustomed to doing things on my own. I came to England on my own and planned on coming to Scotland by myself as well, because I really have so many things I need to do. But . . ." Jesse hesitates.

Alicia picks up the pot. "More tea?"

Jesse shakes her head. "No. Thank you." She dithers, then surrenders. "You see, it *is* true that Rory's made a difference. To recovering from the accident, I mean. And I didn't want to seem ungrateful. *Plus* I do want to get better, so I'd like to say yes. Just for a few days. If that's okay?" Jesse finishes in a rush.

Alicia butters another triangle. Applies jam. "It seems to me Rory owes you. That could be good." A brief, quite wicked smile as she takes a bite.

Jesse exhales. "Um . . ."

"Yes?" Alicia is patient when she has to be.

"Rory did say there's a village quite close."

"Newton Prior. Yes, it's not far."

"Walking distance?"

Alicia shakes her head. "Not unless you'd enjoy a really, really long hike. It's a decent ride too, only we don't have horses these days."

"Oh." A crestfallen silence.

Alicia decides to be nice. "I'll be going to town a bit later today. I can give you a lift if you like."

"I don't want to be a pain, though." Jesse smiles briefly; being dependent for simple moving around is not her idea of a good time.

"Or I could just get what you need?"

"It's only an aerogram."

Alicia doesn't ask what for, and Jesse doesn't tell her.

"You don't have to go to the village for that." Alicia gets up and rummages in a kitchen drawer. She puts a couple of flimsy blue sheets on the table.

Jesse looks at them. Okay, it's decided. She'll write to her parents and post it today. "Thanks. That's great. By the way, is there a library in . . ."

"Newton Prior?"

Jesse nods. "That's it. Is it a big place?"

"Not very. But there is a library."

"Final question." A nervous grin. "How far is Hundredfield from Jedburgh?"

"An hour, maybe more, maybe less, depending on traffic once you hit the main road." The expression in Alicia's eyes is kind.

"Good to know." *Maybe I can get a bus.* "Thanks."

Something cold nudges Jesse's knee and she jumps, dropping her knife.

Alicia ducks under the table. "I warned you. No cadging!"

"Me or Ollie?" Rory strolls in from the passage.

"Ow!" Alicia hits her head as the dog scrambles up, wagging and barking. "Ollie! Be quiet."

"Sleep late?" Jesse's suddenly busy with her toast.

"Me? Never. Had a quiet stroll, that's all." Rory swipes what's on Alicia's plate.

"Get your own." She slaps his hand.

Jesse watches the byplay. Alicia's enigmatic, but now Rory's arrived, she seems happy.

"So." He drops into a chair, pulling the toast rack toward him. "Going to stay?" He selects a piece and lays butter down in slabs.

Shameless. Jesse says, "I'm fine, thanks for asking."

"Jesse's agreed to stay for a few days. I'd say you're one pretty lucky doctor." Alicia smiles faintly.

The butter knife stops moving. "That's great news. Really wonderful."

He means it. Jesse remembers the hospital—the professional young specialist-in-training, not exactly the warmest man on the planet, and now he's morphed into something else, and the power relationship between them has changed; it's almost as if he's a supplicant. That's confusing.

"In that case"—Rory beams—"why don't I take Jesse into the village? Show her the sights before we get stuck in." His general benevolence sweeps up both the girls.

"You could introduce her to Helen while you're there. She'll be delighted to meet Jesse. She's always so proud of your work."

Jesse feels oddly put out. *So, I'm work.* "Helen?"

Rory flicks her a glance. "My mum." He leans forward. "She'd love to see you too, Licia. Why don't you come with us?"

Alicia says steadily, "Oh, I've got more than enough to do here." It's a definite no.

Rory goes to say something, but instead plucks more toast from the rack and scoops butter beside it.

Alicia pushes the jam pot across the table. "You might like this. Vary the taste."

"Thanks." The irony heads straight over Rory's head. Or not. "So, Jesse, what do you think? Nice relaxing drive?"

She eyes him with suspicion. "Actually, I've got things to do. Alicia's told me there's a library in the village."

Rory grins. "Before we go, though, you might like a walk around the castle? Give you a feel for the place."

He's trapped her and they both know it. Staring out at the stars last night, Hundredfield had seemed enchanted; today, in the bright morning, nothing hides the bones of the buildings she drew whole. They're waiting. *Don't be so fanciful!*

"Ollie loves a walk." Alicia scruffs the dog's ears and his tongue lolls in a dog smile. "We could all go together. One big happy family."

They're talking over her head again, as if Jesse were a child. "Um . . ."

"We fight too much for that."

"Okay. Yes. It would be good to walk around Hundredfield." Jesse didn't mean to speak so loud. Half apologetically she says, "But I need to write something to post. Before we go into town."

In the small silence, Alicia stands. She's looking at Jesse's sneakers. "You'll need some Wellies. The spring under the keep is misbehaving again. It breaks out just when we think it's gone to sleep; mind of its own, always has had, though it's worse if rain's on the way." She gathers plates and takes them to the sink.

"I thought I heard rain last night."

Drying her hands, Alicia abruptly says, "You're mistaken. I'd have known. You can stack the rest, Rory." She holds the door open and ushers Jesse along the passage to another vaulted room. "The boot room was the buttery once."

"As in butter?" Jesse has vague thoughts of milkmaids. She chafes her arms. It's certainly cold enough to keep milk fresh.

Alicia, sorting through a large basket, dives deeper. "Try these." She holds up a pair of green rubber boots. "As in butts. Wine butts." She waves the Wellies. "Beer and wine were kept here for the household."

"It's a big room. They must have drunk a lot."

"Big castle." Alicia sits to pull on another pair of scuffed Wellingtons. "The water wasn't safe, that's why everyone drank beer."

"Even the kids?"

Alicia nods. She stands. "Your turn."

Jesse wriggles her feet into the boots; oddly difficult with only one hand. "What are all the buckets for?" A collection of steel and plastic pails is stacked high in one corner.

"Oh, this and that." Alicia leads the way up the stairs and pulls open the great front door. Outside, she shades her eyes against the morning sun. "You get a good view of the whole site from here. A lot of the buildings are ruined and some that existed once are entirely gone, but it's easy to see where they were."

I know. Jesse chokes off the thought.

"Shall we take Jesse as far as the keep?" Rory has joined them. He speaks quietly, the joking tone gone. "She might like to see it."

Only might.

Alicia looks at her guest appraisingly. "Don't let him bully you, Jesse."

"He couldn't if he tried." Jesse turns to look at the building behind. "Tell me a bit about this part first?"

"Well, this is all that remains of a much bigger structure, of course."

Jesse nods. She remembers it from the first drawing.

"So, it was built in the early to mid-thirteen hundreds, though it's still called the New Range. In the old keep"—Alicia gestures to the tower in the distance—"the whole household—servants, dogs, family, retainers, all of them—lived on top of one another with almost no privacy. But fashions changed and the New Range gave the family their own house for the first time."

Jesse looks around appraisingly. *House* seems inadequate for four floors of massive stone with at least two more stories below ground level.

Alicia points. "Part of the wall's fallen away. That's where the other half stood."

Jesse cranes to look. It's as if a tooth, a monstrous one, has been brutally extracted, leaving a wound behind.

"The outer walls were part of the structure you see, but as rooms fell into disuse and some of the roof went after a storm in the late nineteenth century, there wasn't enough money for substantial repairs, and that whole section was sealed off. Then one night, a great lump of the building *and* the wall just slid into the river. We were lucky the whole thing didn't go." They're strolling away from the New Range now, Ollie barking his way ahead.

"Wow!" Jesse stops.

Enclosing the whole ridge, a massive wall tops and follows the contours of the hill, and at their feet a cobbled yard stretches away until it narrows like a throat to begin a long climb to the keep in the distance. Below, facing the river, a double-height gateway with battlements above and iron-banded doors below—held open by chains—cuts a hole in the stone defenses. Through the opening Jesse spies a bridge spanning a fast-moving river.

"You were asleep when we arrived so you didn't see any of this." Rory hasn't spoken for a while.

Jesse says breezily, "That's right. All new to me." *As it is now.* "But this yard! You could lend it out to Her Maj for the Trooping of the Color, you really could. Or put the tents up and have 'the wedding' reception right here."

Alicia grins. "Well, it's officially called the inner ward, but they did rather plan for the days when everyone was home. Must have been quite a crowd. Those are the stables, by the way."

A row of roofless barns gapes. Jesse hadn't seen those in her drawings—they'd been hidden by the point of view of the sketch—but they're huge. Her breathing ramps up. *Getting closer . . .*

"There are cellars under there that go for a really long way, each one linked to the next." Rory flashes a glance at Alicia. "We weren't allowed in as kids on pain of, well, pain, because they were unsafe even then. But you can still see where water from the spring was diverted into a cistern down below; it supplied Hundredfield with water and drained into the moat."

"A moat. You talked about that." Jesse so wants to look at him, but does not. *Closer still . . .*

Rory nods. "They dug the bed halfway up the hill. You can still see the workings."

"And when the castle was extended, the river was diverted to circle the base of the hill. They drained the old moat and left it as a defensive ditch, but they never did solve the problem of the spring; it's still there and sometimes the old moat fills up again and overflows."

"They?"

"My ancestors." Alicia's quite curt.

"Must have had a lot of labor to build all this." Something about the scale of this place is horrifying. *So many deaths to build it.* Jesse stands still. *Close. Really, really close.*

Rory puts a hand on her arm. "Are you feeling okay?"

"I'm fine." Jesse transfers her attention to Alicia. "You were saying?"

The other girl sweeps an arm toward the castle's perimeter walls. "Once, you could walk all the way around that parapet, from here to the keep and back, and it was wide enough for four men to march abreast. The point was, you could see your enemies coming. The stone's too dangerous now, of course, and the enemies long gone." But she narrows her eyes.

Jesse so longs to ask, *Define dangerous?* "It all looks spectacularly old."

The trio saunter on, Alicia and Rory matching Jesse's slower pace.

"The Normans. Who were they really?" Jesse's staring at the keep.

"Invaders. Dressed up in fancy rhetoric to justify William stealing the throne and the country, but that's what they were. It's the old story: the victors take everything from the original people and murder or enslave all those who stand in their way whilst rewriting history. They were brutal—the times and the men." Alicia could be speaking to herself.

A quick glance at Jesse's white face, and Rory taps his watch. "Maybe we should come back and see the inside of the keep another time?"

Jesse's happy to go, though she tries not to show it. As they walk away, wind ruffles her hair like fingers and she turns to look back. There's nothing to see. Just an old tower scarred by a thousand years.

Ruin.

The word whispers in her head, like the sound of a quiet sea.

Dear Mum.

That's not right. Jesse puts the pen down and peers at the fingers of her left hand; they wrote those innocent words. Correction. Her *brain* wrote the letters. Her brain, not her soul. Or her heart. Habit, that's all it is.

Jesse gets up. What does she really want to say?

Dear Mum, why didn't you tell me?

Dear Mum, who are you and who am I?

Dear Mum, who's my dad?

Dear Mum, WHY?

Jesse knows her parents are suffering as she is suffering, and she knows too that they must have had a reason not to tell her the truth. But this is so hard. All her remembered life, she's felt like an outsider, so different to look at from her parents. And she thinks of the answer her mum gave when she first asked the question:

But this is the way God wants you to look, Jesse. You were our gift from Him.

Their gift from God. Her parents had sent her to a Catholic parochial school though they were Presbyterians. Now, knowing what she does, Jesse wonders if her real parents were Catholic and this was a gesture to them.

Jesse stares again at the words she's written. She sits down and leaves the *Dear Mum*, adding, *I'm staying in the borders of England and Scotland and hope to be able to visit Jedburgh soon. Any information you can send would be appreciated. You can address it to me, c/o Post Office, Newton Prior, Northumberland.*

What else was there to say?

I'm well—economical with the truth, that statement—*and looking forward to the future.*

No *Give my love to everyone.*

No *Hello to Dad.* She signs it with just one word, *Jesse.*

19

TWENTY MINUTES from Hundredfield and Rory's Saab idles into the main street of the village of Newton Prior.

"Oh! This is lovely." Jesse twists in her seat, tries to look everywhere at once. The road is lined with pretty houses of gray stone and opens into a paved square. Window boxes spill flowers and a cheery tearoom has checked curtains in the windows. It's an unexpectedly sunny day.

"That's the Beast Market." Rory points to a graceful building with open sides that stands in the center of the square. "Newton Prior's still a market town, by the way. Sheep, cattle, and horses—they're all sold here once a month." He swings the wheel and the car slides into a parking space. "Pub's over there." He waves at an austere building with small windows crowded up beneath the roof. "Quite ancient too, actually. Not as old as Hundredfield, but close."

"You said there was a post office?"

"You go along the lane beside the church, and that leads into the other end of the shopping street. It's halfway down." As he gets out, Rory points.

Jesse stares at the church that takes up most of one side of the square. It has little decoration, and the blunt tower claims the sky as if entitled to the real estate. "That's old too, isn't it? Not Saxon, but . . ."

Rory nods as he opens the car door. "Well done, young colonial."

Jesse just looks at him.

Rory staggers, as if she's shot him in the heart.

"Pathetic, Dr. Brandon. Just, really . . . pathetic." But they're both, finally, smiling.

"*So*, anyway, this whole village basically grew up around a Benedictine priory. Hence the name. And in case you're wondering, that's the Church of St. Michael the Archangel. He was always picking fights on behalf of God. Normans must have loved him."

They peer up at the tower, Jesse shading her eyes.

"It looks like a, well, not quite a castle—more a fortress?" Jess points at the battlements.

"It was violent around here. And local legend says it was built on the site of a Roman temple. Mithras. Another god who rose from the dead—he was a warrior too. Churches were often built on top of the sacred places of other religions."

"Interesting." Jesse sneaks a look at her watch. "By the way, what's the name of the street I should look out for when I come back?"

"Same as this. Silver Street. You won't get lost. The village is a grid. Keep turning left and you'll find yourself back here. That's the Romans for you."

"Romans?"

He nods. "This was a garrison town in Hadrian's time."

"*The* Wall."

Rory nods. "What about we meet back here in half an hour?"

"An hour might be better." Jesse doesn't say why.

"Right. And I'll introduce you to my mum, and Mack."

"Mack?"

"My half brother from Mum's second marriage. He's a few years younger than me."

"Okay. Where?"

Rory points at the pub. "My mum's the licensee; Mack runs the business."

Jesse stares across the square at the name board of the old gray building. "The Hunt?" She squints, puzzled by what she sees.

"Not the red-coat kind. I'll let Mack explain."

"See you in a while."

He calls after her, "Take things gently. Doctor's orders."

Take things gently. Jesse ponders the indirectness of polite conversation as she lengthens her stride across the square. Her mood lifts. She's alive and that's so much better than the alternative.

The façade of the church looms as the tower casts a shadow across her path. Jesse pauses and tips her head back. The archangel's expression, even after a thousand northern winters, remains severe. Jesse's tempted to call out, *Cheer up, Mike,* but she doesn't; she's trying to be English, and English people don't talk to statues. She waves instead—when no one's looking—and walks on.

Trying to be English. That sets Jesse thinking about what she has to do, and, preoccupied, she looks up to find she's almost walked the length of the other end of the shopping street. She turns around. There's the post office, a modest building of red brick squashed between a cake shop and a boutique, and even here, in this tiny place, "the wedding" lurks.

On one side of the post office there's a towering cake in the window, with CHARLES & DIANA, LOYAL CONGRATULATIONS FROM NEWTON PRIOR written in icing around a pair of glass-eyed figurines. On the other, a dummy wears a face mask of Diana, plus a blond wig and a tiara, and sports a gown so fussy—such a froth of lace and bows and frills—it might stand up by itself.

The dress cheers Jesse up. She likes the way the whole country has embraced the story of an obscure, blushing girl being made into a princess with the wave of a royal wand. A genuine fairy tale, coming to life, right here, right now.

But fairy tales aren't real. Jesse's turned her back on the only family she's ever known in search of—what? Truth, not fantasy. Shocking, unwelcome, but still the truth.

She stares at the small blue rectangle in her hand. She wrote the address without a wobble; now all she has to do is post it.

Jesse draws curious looks as she stares at the red letter box. Then, as if wet, she shakes herself and drops the lettergram through the slot.

What will they think when they open it? *Too late now.* She looks up and down the street. "Excuse me." A woman with too many shopping bags pauses. Jesse picked her because she has a nice face. "Sorry, but could you tell me where the library is?"

The library is a 1960s building and very ugly. A brutal concrete box that's someone's idea of a suitable prison for books. It's as if the knowledge and wisdom trapped inside are medicines—things you swallow to make you better even if you hate the taste.

Jesse walks through the tricky revolving door—it snatches at her skirt—and in the foyer is the ghost of wet winter coats and the dank sense of mold growing somewhere out of sight.

"Do you keep copies of past phone books here?"

The girl behind the INFORMATION sign draws her cardigan close, as if Jesse's brought a cold breeze inside. "How far back?" She starts to cough and, hunching, turns away.

Jesse has the odd feeling the paroxysm's her fault. "The midfifties? I want to find a family who may have lived somewhere in the borders area. Have to start somewhere." She smiles apologetically.

The girl coughs again, shakes her head. "Stacks."

"What?"

"The stacks. In the stacks. Phone books from then." A cascade of hacking barks.

Jesse winces.

Breathing in gasps, the girl pushes a form across the desk. "We . . . can . . . get . . . them . . . in a few days. Different building." The last words tumble out. She offers a pen. "Years. Which ones?"

Jesse starts to fill in her name and then realizes she doesn't have Hundredfield's number as a contact. "I'm staying locally but I don't have the number of my host."

The girl behind the desk stoops and hefts a thick telephone directory from under the desk. She watches as Jesse thumbs through to find *Donne*. "Hundredfield?" She taps the name. Jesse looks up, confused, and the girl nods. "Donnes. Everyone knows everyone around here." It's said in a rush but is an actual sentence.

"So do you ring me, or . . . ?" Jesse hesitates to ask anything more.

"Yes."

"Oh. Okay. Thanks." Jesse nods and starts to turn away, then: "Apologies again, but I'm interested to find out about a place in Jedburgh. A house, actually, in Priorsgate. Probably quite old?"

This time the girl pulls a pad closer and writes, *Upstairs, first room on right. Architectural History, Borders Region.*

"Births and deaths for the same period?"

"Try churches." A half smile and a wheeze.

Jesse, not wanting to set off another coughing fit, says hastily, "Thanks again." She walks away, then stops. Hurries back.

"Really, really sorry, but is there a local-history society in Newton Prior?"

Another heaving wheeze, and the librarian writes, with some effort, *Helen Brandon. At pub.*

Jesse stares at the name. Has to be the same person, doesn't it? That's a good omen. "You've been very kind. Thanks."

The girl tries to say something, can't find the breath.

Jesse looks at her encouragingly.

Another chest-quaking effort and the words are finally expelled. "No trouble at all. Here to help."

"Did you find what you wanted?" Leaning against a wall, Rory's propped at the corner of the lane leading back to the square.

Deep in thought, Jesse stumbles when he speaks.

He grabs her before she falls. "Oops. Thought you might be lost."

Lost, that very word, strikes hard. She'd had so much faith she'd find clues at the library, a beginning, something to set her on her way. But she hasn't. Jesse's face crumples.

Rory's confused. "Sorry." He drops his hand.

If she weren't so close to tears, Jesse'd laugh. It feels as if she's been apologizing all morning. "No. I'm fine."

But she's not, and Rory's not sure what to do. He fills the silence. "In Roman times, you could buy lions and tigers here. And bears too. Did I say that?"

Jesse shakes her head, trying not to sniff. She longs to wipe her nose, but there's only the sleeve of her top.

"Here." Rory pulls a little packet of tissues from a pocket. "Yes. I always come prepared."

"Thanks." Not much of even a mumble.

He begins again. "So, yes, the Roman garrison put on animal shows. You know, boys away from home—keep them out of trouble between shifts. That sort of thing."

Jesse nods. She doesn't care. But she blows her nose. Once. Again.

Rory clears his throat. "And gladiators. They had those as well." The facts run out.

She wipes her eyes. "This is silly."

"What is?" he asks quietly.

"The substance of my life. It makes no sense at all." Jesse looks braver than she feels.

A flash of something crosses Rory's face, concern, consternation, and he goes to put an arm around her shoulder, but she says, "Don't." It's hard to avoid crying again. That's embarrassing.

To shield Jesse from strangers' eyes, Rory steps in front of her. Once or twice he says hello to people he knows or raises a hand in greeting, but he does not abandon her. He stands quietly, waiting for the gust of emotion to ebb.

It's an overreaction, Jesse knows it is, a letting go. She breathes deeply and *makes* herself stop crying. "The librarian said I should talk to your mum. At least I think she meant your mum. Helen Brandon." A watery hiccup.

"Why would she say that?" Rory's making conversation, just providing space and time for Jesse to get herself together.

"Local history. Might help tracking my parents."

"I should have thought of that. Mum knows pretty much everyone around here." Rory clears his throat nervously. "Lunch?"

Because she doesn't know what else to do, Jesse lets him lead the way.

The dining room in the Hunt is crowded, the tables shoved close together to handle the rush.

Rory surveys the room. He says uneasily, "I forgot about the tourists. Summer rush."

Swollen-eyed, Jesse's dismayed by the sight of so many people.

From behind the bar, a voice calls out, "Who let you in?" They turn as a man flips the counter up and hurries over, one large hand outstretched.

Rory's face clears. "Mack!" They hug with much slapping of backs and arms.

Mack has the thick shoulders and wide chest of someone who's played rugby, plus the broken nose. But his eyes are dark brown, so dark they're almost black, and in the flurry of greeting, Jesse registers an odd fact: Mack has a strand of white hair among the dark—a bright flash above one eye.

"Putting on a bit, I see, Dr. Brandon." Mack throws a punch at Rory's diaphragm and dodges a faked uppercut in return as the two laugh, great whoops that silence the room.

But Mack's registered Jesse, and after a moment's hesitation Rory says, "And this is Jesse Marley. She's staying at Hundredfield with Alicia. Jesse, this is my brother, Mack."

"Mack, Jesse; Jesse, Mack. We could sing that, if you like. I hear a Welsh male-voice choir, one hundred strong." Mack grins, but he doesn't make a big thing of looking at her face.

Jesse swallows. His whimsical kindness brings tears too close again. "Is Mack short for . . . ?"

His face creases attractively. "Nope. That's my name."

"As in truck; always been built like one." But Rory draws his brother to one side. He murmurs, "Is there any way we could eat in the private dining room? Jesse's . . ."

Jesse hears him. "The truth is, I've not been well and . . ."

"Of course. No sooner said than— Rachel!" Mack weaves through the tables to a waitress. The woman turns patiently when Mack taps her on the shoulder.

"I wasn't going to tell him." Rory watches his brother as the woman nods.

"But I decided I would." Jesse's tired of feeling ashamed and overwrought; really, *really* tired of the bad psychic weather in her head.

"All settled." Mack's back. He guides Jesse to a door set deep in the wall. "You might have to duck." He points above her head.

"Again." Jesse nods.

"What?" Mack's confused.

"Nothing." She manages a smile. The lintel is certainly low and the thickness of the walls massive, but now she's staring at the stone beneath her feet. It's carved with what seems like a bundle of sticks and some letters: SPQR. She looks at Mack expectantly. "I've seen this before."

Mack nods. " 'The Senate and People of Rome.' Some say we should put it in a museum, but I think it belongs where it is." He gestures through the open door. "Just through here."

Jesse pauses. She'd like to kneel down and press her fingers into the carved letters. Maybe the person who carved these words, this image, two thousand years ago had the usual human problems too; does that put her own transient misery into perspective? Only maybe. She steps carefully over the carving and through into the room beyond; it's an odd space, a truncated half circle with a series of stone seats set into bays in the wall.

Mack says, "This would have been a circular room once, with a seat for each of the monks in the niches. It's all that remains of the priory house."

Grapevines have been carved around the bays, and Jesse steps closer. "Maybe the monks knew the place would end up as a pub? Sorry! What I meant was . . ." She's horrified.

Mack's amused. "Don't think they'd have minded so much. Christ associated with all sorts of riffraff, publicans included."

"Now I really am embarrassed." Jesse's face is flaming.

Rory pulls out a chair from the table in the center of the space. "And I'm hungry."

Mack takes the hint. "I'll send Rachel with the menus. Enjoy your lunch."

Rory calls out, "Where's Mum, by the way? Jesse wants to meet her."

"At the doctor's. Nothing wrong. Just a checkup." Mack closes the door with a soft click and cuts off light from the pub. Jesse sees the room is windowless, though lit with some drama by artificial candles in sconces around the walls.

A knock punctures the awkward silence as the door opens and Rachel peers in. She brings menus to the table. "Hello, Rory. Nice to see you again. Your mum'll be happy." Rachel's smile brightens an otherwise unremarkable face.

"Likewise." Rory grins easily.

The waitress gets out an order pad from a pocket. "So, chef's specials. For starters, we have a shrimp velouté with our own smoked wild salmon, which is very popular."

The words wash over Jesse as she tries to think. She clears her throat. "Actually, I don't think I'm hungry." She hands the menu back.

"Some tea, perhaps?" Rachel is unfazed.

"That would be lovely." It's true. Jesse's thirsty suddenly.

"What about you, Rory?"

"Bouillabaisse sounds good."

The door closes quietly.

Now or never. She feels his eyes on her face. "So, Rory, what's the truth?"

"The truth." Rory says the word as if he's tasting each letter. As if he does not quite like the flavor. "What do you think you know, Jesse?"

Jesse touches her skull. "Everything's getting worse. Today, when we went to the keep"—she shakes her head—"I was frightened."

"Can you say why?"

She swallows, presses her hands over her eyes. "Sometimes"—she shakes her head—"this is all just too much."

He says quietly, "You said you are frightened. Is it the thought of insanity?"

The words go off like a bomb. Jesse tries to speak, and again; finally something struggles out of her mouth. "You're the doctor. *Am* I insane?" The truculence fades to a plea.

Rory leans forward. "If it gives you comfort, I'm almost certain you're not."

"*Almost* certain?"

"On available evidence."

The door cracks open as Mack backs through with a tray.

Rory attempts a smile. "Though everything's relative."

Mack puts the soup in front of his brother with practiced care. "And for you, Miss Jesse, the all-England restorative. Though the tea's actually Scottish Blend." Pot, cup, sugar, strainer, and milk are deposited on the table. "Rachel thought you might like this as well." A plate of scones is put down, jam and cream on the side. "Just to pick at." Mack stands back, the tray clasped to his chest like a shield. "Whose relative?"

"Not who, what." Rory picks up the soup spoon, scoops up a prawn. "Can't have too much saffron in a fish soup, that's what I think."

Jesse stares at Rory. For a few minutes the urbane mask had gone. Now it's back.

"Do you know what he's talking about?" Mack pulls a chair out from the table and sits.

Jesse says slowly, "I'm trying to trace my birth family. All I know is my mother's name, my birthday, and the fact I was born in Jedburgh. I'd be further along, but I had an accident in London and Rory was my doctor. I'm here because of him."

"Rest and rehabilitation," Rory speaks around the soup.

Mack's eyes are sympathetic. "That's no good—the accident, not the doctor. Obviously." He smiles. "Still, Jedburgh's not so far away, and everyone knows everyone in the borders. Not such a grand thing some of the time, but useful all the same."

Jesse's mood lifts. She likes this big, calm man who seems so much less complicated than his brother. "The librarian told me that too. She also suggested I search church registers."

"She was right. Try a scone." Mack nudges the food closer. There's a pat of pale butter and two kinds of jam, plus a dish of whipped cream.

Jesse's stomach gurgles.

Rory deadpans, "I'd say that's a vote in favor."

She laughs. "Seconded." She breaks a scone open and loads it with cream and jam.

Satisfied, Mack gets up. "I could introduce you to the rector of St. Michael's if you like. Good value, if a bit eccentric. Call me when you're next going to be in town. Easy to set up."

"Would you do that?" Hope makes Jesse swallow a piece of scone too quickly. She gasps and coughs.

Mack bangs her between the shoulder blades.

Jesse shakes her head as the paroxysm subsides, and with one more thump, Mack scales back the assault.

Rory murmurs, "Did I tell you about the broken clavicle?" He points the soup spoon at Jesse's sling.

Mack's horrified. "*So* sorry! Really, I—"

She manages the facsimile of a grin. "I'm fine."

"Are you sure?" Poor Mack. He's scarlet.

"I'm a doctor. All will be well." The glint in Rory's eye is wicked.

"Well, if you're sure you're okay, I'll . . ." Mack bumbles toward the door.

"That wasn't very kind."

Rory contemplates the rest of the soup with interest. "No one ever said I was."

The lunchtime crowd is thinning as Rory shepherds Jesse through the bar. "There she is. Mum!" He waves.

A handsome woman somewhere in her later forties stands behind the cash register.

Now that's a smile, thinks Jesse, as Rory's mum leaves her customers and hurries to her son.

"Mack said you were here, but"—those bright eyes glide to Jesse's face—"I didn't want to disturb."

Rory puts an arm around his mother's shoulders. "We'll be at Hundredfield for a couple of weeks, Mum, so I just wanted to say hello and—"

Helen interrupts, "Alicia's not with you? We haven't seen each other in, oh, ages."

"I asked her to come, but she apologized. Things to do."

"That's Hundredfield for you. Eats you up, that place." Helen touches Rory on the arm. "Come and have dinner while you're here. Give me a call."

Jesse clears her throat.

"Of course! Mum, I should have introduced you properly. So, this is Jesse. Jesse Marley." It's rare for Rory to be flustered.

"Nice to meet you." Helen Brandon holds her hand out and Jesse goes to grasp it.

But Helen swings to point at the growing queue stacking up around the register. "Rachel!"

It's odd to be left standing with an outstretched hand.

"Sorry. You're a patient, I gather?" Those cool eyes assess Jesse quite blatantly.

How did you know that? "Yes. I'm recovering from an accident." Jesse lifts the sling slightly. She feels foolish. As if she's pretending. "But I'm researching too, while I'm here."

"We have a very rich history in the borders, of course." Helen's tone says she's only mildly interested; she's had history conversations with tourists countless times.

"Yes. In fact, at the library they said I should talk to you."

"Oh?" Helen's sweeping the busy room with her eyes. "Rory, d'you know where Mack is?"

Jesse feels like she's talking to the wind. "I'm looking for my birth parents, actually. I was told you're an expert in local history?"

"Really?" Helen puts her head to one side when she turns back. She doesn't say she's not. "What's your family name?"

"Green."

"There was only one lot of garlic prawns. You've overcharged us." A man's voice, quite aggressive, cuts through.

"Please do excuse me." A duck of the head, and Helen strides away to the cash register.

Rory glances at the embarrassed girl beside him. "Um, sorry about that."

"It's fine. She's busy." But Jesse's perplexed. Was she just snubbed?

They watch Helen dispensing efficient charm as she takes money and provides receipts as Rachel's banished to clearing tables. Outside, rain assaults the windows of the pub, blurring the view of the Beast Market.

"I can drive the car to the front door if you'd like?" Sometime in the past, a cast-iron-and-glass portico has been added to the ancient building.

Jesse's look is sardonic. "I'm not going to melt, Rory. It's just a bit of water."

"Okay. One, two, three, *go!*" He rushes her from the pub to the car but, in haste, drops the keys in a puddle, and they're both wet by the time they fall into the front seats.

"Been a top day for me so far, I'd say. What about you?"

"Excellent." Jesse is just as good at irony.

20

Tell them I have ridden to the village—if they ask."
Foot in the stirrup, I swung a leg over the stallion's
back.

Hurrying to saddle the mare I had asked for, Dikon nodded.
He did not look at me.

I punched him lightly on the arm. "I have friends there, boy.
And it is the season for a little, ah, joy." He would think I was
visiting Rosa. If I did not return before dawn, the lie might win
me time.

But Dikon's manners were good. He did not ask why the extra
horse was needed if I was visiting "friends."

I threw him a groat and, nudging Helios forward, gathered the
pack rein so the mare walked close behind.

The portcullis was raised for me, and once across the river,
I booted the stallion to a fast canter and allowed the mare more
room on the rein. Helios had left the stable with bad grace, but the
night air woke him and now he ran willingly enough.

Not one light shone from the houses as we rushed through the
village; we were gone so fast only a lone dog heard us pass. But as
he barked, another joined in and then another, until it seemed a

pack of wolves howled on our scent. Most would be chained. Most. But those that were not, we could outrun. Dogs did not worry me. My concern was that I was one man alone, riding at night. One man against a pack of wolf heads and runaways who hated the Dieudonné; if they were there. If they heard me.

The ride was a blur. Where the path was clear, I pushed both animals to speeds I knew were foolish. I did not allow myself to think I would fail. I could not fail.

Not fail. Not fail. Not fail. The words were beaten out by the rhythm of the hooves, and I do not know if one hour or two passed before I saw the priory wall. When I reined to a stop, plainchant came to me through the frozen air. The monks must be singing lauds. There was still time.

"Open!" I beat on the closed gate with my fist. The mailed glove struck hard.

Wind, as it came and went, swept men's voices closer and then away, but none answered the summons.

"Open. Or I will destroy the door." That was presumptuous. I did not have the means or the intention; it was good the brothers did not know that.

The cover of a barred port slid back, and a face peered out. The boy was young. And frightened. "Sir, I cannot let you in. The brothers are—"

I leaned down from my horse. "Fetch the prior, boy. Tell him Bayard de Dieudonné is here. And if he does not come quickly, tell him my brother is close behind with his men. Lord Godefroi. Be sure and tell him both our names."

The boy gasped and the door port closed with a slam.

The horses stamped in the cold, steam rising from their hides. If the prior did not come soon, it might truly mean I must find a way of breaking the door down.

"What do you want?" The port had creaked open again and light shone through. This was a very different face. The size and shape of the risen moon, it seemed to me the prior was too well fed to be a holy man.

"Prior." I bowed from the saddle. "Hundredfield has need of a priest." Helios was cooling and I spurred him in a tight circle, dragging the mare behind.

"Father Matthias has the cure of souls at the castle." The man did not look at me.

I spoke politely. "Perhaps the novice did not tell you my name. I am Bayard de Dieudonné, brother of the lord of Hundredfield. I regret to tell you that the man you speak of is a thief. He despoiled the altar that was in his charge." I crossed myself. "If those holy furnishings are returned to me tonight, and if you provide me with another priest, perhaps he will escape with his life." I shrugged.

The voice of the prior wavered. "I do not understand what you are talking about. Evil is truly abroad in these hard times, but your soul must be corrupted for you to slander a servant of God in this way. I cannot grant the services of another priest while . . ."

So, Matthias had told the prior.

I jumped from the saddle and launched myself at the port, shoving my hand through too quickly for the man to duck. "My brother asks for your help, and he does so courteously. Whatever you might have heard, it is your obligation to provide our house with a priest. If you do not, the endowment of this priory will be removed immediately and given to others more prepared to provide these sacred duties." I squeezed my hand around his throat and with the other put the prick of my dagger beside an eye. "I have been out of my bed for a very, very long time, Prior. Perhaps, from exhaustion, my hand will slip. That would be sad." Another squeeze and the man gurgled. He could not speak, but I heard a chain rattle and felt the door move.

I was never so quick in my life. The prior might be white lard, but he was a big man and perhaps some muscle still hid in those arms; he might try to slam the door on the hand that held the knife.

A neat twist, however, and I was through; and this time, though I dropped the grip on the prior's throat, I had the steel at his kidneys and an arm around his neck.

I said politely, "Perhaps I should meet the candidate you will propose. Just to be certain he is suitable."

That white face flushed. Moonlight made it black. "The bishop at Durham—"

"—is a personal friend of my family, as is the king in London. Perhaps, if it worries you, you may also enjoy a conversation with the warden of the East March? Baron Percy is our liege lord, and therefore yours."

"My allegiance is to Rome. Only the pope is my mortal overlord." A flash of courage.

I allowed myself to yawn. "I should counsel you, Prior. There is a choice here: provide me with an obedient priest and return the furnishings of our altar, and you and the priory will not be harmed. Disobey me in this, and I will call my brother and his men. And perhaps you will die, as will Matthias. I warned him of this; perhaps he did not properly convey the caution." The point of the knife was sharp and cut through the man's habit. I allowed it to sink into the fat of his lower back, though only a little way.

The prior gasped. "By these actions you damn yourself."

I was weary. "Lord Godefroi, as you know from Matthias, is not a reasonable man. Neither am I, though, perhaps, I am kinder than he. And dead men have nothing to say. Do not forget that."

The prior stood very still. "I will instruct my novice." The remark was measured, the tone cold as ice on bone. I heard some of what was said between them, though he spoke softly to the boy; "box" was mentioned and "in my cell."

I permitted the prior to dismiss the child, but I called out as he hurried away, "One moment."

The boy quivered where he stood, his eyes large as a cat's. I did not like to frighten children and said gently, "Your brothers should stay in the chapel. They will be safer there."

The boy nodded, and with one wild glance he ran; skinny legs flickered white as the habit flew up.

We waited. At first the prior held himself rigid and still as a tree, but lack of muscle let him down. So did fear of the knife in my hand. Soon he began to tremble, and his sweat, rank and doglike, drowned the air we both breathed. But I was used to sweat and said conversationally, "You made the right choice, Prior."

Two dark shapes hurried toward us, one small, one larger, and I could no longer hear the service being sung.

The taller was a young man and properly thin. His expression too was mild and certainly anxious. I saw he stumbled under the weight of the large wooden box he carried.

I made shooing motions to the boy. "Back to your prayers."

A glance at the prior, and the child scurried away.

I addressed the priest. "Can you ride?"

The man swallowed, his eyes on the prior. "No. That is to say, not well."

"Then I am the man to teach you. Tell me your name."

"I am called Simeon." He controlled the quaver quite well.

"Father Simeon, my brothers—Lord Godefroi and Lord Maugris—will be pleased to welcome you to Hundredfield as our new priest. As shall I." Perhaps I was too pleasant.

The prior muttered, "No priest can save your family."

I stared at the man and he dropped his eyes as I hustled Simeon through the gate. Outside, the mare had wandered a little way, cropping what fodder there was. I grabbed her reins and got her to stand.

"Get up." I nodded to the saddle. "I'll lash the box behind you."

Simeon shook his head. "It is too far. I cannot."

The horse sensed his fear and began to fidget, throwing her head and snorting.

I bunched the reins tighter, cupping my other hand into a step. "Put the box down. Your foot goes here."

The priest gulped but did as I asked, and as he tried to step up, I flung him into the saddle. This was nice judgment; any farther and he would have fallen over the other side. Perhaps my expression helped him hang on. I cannot have looked especially friendly.

The ride was miserable for Simeon, though he only tumbled off once and that into mud; but the pace was frustratingly slow, and though I had hoped to return before first light, a red dawn blood-ied the river and the sky as we came to the bridge.

"Father, I have good news." I turned to look at the priest. The wretch was hunched over the pommel, his face the color of ne-glected cheese.

"Any words of cheer are welcome, Lord Bayard."

The courtesy of the title pleased me; it said the man was prag-matic. I reined Helios to a stop and hauled the mare close. "As you see, soon we shall be inside the keep, and safe."

"From your brother?" The tone was dry.

"Lord Godefroi will have traveled ahead of us." I dared him to ask more. He did not. So I said, "You have two immediate duties. One is joyful—a mass to celebrate the birth of our Savior. The other, most sadly, is not. The Lady Flore, my brother's wife, must be buried. Hers will be the first service." I crossed myself; the priest did not as he stared at the castle.

I saw what he saw then. Fulk's tower, in that red light, was grim as a skull.

But this time there was no delay—the drawbridge descended when I called out—and we rode into the outer ward in reasonable order.

I had not known I was so stiff until, in the stable, I tried to dis-mount; the priest was in worse condition.

Throwing my reins to Dikon, I hobbled to the mare's head. "Take my hand, Father."

Father. An odd word to describe so young a man.

But if he was weary, the priest had some pride. Avoiding the box, he tried to swing a leg over the back of the mare, but his body let him down; the other leg buckled in the stirrup, and he fell.

I caught Simeon before his head hit the cobbles, though the same cannot be said for his knees. "I have you."

The man was panting as he plucked straw from his habit. Crossing his chest, he muttered, "That is true."

With Dikon carrying the chest, I walked the priest to Matthias's old cell. We passed four girls, pale from their beds. They were going to the byre to milk. As was proper for female servants, they dropped their eyes to the ground, though one was bold enough to look back and she said something behind her hand when she saw Simeon beside me.

I called out cheerily enough, "Good morning, on this holy day." But they hurried on without speaking. I did not know if they were afraid of me or modest.

Built into the castle wall beside the stables, Matthias's cell was comfortless. It had a bench, a plain prie-dieu, and a truckle bed, though someone, perhaps on my brother's orders, had left bread and hard cheese beside a jug of ale.

"Here is food to break your fast, Father, and also"—I gestured at the bed—"a place to lay your head."

Simeon stared around the chamber. "All I require is time for prayer. I cannot eat before the mass."

I said politely, "Lord Godefroi will let me know when he wishes the service to be sung and you shall be told. For now, I will leave you to contemplation."

I closed the door quietly. A key was in the lock outside. I used it.

The damage to the chapel doors was worse than I remembered. My first thought was that the splintered timber and mutilated lock must be removed before the household saw what was there.

A voice called out from inside the chapel—Godefroi's. I hurried to speak to him. But candles danced shadows across the walls and the floor, and in that uncertain light I did not see him at first.

"Flore!" My brother lay beside his wife's bier. He was sobbing her name.

"Godefroi?" Shocked, I did not immediately understand the bier had no occupant—until I saw the dress: an abandoned husk. The girl was gone.

21

BEFORE YOU ask, I do not know where her body is."

I had stumbled against Maugris as I backed away from the bier. He was kneeling in the chancel, directly under the silver Christ.

"You were praying?"

He got up quickly. "Am I not a Christian?"

His tone was belligerent, but I could smell the truth. My brother was terrified.

"What—that is to say . . ." I did not know how to frame the question.

"He was in the chapel all night. So was she."

"Did you see—"

Maugris said roughly, "I saw nothing."

"But—"

He grabbed the front of my jerkin, pulled my face against his. "Understand this. Godefroi kept vigil with her as he said he would." Maugris did not use Flore's name. "I was outside in the annex, watching over him. None came in, and none went out of this place. I did not sleep. Before dawn, I found what you see."

He let go, breathing hard.

I remembered another time—the morning before I fought first as a man. I was fifteen and my gut had contracted so tight against my spine it squeezed my bladder and I thought I would piss myself. I seemed to hear Death breathing beside me; I heard him again on that Christmas morning.

Maugris swallowed. "I have searched the keep, Bayard, every floor. The stables, the cellars. Her body is"—Maugris's face twisted—"it is not to be found."

My expression must have mirrored his, and God knows his was horrified.

Two nights, and the day in between, had upended the certain order of the world. Maugris and I stood balanced on the lip of an abyss we could not fathom, and something lay in wait for us down there. I swear I could hear it stir.

At the foot of the altar steps, Godefroi shuddered a breath and wailed, "Flore!"

"That is all he says. We must make him speak to us."

Maugris was right. And so we knelt beside our brother, trying not to look at the bier, the empty dress. One on each side, we held him upright. A heave, and we stood together like a trio of drunks.

"Godefroi?" Maugris spoke into his ear.

There was no change.

"You must walk, Godefroi. Now."

Bleared and dull, at least his eyes had opened.

"We shall take you to your bed."

Godefroi sighed and drooped between us.

"No, you must walk. The stairs are close." I tightened my grip.

Godefroi mumbled, "Too far."

I leaned closer. He might slur like a drunk and walk like a drunk, but I could smell no wine on his breath.

"First foot, next foot. And again. First foot, next foot. Yes. And again." Maugris talked as if Godefroi were learning to walk.

It was still dark inside the keep, for arrow loops give little light, but with each dragging step Godefroi seemed heavier until Maugris and I dripped sweat like flogged horses; finally, we brought our brother to his bedroom.

Half carrying Godefroi, Maugris and I rolled him over the edge of his bed; he lay on his back, deep asleep.

"And now?" Locking our brother inside, we moved quietly down the stairs.

Maugris led the way to the chapel. "We must take the bier away."

"But what to say if anyone asks where she is?"

"No one will ask because no one will see."

We stared at the abandoned dress, mute witness to so much we did not know. I gestured. "The ropes have not been cut."

Maugris went to speak, but then did not.

"How could she have—"

He spoke over me, "This must all be hidden."

"Yes."

Neither of us moved. As if laid out before dressing, Flore's gown seemed undisturbed, yet this was the winding sheet of an actual woman; where had she gone, *how* had she gone? Even now the damask held the shape of her body in some faint way—the swell of breasts, the suggestion of hips. Could cloth remember? Or was she a snake, to have shed her skin and left it behind? I shook my head, shook it hard, to banish the fantasy. "The Madonna."

"What did you say?" Maugris was staring at the dress. He too seemed dazed.

"In the shrine. We can hide the bier there. And the dress."

"Not the dress." With a quick movement, as if he feared to touch it, Maugris dragged the gown and the ropes off the bier. "Help me." Averting our eyes from what lay on the floor, we carried the door, plain wood, to the hidden shrine.

The Madonna was behind a painted screen, and inside, covering the statue, was a silk hanging embroidered with our crest; this Maugris now drew back.

Revealed, the Madonna seemed almost a real girl with rounded limbs under her clothes. But she was taller than any woman would ever be, and her face was covered with a fall of blue silk. Perhaps Maugris longed to uncover her face as I did, for it was years since we had seen it, but he did not touch the veil. "There is enough space."

It seemed sacrilege to prop the door against the wall behind her, but the niche was large enough. I said, "We shall need this again when we find Flore's body."

"If we find it. It is as if she has flown away."

This was so like my own thoughts, I had no words.

Maugris stared at the chapel's damaged doors. "We will need Rauf's help."

But I remembered last night as the men left. "And if he is not willing?"

Maugris's voice was harsh. "He has no choice." He strode ahead to the altar. "Burn it." He was pointing at the dress.

I hesitated. "But—"

"Do not question me." His eyes were fierce.

A lit candle stood in one of the stands. Maugris took it down. "Then find Margaretta and the child. Perhaps they can bring him back, if we cannot. Go."

I, who so loved beauty, would now conspire in its destruction, but as my fingers touched the material of Flore's gown, there was this. The cloth was warm, as if its owner had only now put it aside. And the surface was, horrifyingly, as smooth as a woman's skin.

I could not do it. I could not pick the dress up.

"What ails you?"

Older brother, younger brother. "This is valuable. Godefroi will not be pleased."

"What use has he for a dress?" But Maugris knew what I meant. To despoil a corpse of its covering was wrong.

But there was no corpse

And so I folded the gown and held it under my cloak as I climbed the stairs.

Where could such a thing be burned, unseen? Straw was stored near the cistern under the stables. So early in the day, it would be unvisited.

Keeping the candle burning as I crossed the inner ward was not easy, but the place was quiet and cold as a winter tomb. In the undercroft beneath the stables, I dragged stooks into the shape of a pyre and brought the candle close among the straw. The wisps would not catch. I knelt and blew, steady as a bellows; a thread of smoke was my reward, then the gleam and spark of fire.

I fed the blaze with care. Straw is quickly consumed but smothers too if not watched carefully. It came to me that if I were seen, I would seem a servant of the devil—my face lit by the flames of burning grave clothes.

I heard something.

Light picked out the glimmer of water as it welled over the cistern's sides and crept toward me like a living thing. Soon, my fire would be engulfed.

As if it were not mine, my hand moved. It flung the gown into the heart of the blaze, and then the rope. Though cloth does not easily burn, the damask might have been steeped in oil, for, writhing, gleaming, it twisted among the flames.

I listened for screams—as if this dress covered the body of a mortal woman blazing on her pyre.

22

As the warm day chills, rain spatters the gravel outside the New Range.

In the kitchen, Alicia's absorbed; a notepad is on the table and she's staring at what she's scribbled down.

Two columns. Pros. Cons.

Pros:

We've always lived here.

Estate should be preserved.

Must be a way to trade through this.

Get advice.

The pros run out.

Cons:

Money.

Alicia stares at that one word. And underlines it.

Staring at what she's written, she doodles something else. *RORY.* They're big, bold letters, and she underlines his name as well. Then, like a schoolgirl, she draws a trailing border of little hearts.

Abruptly, she rips the sheet off the pad and hurries to throw it into the firebox of the stove.

Something's tapping on the window above her head.

Alicia looks up. "No!"

Rain streaks the windows.

Alicia grabs a flashlight and takes the back stairs at a run; five floors and she's panting. At the very top is a last extension, a wide ladder that's propped against a landing high above her head. As Alicia climbs the final rungs, she hears the sound she dreads.

Pushing the attic door wide, Alicia juggles the flashlight. The sound is enormous as water, glittering, falls through that silver beam.

"Please, God, please, God . . ."

Sliding down the ladder, praying, cursing, Alicia's chest contracts like a drum skin, but she makes it to the buttery. Loading buckets, she starts back up. The rain is thicker now; there's a drowned layer to the window glass.

Sweating, she counts the steps, but when she gets to the attic, she's splashing through water.

Catch the leaks! That's what she has to do. That's all there is.

As Rory drives Jesse back to Hundredfield, the world shimmers. The rain has passed away to the west, the trailing edge of the storm flaring in a dark sky as fingers of light walk fields of vivid green.

"How beautiful this is." Jesse's making conversation. The drive's been tense.

"You don't remember from when you were little?" Rory knows, as Jesse does, that they're skirting around what happened at the pub. He shifts down, slows the Saab to walking pace.

Ahead, the road is filled with black-faced sheep. The leaders balk in front of the car, and the rest of the flock banks up behind, bleating.

"I was very young when we went to Australia. Less than one." Jesse leans forward as the car stops, staring through the windscreen. "I couldn't have memories. Could I?"

The sheep, ewes and well-grown lambs, are pushed forward by two border collies and the shouts of the farmer walking behind. A nervous mass, they stream past on both sides of the car calling to each other—the mothers hoarse and anxious, the lambs lighter, sweeter, in reply.

"Do you think they're talking about us?" Jesse winds her window down and half hangs out. "Hello, there." A gust of lanolin and sheep shit hits. Jesse wrinkles her nose and slides back inside. "It's the smell that seems familiar. Is that possible?"

The farmer waves them on.

Rory puts the car in gear. "It might be. Smell's very powerful. It's the last sense to go as you die."

"What about when you're born? Does it arrive first?" Jesse looks back as the Saab speeds up. The dogs have gathered the flock into a milling huddle, and when a gate opens, they flow through, a river of cream and black.

"Interesting thought." Rory accelerates, drops back into a higher gear.

After some minutes, Jesse says, "You told Helen that we'd be at Hundredfield for a couple of weeks, and you said that to Alicia as well. We should talk."

"I'm grateful for any time you'll give me, Jesse." Rory catches her glance in the mirror. "I want you to get well. You've been under a great deal of stress and you've handled that bravely, but you're not bulletproof. Let me take care of you. It's what I'm here for."

Jesse'd been prepared to argue, and if Rory had been anything but kind, she would have. But something's shifted. *A good cry, just what the doctor ordered.* Her mum used to say that. "So, you have a plan?"

Rory nods. "Alicia's said we can use the library. That'll be a good place to work." He flips the sun visor down and points the car toward the ominous west. Directly ahead, the hills are clothed in a haze of gold, and Hundredfield's keep is a stone finger on the brow of its distant, fortified hill. A sign? A warning?

Jesse doesn't know, but if Rory has a plan now, so does she. She closes her eyes against the glare. *Mack's a nice man. I'll take him up on meeting the rector. And then, the phone books will be at the library a bit later in the week. And Helen. Maybe I should try to speak to her more formally.* Jesse frowns.

"Anything wrong?"

She opens her eyes. He's watching her. "No. I'm good."

But she's not. Not really. Helen worries her. It's not often someone dislikes you on sight.

"Licia?" Rory pushes the front door open. Hundredfield has that feel: *empty.*

"I'll go up to my room, if it's okay. I got a couple of books from the library. About the borders." That's an economical lie; they're both about Jedburgh. The girl at the front desk had been right. There'd been shelves of information about the town where she was born.

"I'm cooking tonight. Take your time." Rory waggles the paper-wrapped parcel from the butcher. "Better get organized if we're going to eat before midnight."

Jesse stares around uncertainly. "Did Alicia say there was another way upstairs?"

Rory strides to the far end of the hall and throws back a pair of doors. "Here you go."

Ahead, a monumentally carved staircase rises to a landing before it splits into two flights. Jesse whistles. "Just shouts 'look at me.'"

"That was the twelfth earl for you. Always more money than sense, until both departed around the same time."

Jesse stares. *Earl?*

"These are some of the Gothic 'improvements' Alicia talked about. So, up to that first landing and take the right flight where the stairs split. Next landing up from there you'll find a door straight ahead; that's your corridor."

"You know this place well, don't you?"

"I do indeed." A polite smile. Back to the cool young doctor.

Behind her, the doors echo closed as Jesse begins to climb. Rain-dimmed light slants across the stairs, catching gilded picture frames, picking up painted eyes that stare as Jesse passes. Elizabethan grandees in silks and ruffs hang beside dark-eyed girls in the lace of Stuart times, and generals and admirals in uniforms of red and blue and gold keep company with Victorian beauties in jewel-bright satin. Some look like Alicia, eyes and nose and jaw—a few prettier, some not—but too many seem to sneer as Jesse climbs to the landing.

What am I, a peasant? What would you know? Resolutely turning her back, she comes to a wide door. Here it is. Her corridor. She's quite glad to leave the company of all those dead, grand people.

Jesse turns the handle, steps through. And stops.

Someone's crying. Softly.

Perhaps the hairs on her neck and arms will sit down if she waits for a moment.

No.

The sobs are louder. Utter misery.

Jesse looks at her bag. The door to her room is thick—she can go inside and just read.

But it's impossible not to be curious.

She's in someone else's very, very old house, and what she's hearing could be—what, a ghost?

Once, Jesse would have thought that absurd, but things are different now. *Someone* drew the sketches of this place. And if not her, then . . . automatic art, like automatic writing?

Jesse Marley scowls. Ridiculous!

So, it can't be a ghost.

What, then?

The sobbing stops.

Jesse listens so hard, pain blooms between her eyes.

Not there now. Definitely.

She closes her eyes. Really, really concentrates, doesn't even breathe.

Her ears sing like crickets.

Silence.

It's almost a relief as she tamps down that small flicker of regret, of curiosity. And opens the door to her room.

There!

She doesn't close the door. She leaves it open and follows the sound, those wrenching sobs, all the way to the end of the corridor. Another door. Alicia's door.

This is all too personal.

Jesse turns back.

"Who's there?"

Floorboards creak.

It's hard not to sound snoopy, but she says, "Hi, Alicia. Just thought I'd let you know we're back." A lie, but kind.

The door is wrenched open and Jesse tries not to gasp. Alicia's face is ravaged and her nose is red; she's been crying for a long time.

"Here." Jesse fumbles to extract Rory's tissues from her pocket. "It's the day for it."

"What?"

"Tears."

As she blots her face, Alicia mutters, "Apologies." And blows her nose fiercely.

"Look, I know how you feel." Jesse hovers in the doorway. It does not occur to her that she should not speak the truth.

"You don't. You really, really do not."

Uncertain what to do, what to say, Jesse toughs it out. "All right, I'll match you, and raise you. Trust me, I can." It was meant as a bit of a joke.

Alicia's eyes flare open. There's fury there.

Jesse takes a step back. She mumbles, "Oops. Thought it might help to laugh." She says humbly, "I keep feeling I should apologize for even being here, but I don't know what to say and I don't know how to say it. I'd like to make things better if I can." That ends with a wobble.

Alicia softens. She hesitates but says, "Come in."

Now Jesse's having trouble holding herself together as she ducks her head and walks into Alicia's bedroom. It's lived-in, and shabby, but the grace of furniture passed down through generations and a mantelpiece crammed with photographs is charming.

"It's untidy. Sorry." Alicia drops into a window seat, folds her arms around her torso. "I haven't been here for six months."

"Rory said that."

"Did he?" Alicia's back to cool.

There's a pause neither knows how to break.

Jesse clears her throat. "This is similar to the room I'm in. But it's bigger. They're both lovely."

"It was my parents' room." Alicia points at the largest photograph on the mantelpiece.

The black-and-white image of a young couple dancing together is in a silver frame. She in a filmy dress—all tulle skirt and lace bodice—he so classically handsome in white tie and tails. The girl in the picture is a version of Alicia, though her face is beautiful as she laughs with delight.

"That was the night of their engagement. The last real ball Hundredfield ever had. They were so happy then." Alicia's eyes fill with tears.

Jesse thinks about taking the other girl's hand. And doesn't. But she sits down beside her. And murmurs, "Don't talk if you don't want to."

"It's been so long since I've even said their names." Alicia stares out through the window. "It wasn't a very good marriage, in the end, though I didn't know that for a long time. No one said anything. I never even heard them raise their voices." Perhaps she's talking to herself.

Jesse would like to say she knows about the silence of marriage.

"Pa liked a certain way of life, you see—all the good things." Alicia waves a hand around the room. "He'd been born to it. Land was more important than money then, and you never run out of land, do you—place like this. And they're not making any more." A sharp laugh.

Jesse's not sure what Alicia is saying.

Alicia sighs. "The thing is, no one ever taught them how to *manage*; other people had always done that. Estate people, stewards, housekeepers. It was vulgar to talk finance, I suppose. And after the war, when Pa came back and things where so different, I guess he couldn't face it. Just went on spending because that's what you did. He sulked if he didn't get his way. Tricky." Her voice fades.

Silence rests on the air.

"Are they, that is . . ." Jesse doesn't know how to ask if Alicia's parents are still alive.

The other girl gets up, goes to the photograph, picks it up. It's as if Jesse isn't there. "In the end, Ma must have seen it coming, I'm certain of that." Alicia swings around. And hesitates. "Did I say they were together when it happened?"

Jesse shakes her head.

"Maybe that was something good." Alicia puts the photograph back carefully. "But I don't know why she even got in the car. It was a storm, you see, and they were coming back after a party last winter, just after Christmas. Daddy had insisted they leave, though they could have stayed the night. And of course, it was dark." Alicia trembles a breath. "Pa crashed through the rails on the bridge and into the river." She gestures *down there*. "The car wasn't found until the next day, so no one knows if they could have been saved. I wasn't even here."

Away to the far west, the sky is burning as day subsides into night.

"Do you ever feel you've disappointed someone—someone important?"

"Yes. Doesn't everyone?" Jesse thinks *disappointment* is a tame word for some of the things she's done.

"But what if it's your ancestors?"

Jesse says the wrong thing. "They're dead. How can you disappoint someone who's dead?"

Alicia turns away, her shoulders hunched. "By betraying their trust."

"Hey." Jesse gets up, and this time she takes Alicia's hand. "It's okay. It will *be* okay. Time heals all." *And other awkward clichés.*

"Time is the enemy when the past won't lie down and die. There's the roof, you see."

"Okay." Jesse tries not to look confused.

"What I mean is, it leaks, and it needs replacing. There's just miles and miles of it, here and on the keep. Then there's the flashing and the windows, *and* the plumbing, plus the ceilings in the upstairs rooms. That's *before* you get to the damp in the cellars. That has to be fixed before it destroys the stone—no foundations and no damp course in the fourteenth century, so that's become a twentieth-century problem—*and*"—Alicia stares at her elegant, happy father, her radiant mother—"well, Pa stuck his head in the sand about Hundredfield. Ma tried to get him to concentrate on what had to be done, but he thought it would all come right in the end. Always the optimist, Pa. And he's gone. And I have to sort it out."

Jesse thinks about the size of the castle, all the buildings. And the keep. "So, what now?"

There's a pause. "Now?" Alicia squares her shoulders. "I think we should see what Rory's doing. Did he talk about making béarnaise?"

"Not precisely, but he seemed keen to get dinner happening."

"It's his party trick, and it's always a disaster. *Absolutely* no idea, that man, about a good sauce."

Alicia sweeps from the bedroom, head held high.

For a moment, Jesse can see the train held in that long-fingered hand, the skirt trailing over the boards as she goes. Fanciful non-sense.

Maybe not, if you're the daughter of an earl.

Before she leaves the room, Jesse stares at the photographs. These are the Hundredfield family, the portraits on the walls in modern form. And Alicia's parents, so in love and untouched by time; *the best of it.* How lucky Alicia is to know she's their daughter.

Jesse stares at the earl—that handsome face, dark hair, dark eyes.

Her real parents—were they ever such enchanted beings?

Who do I look like? Can you tell me?

23

ALICIA BRINGS peas to the table in a silver bowl as Rory sharpens the carving knife. He looks at her red eyes, goes to say something. And changes gear. "Shall I?" He nods at the fillet of beef.

Alicia's inspecting the contents of the sauceboat Rory's put on the table. "You know, this actually looks okay."

Rory snorts. "Learn to trust, Alicia. Enough, Jesse?"

Jesse takes the plate as she sits. "More than. Thanks so much." The conversation is as polite as an old-fashioned play.

Alicia asks brightly, "So, what did you think of Newton Prior, Jesse?"

"I'm not sure." It comes out awkwardly.

"Interesting answer." Rory offers a roasted-tomato salad.

"I didn't mean, um—the village is lovely, of course, but . . ."

"Don't let it get cold." Alicia offers the sauce dish.

"Carrots?" Before she can reply, Rory dumps a heap on Alicia's plate.

"Did you meet Helen?"

Jesse swallows. And coughs. "Yes."

"And Mack. We had lunch at the pub." Rory's watching them both.

Alicia says cheerfully, "That must have been nice."

Or not. Jesse says nothing.

"What was the *but*, by the way?" Alicia nods encouragingly.

"Silly as this sounds, I think it was the archangel. He just seemed, I don't know, grumpy or severe. Or something. Lame, I know."

Alicia nods. "It's his eyes. I could always feel them on my back when we went to church, as if I'd done something wrong. Mummy understood, Daddy didn't get it. Kid's imagination, I suppose. I was always worried about something." She eats, lost in the past.

Rory says, "And did that work?"

"What?" Alicia snaps back into focus.

"Worrying."

Chewing, she shakes her head.

"It's a habit, that's all. Never change anything by worrying. Trust me, I'm a doctor." He smiles at his own joke.

Alicia says carefully, "I think that depends, Rory. It can be constructive, sometimes."

Jesse stares at her plate with great interest. *They're doing it again.*

"Really?"

Alicia fires up, cheeks pink as her eyes. "Yes. Really." She puts her knife and fork down deliberately. "Jesse, apropos of what we were talking about before, I've made up my mind. It's time Hundredfield went to a good home. And before you say anything, Rory, the roof's failing again."

Rory murmurs, "This house is not a dog, Alicia."

She says passionately, "After the war, people pulled buildings like this down or let them fall down. I will *not* let that happen to Hundredfield. I just can't. It's my responsibility."

Rory's face quirks agreeably. "Of course, there's one easy way to solve the problem."

Alicia makes an effort. "And that would be?"

"Let someone else's money fix the place. Marry an heiress. Or heir, I mean. There. Simple."

"Long time since I did the Season, Rory. No one swept me away then, and they haven't since. Think I'm a bit of a dud in the suitor department."

The smile is gallant, but Jesse sees the glance Alicia flicks at Rory when he's not looking.

Jesse asks brightly, "The debutante Season? Were you actually presented at court?"

"Presentation finished at the end of the fifties, but there's still the London Season, even if no one calls it that anymore. Balls, Ascot, Glyndebourne, charity fashion parades. Honestly, opera? All that singing and prancing about. And me, marching up and down in sequins and chiffon in someone's idea of a ball gown. I just felt bloody ridiculous." Alicia squirms with the memory. "Poor Ma. She tried very hard and it cost a great deal of money we didn't have, but I've zero talent in the social arts; still can't dance to save myself, and small talk?" She rolls her eyes. "London. Drove me crazy. And now, look at me. Welded to the place."

Rory laughs. "Never your forte, Alicia, useless chat. So, what are you going to do?" He gestures at the ceiling.

"Can't fix it, can I?" Alicia's tone is just a bit truculent.

He leans across and grasps one of her hands. "A second opinion's always good."

"Oh, Rory, what's the use?" Abruptly Alicia gets up to clear the table.

Jesse jumps up to help, scoops the plates one-handed. "My turn."

"You're a guest." A minor tussle ensues. Jesse wins and heads for the sink.

Rory interrupts, "All right. What have you got to sell, apart from the land?"

Alicia stares at him. "Nothing. Most of the good stuff went

years ago—Ma's jewels, a lot of the silver. Even some of the portraits are copies."

"There's the fourteenth-century armor in the hall—what about that? And the state furniture in the great rooms?"

Her face pales. "I will *not* sell what's left of the heritage of this place just to fix a roof."

"Well then, what's in the attics? Or the cellars? A place like this, there could be long-lost, oh, I don't know, *things* stashed away." Rory pauses, then says quietly, "You cannot just turn your back and walk away."

"Ah, but I have."

"Six months in London? That's not walking away. That's thinking time. You needed it. But this is different, Licia. This is serious."

At the sink, Jesse tries not to clatter. British restraint. *When it's gone, it's gone.*

"It's not tens of thousands of pounds I need, Rory, it's millions. You know that. Anyway, why should you care what happens to Hundredfield? It's not your home."

"I was born here too, just like you. That's why we both come back."

That statement deflates Alicia. She plumps down on a chair. "Look, I've thought about this. I chickened out when I first talked with the National Trust."

"You didn't tell me you had."

She just looks at me. "*But* if I don't gift the estate soon, it'll be too far gone and—"

"Hundredfield should stay in your family, Licia. It's what your parents would have wanted." Rory's quite heated.

She flares back, "No, it's not. Dad was going to sell half of the land because he couldn't see a way out, and neither can I, now. Half won't do it, either. I should have listened years ago, I should have paid attention." Sudden silence.

This means something, Jesse can feel it.

Alicia hesitates, then says more reasonably, "Look, the trust has to be convinced the house can be self-supporting before they'll take it on. We've never properly opened Hundredfield to the public, but that's the only hope now, and it absolutely will never happen if that roof goes." Without rancor she adds, "And it's not for you to tell me what my parents would or would not have liked for Hundredfield, Rory."

In the deeper quiet that follows, Jesse's not sure what to do. She hesitates. And turns a tap on to fill a kettle.

"Jesse, I am so sorry!" Alicia hurries from the table. "Really, what unforgivable bad manners."

Jesse puts a hand on Alicia's arm. "I'd say you're going through utter, utter shit right now. Can't pretend it isn't happening."

The plain speaking robs Alicia of words.

Jesse turns the tap off. "I'll put this on the stove for tea, but I might just take myself off to bed, if that's all right? You said you wanted to get started tomorrow, Rory. Straight after breakfast?" She doesn't give either of them time to reply. "Good night."

Her last sight, as she closes the door to the kitchen, is of Rory. He's standing beside Alicia, an arm around her shoulders.

Shivering, Jesse stands on the mat in the bathroom and looks at herself in the mirror.

Behind, steam rises as the tub fills. She doesn't want to have a bath, but getting into bed clean after all the dramas of today will make her feel better. She needs to sluice the tension—so many tensions—away. Yawning hugely, she starts to clean her teeth, remembering a semiserious boyfriend from a few years ago.

Geoff was such a romantic. He liked to surprise her with candles when she came home from work. She'd enjoyed those candlelit baths, the petals scattered on the bed, and they'd lived together happily enough for a year, even if her parents had been upset; cohabiting before marriage was a shameful thing to them.

Jesse wonders now if her birth mother's being unmarried had been an influence. Perhaps they thought she'd head in the same direction? In the end, she'd asked Geoff to move out, but that had been for her own good reasons.

Jesse breathes on the mottled glass, draws a heart with a finger-tip, and writes *J + G 4 eva*.

Her hand drops. *Be honest.* Scented candles had not been enough. And Geoff had been one of the good ones.

Why does she always want more? Maybe this mirror—so strangely mottled—is some kind of symbol. An actual demonstration that she doesn't recognize herself anymore—doesn't, really, know who she is.

And that's the truth.

Can you really see yourself as others see you? This face—what does it actually say?

Jesse turns side-on, looks at herself over one shoulder. She's been told she's pretty quite often. Geoff even said she was beautiful. Actually, he repeated it so many times, it began to annoy her. She doesn't think she's beautiful. What does the word actually mean?

She peers more closely at her image, feature by feature. Something about the nose she's never liked—too strong, and it's got a bump. Her chin as well; there's a bit of a cleft. How could that be beautiful? To be fair, her skin has always been an asset—though Alicia's is finer, more creamy somehow—and her eyes. Jesse's never minded when people comment about their color. Geoff said her eyes were like an Australian sky when a storm's on its way. She liked that.

Australia.

Abruptly, tears well and overflow. Her heart hurts.

Sniffing, Jesse stands back. And sees the silver candle sconces. They're fixed to the wall on each side of the looking glass, and the candles are part used. Someone else has stood here and lit those wax tapers. No way of telling when, or who. Or why. Alicia?

Jesse shakes her head. Alicia's not the romantic type.

But she is.

Jesse looks around for matches, finds a box in a little lidded pot. Once lit, the mirror and the holders complement each other; it's surely intentional that this riot of glimmering roses and twining leaves was made to frame the surprised viewer in a silver garland. The effect is magical, as if Jesse's some sort of nature spirit half discovered in dappled light.

As if she's another person. A different girl.

She leans closer. The face in the mirror, the face-that-could-be-her-face, is smiling. But she's not smiling.

Don't be so *ridiculous*! Jesse shivers violently and chafes her arms. What *is* this? Emotional exhaustion, it must be. And, of course, whatever the effect was, it's gone.

She strips off and gets into the bath, slides down until her nose is just above the water.

So. Candlelight is dangerous. Who knew?

24

WHEN I returned, the chapel was empty. I was grateful, for I had not found Margaretta or the children.

But Maugris had been more successful. The broken doors had been removed, the floor swept, and the walls hung with branches of holly and pine. Fresh resin—the scent of a winter forest—and sweet wax perfumed the air from all the lighted candles.

Unwillingly, I stared at where we had placed Flore's bier. There was nothing to see, no sense of the tragedy or the mystery.

Set into the floor a pace away was my mother's tomb. Candle-light found the crystals in the stone, as if she were buried beneath a coverlet of stars. Unsheathing my sword, I knelt beside her grave. *Bless us, Mother. Help your sons so that Hundredfield does not fall.*

Was it blasphemy to pray to a mortal woman as if she were a saint—as if she could intercede with the Christ, who hung above me? It was, and I knew that, but somewhere distant, I heard someone singing. The refrain had no words, but the sound was soft and sweet, each note formed as if it were liquid grace.

My mother had sung in such a way.

Enchanted, half terrified, I did not dare to look up. *"Ma mère?"* Tears stood in my eyes.

The song ceased, but the silence rang. And a baby laughed.

I turned my head to the sound.

Margaretta stood behind me. I thought she must have come from the entrance to the chapel. She held a newborn in her arms.

Embarrassed and, yes, angry not to have found her earlier, I stood to speak harsh words. But the baby stared at me, and I was silenced.

Margaretta had seen the sword in my hand. "Aviss!"

A small boy was hiding in her skirts, and she scooped him up. The child wailed at her frightened expression, and that set the baby crying too.

I backed a little way off and laid my sword on the tiles. "I will not hurt you, girl. Or them."

Margaretta tried to console the boy. "Hush, hush. All is well. This is the nice brother."

I was surprised into a smile, though Aviss still stared at me with great, drowned eyes.

"Your son?" I made the sort of face one does to a puppy, or any young animal.

She set him down on the floor again. "Yes." He hid behind her knees.

I displayed empty hands. "May I see?" I meant the baby.

Margaretta hesitated, then nodded.

I stepped closer and held out a finger to my niece. She seemed to inspect it, and then me—as if considering what I might be. Confused, I said, "It seems to me that much has changed at Hundredfield."

"May I sit, lord? I am weary and the baby . . ."

She did not want to answer me. I nodded. "The little one must be heavy." I waved at the altar steps. The priest would not like it, but he was not here to see.

As Margaretta settled her son behind her, the infant smiled at me. Perhaps it was wind. I knew little of babies. "A fine child." I forced civility into my voice. "Robert told me you were with your mistress when my niece was born."

"Yes." She arranged the infant in the crook of one arm.

"Has my brother seen her?"

Margaretta hesitated, then said, "He was there."

"As the baby was birthed?" My voice rose.

"My mistress was dying, and he would not be kept away." She was trying not to sniff and dropped her head. "There was no time. After the child came, I put her into the arms of my mistress. And the Lady Flore held her but . . ." Tears slid down her face, and she could not speak.

I was surprised by a churning wash of emotion. "Forgive me, but why did Lord Godefroi have you wait on his wife?"

"I do not know." The girl wiped her face with a hand. "But I miss her. So much. Aviss does also, for he loved her as he loves me. She was a dear friend to us both."

"The Lady Flore was your friend?" I tried to understand what this might mean.

"She cared for me as if she had been my mother. More than that." To see Margaretta so sad, Aviss began to cry again, and the baby, that strange little being, tried to pat her face. Truly, I was astonished.

As the girl pulled her son close, I spoke above the noise. "What more do you know of her?"

"Forgive me, lord. Aviss must be comforted. He is hungry." The girl gestured helplessly.

"Of course." I turned half away as she opened the bodice of her dress.

As the boy settled to the breast, his sobs turned to snuffles and I felt Margaretta study my face. Her glance touched my skin like a hand. I flushed with the sense of it, though I did not look at her.

I tried again. "Did the Lady Flore seem . . ." Words eluded me. "Was she a good woman?"

"I do not think she was a woman at all." Margaretta spoke low, gazing down at her son's nestled head, his hair like feathers against the curve of her breast.

I swallowed. "Why do you say that, woman?"

Margaretta hesitated. "Once, I saw her fly."

I remembered the feast all those months ago. *She did not eat.* Was Matthias, therefore, not just a vindictive fool, jealous his influence had been usurped? *Was he telling the truth?*

Margaretta must have seen my expression. "It is true, lord. It was before the little one's birth." As her son sucked, she hitched the baby closer. "Greatly pregnant, the Lady Flore yet flew across the river at dark one night."

"Did she have wings, then?" I thought it a sensible question, considering.

She transferred her gaze to the baby. "My mistress was not an angel, if that is what you are asking. And now she is gone." Margaretta shook her head. "Because of the priest, and what he said, the people here would have killed Flore, and her daughter. Aviss also." She put her hand on the boy's head.

"Because he is Godefroi's child?"

Margaretta did not raise her eyes. "The Lady Flore said we must hide when it was needed." Her son's eyelids fluttered as he remembered to suck, fighting sleep.

"And you have had need?"

"I think your brother would have killed me after my father . . ." She could not cobble the words together. ". . . after the soldier was killed. His fury was very great. But I could not leave her—how could I leave Flore? She needed me. And her protection, her care for me and for Aviss, saved us both. She convinced Lord Godefroi to let me live."

The boy had ceased to suck and slept peacefully against her chest. I tried not to watch as Margaretta laced her gown.

"Her daughter will continue what the Lady Flore has begun."

I did not know what she meant. "Margaretta, if you know where she is—"

Margaretta cut me off. She stood with both children in her arms. "Will you let them live? Will you protect them?"

"Am I a monster that would kill children of my own blood?" I was offended.

Margaretta searched my face, feature by feature. "No. You are no monster." Her voice was flat. "But you must speak the truth, or I cannot tell you what the Lady Flore told me."

"What do you mean?" My family owned this girl and her son, yet I spoke to her as if I were the supplicant.

There was a pause, and then she said, "Lord Bayard, when did the Lady Flore come to the keep?"

I said slowly, "I have never known."

"On the day of her daughter's birth, it was one year and one day since Lord Godefroi found her in the forest." The expression in the girl's eyes was eerie, as if a fire had kindled there.

"And so?"

"The Lady of the Forest comes when she is needed. She shares the bed of the man she must and has his child. The baby is always a girl. That is very important."

Perhaps I laughed. "A boy is better." But I looked at Godefroi's daughter and was less sure. The child was staring at me as if she understood each of my words.

Margaretta stepped closer. She stared at me as if we were equals. "I brought this child, your niece, out of the body of my mistress and into life. And I say to you that though the Lady of the Forest always seems to die, she is never buried. On the day after the child is safely born, her body disappears."

I was shocked to silence. No one, so far as I knew, had seen what Maugris and I had in the chapel this morning. Or spoken of it, either.

So much pity was in Margaretta's eyes. "The child of the Lady of the Forest will bring abiding good fortune to your family, or she will be the destruction of your house. It has always been so. That is the truth you must know."

I shook my head. "And I thought you a clever girl, Margaretta. This is nonsense."

Her expression hardened. "You do not think me clever, Lord Bayard. You think me a peasant, and peasants are animals incapable of thought; all of us at Hundredfield are property to you and your brothers, things, not people."

Had she seen my thoughts?

Margaretta spoke urgently. "The Lady Flore chose *me*, Lord Bayard, and she chose this place. She chose your brother too, and your *family*. But I guard her daughter with my life and even the life of my own child, if that must be given. This was the trust she gave to me. I will not betray the Lady of the Forest and I am not afraid."

"If the priests hear you speak in such a way, it may come to that." I went to pick up my sword. "Where is the body of your mistress?"

Margaretta's face worked. If it was distress, or happiness, I could not tell.

"Did you move it from the chapel as my brother slept? Tell me!"

Margaretta said in an awed whisper, "Then, it is true. All of it is true. She is truly gone." Her face shone white and dazed. "Time will pivot now, and fortunes change. She told me that."

"You speak in riddles."

She shook her head. "There are no riddles here. Not anymore."

I pulled the sword belt tighter by a notch and turned to the opening of the chapel. "Stay here. When Lord Godefroi permits it, I shall send men to bring you to him."

"You do not understand. The men here will kill us all if they can, the children and me. And you as well."

I ignored her. "You are safe by the altar, Margaretta. You have sanctuary in this holy place." I hurried to the stairs.

"Lord Bayard," Margaretta called. "You believe more than you say you do. She spoke to you."

That brought me back to the chancel at a run. "What did you say?"

But the chapel was empty.

25

RORY PUSHES the door open and Jesse peers past his shoulder.

With long windows at the far end, the room is twice normal height, and all around the walls, shelves carry books—thousands and thousands of volumes, their titles stamped in gilt on leather bindings. There are no modern books at all. Not one.

"Who has enough time to read all this?" Jesse's nervous as she wanders from bookcase to bookcase.

"Not me." Rory beckons. "I want to show you something."

She follows him to a fireplace on a side wall.

Rory points. Above the mantelpiece is a tall glass case. "This is a map of Hundredfield, with the country around it."

"Really?" She cranes to look.

He nods. "It's hand-drawn and made before anyone knew about latitude and longitude. No real scale, as you see."

They stare in silence. "What's that?" Jesse points at a bold black line.

"The border between England and Scotland."

"It looks close."

"Yes. The border shifted quite a bit, back and forth. This

map's never been properly dated because carbon-element-decay analysis means you'd have to snip a bit off and destroy it. Alicia's dad wouldn't let it be done. Fourteenth century, or possibly earlier. Before printing, anyhow."

"It's rather nice, though, isn't it? Like a kid's drawing. The estate looks huge—the amount of land, I mean."

"It was. Even the plague, when it came, couldn't destroy this family."

"So the Donnes of Hundredfield were tough." Jesse can't bring herself to ask if Alicia really is the child of an earl. It seems so much like fantasy. A waitress who's an aristocrat living in a ruined castle?

"Only, they weren't called the Donnes then. Names change over time." Rory switches the subject. "I think I'll set up over there. Okay with you?" He points.

Anxiety. *My constant friend*. Not. "Yes. That's fine."

In a slant of sun, chairs crowd a library table. With magazines strewn over its surface, it's as if someone got up, forgetting to tidy away.

Or expecting the servants to do it, thinks Jesse as she watches Rory stride over with a reel-to-reel tape recorder. Placing the equipment with some care, he says, "Pick somewhere comfortable; you'll be sitting for a while."

Jesse folds herself into a low armchair with scrolled arms. "No rush." She brushes dust off the cover of a magazine. *Tatler*, August 1956. Her eyes widen. The month of her birthday. Spooky.

She flips through the pages as Rory pulls an extension cable out of a canvas bag and looks around for a power source.

Jesse points. "On the wall beside the windows."

"Well spotted."

Jesse doesn't hear him. She's found a photo of a ball in progress. "Wow."

"What?"

"Look at this."

The caption says it all. *The Earl and Countess of Hundredfield at the Lorton Melbreak Hunt Ball.*

Jesse taps the page. "Alicia's parents. I've seen a picture of them." But the beautiful girl is no longer young in this picture and she's too thin. And too tense.

Rory doesn't comment. "You're sure that chair is comfortable?"

"It's fine."

"Right, then. I think we're sorted."

With the mic in place, Rory sits across the table, a pad and pen close to hand. "I'm going to keep this simple."

Jesse nods cautiously. "Okay. How simple?"

He taps the reels. "Record everything and I'll transcribe each night as we go. You responded really well in London to hypnosis, by the way."

"Yeah, right." Jesse's surprised.

"You certainly did. An excellent subject. And if you're agreeable, by using this same technique, I think we've got every chance of assessing how this odd situation has come about for you, and getting some answers."

Jesse puts the magazine down. She mutters, "Odd is right."

"So, I'll ask questions under hypnosis, just as I did in London, and see what replies you give me; we'll take it from there."

Jesse shifts uneasily. "But, Rory, I don't know any more than you do. Less, in fact. You, at least, have some understanding of how a brain is supposed to work. And you know all about Hundredfield. I don't."

"When I say *you*, I mean let's ask your unconscious to explain what *it* knows. That's what hypnosis does so well—it gets down there by bypassing your busy, workaday mind. I'm very confident we'll obtain"—Rory pauses, thinks about the next phrase—"interesting material. At the very least."

"What about the drawings, though?"

He says easily, "Jesse, the drawings were an anomaly, and anomalies by their nature aren't usual. This one may have run its course as you've been healing. I'm more interested in the fact that you began to draw at all."

When he talks about the pictures, it feels to Jesse like thunder lurks, half heard, in the distance. They're not close, the drawings, but not so far away, either.

"Now, I want to be sure that you're completely comfortable, completely at ease." Rory's voice alters. It's softer, more even, and the tone has dropped to a deeper level. "And just to be sure, I'm going to cover your legs with a rug. Sitting for a while can make you cold. Is that all right?"

Jesse nods. She sighs and her eyes begin to close as Rory unfolds a rug over her knees.

Rory's watching Jesse closely. "Are you ready for us to begin?" He's completely focused now.

"Yes." The word is a sigh.

"Very good. So, I'm turning the recorder on." A click and the spools begin to turn. "And now I'll identify the tape."

Rory clears his throat, "Sunday, June twenty-eighth, 1981, interview under hypnosis of Miss Jesse Marley conducted by Dr. Rory Brandon at Hundredfield, Northumberland"—he inspects his watch face—"commencing at eight forty-seven a.m." He pauses to check the spools are turning correctly. "And now we shall begin." He leans forward a little. "Jesse, I'm going to count from ten down to one, and when I reach the number one, your body will be asleep but your mind will be awake. You'll be completely relaxed and ready to listen to my questions, a happy participant in our joint research. Nod if you understand."

Jesse nods, her head moving up and down like a sideshow doll's. She goes on nodding, eyes closed, face at peace.

"Good, Jesse, very good. You can stop nodding now."

Jesse stops and her head lolls back against the chair.

"Ten. Feeling relaxed and happy. Nine. Happy and comfortable. So comfortable. Eight. You're in a delightful place, a place you really love. Look around, familiarize yourself." Jesse's mouth curls happily, and Rory eases back in his chair. "That's good. Seven. You're standing at the top of a short flight of steps. You'd like to see what's at the bottom. Six. Walk forward, there's a light down there. Five. You walk from the top step to the next step, closer to the light. Happy and relaxed and interested. Four. Down one more, the light is brighter. Three. And the next; brighter still. Two. Walk down the last step. One. You're at the bottom and the light is like warm water all around you. Like a child in her bath before bed, you feel secure and happy to be here. And completely relaxed. More relaxed than you've ever been before. Nod if you can hear me."

Jesse starts to nod.

"Just once. That's it."

Morning light models the cheekbones of Jesse's face, and Rory smiles. She does look like a sleeping child. "Now, Jesse, I'm going to take you into the past. Only a little way, and you'll enjoy the short journey we'll take there together. We're going back to the day of the accident in London."

Jesse shifts restlessly and her face changes, eyes moving quickly under closed lids.

"Happy and relaxed, Jesse, because you're just an observer and nothing can hurt you. Your life is like a movie you can watch anytime. You enjoy seeing the story unfold, and each time you see a little more. Different things. That's better. So serene, so tranquil."

Jesse's face is calm again.

"Now, see yourself just before the accident. Tell me how you're feeling."

"I'm nervous."

"Why do you feel nervous?"

Jesse lifts her left arm. Her fingers curl as if she's clutching something. "Because I've got this."

"Tell me what you have there. I can see it makes you happy."

A radiant smile. "Oh, it does. It's my birth certificate, and when I open the envelope, I'll know who I am. Who I really am. But I'm feeling scared too."

"Remember, absolutely nothing can hurt you. What happens next?"

Her expression changes. "There's a man. His name's George. He's very nice. He's got a motorbike. But"—there's almost a one-shouldered shrug—"he runs me over because I don't look when I'm crossing the road. I try to explain it's my fault, but he doesn't listen. Everyone's helping now. They're all talking at once." She flips a hand in front of her face, as if to brush away flies.

"Don't listen if it bothers you, Jesse. Where are you now?"

"I'm on a bus. Now I'm in a church. It's a beautiful place, but I don't feel good. I'm falling." She flutters fingers through the air. Her face is anxious. "Now . . ."

"Are you somewhere different?"

"Yes. I'm in hospital. My head is very sore, my shoulder too." She winces.

"But you're not sore now, Jesse. There is no pain at all, and your shoulder will be healed very soon." Rory makes a brief note. "Now we'll go forward in time, just a few days. This will be an easy process and you'll remember everything perfectly. Do you understand what I'm saying? Say yes if you do."

"Yes."

"Good, very good." Rory leans closer again. "Jesse, why did you draw with your left hand when you came off the ventilator in hospital?"

Jesse looks pleased. "Oh, that's easy."

"It's good that this question is an easy one."

He adjusts the mic fractionally, making sure it's catching everything Jesse says. "So, why did you draw with your left hand?"

"Well, I couldn't draw with my right, could I?" Jesse points at her right shoulder. "It hurt too much."

"Yes. That's true. A very good answer."

The sleeping girl smiles.

"Here's my next question. In the hospital, the first time we talked about it, you said something about drawing to me—do you remember what that was?"

She nods. "I said I could not draw at all."

"That's right. But yet, with your left hand . . ."

Jesse's face clears. "Oh, I understand. You don't know why *I* can draw with my left hand?"

"That's correct. Why could you draw with your left hand so well after the accident?"

"Because that's her hand. It's not mine. She can draw, I can't, so I let her use it."

In the silence that follows, the whir of the spools is suddenly clear. Rory coughs. "You're still warm and comfortable and re-laxed, Jesse. Body asleep, mind awake. Can you tell me who *she* is? The person who uses your hand."

Jesse puts her head on one side. She doesn't say anything.

"Did you hear the question, Jesse?"

She puts a finger to her lips. "Shush."

"Why do you want me to be quiet?"

Jesse turns her face toward him. "That's a different question."

That eerie feeling washes over Rory again: a person without eyes is inspecting him. "It is. Let's answer this one first, and then the other question, the one I asked just now. Why do you want me to be quiet?"

She sighs patiently. "Because I'm listening. She's telling me something but I can't hear her when you speak."

Rory waits for a moment. Then says, "We can go back to the other question now, Jesse. Who is the person who uses your hand?"

"I don't know her name, but she knows who I am. We've met before." An expression of wonder transforms Jesse's face.

"Now, I'm going to ask you another question, Jesse. It might not be easy, but I'd like you to try. Is that okay?"

Jesse smiles seraphically. "Yes."

"How long since you have seen one another?"

Jesse says nothing.

"Can you hear me, Jesse? I'll ask again. How long since you've seen the lady you've been listening to?"

The girl in the chair breathes deeply. Her mouth moves but there's no sound, as if it's a struggle to form words.

"Speak when you are ready. You'll find it's easy, so easy to talk to me."

"No, it is not easy." The girl turns her head, and this time, that strange inspection is different.

Rory sits forward. Feature by feature, he inspects Jesse's face. And starts to sweat. The girl looks different. He stares at the tape counter as he says, "Why is that?"

A laugh, lower than Jesse's usual giggle. "Because this girl is not your servant. You may not command her as you wish to do. I shall not permit that."

Eyes closed, Jesse sits up as her left hand gropes until it finds his pen, and the notepad on the table. As she begins to draw, her face changes, becomes more and more happy.

The woman's face emerges on the page. It's the eyes that catch him; shining as if lit from within, they look directly into his own with calm authority.

Rory swallows. He makes an effort to take in the other details of the drawing. The woman's wearing something on her head; the outline of the flowing shape, like a nun's veil, defines her against the shadows behind. The dress below is sketched in—a darker block—and behind the woman's shoulder the unmistakable outline of the keep rears up.

"Relax now, Jesse, and put the pen down."

Jesse opens her hand and the pen drops to the table.

"Lean back. Rest."

Obediently, the girl slumps against the upholstery, her head drifting to one side.

"That's very good. You're so comfortable in the chair, it's soft and welcoming and you feel warm and safe. Now I'll count down from five to one, and when I reach one, you'll answer the questions I ask, easily and happily. Five, more deeply relaxed than you've ever been; four, content and pleased to be here; three, each breath takes you deeper; two; and one. Body asleep, mind awake." He stares at the girl's blank face. "I'm going to ask you some more questions now, Jesse. And you'll be happy to answer them so we can both understand more. Raise your hand if you understand."

Jesse's left hand floats up from the arm of the chair.

"Good, Jesse, very good."

The hand continues to hover.

"You can put your hand down now."

It descends like a leaf.

"First I want to be sure that you"—Rory stops, reframes the question—"that I am talking to Jesse Marley?"

The reply is a giggle, Jesse's giggle. "Of course you are. No one else is here."

Rory swallows. "You've drawn a lady in your picture. Is she a nun?"

"No." Jesse's expression is amused as she turns her head, eyes closed, toward the piece of paper.

"Did I ask a funny question?"

Jesse hesitates, then shakes her head. "She's never been asked if she's a nun before. That makes her laugh."

"I thought you were here alone. Is the lady with you now?"

Jesse's expression changes. "Yes. She is, in a way, because she's in the picture."

"Tell me more about the lady you've drawn. Her clothes are unusual."

"Not to her."

"Can you tell me her name?"

Jesse doesn't respond.

"Do you know her name?"

Jesse says reluctantly, "I'm not sure. But she came here to speak to me, to tell me the things I need to know." Flexing her back, Jesse winces.

Rory says quickly, "You're feeling no discomfort, there's nothing to hurt you, and you have no sensation of pain anywhere in your body." The girl's face relaxes as she settles. "Remember, Jesse, you don't have to feel anything unless you want to."

But Jesse's expression alters, her face suddenly anxious.

Rory's voice deepens and slows even more. "Feel yourself breathe, Jesse, in and out. In and out. There's no anxiety, none at all. See the air as it enters your mouth, follow it down, down into your lungs. And breathe out. Watch the air, just like a pretty silver stream. Each breath takes you deeper, far deeper, to a safe and happy place."

On the arms of the chair, Jesse's hands flutter.

Rory tries again. "You're looking down on what you want to see, Jesse, as if it's a movie and you're the director, way, way above the set. Describe what's below—you'll find it's easy, really easy."

But Jesse's expression is anxious. "It's dark and cold down there. Really cold." She hunches forward. "I don't like this place. It's unhappy. And there's something . . ." She's shivering violently.

"See the breath, silver and warm. In and out, in and . . . out. That's good. Describe what you see, Jesse. Like a picture."

"It looks like a man but . . . not really. He's the wrong color and he's in the air. He's shining!" Jesse's left hand reaches above her head as if to brush something away.

"Remember the movie; this is your movie."

She moves her head from side to side. "I don't like this."

"No need to worry, no need to feel anxious. Can you draw what you see?"

Her face clears. "Yes." She starts to sketch, the strokes quick and confident.

Rory watches. His eyes widen.

26

WHAT HAPPENED?" Jesse sits up in the chair, blinking. "That felt different."

"In what way?"

Jesse's focus shifts as she tries to catch something elusive. "Just . . ." She struggles. "It wasn't very happy, was it? At the end, I mean. In the beginning it was different." She doesn't want to tell him what she felt then—that sense of tenderness, of love without boundaries. It's too precious to talk about.

"You became a little anxious so I brought you out earlier than I'd planned. We made progress, though."

"Oh?" Jesse's not sure. It feels like she's walking an emotional high wire between light and dark.

"I want to show you something. Two somethings." He hands her the sketches. And watches.

Jesse stares at the woman's face first. Her eyes soften as she touches the paper.

"How does this make you feel, Jesse?"

"Happy. If she's an anomaly, I'm glad."

"And this?" Rory gives her the second drawing.

"I . . ." She hesitates. "I don't know what it is."

Rory waits.

"Is it a crucifix?" Jesse rations the words. "He looks real, though. Like he's a real person."

A quick glance at Rory, and she puts the image down, picking up the first drawing again. "But this . . ."

"This?" Rory speaks softly.

Jesse shakes her head. She knows. She really does. This is the woman she dreams about, the one who was there when she was on the ventilator.

"What do you think of when you look at her, Jesse?"

There's a jolt. "It's hard to put into words." That's true. *How do I say I know this face?*

Rory doesn't push her. "Would you be okay with me showing the sketches to Alicia?"

"Why?"

"Maybe she can help. She knows the history of Hundredfield better than anyone. Since you've drawn them here, they might mean something to her."

Jesse thinks about that. And nods. "But if you don't mind, I think I need some air." She gets up and almost stumbles toward the door, as if her legs have gone to sleep.

Rory waits a moment before he strolls across to the windows. Minutes later, Jesse walks along the terrace outside. She doesn't notice him. He watches her until she's out of sight and goes back to the table. Picking up the drawing, he tries to make sense of what he sees.

It looks like a man but . . . not really. He's the wrong color and he's in the air. He's shining!

He stares at the tape recorder, flicks rewind.

Gibberish chatters as the tape goes backward. He's watching the counter. Abruptly he hits STOP, and then PLAY.

This girl is not your servant. You may not command her as you wish to do. I shall not permit that.

Rory hits STOP again. He stares at his notes and writes, *Who are you, Jesse Marley?*

She stares into the sky, right in the eye of the sun. When she drops her head, black dots obscure the world. A hand over her face, Jesse walks, just walks, trying not to think, staring at the ground as it slowly turns into what it should be, the cobbles of the inner ward as the ground begins to rise.

Jesse stops. She's come farther than she thought. In her cloud of unknowing, she's begun to climb the path to the keep. She drew this view in the hospital, and the new sketch of the woman with the tower behind her seems to be of this same place.

Clear, cloudless sunlight mocks Jesse's confusion—it warms the stone of the keep, makes it normal. Jesse shades her eyes. "You're just a battered old building, you."

Ahead, a gate leads to the tower and, on the other side, the stairs—and the door in the wall.

Jesse's feet take responsibility.

There's the path right under the gate, walk further, climb the stairs. Only the handle now.

It's a bird's-eye view somehow when her hand stretches out and hovers.

Jesse snatches it away. It's a conscious effort—her fingers want to grasp that iron ring.

But *she* does not.

The sun is no longer warm and color has bleached from the day, leaving it flat.

She wants to run.

27

"BAYARD!" MAUGRIS was behind me in the stair tower.

"You found the girl?"

I nodded. I did not want to say she had found me.

"The child is healthy?"

"Yes."

He searched my face. "Why did Margaretta hide?"

"She thought the baby would be murdered. I asked her to stay in the chapel." That at least was true. Before she vanished.

He spoke over me. "What else did she say?"

I rubbed my eyes, no longer able to tell real from unreal. "She spoke nonsense."

"Tell me what she said!" He grabbed my shoulders.

I struck his hands away. I was no longer the runt of our litter.

Maugris stepped back, breathing hard. So was I.

"She said Flore was . . ." What words did I have?

"Bayard! Tell me."

I sighed. "She said Flore was known by another name."

"What does that mean?"

"I do not know. I am repeating what she said, that is all."

"And?" His tone was dangerous.

"She said Flore was the Lady of the Forest."

Maugris stood very still. "Well?"

"This *lady* comes when she is needed." I waved a hand as if to sweep away cobwebs. "And it seems Godefroi's daughter will bring great fortune, or disaster, to Hundredfield. No telling which. Peasant rubbish."

"There was more." Maugris stared at me intently.

I did not know how to read the expression in my brother's eyes. "Why should you think that?"

"Please, Bayard." It was like the grating of a key in a lock. My brother never *asked*.

I thought carefully on what Margaretta had said. "The girl told me Flore's kind do not die, though they seem to. Their bodies vanish after they bear a living child, and they cannot be buried like a Christian woman. The child is always a girl. Make of it what you will."

Maugris leaned against the wall. "So that is why." He stopped. "You *believe* this?"

"Others will, even if we do not. Our mother knew this story. She got it from our father's old nurse and told it to me—a bedtime tale when I was very young. She said the Forest Lady was the guardian of our family and she would help me when I was frightened in the dark."

I snorted. "Our mother was a good Christian woman and these are pagan lies." Why did our mother not tell me of a guardian? I too had feared the night.

Maugris shook his head. "Our father heard her tell me. He struck her for it."

"Why would he do that?" I was suspicious.

"He was frightened of the priests, that they would burn her as a witch. Our mother cried, and I remember." Maugris stared at me.

"What?"

"She said she had no daughter and, though it was forbidden,

she must tell her sons if our house was to be saved." He glanced furtively up and down the stairs.

"You think Margaretta is right." I was incredulous.

"No. I think it a children's story. But we have enemies inside and outside Hundredfield. One spark to light a fire, that is all, just one. And if they hear what this girl said to you—"

I interrupted, "An apostate monk and peasants with billhooks. These are our enemies. You fear a monk?"

"A billhook is still a blade. We are few and may be overwhelmed. And in the forest"—Maugris waved at an arrow slit—"they wait. Do you think our household will stand with us in a fight? I do not."

I stared at my brother. "Our cause is not so hopeless we cannot outthink a rabble, protected by these walls. What have we been doing all these years?"

He said stubbornly, "Matthias refused to bury Flore, and they know why. Margaretta is right. The disaster of this birth can certainly destroy our family, and her prophecy will be fulfilled. That is the spark." He paused. And sighed. "This child should not survive the winter. Babies are vulnerable, everyone knows that."

"I will not kill an infant."

"So scrupulous, Bayard." He pointed. "In the service of the Percys that hand has murdered—yes, *murdered*—children. I have seen it."

I flared at him. "This baby is our brother's daughter. Our *niece*, Maugris."

"But perhaps it must be done."

"You do it, then." I did not want to think he was right. I remembered the little one, staring up at me.

Maugris was silent.

I said, "What happened last night? Where is Flore's body?"

"Godefroi does not know." Maugris flexed his neck. And blinked. "He can talk but says he remembers nothing."

"Yet she must be properly buried. With honor."

Maugris stared at me, red-eyed. "What do you mean?"

"A coffin with close-packed rocks inside, nailed and sealed over with lead. It shall be buried beside our mother, in her grave."

"The priest will never agree." But Maugris straightened and some kind of hope was in his eyes.

"Simeon will not know, and, yes, he will agree for I shall ask him. Politely. Then he will say a Christmas mass and be sent back to the priory. How sad it would be if he was attacked on the road." I crossed myself.

Maugris absorbed what I said and finally nodded.

"But you must make the coffin, brother."

"I?" He looked at me, puzzled. I had always obeyed *his* orders.

"Yes. Ambrose left planks in his workshop. It must be done quickly while I talk to the priest. Then there is the grave to be dug—before the burial."

My brother crossed himself and pounded his chest with a closed fist. "For our sins, Father, we seek forgiveness."

I muttered, "And with speed."

As I unlocked the priest's cell, I said heartily, "Father, it is good you are at Hundredfield on the day of Christ's birth."

The man got up from the prie-dieu. His face was pinched and white.

"It is cold in here. I shall have a brazier brought." Breath was mist on the air.

"That is not necessary. Cold concentrates the mind on God." Simeon folded his hands into his sleeves. His expression was wary.

"Father, I know your welcome here has been a strange one, but sorrow makes men less courteous than they should be."

"I have prayed for your family, Lord Bayard, and all here at Hundredfield. God will support your suffering as Christian men."

"I am grateful. The mass you give to celebrate the birthday of our Lord and Savior will provide even greater comfort in these dark days." I crossed my chest.

The priest echoed the gesture fervently. "Amen, Lord Bayard. Amen to that."

I nodded piously. "Another service is required also, Father, as you know. A private requiem for the Lady Flore must be sung, since she has passed into God's keeping."

The man put his hand on the prie-dieu. Anxiety flickered like fire in his eyes. "Lord Bayard, we are all civilized men. Devout men." He paused on a breath. "However, Father Matthias brought reports to our prior"—Simeon swallowed—"that could not be ignored. He said your brother, your whole family, was cursed by the presence of evil in this place."

I responded confidently, "The man was criminally deranged, Father. That is why we sent him away."

"But Father Matthias spoke of a succubus preying on the soul of a Christian man—your unfortunate brother, Lord Godefroi. And this thing that became his wife oppresses him still in spirit. My brother-in-Christ even saw that fiend fly out at night. Without wings." The priest's eyes were the size of eggs.

"You would know that Matthias robbed the altar of our chapel?" My tone was tolerant.

Simeon opened and closed his mouth.

I prompted gently, "Those were the articles you carried from the priory."

How reluctant he was to agree. "It is true I was instructed to remove certain holy items from our priory and provide them to you; however—"

I raised my voice. "For that crime Matthias was lucky to escape death. You know this. But to blame others as an excuse for what he had done, to destroy the reputation of my sister-in-law with gossip so foul that she died from very shame giving birth to my niece? Heinous!" My tone was harsh.

The priest blinked.

I said more calmly, "The Lady Flore was married to my brother by this same false priest in the proper way. He did not speak of her in those terms then."

Simeon's expression wavered. He said cautiously, "My brother-in-Christ cannot have lied."

I paused as he dwelt in uncertainty. "We bear no ill will to this man—how can one hate those who are mad?—but you are Hundredfield's priest now, Father. Will you not help us? Our brother Godefroi most particularly."

The man's expression was confused. "But if your brother *has* been cursed, it is my duty to expel the succubus that plagues him. It is my duty before God."

"Father, tell me. Have you ever seen a succubus?" I asked the question innocently.

The man's eyes snapped wide with horror. "No!" He gripped his rosary beads.

"Neither have I. Nor has any man. Can an educated person seriously allow himself to think such things exist?" I solemnly, sorrowfully, shook my head. "No. The truth is this. My poor sister-in-law has most tragically died in childbed, and my brother is ill from sorrow and from the lies that have been spread about his wife. Mortal despair afflicts him, and for this, prayers are the best cure. And also to see the burial of his beloved wife performed with reverence. The Lady Flore is to be buried in our own mother's grave—to lie beside her mother-in-law for all eternity. Would he, would we, permit such a thing if we believed the foulness of these rumors?"

Simeon's face was profoundly troubled. He looked with longing at the prie-dieu. "Lord Bayard, will you allow me to pray on this?"

"The place for your prayers is the chapel, Father. My brothers and our people wait for you there."

The gathering in the chapel was quiet as the bell was rung and the host elevated before the altar. Beyond the rood screen, outside the chancel, men on the right, women on the left, Hundredfield's garrison and all our household servants stood in rows behind Godefroi, Maugris, and me. In unison, all of us bowed as Simeon uttered the final words of the Christmas mass and turned earnestly to bless and cense the congregation as the service finished.

I could finally breathe out.

At my side, Maugris muttered, "The hall."

Half listening to Simeon's final words, I said, "Yes. All is prepared."

Maugris whispered to our brother, "Godefroi, you must lead the household to the feast. Bayard will see you settled on the high dais with Father Simeon."

Our brother was pale and had spoken little since I had brought him from his chamber. He stared at Maugris. "Where shall you be?"

"I will join you soon." Maugris did not look at me.

Now the service was done, a soft mutter moved from the men's side to the women's. It cheered me to see that some of their faces were bright. The familiarity of the mass, and the custom of we three brothers standing with the household for the service, had done its work.

Maugris beckoned the priest. "Father Simeon, this is Lord Godefroi."

"Sir, I am sad indeed to hear you have not been well." The man's expression was kind as he sketched a cross in the air over my brother's head. "However, it is my duty—"

I looked at Simeon keenly.

His face colored, and he stuttered, "It is my duty to commend you to the Lord's good grace on this glorious day. I shall pray for your health and, er, happiness."

He paused before he said the last word. Godefroi's haggard countenance, his red eyes, spoke only of misery.

"In Christ's name it is time for you to break your fast, Father." I turned to the household. "Join Lord Godefroi in our hall, friends, for the yule wassail." Without asking his permission, I took Godefroi's arm and led him from the chapel. We were followed by the priest with the crowd streaming behind. Maugris stayed in the chapel, kneeling as if to pray privately at the altar rail.

Outside, I picked out Dikon in the throng and signaled him quickly.

"Yes, lord?"

"Go to my brother, boy. He needs you. Do as he says."

The boy's expression cycled from anxious to dismayed and back again. Even in the chapel, we could smell the meat roasting in the kitchen.

I patted him on the shoulder. "A silver penny will pay for your pain. And your discretion."

The boy dropped his eyes, but the money made a difference and he waited happily enough for the tide to surge past as the priest and I helped Godefroi up the chapel stairs.

I trusted the boy. I hoped he trusted me.

An hour and more had passed, and I made sure that ale and Rhenish wine flowed better than our river; no goblet was to remain unfilled, and food was always to be before each man and each woman on the benches.

With mutton and salt pork heaped up in mounds, with roasted eggs—so rare in winter—and sausages, with fritters and fricassees of salmon and trout and pike on salvers, and ale slopped all over the tables set below the high board, the household grew boisterous. One or two friendly glances were thrown to me from some of the girls—which I returned, along with choice dishes as marks of favor (to the chagrin of their beaux)—and I was beginning to relax.

Too soon.

Maugris entered the hall, Dikon at his heels. Both were sweating.

"Where have you been? You smell like a winded horse." Godefroi's tone was waspish. He spoke in French.

"Brother." Maugris dismissed Dikon as he bowed to Godefroi, and then to the priest. "You seem much improved. God grant you even better health tomorrow." He used English loudly, so that many of those present would hear his words.

Scanning faces in the hall, Godefroi replied in French, "Only if I survive the night. Some here will not like that."

Perhaps they did not understand what Godefroi said, but his sour expression punctured the mood.

Maugris said hastily, "Father Simeon? Private prayers will help our brother rest." He met my eye.

I stood. "After the blessing, perhaps you will lead us to the chapel, Father."

The priest's expression was strained but he rose politely enough. "*In nomine Patris, et Spiritus Sancti*, amen."

As the sonorous words rolled out into the smoky air, I watched men's faces. Some were hostile and, as the blessing finished, one, then two, then more of the keep's household left the hall as if going to the kitchen, or to relieve themselves. They thought themselves unnoticed.

Perhaps Godefroi was right.

"Why have you brought me here? I do not wish to pray."

On trestles before the altar lay a long, cloth-covered box. A hole had been dug beside it in the tiles, immediately beside the grave of our mother.

"Father, are you ready?" Maugris did not answer Godefroi's question.

Simeon's face was pale. "Lord Maugris, I—"

Godefroi said loudly, "What is that thing?"

Maugris led our brother forward. "Your wife lies here, Godefroi. See, this will be her resting place, with our mother. As we discussed."

Godefroi shook off Maugris's hand. "You told me that she, that her body . . ." The confusion was pitiful as he tried to put his arms around the casket.

I stepped closer. "Come, brother. Our mother will care for her now."

Godefroi wailed, "But you have closed her in. I cannot see her face." Tears gathered and began to fall.

The priest, discomfited, said, "Your brother is distressed, Lord Maugris. I do not feel that—"

"Lord Godefroi's wife is to be buried, Father, as you agreed. She died some days ago. It will not be good for the health of those in the keep to delay further." Maugris was courteous but he was also armed and his face was grim.

Simeon tried to light the candles on the altar—it was hard with hands that shook—but he began to prepare for the requiem mass without further protest. Maugris and I, one on either side of Godefroi, helped our brother kneel at the altar steps, and his sobs, so loud at first, grew quiet.

The priest, at last, faced the altar and, lifting his arms, began the mass. As he found the rhythm of those eternal words, their blessing and forgiveness, the hope and acceptance they offered, Godefroi became calm. And after the host had been elevated, and we had shared the bread and wine, Simeon called us forward for the last of the rite.

Maugris and I sweated to lower the rough coffin decently into the hole in the floor, and as the box descended, I muttered silently, *Forgive us, Mother, for what we do here.*

"Lord Godefroi." Simeon beckoned our brother to stand beside the open grave. There was earth to sprinkle on the coffin lid.

I saw Godefroi's face change.

"Maugris!"

Godefroi was quicker than a cat as he tried to jump down, but Maugris and I caught his arms.

"I want to go with her." As he struggled, soil from the banked-up sides showered the coffin.

"Lord Godefroi, please! You disgrace your wife and your mother." Simeon's face was a horrified mask.

"Whoreson!" Godefroi wriggled from our grasp. He had flushed a dangerous red and would have struck the man, but we hauled him away and I put my hand over his mouth.

Simeon threw a reproachful glance at me. "Your brother *is* possessed!"

"Come, Father. I shall take you to your cell." Maugris turned the priest neatly and walked him from the chapel.

Godefroi bit my hand.

"Brother!" I tore it from him. He was growling, and marks from his teeth tattooed my palm.

His eyes bulged. He spat as he said, "I curse you. I curse Maugris. And the priest. All priests!"

He spoke with such venom that I considered, seriously, if Simeon was not right. "Calm yourself."

"You took her from me!"

I ducked to avoid his fist.

"No, Lord Godefroi. They did not." We both turned at the sound of that voice.

Margaretta stood there, the baby in her arms. As before, Aviss clung to her skirt. "The lady chose the time and place of her leaving."

Sunk deep in pillows of flesh, something glittered in my brother's eyes. "Speak plain."

"Your wife is not here."

"The Lady Flore's body lies in this grave." I was angry, and that upset the little boy.

"No." The girl shook her head.

"Enough!" I blocked her with an arm as Aviss began to howl.

Glaring at his son, Godefroi roared, "She will speak."

With a shake in her voice, Margaretta said, "Aviss, bow to your lord father." The child gasped into sobs. He would not look at Godefroi's face.

His distress touched me and I held out a hand. "Give the boy to me."

His face streaked with tears, Aviss peered around his mother's legs. His eyes were huge and of a brown so dark, they seemed black. Our mother's eyes. Surprisingly, he let the skirt fall and took a step forward. I scooped him up, and as I did, he put one dirty thumb in his mouth and turned his face to my neck, hiccuping. His breath was sweet.

I do not know why, to this day, I was so affected by the beat of that small, steady heart against my chest.

The girl held Godefroi's baby close. The child was still deep asleep. "I have some knowledge of the Lady Flore."

I snorted.

"Then you must speak." Maugris had returned without the priest.

"Lord Bayard thinks I will lie to you." Margaretta did not look at me.

Low and dangerous, Godefroi said, "That would be foolish. Where has she been taken? Tell me."

I opened my mouth, but Maugris silenced me with a look. "He has a right to know."

Godefroi's face leached of color. "It is true, then. She is not here." He stared at the grave in the floor, then at each of our faces; his own was stark as any corpse. "Why have you done this?"

Maugris did not apologize. Godefroi had brought us to this pass. "The household must see that Flore has been properly buried by the priest. Rumors are dangerous things."

Godefroi's voice rose. "What is in this coffin?"

"Rocks."

Silence dropped as if it were a physical thing.

Godefroi said finally, "I do not understand."

"The Lady Flore said . . ." Margaretta hesitated.

I shook my head.

She ignored me. "Her true home is not in the houses built by men. She comes from the water and the trees and the sky. You must go to the river, Lord Godefroi, and ask at the ferry."

"Ask what?"

"For knowledge of your wife." Margaretta was pale; her expression said how frightened she truly was of Godefroi, of what he might do.

Our brother stared at the girl. "My wife is dead, her body is missing. Why would the ferrywoman have anything to say to me on this?"

"Lord, I have told you the truth. The ferrywoman"—Margaretta swallowed—"knew the Lady Flore."

Watching the girl as if she were a snared animal, Godefroi plucked the baby from her arms. He went to hand her to Maugris, but the child opened her eyes. She did not cry but stared at her father. That same serious inspection I had endured.

Godefroi offered a finger. His face was tender. "You are all I have now."

I watched Maugris's expression congeal into shock as the baby grasped what was offered and smiled.

"She knows me!" Godefroi was transformed.

A sound grated in Maugris's throat. He was staring at Flore's daughter and watched, bemused, as this days-old infant reached up to touch her father's nose.

"You wish to say something, Maugris?" Godefroi seemed to speak as he once had. Bland—and withering.

"No." As the infant was put in his arms, Maugris glared at me as if the baby's actions were my fault.

Over my nephew's head, my eyes met Margaretta's. This baby

had brought Godefroi back to the man he was; how else to explain the change?

"Hold the keep. Guard them well. I will know more when I return." Godefroi flung the order to Maugris over his shoulder as he strode from the chapel. "Bayard. Come."

28

CAN I speak with Mr. D'Acre, please?"

Alicia's on the phone in the kitchen. She listens. "Tell him it's just a quick call. . . . Yes. Alicia Donne. Thanks." She waits. "Allan?"

"Lady Alicia. What can I do for you?" In his office in Newton Prior, Allan D'Acre suppresses a sigh. His wife calls Alicia one of his lame ducks. The Donnes ran out of money long ago, but he helps with legal advice from a sense of duty to the once-great family they were.

"Advise me. About Hundredfield."

"Ah." The lawyer's pretty secretary puts her head around the door and taps her watch. He nods. "I haven't got very long. Perhaps you'd like to make an appointment and we can go over the options?"

"That's just it. It's rained again." Alicia stares up at the windows—it's a bright day out there. Today.

"The roof?"

She sighs. "Yes. I really have to find a substantial, a very substantial, amount of money from somewhere. And soon."

The solicitor interrupts, "I said this to you six months ago, and I know you don't want to hear it—sell the estate. That's my advice."

There's silence on the other end of the line.

"You may say that no one will buy it, you may say the building needs thousands spent on it . . ."

She mutters, "Millions."

". . . *but* it is irreplaceable, part of the fabric of the country. In the right market, that will always have cachet."

"The land's mostly leased."

"You say 'mostly.' What remains is still a substantial amount in this world's terms. And leases, my dear, can be broken—if enough money is involved."

"I can't sell Hundredfield, I just can't." Tears are standing in Alicia's eyes. "Who knows what a buyer would do to the buildings?"

Allan suppresses a sigh. "Your father considered it."

"But only half. And we didn't agree about the sale. It caused a terrible quarrel."

He says gently, "There's just you now. You can do what you like. Cut your losses. Put this burden down and move on with your life; enjoy being young. You won't be alone. Many of the grandest estates have changed hands since the war. You'll find the right buyer, believe me. There's always a way."

"But"—and then she says it in a rush—"how would I begin to do such a thing?"

"Ah. Now there I can help." His secretary is at the door again. He waves her away. "I know an estate agent who might suit." He flicks through the Rolodex on his desk looking for one particular name. "You'll like him, reliable and discreet. And not at all pushy. Get him to come and see the place; there'll be no obligation to do anything more."

Alicia grips the phone cord. Tight. "No. Yes. Oh." This is hard. "All right. What's his name?"

"Hugh Windhover."

"I've met him." Alicia worries her bottom lip.

"Excellent. I'll have him call you." There's a pause. "You're doing the right thing, Alicia."

"Am I?" She puts the phone down quickly and stares at it.

"Anyone I know?" Rory's standing in the doorway. He's watching her.

"Don't be so nosy." Alicia takes a loaf from the old-fashioned bread bin. "Sandwiches for lunch." An automatic smile.

"No need to go to any trouble. We can help ourselves." Rory washes his hands. "Are you okay?"

"Of course. But it's your duty to eat some of these; we have to keep up with the crop somehow. I shouldn't have planted so many." A bowl of tomatoes is plonked down. "How was the first session?"

"Not quite the first. We spent a couple of hours scoping parameters before Jesse left hospital." *One way of putting it.*

Shuttling between the fridge and the table with cheese and cucumbers, Alicia says brightly, "Oh?"

"Yes. And I think I should show you why."

"I'll just get the plates. Won't be a—"

"Sit down, Alicia." He's rarely this intense.

Alicia subsides into a chair. "Yes, sir."

Rory puts a folder on the table and takes out Jesse's sketches, lining them up in the order they were drawn.

Alicia leans in. "But these are excellent. Did you draw them?" She's genuinely interested.

"Look closer." He offers her the first drawing.

"Don't want to get it dirty." Alicia wipes her fingers on a napkin. As she takes the sketch of Hundredfield, her face changes. It's some time before she says, "Can I see the others?"

The only sound in the kitchen is from the kettle on the hob, winding up to a scream. Rory pulls it off. "Coffee?"

"Tea." Alicia picks up the last drawing very, very carefully. "This is a crucifix. A Christ figure."

"Yes. I think you're right." A glance over his shoulder.

"Tell me again. You didn't draw these?"

Dunking tea bags in separate mugs, Rory brings them to the table. "No. I did not. Milk?"

She shakes her head.

"Jesse did. Though she wasn't sure at the time." He points to the sketches of the castle and the keep.

"What does that mean?" Alicia frowns.

"She drew these two this morning." He ignores Alicia's comment as he taps the portrait and the crucifix.

Her eyes widen. After a pause she says, "What is this really about, Rory?"

Rory stares into the tea whirlpool he's made with his spoon. "I'm trying to understand what's happened to Jesse after the accident. And I brought her here since at some level she seems to know this place, though she says she's not been here before."

Alicia stands abruptly. She's pink with anger. "You've been conned. It's some sort of scam, that's what it is. This, this is just . . ." She's staring at the suffering Christ. "It's rubbish! You don't know anything about her, she could be anyone, she could be a thief, and—"

"Hey, calm down. I'm just trying to help her."

"Help?!"

Rory says patiently, "It's what I do. And besides, you said there was nothing worth stealing." He's trying for a joke.

The flush is gone. Alicia is icily polite. "It's been delightful having you stay. Unfortunately, I now think it best if you both leave and . . ."

A pause before a cool shrug from Rory. "Forgive me, I think you're overreacting."

Alicia snaps, "That's enough." She brandishes the drawing of the crucifix and then slaps it down. "She's sucked you in with this . . . whatever it is. People do that, they inveigle their way into old houses, they take photographs and come back and rob the place!"

Abruptly, she marches out.

"Alicia, there's no need—" Rory half stands. But he hears her boots on the stairs.

"Rory?"

He swivels.

Jesse's standing inside the back door of the kitchen. There's no way she hasn't heard at least some of the conversation. "I should leave."

"Sit down. Make yourself a sandwich." Rory starts slicing cheese. "Why don't people sharpen their knives?" He riffles through a drawer looking for the knife steel. "I'll start on the transcripts this afternoon, by the way." He strops the edge of the blade with vigor.

Jesse's misery deepens. "I'm not staying, Rory. Alicia wants you to leave too. You heard her."

"She'll get over it. She's a bit surprised, that's all—I was too when I first saw your drawings." Rory runs a finger along the knife edge. He eyes a tomato and with four quick strokes opens it like a flower.

Jesse feels a breeze as the door to the house opens. Alicia is carrying a large, leather-bound book. She doesn't acknowledge Jesse. "This is *A History of Hundredfield*, written by my great-grandfather." Alicia leafs through it rapidly. "In this book, a crucifix is described." She darts a look at Jesse. "The figure was worked in silver and it hung on a carved screen in the chapel of the keep. It was lost almost seven hundred years ago." The tone is icy. "And this is a sketch he made of this crucifix constructed from historical records." Alicia places the open book beside the drawing. She taps Jesse's sketch, then the illustration. The similarities are clear. "Garnets. Here. And here too. The gash from the spear, the gore from the crown of thorns, the nails, that's what they represented. You've shown them as he did. Did you know the figure was greater than life-size?"

Jesse swallows. "No. That is, I don't know anything about it.

And I didn't copy the drawing, Alicia. I've never seen this book." Jesse can just imagine how guilty she looks. It will be written on her face, it always is, when she tells the truth.

Alicia flips through the pages. "You replicated these images of the castle too." She holds them up, one, another, and another. "What do you want from me?"

Jesse protests helplessly, "I didn't know about Hundredfield or your great-grandfather's book. How could I? I've lived in Australia my whole life. I don't understand what's happening." She fades off unhappily.

Alicia just stares.

"Can I borrow your car, Rory?" It's the coward's way out, but Jesse's too upset to stay.

"Um. Sure. If you think you're up to it." He stands, patting his pockets. "Have a look on the table in the hall."

"Thanks." Jesse can't meet Alicia's eyes.

They hear her footsteps disappearing up the stairs.

Rory coughs. "I should let you know a couple of things."

Alicia sits back with her arms folded and a *this had better be good* look on her face.

"So, in the hospital after the accident and when Jesse had been taken off the ventilator—"

"I'm not interested in what happened at St. Barts."

"That's just it, though. Jesse's accident, the fractured skull, that, I think, is key and . . ." He hesitates. "I don't see she's after anything. I suggested we come here, and I've seen her actually draw with her left hand and nothing to copy from. The crucifix, for instance. I watched her do it this morning. And I know she's naturally right-handed."

Alicia opens her mouth. And closes it. Then, stubbornly, "She's setting you up. Setting us both up."

"To do what? Jesse's not faking, Licia. I think she's become a savant after the accident, and though that's incredibly rare, it does happen. Besides, if this *is* all some sort of elaborate performance, it's worth an article in *Psychology Today*, but I can't understand why she'd want to do it. She's doing *me* a favor because she's curious. And frightened by what's happening to her. And because, at least geographically, she's closer to finding her parents here." He hesitates. "Don't you want to know more, Alicia? Because I tell you, it's gone past research for me, it's . . ."

Alicia stares at him. "What?"

"Well, it's not magic, obviously." He laughs. "But I can't explain what's happening. I really cannot." He says, thoughtfully, "I've just got to keep Jesse engaged for as long as she'll permit me to work with her. That might not be easy now."

Alicia is silent. Her face is faintly guilty as Rory says, half to himself, "This place is the key."

"To what?"

"I don't know, but I'd like to find out, that's for sure and certain."

Alicia closes the book. "You think I should apologize."

"Up to you. This is your house."

That statement sits between them.

After a pause, she says grumpily, "Oh, all right. Jesse can stay. But only if you help me smooth things over when she comes back."

"Love to, but when I've got the car again, I'll be off. Mum's expecting me for dinner."

Alicia rolls her eyes. "Typical. Scoot out from under when you've created havoc *and* expect someone else to clean it up." She stands. "If you're finished, you can clear the table." A haughty sniff.

Grumbling, he pushes back his chair. "You don't play fair, Alicia Donne."

"And who taught me that, Rory Brandon?"

But they're grinning.

29

TIRES SPIT gravel as Jesse steers the Saab toward the inner ward. Crossing the bridge, she's grateful the drive to the front gates of the estate is so long. Despite what she said, she needs every bit of that oak-lined mile to get used to driving with one hand. But she'll cope. There's no way she's going back right now.

Once out of Hundredfield's gates, Jesse finds the road to Newton Prior without trouble. Along the way, she makes one false turn—and ends up at the entrance to someone's field being stared at by cows—but it's still quite early in the afternoon when she drives down Silver Street between the old, gray houses.

In the Beast Market, Jesse stops the car and, sweating as the tension ebbs, leans her forehead on the steering wheel. She's sick of thinking, sick of trying to work out what's going on, sick of . . . An impulse makes her look up. The Archangel Michael is frowning from his perch on the façade of the church. He's not offering any kind of welcome, but right now Jesse declines to pick a fight with anyone. She gets out from behind the wheel with some awkwardness and, as she locks the Saab, stands back and looks more carefully at the church.

"And do you find you like this building?" a cultured voice intrudes.

Jesse swings around. "Pardon?"

The man's dressed in a black cassock with a pectoral cross, and he's carrying a lit candle in a silver holder. Odd, in daylight. "*Like*. It's a useful word. Noncommittal when you don't want to say what you really think."

"Um. Well, I suppose it is a bit intimidating." Jesse's bemused.

"That's what they were, the Normans. Professionally so." He turns to look at her. "You don't like it all, do you?"

"No. I must admit I don't."

He grins. "Fred Stewart's my name. I'm the rector. Come inside. It gets worse."

There doesn't seem to be another option, so Jesse follows.

Closing behind them, the sound of the door echoes like a handclap. Fred waits for Jesse to speak.

She whispers, "What's *that*?"

The interior of the church is dim, as if natural light is somehow not permitted, and it's not just Fred's candle that flickers in the gloom—ranks and rows of candles are everywhere. But that's not what Jesse's pointing at.

"It's called *The Harrowing of Hell*."

"The what?"

Fred leads Jesse to the altar, where she genuflects unself-consciously. He says quietly, "A one-of-a-kind survival in the north, this." He gestures at the fresco covering the wall behind the altar. "It was lost for centuries and thought to have been destroyed in the dissolution of the monasteries, but when the Victorians got stuck into renovation here, they found it behind Tudor paneling."

Jesse takes in the monstrous images of devils eating women, demons pushing children into flaming pits, men skewered by tridents and torn apart by monsters. "It's just"—she searches for a word—"terrifying." What she'd really like to say is that she's revolted. "I mean, what must the congregation have thought? The children's nightmares!"

"That was the point. It helped keep everyone in line when people couldn't read. Their version of cartoons, I like to think."

Jesse turns in a circle. "I've never seen a church like this. Don't think me rude, but it's dark." *And I'm not talking about the opposite of light, either.*

"That's why I've got this." Fred holds up his candle. "I had spares in the car."

She sniffs. "Is that incense?"

Fred nods.

"This is a Catholic church?"

"No, but they all were once. So, how are we going?"

"Pardon?" Jesse's confused. But Fred's asked the question of the dark above their heads.

Someone answers, "Pretty much done."

Jesse swings toward the sound, can't place its origin.

"Up there." Fred's amused. "In the pulpit." As Jesse looks up, a disembodied head floats in the shadows of the canopy. The head moves and reveals itself on top of the body of a man dressed in dark coveralls. He's packing up an electrician's tool kit.

Fred says conversationally, "Actually, the church is darker than it normally is. We had a power failure and that's where the fuse box is." He protects the candle flame with one hand as he gestures toward the altar. "I agree about the fresco, by the way. What were they thinking? So, you know my name. What's yours?"

With such a contrast between his ceremonial clothing and the informal way he speaks, Jesse's nonplussed, though she shakes the proffered hand. "Jesse Marley. Hello."

"Call me Fred. Everyone does."

As if by sorcery, a blink of light flickers—on/off, on/off—then stays on; and the interior of the church jumps into being, all shape and form and height.

"There. Much more cheerful. You can see all the colors now." Fred's staring at the fresco, smiling slightly.

"Yes, you can." *All those flames and blood.* "Isn't that good."

"Now, is there anything I can do to help?" Fred's looking at her encouragingly.

She says cautiously, "Maybe." *He has such kind eyes.*

"Good. You looked a bit lost out there." He gestures to the door of the church. "I can spot that, you know. Years of training." Another smile, dispensed free.

Jesse hesitates. "Well . . ." *What have you got to lose?* "Parish records. The lady in the library says there's still quite a good collection among the border churches?"

"The lady at the library is right."

"I'm looking for my birth family, actually. I was born in Scotland, you see, but was adopted and brought up in Australia."

"Ah. Well, since I don't have any customers right now, perhaps we can shed a bit of light together." A gracious sweep of the arm shows the way as Fred strides to a side door. "A lot of church records have been stored in the larger towns for easier access, but you're very welcome to see what we still have. We've microfiched many of the oldest records. There's so much interest in ancestry these days, and I was concerned about damage to the physical documents. This way. I'm just next door in the parish hall."

Fred's office is long and narrow with high windows and walls painted a drab beige. It looks like a converted corridor, and what available space there is is crowded by pigeonholes on both sides.

"There's just too much stuff in here. Space. Such a problem. The ladies of St. Michael's Auxiliary had already colonized the hall before I arrived; didn't want to give much of it up. So I got this. Never mind. Do sit." There's a visitor's chair, but the seat's been slashed. "Sorry about that."

Fred doesn't explain, and Jesse doesn't want to ask.

"So, this is the business end of what you want." He pats an odd-looking metal box with a hood and some kind of screen in its depths. "Much quicker than going through all that paper, the microfiche. Now, information. What do you have?"

"Green. That was my mother's surname. Her first name was Eva. I don't know where her actual birthplace is, though it might be in the borders somewhere because I was born in Jedburgh. Just have to start somewhere."

A polite nod. "And your father?"

Jesse takes a breath. "It's not recorded."

Fred doesn't react.

"But I'm planning to ring all the Greens I can find in Scotland. Someone must be able to help me." She's speaking too fast. Nerves.

Fred considers what she's said. "As good a plan as any, to get you on your way. I should just explain something, however. The more common names will often need a little work to track down the correct person. You're lucky Eva is less usual, so let's see if we can find any information about your mum in our records. Do you have her date of birth?"

Jesse unfolds the birth certificate from her bag. "It says 1940. And I was born in 1956—Jesse Mary. Here I am." She offers the piece of paper.

Fred doesn't comment.

Jesse aches when she thinks about it. Sixteen? So, so young. Of course, it must have been impossible, *of course* Eva would have given her to other people. How could her mother, still a child herself, have kept her in those days?

"Your mother was born during the war, of course." Fred wrinkles his brow as he pulls open a filing-cabinet drawer. "*G, G* . . . Let me see." Another drawer. "Here we are. All the *G*'s I have." He sorts through hanger files at a rapid rate. "Graeme, Grahame—a lot of those—Grayling, Grave, Gread, *Green* . . ." He pulls out a folder of transparencies and puts them next to the microfiche reader. "You'd appreciate that a number of births were, shall we say, irregular during the war? We had both army and air-force bases close to the village."

"So, is 1940 likely to be a problem?"

A kind smile. "This was not my parish then, as you'd understand, but I do know there was a fire in the hall after blackout one night; a cigarette, we think. Not serious for the building, but an annex was burned out. That was where church records were stored, and some were lost. I'm hoping that's not the case here. Green, Green, 1940, let me see . . ."

Jesse wills her heart to slow, wills the blood to be still in her veins. If she thinks of waterfalls, the sea, snow falling, as the minutes pass, she'll center herself. Her mum taught her how to do that when she was stressed or unhappy. Her mum in Sydney.

"Hmm. Nothing for January to March 1940." The rector swaps cellulose sheets under the lens of the microfiche. "So, April."

The kindness of strangers. Jesse doesn't know how to respond as she watches the priest; his hands are magnets.

But it's unbearable just to sit and observe someone trawling for evidence of her life, or her mother's life. Jesse gets up quietly and mimes going back to the church. Fred nods, absorbed.

She picks a chair in a tiny side chapel. The altar is no bigger than a card table, but votive candles flicker before a statue in a wall niche. Carved with more faith than talent, the paint and gilding have mostly flaked away from the Madonna and her son, and wormholes pock the ancient wood. But Jesse finds the simple image comforting, and the jaunty baby in Mary's lap makes her smile. She'd intended just to sit quietly, but the kind expression on the Madonna's face slips under her defenses. Without thinking, she kneels and joins her hands. And prays. *So many women must have asked you for help. My mum. Was she one of them? She was just a girl and I don't know if anyone cared.*

Our Lady of Sorrows. The name floats into Jesse's head, and she sees her mother's stricken face in Sydney; the moment when, sobbing, she'd slammed the bedroom door. And shut Jesse out.

Being in that house had been impossible from that afternoon on. And now she's here.

Jesse opens her eyes. Even this far from the altar, the power of the fresco is enormous. The barbarism, the cruelty, the sheer *relish* in God's vengeance against the so-called wicked. It's an assault to the eye and the soul. Angry, upset, she scrambles off her knees.

"Apologies." Fred's been waiting for her. "Hoped I wouldn't disturb."

Jesse wipes her hand across her eyes. "I'm sorry. It's—that is, I should be apologizing to you. What a ridiculous world this is."

The priest says gently, "No. Just full of surprises." He smiles and she responds. A little. "Come back to my office."

She knows, looking at his face. He would have said he had good news, but it's still no easier hearing the truth.

"I'm sorry, Jesse, but I haven't found Eva Green or, indeed, any records that mention you."

She slumps.

"Not yet, that is. *But*"—Fred turns back to his desk, picks up a piece of paper—"I hope you don't mind, but I've made a quick call on your behalf." He taps the number that's written there. "I saw you were born at Holly House. It's a private home now, but I was able to find the number through a colleague—a Catholic priest. I rang the contact he gave me, and the owners were very helpful." He offers the paper to her. "This is for a nursing home in Jedburgh."

"Nursing home?"

"Yes. They have a resident whom you might like to meet. She was a nun—a nursing sister—at Holly House in the fifties. Her name's Sister Mary Joseph. She lives there in retirement with a number of her former colleagues. I knew her slightly some years ago. A fine person. Very compassionate."

"I don't understand."

"Holly House was a home for unmarried mothers when you were born. It was run by the Catholic Church, and the pregnant girls worked in the commercial laundry that was managed by the sisters."

Jesse stares at what he's written. "This is very kind of you, Reverend Stewart."

"Fred, as I said. Just my job. The nursing home has liberal visiting hours; you can make an appointment or just turn up as it suits you."

Jesse stands. "I feel so lucky, meeting you today."

Fred beams. "Let me know how you get on. Remember, this is just the beginning: you've made a start." He says that as if she's been awarded a prize.

Jesse finds the muscles that make a smile. "With your help." A beginning. It's true.

On her way back to the square, Jesse finds the little Madonna and her baby again. She lights a taper and kneels at the altar rail.

Let me find her. Please. Just let me find my mother.

She knows that praying's a relic of childhood habit. She knows it's idolatrous too—beseeching a statue for help—but Jesse still opens her heart to that kind woman. And hopes.

The Hunt is busier than yesterday when Jesse finds her way inside.

Rachel's hurrying from table to table, past another girl who's working today as well: a teenager with the startled pink eyes of a rabbit.

Mack whirls past with a wave. "Table won't be long."

Jesse calls out, "Thanks!" The people, the food, the noise, it's all cheery, all so alive, so *normal*. Normal is good today. And comforting.

"This way, Miss Marley." Rachel leads her to a table for two. She offers menus. "Anyone joining you?"

"No, it's just me." Jesse feels as if everyone's staring. Afternoon at the Hunt is a coupled world, and people seem to know each other, companionably leaning between tables to catch up on gossip.

"Thanks, Rachel." Mack appears behind the girl's shoulder.

"Sure." The waitress gets the hint.

"May I?" Mack taps the back of a chair as the waitress plunges back into the scrum.

"Of course." Jesse's mood lifts. "But you're very busy." *Let him sit. He wants to!*

Mack grins. "Always. Wasn't expecting to see you quite so soon."

"No." Jesse fiddles with the menu as he slides into the seat.

"So, what brings you to town?"

She's grateful he doesn't ask about Rory or Alicia. "Oh, you know. A bit of sightseeing. I met Fred Stewart, by the way."

"He qualifies. Definitely. Should be declared a national monument, Grade I listed."

Mack's got good teeth when he smiles. Jesse likes that—it's unusual enough to notice in Britain. "He's nice. He showed me some of the parish records for St. Michael's. It was a long shot, but we looked up my mum's name."

"Any luck?"

Jesse shakes her head. "He's given me a lead, though. Someone he knew who worked at Holly House at about the right time; that's where I was born. She lives in a nursing home now, so I'm going to visit her."

"In Jedburgh, right?"

"Yes. I guess I can catch a bus."

"Tell you what. I've got a day off due, how about I take you when you're ready?"

"Wow. Really?"

He leans across the table. "Do you a deal."

Jesse finds she's grinning too. "What are the terms?" Close up, the eyes are a shock. So dark, the pupils cancel out.

"And here's me thinking all Australians are risk-takers."

"But I'm not Australian." A twinge of disloyalty.

"Ah, yes. You said that." He's looking at her expectantly.

Jesse rallies. "What have I got to give to get?"

"Eat lunch. On the house. A proper meal. You need to build your strength."

He has the wrong idea, plainly. "Actually, I like eating." She smiles nicely. "Sold to the girl in the very old jeans. With thanks."

He says amiably, "I didn't notice. Not the jeans."

The brief silence is filled with noise, voices, the clatter of cutlery, and Jesse doesn't know what to say.

Mack taps the menu. "Let Rachel know what you'd like. The Eccles cakes are good today. Personal recommendation."

Eccles cakes. It seems like a sign, an approval of some kind; as he gets up, Jesse says hastily, "Just one thing, Mack." There are so many things she wants to ask, such as *What* is *it with Rory?*

"Yes?"

It's not easy matching his glance. She temporizes. "Um, Helen. Is she around?" Maybe she's on a hiding to nothing asking Mack's mum for information again, but that strange moment yesterday could have been a misunderstanding.

Or not.

"I'll find her."

Jesse says hastily, "No rush. Truly don't want to get in anyone's way."

"Impossible." That smile again.

Jesse would like to pretend the menu takes all her attention, but her glance strays at least three times over the top of the card. She's watching Mack as he winds through the dining room, chatting, pouring drinks, clearing tables where he can.

Is it the streak of white hair? No. It's the eyes. Definitely the eyes. He catches her looking his way. He smiles and she blushes. Then it happens again, though this time she catches him looking at her.

Mack's not the only one taking an interest. As she dawdles over the Eccles cake, Jesse brushes the back of her head; it feels like an insect's caught in her hair. When it happens again, she checks over her shoulder.

A man is sitting at a table directly behind her, almost within touching distance. Somewhere over sixty, the spare frame and the deep-sunk eyes speak of suffering and will, but an interested glance swings Jesse's way. "Hello there. Have we met?"

She turns a little more in her chair. "I don't think so. I'm a visitor. Jesse Marley is my name."

"Australian?"

"Well spotted." She doesn't mean to get into explanations.

"Alistair Nicholls, physician." He half rises. "Don't let me interrupt." He waves at the last of the cake. His smile is attractive and brings warmth to those mournful eyes.

"I've eaten too much already."

"May I offer you a cup of coffee?"

Jesse's slightly startled. "That's very kind. Tea, I think."

"Very wise." He swivels in his seat and beckons the other waitress. "Another pot of tea please, Jewel."

Jesse tries not to stare, but the rabbit analogy from earlier is inescapable—something about the nose, never mind the eyes. And the girl walks with a lollop. Definitely. *Stop that!*

The doctor winks. "And I'll have what this young lady's having."

"Eccles cake." Jewel scribbles diligently, but as she turns to go, the doctor beckons her back and murmurs, "Did you not take all the antibiotic I prescribed?" Jewel half answers as she leaves, a mutter Jesse can't quite understand.

The doctor sighs. "Conjunctivitis."

"That's contagious, isn't it?" Jesse's alarmed.

"It shouldn't be if she's taken all of the course, but . . ." He shakes his head. "Patients forget. Or they don't really listen." Dr.

Nicholls stops himself. "Forgive me. One of the duties of the old is not to be boring. Doctors can be tedious about their work, especially, perhaps, to strangers who are kind enough to listen." A faint smile.

And there it is again. That sense he's inspecting her quite closely.

Jewel arrives with a tray, and Dr. Nicholls captures the teapot as a cup clatters down. "Shall I pour?"

Jesse sends Mack a silent prayer: *Rescue. Help!* "Um, thanks. Do you practice locally, Dr., er . . ." She's forgotten his name.

"Nicholls. Yes. For many years, though originally I had rooms in Edinburgh."

Jesse struggles. "It must have been something of a contrast. There, I mean, and, er, here." She's properly trapped.

"Ah, yes. But babies, you see, have been a constant in both places. Tell me about yourself, Miss Marley." Dr. Nicholls nudges her cup across his table and pours one for himself.

"Oh. Well, not so much to tell." She sips the tea.

"On holiday?"

"No. It's beautiful here, though; that's like a vacation." Inside Jesse's cringing. She *so* hates useless chat.

"A refreshment to the soul, I always think. Beauty. And it must be so different from your home." His eyes crease encouragingly.

Jesse puts the cup down. "Actually I was born in Jedburgh."

His looks interested. "Is that so?"

She nods. "I'm adopted. I found that out just recently. It's why I'm here."

Something has changed. They're engaged with each other.

"Perhaps I can help. We're a close community here."

"You're the third person who's told me that." Jesse smiles, but it occurs to her that Dr. Nicholls is just the slightest bit nosy. "I've only just begun to look."

"Is everything to your satisfaction, Doctor?"

Jesse turns in her chair.

Helen Brandon is standing behind the table. "Miss Marley, lovely to see you again. So soon."

"Hello, Mrs. Brandon." *So, no first names.*

"A moment of delightful respite, Helen. As it always is, coming here."

Rory's mother goes to say something and hesitates. "On your way out, if you have a minute, Doctor? Just a quick question."

Alistair Nicholls nods. "Of course."

"Miss Marley." Helen's smile is perfunctory as she walks back to the till.

That's that, then. No way Jesse is going to ask Helen anything. Not now.

Alistair pats his jacket, searching a pocket to find a slightly scuffed card. "If I can help you in any way, the number's here. Good luck with your search." He stands with a courteous smile.

"Thank you." She accepts the card and watches as he pays Helen and they talk.

"Excellent result."

Jesse jumps in her seat and tea spills on the front of her shirt.

Mack grabs a table napkin.

Jesse takes it from him. "It's okay. Really. The pattern's very forgiving." She mops her chest.

"Look, can we start this again? I promise never to hit you or spill things on you, so if you'll just wipe your memory tapes, we can—"

"You blush like me! I've never seen that. In a man, I mean." Jesse feels quite bold.

"Fair call. Right." Mack holds out his hand. "My name's Mack. Pleased to meet you."

"Me too. Call me Jesse." She offers her left hand and he takes it awkwardly. They laugh.

His grasp is warm. "Give me a call when you're ready to go to Jedburgh, Jesse."

"I will. Thank you."

"My pleasure."

He still has her hand. Jesse takes it back. She stands and he jumps to help.

"It's okay. My arm's the problem, not my legs."

He can't help glancing down. And says absently, "No."

That makes Jesse laugh out loud. So loud, Helen looks up.

She knows Helen's watching as she strides from the dining room. And Mack is too. She can feel it.

The Saab starts reluctantly, and something about that unwillingness punctures Jesse's mood.

She's in no hurry to face Alicia because it all feels so outstandingly awkward; as if she's just busted up with a flatmate and all that's left is to pack and make a dignified exit, hoping she can get through the door without a screaming match.

Time's come. Walk away. Think about Hundredfield from a distance, when she's staying somewhere less fraught. Less odd. Less, to be honest, scary.

There'll be a hostel in Jedburgh. Maybe she can take Mack up on his offer of a lift sooner than he thinks. If Rory wants to keep going with the research, he can come to her there.

Helen Brandon's face swims up from somewhere. "So, how would you feel about your baby boy taking me to Jedburgh, Helen?" A bitchy little laugh.

But it's hard not to be hurt when people don't like you and there isn't any reason.

Except a good-looking son. Two good-looking sons—though Rory doesn't count (that's not remotely the way things are between her and him).

Mack, though—*admit it*—Mack could be different. And then Helen might really have something to worry about.

Yes, Jesse's looking forward to seeing Mack again, one-on-one. No mum, no pub, no brother. Awkward, though, when such a good-looking bloke's playing piggy in the middle and he has no clue. Not yet.

Jesse's not about to tell him, either.

30

THE FERRY across the river was reached by a path from a postern gate in the wall of my mother's pleasure garden. I remembered this as a sheltered place, a green bower where bees robbed flowers of pollen. But no bees cheered us that freezing Christmas afternoon as Godefroi and I walked away from the keep—away from the noise in the hall, the fire on the hearth, and the beer soaking through the rushes. There was only the jangle of thoughts that must find words.

"Aviss is a fine child, Godefroi."

Godefroi grunted. "A bastard has no place in succession." He had stopped for breath beneath the branches of an ash. In the cold light, his face was gray.

"But a girl-child is—"

He flared at me. "I am not shamed by her sex. She will be my heiress."

"Then she must be baptized, brother, and acknowledged before the people as yours. To protect her."

"My daughter will always be safe within Hundredfield's walls."

There was no escape. "She is Flore's child and at the heart of the rumors. The keep is unsettled and—"

"Pagan rubbish. *You* called it that, Bayard."

I tried again. "Superstition is hard to fight, harder to suppress, I will agree, but—"

Godefroi spoke with great force. "These were the terrors of a woman facing childbirth, fanned by ignorance in those who served her. She was right to be fearful." He stared back toward the keep. "Flore died in her birth-blood up there, in my bed. Her daughter is true-born, flesh of her mother's mortal flesh and of mine."

"Then why do we go to the ferry, Godefroi?"

"To find Flore's body! And the people who stole her from me." His voice cracked.

Godefroi's suffering was raw, and I was touched. I said quietly, "Perhaps your daughter might be sent to the sisters at Berwick."

"For what purpose?" The hauteur returned.

"Until our difficulties here are resolved."

"Difficulties? Bah!" Godefroi stamped on.

I called after him, "You spoke of succession. Your word. Yes, your daughter is the heir to Hundredfield, but infants are tender and many die in a harsh season."

Godefroi stopped. "What do you mean?"

"Nothing more than I said. If you will not consider Aviss, then Hundredfield needs a legitimate son." I did not say, *And you need a different wife.* "You must marry again, Godefroi. For the good of us all."

"You will not tell me my duty to this place." He ripped his sword from its sheath.

I danced back as he came at me, drawing my own. "Who else can tell you the truth?"

A heaving slash from Godefroi, badly timed.

I parried.

He was panting. "Do not—"

My blade slid on his.

"—presume—" Godefroi sobbed a breath and rushed on. "—to dictate to me!"

I pivoted, raising my sword. As Godefroi blundered past, his neck was undefended. For Hundredfield, I could have killed him. Who would have known?

But I did not.

I stood aside and waited.

"I go to the ferry." Godefroi was panting. "Be gone when I return."

I planted the tip of my sword in the earth. "Brother, I am sworn to protect and defend our house. Take my sword if that duty is extinguished and I will agree to go. But I will not come back."

To destroy takes no time, to build is another thing.

There was silence except for the wind and our breath.

After a time, Godefroi shook his head. He said heavily, "I will not take your sword." He did not apologize. He never did.

Behind the walls of the garden the sky was clear, but shadows had begun to grow on this short day; they crept on like fingers toward the postern gate, so long unused and nearly overgrown. This had been our mother's private way to the river when she wished to cross unseen by those at Hundredfield; now it was almost lost to human sight. As she was.

Godefroi watched as I cleared the overgrowth of briar and woodbine. Below, we heard the river move in its cold bed. Rain falling in the west had swollen its margins.

Rusted metal groaned as I pushed against the gate to force it open. Then I saw the world from on high.

On the other side of the river was a hut—an outlier from the village that lay beyond sight behind the trees. When I had been a child, a woman, Hawise, lived there. Strong and brown as a donkey, she dwelled alone, never having married and poled a punt across the water when called by our mother; a bell was kept at the wharf for that purpose. Hawise was given a tiny sum for her service and permitted to forage firewood among Hundredfield's trees. A goat for milking, a patch for growing greenstuff, a bee skep, and an orchard with a collection of shabby hens kept flesh on her bones most years. In famine, she begged at the gates of the keep like everyone else.

I asked, "Is it Hawise still who pulls the punt across?" I was thirteen when our mother died. The years since seemed very long.

Godefroi stepped through the gateway to the path. It was steep and, from little use, narrowed by brambles and gorse. He said grudgingly, "I do not know. She was old when we were young."

Our mother would often visit the village beside the river unannounced. Because our grandmother had been the daughter of a Saxon noblewoman, our own mother was well liked. Or liked better than we at least, the men of the family—and it was she who had arranged for the hut to be built and for Hawise to be given animals from which to feed herself. So that lonely woman—an outsider because of her size and her strange ways—was personally devoted to "the lady of the keep." If she were there still, I hoped she felt something for her sons.

I arrived at the wharf before Godefroi. Jetting out over the water, elm planks were fixed to trunks rammed into the shallows. It was old, but the structure seemed sturdy, though the bell had disappeared. I cupped hands and called out, "Hawise!"

Nothing stirred on the far bank as Godefroi joined me.

I tried again. "Hawise?"

Something moved beside the hut, dark against dark. We strained to see, for mist was rising as daylight dimmed.

After a splash, a wide, low shape began to glide toward us.

I milled my arms around my head. "Over here!"

The punt drew closer. The rhythm of the cloaked figure was hypnotic: plunge the pole, walk forward; plunge again, walk forward. We could not see the face in the shadow of the cowl.

Ready to catch the rope, I bent down. But the figure dug its pole deep—and kept it there. The punt rocked in the stream but came no closer as a voice called out, "Who are you?"

"I am your lord." Godefroi was not by nature polite to peasants and spoke French.

The figure did not reply.

I called out, "Are you Hawise?"

The cowled head swung toward me. It was eerie to be inspected by that unseen face.

"I remember you. You are the youngest one." The cowl dropped back from the head.

I stared. It had been a long time, but the woman seemed unchanged. I thought of Rosa. How could a girl become a crone sooner than Hawise?

"I have business with you." When Godefroi spoke again, in English, his tone was less gruff.

"Yes, Lord Godefroi, we shall speak. But on the other side." The woman lifted her pole and plunged it into the rushing water. And again. I caught the landing rope as, with a neat swirl, she brought the punt along the wharf. "You must pay for the passage."

"I have no coin." Godefroi turned to me.

"I, neither." My last penny piece had been given to Dikon.

"She does not ask for metal money."

"Of whom do you speak, woman?"

"The river asks you, Lord Godefroi. Three drops of your blood is her price to cross."

Godefroi reared back. "Blasphemy!"

"Then you will never know." With a sharp jerk, Hawise pulled the rope from my hands and drove the pole deep, walking the punt away from the Hundredfield shore.

Godefroi called out, "I will pay the fare." Kneeling with some trouble, he took a dagger from his belt and drove the point into the skin of one wrist. Blood dripped into water dark as steel.

Returning, the woman threw the rope again and I caught it; she reached to help Godefroi down into the punt.

Holding the craft against the wharf, I waited to climb on board.

"No." Godefroi pushed the punt away.

I hauled on the rope to bring it back. "Brother! You should not go alone. The monk—"

"—does not concern me. Guard my daughter. Keep her safe."

Hawise called out, "Throw the rope, third son."

"Do it!" Godefroi's shout startled rooks from their roosts.

And so I did as I was asked. I threw the rope and watched as the woman caught the coil and Godefroi lifted an arm in farewell. And I let my brother go.

The sound of men's voices pulled me to the hall of the keep, but as I opened the great door, the chamber fell silent.

Too late. The phrase stung my soul like a venomous fly, but smiling to left and right, I strode to the dais as subdued conversation followed me.

I beckoned a kitchen girl and said, loud enough for all to hear, "Lord Godefroi is resting. He asks that wassail continue. Bring beer! Ale for all!"

Pulling out a stool, I sat beside Godefroi's chair and beckoned Rauf—he had been sitting with several of our fighters, separate from the other folk.

"I hope Lord Godefroi improves?"

I nodded. "His situation is better."

The girl returned with several kitchen servants, all bearing skins of ale. She hurried first to me.

"A drink for my friend, to toast the season." I pointed to the ale horns hanging from her belt. She was young, not much more than a child, and frightened. I remembered being ten and scared, and so found her a smile.

When it was filled, Rauf raised his horn to me. "To what must be done."

I nodded, lifting my own. "And it will be done well, God willing." I owed Rauf much. But then, I had saved his life also, and not only once. I leaned across the board. "Tell me the mood."

Rauf smiled as if I had said something funny. "Nothing changes unless it is worse."

I laughed, and Rauf joined in. "We must set a watch on the postern. Also it must be repaired. I had to force it open."

Rauf nodded. He did not ask me why.

"And?" Beaming, I raised the horn to his. We knocked together and ale fountained as we threw the rest down our throats.

Wiping a hand across his mouth, Rauf said through a smile, "I have reports there's a proper camp in your woods now. Well hidden, well defended. No doubt the monk holds his own feast there today." He beckoned the girl for more ale. "And tonight, the village will empty. He tells them he will feed their children if they fight for him."

The hall grew silent. Maugris was striding from the door. As I stood to salute him, I muttered, "Then we must find the monk." As Rauf withdrew, I raised my voice and called, "Brother!"

Maugris stared at me, eyebrows raised.

As the ale-girl filled a silver goblet, he sat. When she had gone I murmured, "He went alone."

Maugris raised the goblet to the hall; one or two responded. "Why?"

"Pride. Foolishness. I could not tell. He says he wants to find her body."

"Not foolish. Godefroi is hard. He does not believe he will be harmed. He thinks no one on Hundredfield would dare."

I muttered, "Then he courts his death."

Maugris swallowed the last of his ale. "And ours, brother. Kill him, and they will come for us."

"Let us in, girl." Maugris tapped urgently. Only he and I knew Margaretta and the children were behind Godefroi's locked door. As she pulled it open, he brushed past. "Here. This is for you."

The girl took the napkin he offered, filled with food—bread, cheese, sausage, and a large piece of a raised pie—and set it down on a coffer.

"There are pallets under the bed. I will get them for you." She spoke quietly. Aviss and the infant were asleep together in the middle of Godefroi's vast bed. A sight to touch the heart.

Maugris surprised me. He said quite gently, "Eat, girl." He gestured at the sleeping children. "They need you strong."

Margaretta hesitated, but nodded. It pleased me to see the delicate way she ate as Maugris and I pulled pallets from under the bedstead and found coverings in the coffers.

Maugris yawned mightily as he pulled off his boots and, rolling into a fur-lined cloak, turned his face to the wall. Soon he was snoring.

"We are all to sleep here tonight?"

"My brother wishes it so. For safety." I waved to the sleeping children. I did not say which brother, and I did not say which child.

"Then I shall put them to bed." Over her shoulder as she made up the two cradles with fleece and woolen covers, she said, "Where is he?" She did not name Godefroi or call him lord.

"We went to the ferry and Hawise brought the punt across."

"She took him to the other side?"

I nodded.

In the shadows, it was hard to see Margaretta's face. "Would you bring Aviss to me, Lord Bayard?"

The child muttered as I picked him up. He was so deep asleep, he did not stir as his mother put him in the plain little cradle and tucked the fleece around his shoulders.

I picked up my niece also. When I transferred the baby from my arms to hers, Margaretta's face was transformed for a moment by tenderness.

"Thank you." My niece was placed in the larger carved cradle and she too was carefully covered. "The nights are cold. They sleep better if they are warm." We both gazed at the sleeping children, flushed like roses. Margaretta whispered, "You are good with babies. You must have been well taught."

We stood so close I could have touched her face.

But I did not.

"Godefroi is a lucky man, Margaretta."

Margaretta looked at me sadly. "He has never thought so. Not with me." She dropped her eyes.

I put another billet of wood in the brazier. "You must have been very young when Aviss was born."

"Yes."

In the silence, I thought how it would have been for her. Perhaps she had gone willingly to Godefroi's bed, but I knew my brother. From her manner with him, I think she had been forced and was disgraced, even though she was the daughter of our reeve, a respected man at Hundredfield.

"Lord, may I ask you something?" Her tone was humble.

"Speak."

"I am worried for Aviss. Your brother does not love him."

No. He does not.

"What should I do?" In that flickering, rosy light, Margaretta's face had the softness, the sweetness, of her own child.

"I trust my brother loves both his children." I did not answer the second part of the question. Godefroi was a spider. He did not let go those whom he had caught.

"I did what I was asked to do, but if he does not find the Lady Flore . . ." I heard the fear in her voice.

To soothe her, I said, "All will be well, Margaretta. No harm will come to you even if he does not find your mistress." I would not willingly allow such a thing; yet Maugris and I could not stay at Hundredfield for longer than the twelve days of the Christmas celebrations. We were expected back at Alnwick.

Margaretta did not speak again, and I heard the soft rustle as she lay down between the cradles on a pallet of straw. It was warm and dark, for the shutters had been closed, and soon all I heard was the sigh of the wind.

As the night grew old, I woke once when Margaretta fed the little girl, but the child's snuffles became part of a dream. Soon the silence was filled with breathing, which became the sound of the sea, and . . .

Maugris shook me.

"What?" It was cold. Someone had pulled the shutters open, and ice blew in with the dawn.

"She has gone." Maugris jerked on his boots.

"The children?" A glance supplied the answer. The cradles were empty.

Maugris buckled his sword to the hanger at his waist. His face was grim. "She is Swinson's daughter. And the sister of the monk. I should not have been so trusting."

It was clear he blamed me. I said, "She could have gone to him before and did not. Explain that." I hunted for my sword.

"She has Godefroi's daughter. And his son. Hostages." Flat. And tired.

"Godefroi does not care about Aviss, Maugris."

"But he cares about the baby. Too much." Maugris made up his mind. "They must be found."

"She will not have walked far, carrying two children." I hesitated. "Last night, Rauf said Alois and his men are camped in the forest. Many of our people have already gone to him. I saw some leave the feast myself."

"A camp on our lands? That is brazen."

I stuck a dagger through my belt beside my sword. "What would you have me do?"

"Take Rauf and some of our men, find the girl, return quickly. If Godefroi does not come back, we will go out to them in strength, but I will send to Alnwick for support first." My brother's face was bleak. "Hundredfield is in play, Bayard."

"At least we know that now." I scooped up my cloak.

"Is knowing enough?"

I gripped his hand in mine. "It is for us. We are who we are."

The path to the village wound between the forest and the water meadows on which our cattle grazed in summer. But winter has a dead and bony hand, and that day puddles were muddy glass, the grass withered where it was not covered by snow. This world was bleak and white and cold. And unforgiving.

"Weapons."

Rauf echoed, "Weapons!" Behind, four of our fighters formed a tight troop and I heard the swords unsheathed.

I gathered the reins and spurred Helios on to the settlement. Ahead, a man was walking to the first of the houses. He heard us, for he dropped his load of wood and ran inside.

I signaled the halt. Rauf jumped from his horse and striding to the house, banged his fist on the door. Inside, I heard a child cry, quickly hushed.

A look from me, and Rauf stepped back. "We shall not hurt you. We seek information."

The door opened a crack, and the man inspected us. Behind his shoulder a woman gave suck to her fretful baby. I called out, "Dame. Good day to you. We search for a girl and two children. They may have asked for shelter last night, or food."

Large-eyed, the woman stared at her husband. His face was bitter. "We have no food here. Not for strangers, not for us."

And the door was pushed shut.

Rauf remounted his horse.

"Easy matter to fire the thatch, lord."

"Leave them."

Hearing the voices, others had come to their doors. Old women with children in their skirts and toothless men too frail to work. Or fight.

I asked the same question three times, and each time was denied an answer.

And then I thought of Rosa.

Cantering to the House of Women, I threw the reins to Rauf and jumped from the stallion's back. "Wait."

I went to push the door open and found it ajar.

"Rosa?"

A fire had always been lit in this house—to light the gloom, to warm the drafts. Now, the hearth was dead.

"She has gone." A heap of rags in one corner had grown a mouth.

"Mary?"

The old woman levered to her knees. "There is no food, and no ale, or I would offer it."

I helped Mary stand. She was dirty and feeble. A shadow held up by bones.

"Where is Rosa?"

The old woman collapsed to the settle by the hearth. "They stopped coming from the village. She's gone to the forest. At least she'll eat there."

"She left you here?"

"I would not go." Mary turned her head and I saw sores beside her mouth and the skull was sharp under her skin. "The witch did this. Rosa told me that. But *he* has said he will save those who can be saved. Him out there." She nodded and mumbled to herself.

I swallowed. The old woman was dying from starvation, but she would not burden her daughter. "There is a girl. And two children. I am looking for them."

"Who would come to this place? Children die at Hundredfield. She has cursed us all."

What point was there to argue?

The men were silent as I remounted and wheeled Helios to face the meadow where the fringe of trees began. Would the children survive this bleak weather? I remembered Margaretta wrapping

Aviss and the baby in the cold of last night. Time was not our friend in any way.

"Rauf." I beckoned him closer. "We must find the camp, see what men they have." *And if she is there with the children—what then?* "We see them, they do not see us."

He nodded. "And?"

I sighed. There was always *and.* "If we are unlucky, I'll hold the men, you ride for Hundredfield and bring strength to us. Take this to Maugris." I had a ring on my left hand with our crest. I put the finger in my mouth; heat and spit made the ring slide off.

Helios was a heavy horse and ice cracked under his hooves as I held him at a canter. Behind, the others rode lighter, but men moving fast in battle array is still thunder of a kind. I was grateful the forest was leafless. We would see men moving among the trees if they heard us coming.

"There!" Rauf pointed. We were looking for a used track, a way the raiders would have taken into the forest, and there it was: a wide path that led the eye through the dim spaces between the trees. Men had been here, and horses also, for there was fresh dung and the marks of iron-shod hooves. As the day turned sullen, we rode onto the rutted way.

Rain that began as mist thickened, and pellets of ice drove into our faces. The only sound was the splatter of sleet against our breastplates and the wet hit of hooves in the mud. Yet there was—something. I looked up.

Above, in the trees, were ravens. I had seen too much of their work on the battlefield, but before that day they had only been scavengers, creatures that did what was necessary when the dead were abandoned. Now, as each black head turned, each yellow eye followed our progress, they seemed to wait as the trees all around became steadily greater until, at last, we moved among the pillars of an unbuilt cathedral where men were beetles and ravens the size of fleas.

I did not know this part of the forest, and fear whispered we would all soon to be dead and would lie here for all time. Under my breath, I prayed the Paternoster as trot became canter, and canter, gallop. Time was lost in the hit of hooves. I only reined our troop to a stop because I came to a fork in the path.

"Stay here."

Rauf nodded and the men closed up behind as I walked Helios forward. Closer to the dividing of the ways the stallion stamped and danced, tossing his head.

I pulled a withered apple from the saddlebag and the animal lipped it from my hand. "There. Not so bad." Dismounting, I looped the reins around a branch.

It was not hard to understand the signs. The path was cut up on the left-hand fork; horsemen had traveled that way fast. The right-hand way was less disturbed, so the choice seemed clear. We would take the left.

The air was bitter, and like a child's rattle my jaw clattered as I walked away from the path to relieve my bladder.

Retying points, I saw, at some distance, an ash tree with a noble trunk. Disturbed earth was around its roots, and closer, the prints of naked feet were clear. A running man had passed this way, for the forepart of the foot was deep and clear, the heel less so. I matched my own foot to the shape. A person bigger than I had made these marks, and from the depth, heavier too; he had fled from something, or to something.

Only the poorest—serfs and outcasts—went shoeless in winter, and they were smaller than most; food was scarce from birth for such as they. Yet only the most extreme want would cause a man to enter my brother's forest in search of fresh meat. To be caught was to be hung. Perhaps, therefore, this man was desperate. And he had had company: men on horses, and not long gone.

"Bayard! À moi, à moi!" Rauf.

There came the clang and clash of blades, the roar of men as they died.

Had I been cold before? Heat drove my legs as I ran to where Helios had been.

And was no longer.

I looked for our men. They too had gone.

A hunting horn sounded far away among the trees.

I was more surprised than angry. Bold raiders indeed to chase deer in our forests, as if they were the lords of Hundredfield.

A hand clamped on my mouth and I was dragged down, my face against the frozen earth. I struggled, twisting and thrashing, but my hands were pinned as a man knelt on my legs. Rauf. I knew his smell.

The horns sounded again. Closer. The palm was removed, so were the knees. "Run. Now!"

In the ancient past, a crack had fissured the massive girth of an oak.

Half hunched, Rauf ran and was swallowed by the tree. I followed. Pressed together like lovers, we breathed each other's sweat. And listened.

Like thunder that moves close, closer, until, at last, it bursts in light and fury overhead, we heard them come, a galloping mass; but there were no hounds. Who hunts without dogs?

Rauf whispered, "They will know. They will smell us out."

"We are hidden. They are only men."

"They are not." He was terrified.

Something crashed past. A single animal. Large. A stag? And then the hunt was on us. It flowed like a river in pursuit of the prey, *but on the other side of the tree.*

And then the sound faded, washed on and away.

We stayed inside the fissure until there was nothing but the play of wind and branches. They creaked like old bones.

We squeezed from our hiding place. The trees were empty of life. "Where have they gone?"

Rauf shook his head. Rounding the oak, our boots were the only prints we saw. And then I understood his fear. This was the hunt that men must never see.

"But we are safe, lord."

"From the forest hunters." I would give them no other name. It was unlucky. "Our men. Where are they?"

Rauf shook his head. Blood was on his hauberk, and loss and fury in his eyes.

"Then they will die, Rauf, the ones who did this. I promise you."

"And I will be there."

Easing around the oak, we saw the crossway on the track. Red pools, black mud.

"Where are the bodies?"

Rauf stared. "I do not know."

"Go to Hundredfield. Tell Maugris."

"You will die for nothing."

"Do as we agreed, old friend. The path will be marked."

I took the right-hand fork in the track and did not look back. I snapped the first of many branches for him to find. In time, I heard footsteps as he ran back the way we had come. Then I heard nothing at all.

Notching my belt tighter, I thought about the monk's camp. It could not be far if the villagers had gone there for a feast.

And I thought about Hundredfield's forest. Broad avenues had been cut through the trees in Fulk's time and maintained so that a full hunt, with dogs and servants, could ride out in pursuit of game. To find such a chase might help me find my way deeper through the trees, and I was less likely to get lost. I stepped out cautiously. The leaves of last autumn were melted into earth or skeletons beneath my boots. Yet naked trees brought in more light. I thought this luck.

But I looked up and around, not down, and so my boot found the rabbit hole, not my eyes. And I fell, the air driven from my chest as I ate wet earth.

A branch snapped. And another. Then came the shuffle of feet.

I could only sip air, and that was meager, not enough for breath. Yet I rolled, and I spat. I would not die on my face, dirt in my mouth.

A man's shape blocked the light. He leaned down as I rose up, and something was in his hand.

31

I DREAMED OF the wild hunt, the silver riders with pitiless eyes. I ran from them, but they chased me down. I tried to wake before they took me under the hill.

And I thought I had, for the air now rejoiced in the scent of roasting mutton. And there was not just the smell; my mouth filled up with the taste of it, and I bit down to savor . . . but that was the last, kind, part of the dream. True, the ghost of lamb fat *was* still in the air when I opened my eyes, but the hearth I saw was unlit, and only a pile of ashes remained.

I lay in a windowless hut. Above, stone had been piled up, circle on circle, like a skep woven for bees. I had seen ruins of buildings like this before. The people of Hundredfield had abandoned them for huts of mud and wattle in Fulk's time.

I rolled to my side and levered to my knees. And stood. I was dizzy, and my head—I touched my scalp with bound hands, which came away wet—yes, there was a wound, and a nest of pain. But I could see and I could hear. And if weapons had been taken from me, also boots and armor, stones in the hearth would fit my hands. I was not defenseless.

I walked my cell to find its extent and heard nothing but the scuff of naked feet on earth. Could I burrow beneath the walls?

"Dog!" Stone muffled the shout.

Then came a howl and the slide and clash of steel. And a roar from many voices.

"Mourrez!"

Godefroi! I groped to the door and banged, kicked, yelled.

No one came.

The scream of the crowd grew louder, but louder still was his voice. If he sold his life today, good coin was being paid.

I shook my head to clear it and kicked the door until it splintered.

The howling stopped. Then came groaning and a sound I did not understand.

I kicked the door again, and light bled through the gaps in the planks.

"Stand away." A voice I did not know.

"And if I will not?" Bravado. But they would expect attack now, when the door opened.

"Then you are a dead man."

"What, you will risk another fight?" I forced a laugh.

"You have no weapons."

I did not answer.

The light under the door wavered.

"It takes a long time to starve to death. And you will. Yet we eat well in the forest. Hundredfield's sheep. And deer." The man was taunting me. He had his mouth pressed close to the wood.

"You need me to live."

"Why?"

"Guess."

I heard breathing. Two men, no more. Unless others were standing behind.

"Only the rich have time for games." Another voice. The sneer was too obvious.

I said, "A girl may have come this way with children. She has value to my family; you may profit from that. If I live. There was another woman also. My brother's wife." I did not speak Gode-froi's name.

"If she comes to the forest, she'll be no one's wife." A coarse guffaw. The light withdrew, and at a distance I heard voices but not words; it was a dialogue—one man angrier than the other.

I felt myself settle—that alert silence of the soul before time shatters into violent fragments.

The light returned and the lock bar outside scraped as it was lifted from its keepers.

I had a stone in each hand, and stepping back—one pace, another, a third—my back brushed the wall.

Each sense stretched out in the dark. What did I hear? Breath. What did I smell? Sweat. Perhaps it was mine.

Light cut an edge to a man's shape as he stepped inside. His companion stood close, a torch of pitch pine in one hand; he was taller than the first, and as the flame dipped and flared, it kindled his eyes. I had never seen an angrier face.

Blocking the exit, the first stopped a pace away. "Why did you ask about the girl?"

Behind, the other man moved. An ear had been hacked off, the blood still running. He stared at me, a focused glare.

"I told you. She has value to my family." I leaned back, my shoulders against the stone. If I had to run, the wall would launch me.

"Value? As if she were coin?" The other man waved the torch and agitated shadows fled as a knife flashed in his hand and . . .

. . . his head hit the floor. Winded, he gasped at my feet like a fish. The shorter man had tripped him as he sprang.

I scooped the torch from the floor. Holding it above my head, I stared at the smaller man. "I know you."

"Then you have the advantage." A pleasant tone.

"I am Bayard de Dieudonné. You are Alois, the son of our reeve. You almost killed me once."

Alois stared at me. I could not read his face. Blood was on his clothes.

"I heard the fight."

Lips peeled back from his teeth, like a hound. "Your brother knows how to defend himself, even if you do not."

Knows. Godefroi was not dead.

The earless man stood. Close up, his head seemed butchered. "He did this to me." Gathering phlegm, he went to spit.

"And what did you do to him?"

"Dog!"

Alois wheeled and kicked, a hit to the ribs with his weight behind it. "Enough!" He snatched the knife and shoved the man ahead.

I stepped out into a clearing lit by fire. Flame showed me ranks of men, some I knew. Badly clothed, their faces thin, they clutched well-honed blades in their hands, even billhooks. There were too many to count. They watched as Alois prodded me forward, the sting of the knife in my back.

"Bring the other one."

At first I thought they had a flayed buck, for something like an animal was dragged from the shadows and dumped into the light.

I have seen much in my time, living men hacked open, split, or beheaded, but those were strangers. This was my brother. Snatching the torch from the earless man, I ran to Godefroi, the flame my only weapon.

Kneeling, I cradled my brother's head. Godefroi's blood soaked my jerkin to the skin. He was dying, life escaping from a dozen wounds; night turns red to black, and I could not dam that dark flow.

"Ask me why." Alois was standing at my shoulder.

Godefroi opened his eyes and stared at me; words were not words, only sounds. He had no tongue.

"Ask!"

I stared at Alois. "I will remember each thing that you have done." In the end, a man can only die once.

"Your brother has been tried. And sentenced."

Oh, I should not have laughed.

Godefroi's mouth bubbled blood as Alois kicked him in the back—he could not scream. "Murder." Another kick. "Dispossession." I lunged, but could not deflect the blow. "Rape. Many rapes. My sister among them."

Godefroi's breath rattled as I scrabbled to hold him. His eyes opened, the whites like raw flesh. He tried to move his hand and I grasped it. He sighed and blood puddled in his mouth.

Alois called out, "Now!"

Something moved, flashed in the flame light. When the blade sliced down and wide, iron cut to the spine, and Godefroi's neck yawned open as the earless man jumped back.

And I was hauled away, death-red, howling, and thrown into the hut.

Godefroi's blood dried on my clothes and on my skin, and for the first time I, a man, cried like a child.

32

RORY LEANS back in his chair and rubs his eyes. He's nearly finished transcribing the first Hundredfield tape. Flexing his shoulders, he clicks the spools into action.

"It is dark and cold where I am. Monstrous cold."

He winds back. Replays. *"It is dark and cold where I am. Monstrous cold."*

There it is again.

The voice he's hearing does not sound like Jesse's. The cadence of her speech has altered, and did she really say "monstrous"? He doesn't remember that, but this tape is the only true record he has.

He writes a careful note of what he's heard, and what he thinks she said. Clicks the PLAY button again.

"I do not like this place. It is unhappy. And something lies here. It has the form of a woman but she has the wrong color and she shines! Aaaah. How she shines."

Rory flicks STOP. Jesse definitely said "man" before. He's certain she did.

She has the wrong color.

Who says *has* for *is*? He stares at the spools, utterly perplexed. These are not all Jesse's words; it does not sound like her voice and at least some of the phrases are archaic.

"Remember the movie, this is your movie." Rory jumps at his own voice. He's pressed PLAY without thinking.

Then that other woman, the possible un-Jesse, says, *"Oh, I do not like this."*

"No need to worry, no need to feel anxious. Maybe you'd like to draw what you see?" His voice again; the struggle for calm.

"Yes. That will be easier for me." She seems relieved, almost grateful.

He flicks STOP as his eyes stray to the other side of the table. There are the sketches, the woman's face framed by a wimple.

You aren't a nun, are you?

Here are his notes in an ordered pile, the writing even and legible just as it always is. And the recorder—metal and plastic and chrome, powered by electricity—is man-made. Something that does what it is supposed to do; not something that—what?

Records the voice of an unseen, unknown woman?

That's ridiculous.

So, what does he do now?

Look for the logic, note what is known, highlight what is not.

Very well.

He will go back to the beginning, the very beginning of this case, and search for explanations of the symptoms manifested by his patient. Scientific explanations, not subjective interpretations. That's his job.

Rory pulls the notebook closer and puts the sketch of the woman's face beside it. He begins to write, reviewing what he knows.

Following injury, Jesse displayed the traits of a savant.

Yes. What he said to Alicia is true in his professional judgment.

*Savantism seemed to be expressed in three ways in this case—
if there is no other explanation:*

*First, with a newly developed photographic memory, Jesse
now manifests the ability to call up details from sources—
books, paintings, television programs that she does not
remember—though she denies that as an explanation.*

*Second, she is able to draw objects, faces, and places with
her left hand, and also write, where before she was right-
handed.*

*Third, drawing is a talent she has not previously exhib-
ited (and denies having, saying another "entity" uses her
hand).*

Rory's attention has strayed to the picture of the woman, and
he feels the skin on his forearms pucker. Staring in disbelief, he
watches the hairs stand up like so many bristles. What does his
body know that he does not?

Outside, he hears a car drive up on the gravel. With a crunch
the wheels stop, and the engine is turned off. Rory strides to the
window and looks down. He watches as the driver's door of the
Saab opens, and after a delay, Jesse gets out with no grace at all.

Rory goes to the recorder and switches it off, hurrying out of
the room and downstairs to the great hall.

"Welcome back. How did you find driving?"

Jesse ignores Rory. Marching past, she goes toward the great
staircase.

He calls after her, "I was starting to worry."

She faces him. "Do you know I thought of running away? Just
never coming back. But I'm not going to do that. I'm doing what
I should have done when you first brought me here, Rory. Get on
with my life, and get out of yours."

He says hastily, "You were embarrassed this morning, Jesse. Both of you were. That's my fault. But Alicia sees things differently now."

Jesse misreads his expression. "Don't you dare!"

"What?"

"Try to manipulate me." Jesse stamps off. "I've decided. I'm going to Jedburgh tomorrow. And I'm going to stay there, as I planned."

He raises his voice slightly. "It's true, what I said."

She rattles the door handle. "So?"

"Licia and I talked about this whole situation and I tried to explain." A grimace. "Well, explain what I know. I haven't finished transcribing the tape, by the way." He hesitates. "Would you consider staying just till that's done? There's some stuff you should know about."

"Don't play games, Rory. I did not want to come back, and I do not want to stay at Hundredfield. How else can I make you hear that?" Jesse's exhausted.

His eyes soften. He goes to put a hand on her arm. "Hey. It's okay."

Jesse steps back, says sharply, "It is not."

"Please. Would you at least consider talking with Alicia? I promise you'll feel better if you do."

Jesse stares at him suspiciously. "Where is she?"

"In the kitchen getting dinner. A peace offering."

Jesse says nothing.

"Just you and her. It'll give you both a chance to get to know each other better."

"And where will you be?"

"Bad timing, but I promised to have dinner with Mack and Mum tonight." He changes gear abruptly. "Don't go in the morning." Rory never pleads.

She opens the door without answering and leaves him standing there.

⚭

In the open doorway to her room, Jesse listens as the Saab drives away. Going to Jedburgh, following the lead Fred has given her to the nursing home, that's what's important, what's *really* important, rather than this strange game of cat and mouse and rat she's been suckered into.

Where Rory's the rat. *Am I the cat? Or the mouse? And Alicia?*

Jesse is angry. She has two immediate choices. Go downstairs, eat dinner. Make peace. Leave in the morning.

Or. Don't go down. Stay in the room, write up everything she remembers from today—she's learned that much from Rory— and . . . just leave Hundredfield when she wakes up.

It's a long walk to Newton Prior.

How *much* would Jesse like to kick something! Everything she's facing is difficult. And fraught.

"And I'm really, *really* sick of it!"

She stamps into the room, thinks about slamming the door. And doesn't. But she opens the armoire with unnecessary force, pulls out her case, and slings it onto the bed.

Shirts, jeans, skirts, knickers—not much to show for twenty-five years on this earth—but she strips the first armful off the hangers and starts to fold the clothes. And finds she's staring out the window.

Stars are in the sky tonight, and a discolored ring around the moon. More rain on the way? Poor Alicia.

Angrily, Jesse rips more clothes off the hangers. Why should she care? She's got nothing to do with this woman, nothing to do with this place. Except the craziness.

But if I walk away, I'll never know.

Jesse slumps down on the bed, face in hands. Why does she have to do the hard stuff all the time?

She sits up abruptly. She's not doing that. She's not a victim here.

"That smells nice." Jesse's standing in the open door to the kitchen. She's nervous.

"I never manage to make enough, somehow." Alicia's stirring a large pot on the stove. She doesn't look up. "Everyone loves real tomato sauce." She takes a sip of wine, bangs the spoon on the edge of the pot, and puts the lid back. "Come in. I have a chicken pie in the oven. Drink?" A half-full bottle of wine is on the table. And an empty glass beside it.

"Thanks." Jesse pours.

Neither of them knows how to begin this conversation.

They both speak at once.

"I apologize for being such a cow."

"Alicia, it really was a misunderstanding and—"

An awkward pause.

Alicia nods, *You first*.

"You weren't a cow. Truly. I'd have been suspicious too."

Alicia says stoutly, "Let's just call a spade a spade."

"Can a cow be a spade?" But Jesse swallows a large gulp of wine the wrong way. And splutters. And tries to say, "I don't understand any of it."

Alicia bangs her on the back. "Rory told me that." She sits at the table as Jesse catches her breath. "Look, you're here because of him. And once he explained what happened, and I actually listened, I must say I was curious. This is so mysterious and . . ." Alicia waves an invitation. "Sit. Do."

"You mean it's eerie." Jesse wipes watering eyes as she pulls back a chair.

Alicia looks uncomfortable. "Yes."

They both ignore the book; it's lying on the table between them.

"Let's just say I massively overreacted. Doing a bit much of that at the moment, so I'm sorry. Really. Please stay. I'll be embarrassed if you don't."

"That's very generous."

"But?"

A small smile from Jesse. "*But* it is odd, though, isn't it?"

Alicia says fervently, "No shit, Sherlock." She holds out the bottle.

"Why not?" Jesse offers her glass. *Rory was right.* She does feel better. "Do you mind if I ask you something?"

"Don't know till you do." But said with a grin.

"Hundredfield's so old." Jesse dithers. Comes right out and says, "Is it haunted?"

"If I had a pound for everyone who's ever asked me that . . ." Alicia gets up, opens the oven door cautiously. "Maybe. A monk's supposed to patrol the old chapel in the keep. Appears through a door that's no longer there; not happy, apparently, and seems to be looking for something. I've never seen him, though." She peers into the oven. "Another few minutes."

"You don't believe in that kind of thing?"

"The supernatural?" Alicia shakes her head. "I don't really know. Maybe." A bit of a shrug.

"And there's nothing else strange about Hundredfield?"

"Just a couple of border legends, I suppose. The Wild Hunt runs through these woods. Well, that's what they say."

"The what?"

"The 'folk from under the hill.' They go out hunting, and if they see you, they take you back to live with them forever—because you're mortal and they're not. Said to turn up here at times of great danger. It was Helen who rechristened the pub in Newton Prior the Hunt because it makes such a great story to con—sorry, *tell*—the tourists. The priory monks would roll in their graves." The glint of a smile. "And there's also the Lady of the Forest. She's supposed to be my family's guardian. Said to be a portent of disaster when she turns up, or the opposite. Take your pick."

Alicia waves her hand dismissively. "Some people have the capacity to believe ten impossible things before breakfast. I'm not one of them, though I try sometimes when life is particularly confusing."

"You've never personally seen the Wild Hunt?"

Alicia snorts into her wine. "God, no! I'd be much richer if I had—the papers would lap it up. And I might be able to hunt again myself if I had that story to tell." She sighs. "Horses. Very expensive."

Jesse changes the subject. "Speaking of the pub, can I ask you about Helen?"

"Sure."

Jesse gets that uncomfortable feeling again. Alicia's tone is just slightly cool. "Well . . ." How does she say this? "It's odd, but I got the feeling she disliked me on sight."

"Is Mack nice to you?" Alicia doesn't mention Rory.

Jesse blushes. "He makes me laugh."

"Aha. You *like* him. There's your answer. Very protective of her boys, Helen Brandon. She's got some kind of sixth sense where they're concerned."

"I don't think it's that." *Do I?* "I mean, I've only met him twice."

Alicia shakes her head, pours more wine. "All it takes."

Jesse giggles. "Seriously. She really didn't want me to talk to him. And—" Jesse's thinking of Alistair Nicholls.

Alicia interrupts, "If it makes you feel any better, Helen's never liked me, either. Rory and I were such good friends growing up, and she hated that. Sometimes I think she married the second time just to get away from here. From us." Alicia's face is suddenly intensely lonely.

Jesse gets a glimpse of the self-sufficient little girl Alicia once was, wandering around this vast house all alone. And thinks of herself in Sydney. Not so different. Except for the house. And the family legends. And the crested silver. *Ha!* She murmurs, "Must have been hard." A pause. "Where's Mack's dad? I haven't met him."

"He's in the navy. Away a lot. A nice man, though, just like Mack, really. Big. *Very* big, actually. And dependable somehow." Alicia grins. And switches tack. "By the way, have you heard from your parents since you've been in England?"

"My parents?" For a moment, the word makes no sense. "Oh. My Australian family. No."

Alicia says hastily, "Not my business, of course."

No. It isn't. Jesse says slowly, "It's hard to know what to say about all this."

"Tricky." Alicia swirls the wine in her glass.

"They won't tell me anything about the past, Alicia. Nothing at all." Jesse blinks. The wine's making her too confiding.

"Perhaps it hurts too much to, oh, I don't know, deal with the truth? They must have thought about it, telling you, I mean. I can't imagine the mental torture—for them and for you."

"Torture is right. It's like being racked."

"You know, I'm pretty sure we've got one of those. In the cellars. Hasn't been used for a while, but built to last, I'd say."

Jesse cheers up. "I can think of a few people I'd like to test it on. Rory Brandon for starters."

They both grin.

Alicia chuckles. "Why not?"

33

RORY PUTS his spoon down. "That was really pretty good."

Mack snorts. "Damned with faint praise."

"Just saying. Not everyone knows how to make a crème anglaise."

"I do."

"Bet you got the chef to do it."

"Boys, boys!" Helen's smiling. They're play-sparring for her benefit. She enjoys that.

The three are sitting in the family kitchen of the owner's flat at the back of the Hunt. It's been a good dinner and the atmosphere is mellow.

"It's so lovely we're all together. Doesn't happen often enough."

Rory stifles a yawn. "I do my best, Mum."

Helen passes a bowl of chocolates. "Stay here next time you come. We'd see more of you."

Rory says nothing, passes the chocolates along to Mack.

"It's *orange* dark chocolate, Rory. Your favorite."

"I'll have his." Mack winks at his brother.

Rory murmurs, "What are you, a Labrador?"

Helen's not deflected. "There's a spare bedroom now. Plenty of space."

"You're not living here?" Rory looks at Mack.

"I've bought a house in the village."

"No. Really? Great idea."

Helen chimes in, "You see? You're out of touch with your own family."

Mack nods, unpeels another chocolate. "Have a look while you're here. Lots of work, but I'll enjoy doing that. Dad's letting me use his tools." Mack grins.

Rory whistles. "That's a first." The grin is shared. Mack's dad, an engineer in the navy, is famously protective of his workshop tools. "And thanks for the invitation, Mum."

"You're my son." Helen covers Rory's hand with her own.

"No one else's, so far as I know." A sardonic grin.

Something complex alters Helen's expression. "That's not a very nice thing to say." Her voice is suddenly sharp. "And I know why you don't stay here. It's Alicia. It can't just be that drafty old barn you're staying in."

"Mum." Mack looks at her warningly.

"What if I'm fond of that drafty old barn? Hundredfield still feels like home to me." Rory removes his hand calmly. "Alicia's having a rough time at the moment. Just needs a bit of support."

"So, coffee?" Mack gets up. Goes to the galley kitchen. With a flourish, he flips a cupboard open.

"An espresso machine! That's new. I'll definitely have one."

Mack grins. "Straight up or . . . ?"

"Cappuccino for me, if you can do it."

"You'll have bad dreams, and you won't sleep, Rory."

He grins. "One or the other I'd say, Mum. I think you can trust me to know if I'm going to sleep or not."

The chewing whine of beans being ground interrupts.

Mack shouts, "Sorry." The whine stops.

"So, how's your work going? The Australian girl?"

Rory's certain Helen remembers Jesse's name. "Yes, Jesse Marley."

"I got the impression she wouldn't be here very long."

"Too early to say."

Mack starts frothing the milk.

Rory lifts his voice but he's careful with his words. "When you met Jesse, you seemed a bit offhand, Mum. I didn't say it at the time, but I was embarrassed."

"Was I, really?" Helen's eyes are innocent. "Oh, dear, I am sorry. I do hope she wasn't offended. But we were very busy just then and . . ."

Rory just looks at her.

Helen subsides into silence.

Mack calls out, "By the way, I should have said earlier, I'll be taking a day off tomorrow, Mum."

Helen turns in her chair. "But we've got two bus parties booked for lunch."

Mack comes over to the table, coffees perfectly balanced in one hand. "For you." He puts the first in front of his brother, sits with the other. "It's sorted. Tom'll work the bar and Jewel will do the shift with Rachel."

"I wish you'd told me, Mack."

"Mum, it'll be fine. Tom's reliable, he's worked here often enough. You employ me to manage the place. This is me, managing."

"Yes, but still—"

Rory interrupts, "Something special planned?"

"I'm taking Jesse to Jedburgh."

"That was who called earlier?" Rory's eyebrows are raised.

"Yep." Mack savors the coffee. "Tastes great, don't you think? So much better than instant. Thinking of putting one in the bar. Novelty value for the tourists."

"Won't that be expensive?"

"You sound like Mum." Mack's a patient man, but there's a bit of an edge. "It'll be worth it, trust me."

"Why would that girl want to go to Jedburgh?" Helen interrupts.

"It's a pretty place. I thought *that girl* and I might have a picnic." Mack looks pleased at the thought.

"Jesse was born there. Did you know that?" Rory's staring at his brother.

Mack nods. "She met Fred when she was in town today and he gave her a lead. A nun who might know about her mother; the old lady lives in a nursing home there."

"A nun." Helen's face is expressionless.

Mack looks at Helen. "Yes. She was one of the midwives at Holly House—that's the actual place Jesse was born. There's a chance she might remember something." He says helpfully, "It was a home for unmarried mothers then."

Rory half stands as Helen gets up. "Are you okay?"

"Excuse me, would you?" Helen's pale. "So silly. I feel a little . . ." She leaves the room abruptly.

The brothers stare at one another.

"What was that?"

Mack shakes his head. "I don't know what's going on. She's been like this ever since you turned up."

Rory hesitates. "I'd better stay the night." He stifles a sigh.

Mack's relieved. "Great. That'll get her off my back." He punches Rory's arm. "Useful, sometimes, having a big brother."

34

THE MORNING'S turned humid as Alicia waits on Hundredfield's river flats. Shading her eyes, she tracks the shooting brake as it stops at the edge of a field. A man gets out to take the chain off the gate and Alicia waves.

It's some minutes before he arrives beside her. The door opens and green rubber boots descend, followed by their owner, a large, fit man in his forties, wearing a well-used Barbour coat. Though his face is weathered, eyes of a clear, bright gray smile a moment ahead of his mouth as he strolls forward, hand outstretched. "Lady Alicia. Very good to see you. Keeping well, I trust?"

Alicia grasps the offered hand. "I appreciate this, Mr. Windhover."

"Hugh, please. A preliminary assessment. That's what Allan D'Acre said." Hugh Windhover is curious and hopes he's hiding it.

"Yes. I need some information about Hundredfield's market value."

"You're considering selling the whole of the estate, or only part?"

"A lot depends on what you tell me."

He says easily, "I understand. And everything we speak of will, of course, be confidential."

Alicia nods. "Thank you. So, I thought we might drive around the estate to begin with. Give you a better sense of what we have here."

Hugh Windhover is used to buying and selling country properties for wealthy clients, but even for him this is a rare event. It will be momentous in the north if Alicia Donne sells Hundredfield, and for his business too. He can understand why she might want to, after the death of her parents; hard to run a place like this when you've had no training in estate management. "Your car, or mine?"

Alicia's old Land Rover, liberally spattered with mud, stands in the middle of the field.

"I'll drive." Alicia strides ahead.

Hugh falls in beside her. "London treating you well?"

"Sometimes."

He nods thoughtfully but doesn't push. "Where first?"

"I'll do a circuit of the estate, then take you up to the castle. I wanted you to see this first, however. The river flats are called the Champion Lands on the old estate maps. I like that." She puts the old car in gear and takes a track beside the river.

Hugh stares out through the window. "This is excellent soil, and a ready water supply, of course." He's done his research. He knows that at least half the estate is leased out, but as Alicia drives on, he's surprised by how rich the prime agricultural land really is, and its extent. Then there are Hundredfield's woods, remnant tracts of the great forest that once covered so much of the borderlands. He gestures. "These plantings of oak now; this is all valuable timber."

"My great-great-grandfather went through the woodland systematically, culled and replanted. It hasn't been maintained properly, but . . ."

"It's in pretty good shape I'd say, even after, what, a hundred or so years?" Hugh's calculating. "This is a real asset to the estate, Lady Alicia. You're lucky to have so much woodland intact."

"And we still have some truly ancient trees amongst it. The last of the shipbuilder's oaks were planted in the fourteenth and fifteenth centuries, for instance. They're worth seeing. I can show you, if you like. Won't take long." The track they're driving on branches off into the woods.

"I'd like that." Hugh's enjoying himself. Pleasure doesn't always come with business.

Alicia swings the wheel and they bump onto an uneven surface where pools remain from the recent rain; the track, long unused, narrows into the distance, a tunnel of green dark.

Alicia keeps up a stream of bright chatter as they rattle on. "You know, I don't think I've been here for years and years. Looks quite spooky, doesn't it? So many trees, so little light at this time of year."

"Very *Grimm's Fairy Tales*. But no wicked witches lurking today, I'd say. Or lost children." Hugh understands how tense Alicia is, but he's good at putting clients at ease. Somewhere, thunder mutters. "More rain on the way."

Please, God, no. The drumbeat of worry starts up in Alicia's head as the Land Rover hits a large puddle. "Sorry. Deeper than it looks." She drops to a lower gear and plows on. Canted over at an uncomfortable angle, the driver's side of the car is up to the wheel arches in liquid, and the laboring engine stutters.

"Don't stall!"

The engine coughs, as if clearing its throat, and settles to its normal note—ancient fishing boat.

"Good girl." Alicia pats the dash as if the car were a horse. She selects low range and the wheels grind forward, spitting mud. "Some of these estate roads need work, and—"

The crack, when it comes, is very, very loud.

Alicia stamps on the brakes and when the great branch hits

the track in front, its canopy of leaves covers the car as the horn screams a warning. Too late.

"Alicia?!" Hugh lunges across from his seat to hers.

Slumped over the wheel, the girl stirs. She sits up, wincing, and the horn stops. "That hurt."

"When your head hit the wheel, I thought . . . Well, I didn't want to think that." Hugh's appalled.

Alicia touches the egg growing in the center of her forehead; her fingers come away bloody. "Teach me not to wear a seat belt. I'll be a unicorn soon."

Hugh produces a handkerchief. "You're bleeding. Let me drive?"

Pressing the linen to her head, Alicia starts to say, *No, I'm fine.* And changes her mind. "Would you?"

Hugh hurries around to the driver's side and helps her navigate the wreck of foliage. It's a measure of how strange Alicia feels that the branches seem almost like arms and the twigs like fingers that snag and grab as she moves past.

"Up you go."

Alicia allows Hugh to help her into the passenger side of the car; it's such a comfort to be taken care of.

Settling the girl in the seat, Hugh buckles the belt—with a moment of shy confusion from Alicia as he reaches across her body—before he sprints around to the other side. The branch was a whole lot bigger than he'd thought—they were lucky. He says, "It's mostly leaves on the hood, nothing really serious."

Alicia closes her eyes. She has no idea if he's right.

Hugh pushes the starter button and the engine fires up, the wheels bite, and the car moves backward, smooth and steady, leaving a tangle of broken tree behind. A glance at the pale girl beside him, and Hugh ventures, "I think we should get you home, Lady Alicia. It's easy enough for me to come to Hundredfield again when it suits you."

Home. The word jostles around behind Alicia's eyes; she doesn't want to think about home.

"Shit!" Hugh stamps the brakes down and hauls on the hand brake, slewing the car to the right; he never swears in front of a woman.

Alicia's eyes jolt open as an entire tree falls across the road, a carnage of leaves and shattered living timber. But nothing hits the car.

The two sit in astonished silence. After a moment, Hugh gets out to inspect the damage.

From the safety of the car, Alicia peers out at the trees. They crowd close to the track, a silent army dressed in summer green.

"Hugh!"

He hurries back.

"Did you see?" Alicia winds the window down.

He stares in the direction she's pointing. "What?"

"There was someone." Alicia hesitates.

Hugh's seriously worried. "Have you got a headache? Fuzzy vision?"

She'd laugh, except his concern is so real. "Well, yes, I've got a headache. Bit odd if I didn't have one, wouldn't you say?"

Hugh's relieved she's talking sense. "Best thing you can do is stay here, Lady Alicia. We're not so far from where I parked. I'll go for help."

"No!"

He looks at her, puzzled.

"That is, I'd prefer to come with you. If that's all right?"

"If you're sure?"

"I'm certain." Alicia's never been so sure of anything in her life.

His expression is dubious. "We'll go very gently, then. Tell me if it gets too much."

"Gently. Yes. That would be good."

He helps her down and they set off together, his arm around

her waist, her leaning into his shoulder. "And if we see your friend, we'll ask him for a hand." He's joking.

"Wasn't a he."

"What?"

"I saw a woman."

35

V ERY PRETTY country in the borders. I had no idea."
Gaaaargh! He'll think you're an idiot!
"If you like flooded fields." Mack flips Jesse a
smile.

"The waterbirds do." Meadows slip past on either side, and in dips and gullies small flocks cluster on storm-made ponds. "Those are herons?" Jesse turns back to look over her good shoulder. "And ducks and, oh, so many others I don't know."

"Sedge warblers, hedge buntings, moorhen, grebe." A glance in the rearview mirror. "Pretty, but not good eating."

She grins. "You're just saying that. I can see you in a damp hide with binoculars, the secret twitcher of Newton Prior."

That grin again. "If I twitch, you'll be the first to know."

She laughs. "I love the names, though." The smile fades. It's hard not to feel nervous. And not just because Mack's in touching distance.

The sound of the engine fills the silence, until he says, "Always like this, after a good storm. The world's washed clean."

"That's a lovely way to put it." She hesitates. "I really do want to thank you for giving me a lift, Mack."

He grins. "Again? Not such a hardship, I promise."

And, just when you need to be witty . . . "I know I have, but still . . ."

"Waters run deep?"

"Oh, very funny." But she's laughing. And blushing. She can feel it. *Look out the window!* "She's very nice, apparently, Sister Mary Joseph. Fred told me that. And even if she doesn't remember my mother, maybe she'll know someone who does."

Remember my mother. The words set up an echo in Jesse's head. A terrified almost-child. Alone. Lost. "Do you think she was forced to give me up?"

His glance is compassionate. "A powerful force, family shame. Especially then."

Jesse's says quietly, "She could have come from anywhere, couldn't she?"

"But most likely the country."

"Why do you say that?" Jesse blows her nose. She *will not* give in.

"Well, there's always been a high number of unmarried mothers on both sides of the borders. Especially in the southeast. It's a well-noted anomaly."

She turns to stare at Mack's profile. "How do you know?"

"This has always been a turbulent place, and the wars here forced a certain degree of intermingling. Putting it nicely. Still going on. The intermingling, not the wars, obviously."

Jesse watches the benign, green country flowing past. "History—such a litany of horrors."

"And every inch, every foot, of these pretty fields fought over and sodden with blood."

"Cheerful! Is that what they taught you?"

Mack nods. His eyes brood into the distance.

"Did you go to school at Newton Prior?"

"No fancy gentlemen's boarding academy for this little black duck." Said lightly.

"Did you mind?"

He flashes her a glance. "I am who I am—don't need that toffee glaze so favored by my dear brother, the doctor. My dad is a decent man, but pay in the navy only stretches so far, and we didn't have the pub then. Still, he's been a good father to both of us, though I think I've had the better of it. A dad I can truly claim as mine, I mean. Rory never had that."

The words touch Jesse. *A dad I can truly claim as mine . . .*

"And what about you?"

"School, do you mean?"

He nods. "Australia. So hot and bright and exotic compared with Britain."

"Exotic? Really?" Jesse laughs. "It was just home. Funny."

"What?"

"*Was* home. That's the past tense." She's silent as she thinks about that.

"And?"

"Oh, there's plenty of *and*s, and a fair few *but*s in my upbringing. 'A riddle wrapped in a mystery inside an enigma.' I didn't understand any of it at the time. My parents in Sydney didn't tell me, you see."

"About?"

"This."

Checking for traffic, Mack's slowed down for a crossroads. The black-and-white metal sign says JEDBURGH, 11 MILES. "That you were adopted?"

"In one. Anyway, you asked about school. I went to a small Catholic convent. All girls. They made us write 'Mary, Mother of God, save us' on the top of every page."

"You needed saving?"

"I didn't think so. Then. Got me into lots of trouble."

"And now?"

"I have absolutely no idea."

Jesse stares through the windscreen as the drowned countryside slides past. Soon they'll be in Jedburgh. And then what?

Her stomach grips. What does she say, what does she *ask*?

"Sister?"

The wheelchair is placed in a pool of sun, and the old lady seems peacefully asleep. Pale, soft skin; short, silver hair; nothing says she's a nun except the chain with the cross around her neck.

Julie, the care assistant, nods apologetically. "She likes her nap after lunch, Sister Mary Jo. Most of them do." Julie leans closer, speaks directly into an ear. "Sister, you have visitors."

"I'm not deaf, Julie." One eye opens, then the other. "You know you don't have to shout."

That faded blue gaze is mild, and the words spoken with amusement, but as Sister Mary inspects each of her visitors in turn, *No pushover* floats through Jesse's head.

"Please. Make yourselves comfortable. I'm delighted you've come." The nun waves to a line of armchairs that line the wall of the common room, and Mack helps Jesse drag two of them closer.

Jesse notices details. The nun's fingers are long and square-ended, the nails cut short—they speak of a woman who's worked hard all her life. Jesse leans forward. "It's very nice of you to see us at such short notice."

"My diary is rarely full these days." Said with a twinkle. "Julie, I'm sure my guests will enjoy a cup of tea."

The girl, who is kind if hearty, says loudly, "Certainly, Sister." She winks at Mack as she leaves and murmurs, "Bright as a button. One of our oldest residents too."

Sister Mary sees the wink, and Jesse feels the warmth of a blush. Why does she feel it's her fault the nun was patronized?

"She means well, of course. A lovely girl. Now, I am to understand you are Miss Marley?" The glance from those steady blue eyes probes her visitor with some attention.

"Yes." *Technically, that is.* "And this is my friend."

"Just call me Mack, Sister."

"You're Helen Brandon's son, aren't you? No mistaking that streak in your hair. Please do give your mother my best regards. I remember her well."

"You know her?" Mack looks surprised. Self-conscious, he runs fingers across his scalp.

"Yes, indeed. We met, but many, many years ago." Sister Mary's eyes drift back to Jesse. "How pretty you are, Miss Marley. I have always delighted in beauty. I never listened to that nonsense about partiality being a sin."

Mack grins. "You know, I flat-out didn't notice."

Jesse's not sure what to say. Or where to look.

The nun smiles. "Oh, age has some privileges. I can say what I like now. Evidence of senility, some would say, but I prefer to believe I speak God's truth—wherever it seems safe to do so, and don't try this at home." Her voice has a whimsical lilt.

"What's this about senility?" Julie's back and clanks down a tray. "You, Sister Mary?" That wink again. "We can't have talk like that. Defeatist, I call it." She's shouting again.

The nun's wry expression slips a little, and the blue eyes sharpen considerably. "Just pour the tea, Julie."

Jesse bites her lip and stares out the window as Julie, oblivious, does as she's asked, chattering all the while. "*Such* a lovely day outside, Sister. When your visitors have gone I can take you out for walkies?"

Between an astonished giggle and a flinch, Jesse doesn't dare look at Mack, or he at her.

As the girl finally leaves, Sister Mary exhales. "So very determined to help. Now, where were we, Miss Marley?"

"I met the Reverend Stewart in Newton Prior yesterday, Sister. I was doing some family research and he was so helpful. He suggested I should get in touch with you. And Mack was kind enough to give me a lift."

"Dear Fred. Someone else I haven't seen for years and years. Time just slips away, doesn't it?" Those old eyes are far away.

Mack catches Jesse's attention and smiles.

How much she would like to lean over and hold his hand. Just for strength. "One of the things Fred mentioned was that you worked at Holly House in the fifties?"

"Yes. The order paid for me to train as a nurse, and I specialized, after a time, in midwifery. I was at Holly House for many years."

Jesse lowers her eyes as she's inspected again.

"Did you bring your birth certificate, Miss Marley?"

"Please do call me Jesse. Yes. I thought you might want to see it." With her good hand, the girl fumbles in her shoulder bag, then leans forward with the envelope.

"Perhaps you'd give me my glasses?"

A leather case is on a side table, and when Jesse takes it to Sister Mary, the old lady touches Jesse's fingers.

"I am glad indeed to meet you, Jesse. Did I say that? I often think of the babies, even now. And here you are." Another pat. "Now, what have we here?" The old hand takes the piece of paper—that bland statement of facts that has changed Jesse's life so completely—and smoothes it on her lap.

Jesse wants to speak, wants to say *something*, but the words will not form.

Mack mouths, *Okay?*

She shakes her head. And nods.

Sister Mary looks up sharply. "Eva Green. Eva *Green*." She peers at Jesse's face.

Jesse dives in. "Do you remember her?"

The old woman considers what she holds. "It was such a long time ago. . . ." She stops speaking, and her expression changes; pale becomes white.

Mack gets up quickly. "Sister? Can I get you something?" He looks for a bell.

"I'll find the nurse." Jesse is already at the door.

Sister Mary grasps Mack's sleeve. "No. Please do not." Her eyes return to Jesse. "I am perfectly well."

This time, the girl meets the old woman's gaze as she kneels beside the chair. "Anything, anything at all."

The nun strokes Jesse's hair, as if it is the most natural thing in the world. "After the wedding, it will be your birthday. We're all so looking forward to seeing them get married. Prince and princess. What a lovely present that will be for you."

It seems an oddly inconsequential remark, but Jesse ducks her head. "I always thought my birthday was in October."

"So many necessary lies." Sister Mary's hand drops from the girl's head. "Sometimes, in those days, a child was informally adopted."

"'Informally adopted'? I'm not sure what you mean."

"Among family, for instance. A grandmother would say she was the child's mother. Or an aunt, perhaps. Very often details were changed for the best of reasons. For the child's sake as well as the mother's, so she could start a new life without shame."

"Was that what happened to me, Sister?" Jesse leans forward.

The old lady sighs. "Child, I would like to help you, but . . ." For the first time, Sister Mary Joseph avoids Jesse's eyes.

Jesse swallows. "*But* you do remember her. I can tell."

The old woman's face works. "I . . ."

"Please." It's a whisper.

Mack stretches out a hand and Jesse grips it.

Very deliberately the nun crosses herself, picks up the little crucifix that lies on her chest. "Of all the girls at Holly House I could not have forgotten your mother. Or you." She gathers herself. "Eva came to us very late in her pregnancy." She picks up the cup of tea. Her hand is shaking.

Mack goes to take it from her. "Sister, you're upset and—"

"Sit down, young man." The voice might be faint but the expression is straight down the line.

Mack does as he's told.

The nun sips, puts the cup down. "I did not see who brought her to us that night, Jesse. She was dropped off at our gate and the car drove away. I remember, though, that there was a summer storm and the poor child was drenched after she'd walked up the drive. We took her in, of course. In those days, we turned no one away. We were so convinced that we were doing God's work." Her voice ebbs as her eyes close.

There's silence.

Mack mimes falling asleep.

Sister Mary coughs, and her eyes snap open. "Your mother could not tell us her due date—never unusual with young girls, of course—but we assessed there was little time before the baby—you—would arrive. But Eva was too frail to work in the laundry, and too close to her time, so the doctor advised rest and a room to herself. We agreed to that, though it did cause some resentment; we were always crowded, for we cared for so many girls in those days. Your mother was remarkable, Jesse. Yes. That is the only word." The nun swallows. "So young, but so very pretty. You look like her. Did I say that?"

"I really do?" Jesse's eyes are huge and shining with tears.

The old woman nods. "I was midwife on duty the night you were born. It was a difficult birth for you both, and very long." Remembering, she takes another sip of tea, then another.

Jesse prompts, "You were there, Sister?"

With an effort, the cup is placed neatly back on the saucer. "Oh, yes. I was there. We had a new honorary that night—honorary doctor, that is. Most often we managed without, since babies were our business, but your mother . . ." Sister Mary puts a hand to her eyes. "Please excuse me, child. It is easier to remember the past than the present, and yet sometimes . . ." The troubled voice fades again.

Jesse scrabbles in her bag for a pen and something to write on. "Do you remember the doctor's name?"

There's a hesitation.

"You can't recall?" Jesse sits closer to the chair.

"Some things are best left to rest in peace."

Jesse's eyes widen.

The nun sits straighter and grips Jesse's two hands in her own. "Your mother died, Jesse. Not an hour after you were born."

Mack draws Jesse close, puts an arm around her shoulder. She doesn't feel it. She feels nothing. As they walk through the car park, a clamor grows in Jesse's head. *Never hold, never touch, never hear her voice, never, never.*

Something's howling, it's trapped in her chest, and her whole body drums with holding it in.

She cannot look up, she cannot speak as pain distills from tears she will not cry.

Until she hears the child.

She stops. "Listen."

"To what?"

"A baby." The screams grow louder. "She's terrified." Distraught, Jessie hurries along the lines of parked cars, peering through windows.

"We'll find it." The car park is small—Mack stops, puzzled. "Which direction?" He turns a circle.

"Here. She's in here." Jesse's found a Mercedes, expensive, new-looking. Tears cascading down her face, Jesse hammers the button on the lid of the trunk.

A large, well-dressed man is staring at them, keys in his hand. "Can I help?"

Jesse runs to the stranger. "Oh, thank God, thank God! There's a baby in there." Jesse snatches the keys. She fumbles as she tries to push them in the lock.

"Hey!" If the stranger was astonished, now he's angry.

"Jesse, give the man his keys. Please." Mack tries to take them.

She swats his hands away. "Let me, I just . . ." The key turns, the trunk lid pops open.

Jesse's hand drops to her side. The cavity is empty.

Mack takes the keys from her and gently closes the lid. "There you are." He gives the bunch to the nonplussed owner. "Sorry." Mack takes Jesse's hand to lead her away.

"But I *heard* her." Jesse strains to look back as the Mercedes starts up. She tries to shake herself free. "He's taking her away!"

Jesse's tall, almost as tall as Mack, but he's stronger, and for a moment they're almost wrestling.

The car speeds up as it leaves.

"She's gone." Jesse's voice is piteous. "She's lost. No one will come when she cries."

Mack pulls Jesse close. "It's okay." He smoothes the hair from her face. "No one's lost."

"I am."

"No, Jess, you've been found." He puts an arm around her waist as he unlocks the MG. "Come on. I'll take you home."

36

I T HAUNTED me. To have held Godefroi, to have felt the blow as he died but not to have heard his voice, or offered more comfort than I did—these things scarred my heart.

My brother was selfish and certain of his superiority in this world. Some would see it as God's vengeance that he died at the hands of those he so despised. But it came to this. Flore had married Godefroi, and he had loved her with all his soul. And if that love had brought him death, perhaps, in the end, he did not care because she was lost to him.

But I cared. I, who had never allowed myself the comfort that comes from such love. Each day I breathed, Death walked at my left hand; to have a home and children would have tied me to the life I knew I must one day lose, and I had chosen this path—so far as a younger son has choice of any kind.

But I was a Dieudonné. Alois said my brother had been judged. For what *he* had done to Godefroi, I would judge him. He would know it before we both died. . . .

311

Dawn woke me as it slipped into my prison. Since I had lived to see this day, it seemed God must wish it so. Yet, I had no time to brood on fate as the door was flung open, and the hut filled with men. Hands raised me, arms hauled me, and I was pulled into the light, an animal, fighting, taken from its burrow.

"Here." Alois. I could hear his voice, but a naked foot pinned my head to the earth and I could see nothing.

I yelled, "Bury us together or I will haunt you." That I meant.

"You try to bargain with me?" Alois stood near.

"Find out."

A man knelt beside my feet and I felt the knife at its work. It sawed through the rope binding my ankles.

"I know these tricks, Alois." It was true. The raiders were pitiless—as we were. He would want me to run: practice for his bowmen.

"Get up."

I did not move.

"Get up, Bayard."

I saw his hand in front of my face. He wished me to grasp it.

Perhaps I might not immediately die.

I shuffled to my knees and used his weight as my brace when I stood. Soon, there would be strength. I would need it. I was ringed by men with eyes sharp as blades.

"Yes, look well, Bayard de Dieudonné. These are the people you abandoned. You did not think them worth food or shelter. I do. That is why they have come to me."

Behind the men, women and children were clustered, and in their front rank stood Rosa. I looked away quickly. For the sake of our past, I would not show I knew her. But there were other faces. Ambrose the carpenter was there, and Welyn, the smith from the village whom Godefroi had banished. And beside them was Swinson. An eye was closed over with scars and he had crutches beneath both arms, but he had lived, and like Odin's, the stare from that single eye was implacable.

I did not see Margaretta, or the children.

Alois yelled, "Bring it."

Backed by the sun, a boy walked a horse from among the trees beyond. The stallion whickered when he saw me and danced, though the lad tried to hold him.

But when Helios flung up his head, he was thrown like a doll through the air.

Helios scattered the crowd as he came, magnificent as his namesake. Only a fool challenges a warhorse in such a mood.

Alois was not any kind of fool—he too jumped away.

How clever that horse was. He knew to separate me from those who threatened my life and he did that, forcing his body between me and the fighters.

I know what he expected: into the saddle and gone. But that was not possible, though I snatched the trailing reins and gentled him to a stand.

Avoiding the animal's hooves, I yelled out, "Give me Godefroi."

"Yes."

I stared at Alois. I had lived to be astonished. "You will let us go?"

"What is my name?"

I did not understand.

The man barked, "Tell me!"

The shout unsettled the stallion and he brayed a challenge. Turning the horse in a tight circle, I said, "Your name is Alois."

"More than that."

"You are Edmund Swinson's son."

Alois thrust his face against mine. "Swinson. Named for a keeper of pigs. That is what your family made us. But that is not our name." He stepped back, sweeping his arm wide. "You took this land from my family, but now the wheel is turning, Norman. Soon, I will sit in your fine keep, true lord of Hundredfield, and you will find no refuge in the north. The hand of every man and, yes, every woman will be turned against you." He spoke to the crowd. "And I say, let them see. Let them all see what you and your brothers have become." His followers, so many more than I had seen last night, stamped and roared.

Them. Bootless, weaponless, he would send me back with my brother's body. A crude demonstration of power.

"I was born at Hundredfield, Alois, as were my brothers. My father, and my father's father before us. We are not Normans." The tumult died as the crowd listened.

"What are you, then? None of our kind. Your day is done." Alois waved a hand, and with no more respect than for a sack of turnips, Godefroi's headless body was dragged to where I stood. It was naked. A bloody sack was flung at my feet. I did not look inside.

Stay and fight?

To challenge this man meant I would instantly die and two of the three Dieudonné brothers would be raven food. Maugris could not hold Hundredfield alone.

I bent to pick my brother up as our former serfs watched; no hand was offered as I struggled. It was hard. I made myself see the corpse as a slaughtered buck and not a man, not Godefroi.

Helios was trained to blood and did not flinch as I slung the body over the saddlebow. It was stiff as wood, but the seat was built for a man in full armor; I could sit behind Godefroi if I held him hard against my chest.

"Rope." Alois was instantly obeyed and a coil was passed under the stallion's belly to bind my brother's hands to his feet. My captor beckoned the boy who had tried to lead Helios. Alois pointed. "Cover his eyes."

One last sacrifice of pride. A rag was tied so that I could not see and rough hands pushed me up to the stallion's back. The sack with Godefroi's head was looped to my belt. It would bounce against my thigh.

A shout from Alois: "Wait!"

The stallion snorted. He was offended by the tone.

"What is the name of the girl you seek?"

"Margaretta."

The crowd muttered.

Alois raised his voice. "The children are your brother's get on my sister's body. It is good they are not here."

"A fine thing for a man to kill his own nephew." *But Maugris would have killed our niece.* "But the girl is the daughter of my brother's wife. Your sister cares for her."

"His wife?" Alois laughed, others did also. "This mess of carrion thought he had a wife? We know better. She was never wife to him." Alois held up his hand. The laughter stopped. "My father suffered and should have died, but my sister remained when he was thrown out from Hundredfield's gates. She has chosen your kind, Norman. Your family. She will die as you will. Tell her this."

"And yet God is compassionate. You were a monk, Alois. He forgives, why not you? None of this is Margaretta's fault."

"Not my God. He takes an eye for an eye; he does not forgive. You have whistled your fate like a dog, Norman, and it has come to rip you apart."

I heard Alois slap Helios on the rump, and the horse leapt forward. I fought to hold my seat and my brother's corpse. I would not think of what bounced at my knee.

The ride was bitter and bootless; my feet ceased to feel as the day grew colder. Helios stopped at last, and the rag was pulled from my eyes. In the fading day I saw we had come to a clearing in the trees—not one I knew. "I thank you."

The boy, sawing at the ropes binding my hands, spat in my face, and, booting his horse, cantered away into the dim, cold quiet of the forest.

I was alone with my brother's corpse. Death had not shocked me for years, yet this husk was a pitiable thing.

I thought of Godefroi's nameless daughter. She would never

know her father. If we lived, and she lived, Maugris and I must tell her what kind of man he had been. What would we say? In the end, the tears of a woman never disgrace the dead. It is a different matter for a man.

Like a slap, a cold gust stung my face. This was the second day since the fight at the crossroads. Did Maugris know of the attack now, or had Rauf been surprised as I had been and murdered?

Helios whickered and I patted his neck. A stream bolted down a hillside close by. Follow the water and I might find the river that ran past Hundredfield, but we must both drink first, the horse particularly, though he had carried the living and the dead all day without complaint.

It was hard to dismount and not treat Godefroi's corpse with disrespect, though Helios stood quiet as I clambered down. I led him forward and found a place where the stream had cut a basin in a sheet of rock. I bent, scooping water into my mouth, as the horse waded farther into the flow, though the water was no warmer than ice.

Watching the horse drink in great shudders, I knew I must ease his double burden. As long as my feet allowed it, I would lead him; a dead man was enough to carry. Gathering the reins, I coaxed the stallion from the stream and walked him down the hill, brooding on what was to come.

I did not see Helios falter; I felt it, for my arm was wrenched so suddenly, I dropped the reins—and almost lost the contest to regain them. The horse was terrified, blowing and stamping, tossing his head at something I could not see.

"All is well, all is well."

Gently, gently, I pulled him close. And saw the light he had seen. It shone from among the trees. My heart rose. Perhaps there was a hut.

"There, you see, nothing to be frightened of."

But what had seemed fixed began to move and took on form—a glimmering column.

Snorting, backing, Helios tried to tear the reins from my hands. Then he stopped. And snuffed the air.

Faint and far away, a song began. There were no words, but I had heard it before, and as it grew louder, and the light flared bright, both found me where I stood; and the song and the light became one.

It was a knife of air and sound in my chest. I could not breathe. *Bayard.*

I tried to gasp her name in reply. It must be her. But as that blade sliced my soul, I was offered a choice. And a task. And another chance.

My heart was undefended as I opened my arms.

"Yes." The word rolled from my mouth. Like a rising river, it washed out between the trees until all other sound died in the forest. And the light showed the glint of water in the valley below. Then it blinked out. As if it had never been.

With shaking fingers, I felt my chest. There was no blood, and no wound.

Helios brayed. And was answered.

Men were riding up from the river. I saw their torches, I heard them calling my name, and Rauf rode out in front. He had survived.

"Eat."

A trestle was set under a window in Godefroi's room. On it was bread and fresh cheese, and a jug.

My head jangled. Returned to the keep, how could I say what I had seen in the forest? "I am thirsty."

Maugris strode to the board. He poured a goblet of ale and I drank what he offered in two swallows, held it out again.

"I need you sober."

Too weak to stand, I shook the empty goblet.

He hesitated, but went back for the jug and the food.

Snatching the cheese and the bread, I ate and drank with both my hands.

"What happened?"

I mumbled, "Swinsons owned these lands. I did not know."

Maugris snorted. "Before Fulk's time." His glance narrowed as he poured more beer. "Who remembers such things?"

"Alois does. He wants Hundredfield back."

Maugris hunched closer to the brazier. "What happened to you?" His look was evasive.

"I was taken and brought to his camp. There were faces I knew, Maugris, far too many. His men killed Godefroi. And almost killed me." I ate like a wolf. Better to eat than remember, or I would never forget.

My brother's face twisted. "Then they shall be crushed."

"Godefroi already tried. You see how effective that was." I rubbed my eyes. I was weary.

"You called them a rabble, Bayard. You said—"

"They are not a rabble now. They are strong, and they are disciplined. And they all saw Godefroi die. His death has given them hope." I crammed the last of the bread in my mouth.

Maugris paced. He said nothing.

"The defenses of this place—"

He flared. "I have not been idle."

"And?"

"We must bury Godefroi." Maugris had that stubborn set to his face. *It is not for you to question me.*

I sighed. "Margaretta and the children. I did not find them."

"That much is obvious."

"What have you told the household?"

"Nothing. They mutter amongst themselves, but none in the castle knows they are missing. Robert has said the children are sick and that Margaretta is nursing them. None but he or I have been in this room since you left, though he brings food, as if to feed them. And the door is kept locked."

I nodded. Maugris had done what I would have done. "But we must find them." I would not speak of the wordless promise I had made.

My brother hesitated. "This keep has never been taken."

I held my hands over the lighted brazier. They were still cold. "It may be better we bring the fight to them. They will not expect that. Did the rider go to Alnwick?"

"Days ago. The Percys will never allow the fall of Hundredfield."

I hoped he was right, but the loyalty of the great marcher lords was always hostage to greed; some would happily watch as our family was destroyed. I thought of the battlefield ravens. Were we to be carrion—our estates dismembered by those who survived the end of the Dieudonné?

You have a choice.

Maugris looked at me curiously as I rubbed my chest. "You are wounded?"

I shook my head.

Two alive, one dead, we three, the brothers Dieudonné, were assembled in the chapel by candlelight. Such a gathering would never again happen in this life.

Our brother's bier lay at the foot of the altar steps just as Flore's had done. More tiles had been torn up and stacked to one side of a deep hole next to the false grave.

Robert's wife had laid out Godefroi's corpse with care. It was decent and clean of all blood.

Maugris murmured, "It is good he was covered as you brought him home."

"You should thank Rauf." I had not had to ask. As we approached the bridge Rauf had stopped to wrap Godefroi's corpse in his riding cloak so that those who remained at the keep would not see what he had become in death.

My brother crossed himself. "I am grateful to Rauf for his service to Godefroi. In our brother's name he shall be rewarded when this is over." He bowed to the corpse.

"Therefore, let it be done." I echoed the gesture formally.

In full armor beneath a white tunic, Godefroi lay on the same door that had carried his wife so few days ago. Maugris had given his chain-mail coif to disguise the severing of the head, but nothing could hide the bruises and the cuts on our brother's face. These wrote the story of that final melee, and the journey he and I had made together; they would go with him into the earth.

Wearing Maugris's second-best sword and a good pair of boots, I stood beside my living brother. He had provided both since my own had been taken by the raiders.

I was not sentimental about weapons—they are often lost in war—but my old blade had served me well; perhaps I had begun to think it was lucky since I had used it for so long and survived. It was gone now. That was a lesson. A sword is just a sword. Life, so long as it lasted, was true luck.

Maugris murmured, "The priest has made no problem with the mass tomorrow. Godefroi was a Christian, at least."

"You did not send Simeon back to the priory?"

"No." My brother had always been pragmatic. He must have thought more bodies would be buried.

Maugris crossed himself again and knelt.

I joined him. And the night's long vigil began.

In his black vestments, Simeon sang the mass of the dead in a resonant, untroubled voice. He cannot have sensed the mood of the small congregation in the chapel.

I did. Those few men and women listened in silence and made the correct responses, but none sobbed for Godefroi, not even for show. They thought the unthinkable: the Dieudonné would soon be gone, dead or fled. Godefroi, in his coffin, was the symbol of that fate and our fall.

Maugris's expression was grim. When the last of the prayers were done, the homily delivered, and the congregation censed, Rauf and three of our fighters joined us brothers to lower the coffin into the grave.

At the conclusion of the mass, we two stood with the priest and watched as the grave was filled in.

I lingered after the others had left and knelt by the altar rail. "The priory shall pray for your soul, Godefroi. I shall see it done."

I hoped hell was not real, I hoped Godefroi was not there, but if he was, remedies existed; for generations the Dieudonné had paid good coin for all our family to be prayed for.

I crossed my chest and stood.

And heard.

A voice, a lone voice, singing.

Within the stone of the chapel walls.

37

I SHOULD STAY. At least until the doctor comes."

"I'm fine. Really. It just looks dramatic."

Hugh Windhover's standing beside his car outside the New Range. "Lady Alicia—"

"Alicia. Please." A grimace. "Thank God you were driving. If it had been me . . ." She shakes her head.

Hugh brushes the compliment away. "Let me make tea for you at least, or a sandwich?"

The thought of food brings vomit to Alicia's throat, and she so does *not* want Rory to see this man. "You're very kind. But I should clean this up and rest."

"Of course." Hugh's a gentleman. He won't press her. "But may I ring in a few hours? Just to know you're all right?"

"I'd like that." Alicia is surprised. She means it. "Good-bye. And thank you again, Hugh." She holds out her hand and he grasps it as if it were very, very delicate.

If she'd been feeling better, she might have laughed.

Then he's gone.

Alicia has held herself together well. Inside, after she closes the great front door, she leans her weight against it. She's back in the forest. The first tree's falling. And the next. Branches and twigs and leaves entomb and smother and—

"No!" Alicia folds into a chair beside the suit of armor. Hugs herself, rocking. She will *not* let herself see that figure walking among the trees. That woman. Light was all around her. But from where?

Wheels crunch on the gravel outside.

Alicia labors to her feet. *Please, God. Don't let it be Hugh. Please.*

The front door opens. "Sorry. Got caught up. Mum needed me. Hope you didn't wait up." Rory sees Alicia. And runs.

She's sobbing, and trying not to. Great gusts of breath come and go. Each one hurts.

Rory doesn't ask questions. He picks her up.

"I'm too heavy, you'll . . ." Alicia's voice wobbles.

"Shush."

There are real muscles in those arms, and though she's tall, Alicia's slight; that helps, though down and around those treacherous stairs to the kitchen is testing. Panting, Rory puts her in a chair. "Stay."

As he sprints off, Alicia calls out, "Take your time. Not going anywhere." She's feeling less shaky. A bit.

"So, describe how you're feeling." Rory's returned with the first-aid kit from the buttery. He's begun to clean her face with a dressing.

"Physical or mental?"

"Physical. I'm looking for symptoms."

"I keep getting flashbacks. And I feel like being sick."

Rory picks up a flashlight without fuss. "Just going to shine this in your eyes. Right one first. Okay?"

She manages to nod, and he puts a hand over her left eye. It's cool, and firm. And comforting. He flicks the flashlight on. "Good. That's good. Swapping my hand now." He's careful and thorough. When he puts the flashlight down, he says, "Not concussion. More likely shock. What happened?"

The shakes hit her like an outside force. "There was an accident."

"Was Hugh Windhover involved? I saw him drive past just now."

Alicia swallows. "He was very nice. In fact, if he hadn't been driving . . ." She stops.

Rory applies arnica cream to a dressing. "You'll have a nice black eye by tomorrow. Maybe two." He puts the dressing over the lump on her forehead. "Where were you two off to?"

Silence.

"I know he's an estate agent, Alicia."

"It's not a state secret." Anger sparks up, just controlled.

As if the case were settled, he says, "You're here because of your ancestors. Because of all that they did. You're the latest chapter of this particular story, and there'll be another yet to come—your children, for instance. You cannot sell Hundredfield."

Children. "This is ridiculous! Yes, there'll be a next chapter at Hundredfield, but I won't be in it—someone else will. And the Donnes will be gone at last. Some would say that's a good thing and long overdue."

Rory can be as stubborn as she. "You need to make this work, Alicia. It's your duty. There. Said it."

She stares at him, astonished. "That's just, that's . . . rude! Some girl hits her head and you get all these ideas? It's stupid, it's *more* than stupid, it's, it's . . ." Alicia sputters like a kettle, brick red with fury.

"Jesse is not *some girl.* Out of all the doctors in London, *I* see the drawings, and I know what they are because I'm linked to this place. *You* set that up, Alicia. You could have just called 999, but, no, you came and hauled me out of choir practice. If she'd been treated by someone else, none of this would have happened." He hesitates. "This is not random. It can't be. Scientist or not, I've never felt so certain of anything in my life. Yes, we're standing on the edge here, but we don't have to jump off."

Alicia snaps, "We? *I* don't have a choice, end of story. Stop bugging me on this."

He will not let go. "There's always a choice. You stopped your dad selling and—"

"Yes, then he died." Like a child, Alicia claps her hands over her ears.

"You have to hear this. Your father—it wasn't just about selling the land."

"What?" Rage and fear make Alicia formidable.

Rory backs up. "It's true. I was back late because Mum was talking about Hundredfield this morning. Your dad just wanted to clean the place out and walk away; everything was to go, the state furniture, the armor. . . . Never mind the land, he wanted to sell anything that wasn't nailed down. *You* were meant to have this place because you fought him for it."

Alicia's face has gone from red to white. "I will not have my family gossiped about in the village. Your mother has always hated me. I don't know why and I don't care, but if this goes on, I'll—"

Exasperated, Rory shouts, "I said she was talking rubbish. I *defended* your family, Alicia."

They stare at each other. They're standing close.

"So, are you going to tell me what Hugh said?"

She moves away fractionally. "I asked for a preliminary valuation, but we didn't get that far. The trees got in the way."

"Trees?"

"The accident—accidents. I had the strangest feeling when it happened."

"Go on."

She half laughs. "I think they're on your side."

"What?"

"The trees, Hundredfield. I really felt as if the place were turning on me." Alicia touches the bump on her forehead with trembling fingers. "Oh, this is all just mad. Why does no one want me to sell?"

"Hugh does. He'd make a nice fat commission." There's no antagonism this time, just fact. Rory sounds so sad.

"I'm exploring options. That's all I'm doing. I have to." But her voice breaks.

"You're stressed, Licia. Pardon the cliché, but you just can't see the wood for the trees." He holds out his arms.

"Oh . . ." She surrenders, sobs into his shirt.

He holds her at a slight distance. After a minute, he murmurs, "Careful. Good cotton, this. It'll shrink."

"Sorry." Alicia stands back, head buzzing, nose running.

He offers his handkerchief.

Crying does not suit Alicia. Her eyes have swollen to slits and her face is a shade of hectic scarlet. "I must look dreadful." She blows her nose, a painfully loud sound.

Rory conquers a wince. "Not at all." He looks at his watch. "You know what? Time for lunch. And before you say you're not hungry, think of my feelings. I *can* actually make a sandwich without poisoning people." He holds out a hand.

Alicia is overwhelmed. "You're lovely. Have I ever told you that? Really, really lovely." She cups his face in her hands.

The yearning in Alicia's eyes is a shock. There've been clues for years, but Rory's ignored them all. He's her friend, they're *best* friends. You don't fall in love with your best friend.

The silence is brief but it's enough.

Alicia shrinks, shrinks into herself. She'd enjoy dying right now, if that were an option.

Rory pretends not to see her distress. "Come on. Not so bad. You're just feeling the effects of shock. You'll be right by tomorrow."

But the shock isn't physical anymore. Alicia steps back. "Of course. Yes, you're quite right."

"Did Jesse . . ." Rory hesitates. "I know Mack took her to Jedburgh. Is she coming back?"

Alicia does her best to meet his eyes. "I don't know. I guess we'll have to wait and see."

Jesse says nothing as they drive from the car park of the care home. Huddled like a child, she leans against the window and seems to sleep.

Mack lets her be. He's driving fast but with great concentration; they can't get back to Hundredfield too quickly, that's what he thinks.

But he looks at Jesse from time to time. If she is asleep, it's bad dreams she's having. Her face is clenched tight.

Mack tries to imagine himself into her mind, into what she's just experienced. Is it possible to feel, really feel, someone else's anguish? He would have said no, once. Now he just wants to see her smile again.

"Stop. Please stop."

Rattled, Mack almost swerves off the road but does as he's asked, steering his old MG onto the shoulder and cutting the engine. They sit in the ticking silence. Woods crowd close, and the deep canopy of summer dims the light to green shot through with gold.

Jesse asks politely, "Do you mind if I get out?"

"No. Of course." He goes to open his door; he'll sprint around and open hers.

But the girl climbs out by herself. "I won't be long."

"Really, you're fine." Mack leans across to pull her door closed. "We're not far from Hundredfield now."

Sometimes Mack wishes he hadn't given up smoking. Usually he has a big man's confidence around girls, but Jesse's different, so different she might actually be crazy. Her behavior in Jedburgh . . . How does he feel about that?

Common sense kicks in. Jesse's not insane, she's just shocked and desperately unhappy—with good reason; and that sadness, in its own way, is attractive. Mack's surprised by his need to comfort her. Not his usual response.

His fingers drum on the steering wheel. He's feeling anxious. For her. He gets out, looks at his watch. Five minutes yet? He's pacing, up and back the length of the car, kicking the tires.

What did his mother say about Jesse last night? A bird of passage. Not those words, but that's what she meant. Mack stops pacing.

He stares at the woods, in the direction Jesse went.

He doesn't want this girl to go anywhere. And if Helen isn't pleased, that's too bad.

Mack stubs that mental cigarette on the ground and sets off to find Jesse Marley. He doesn't want her to get lost.

There's water close by. Jesse hears it as she sloshes along a muddy path. Her canvas shoes are starting to leak, but she doesn't care; she needs time to think. Alone.

She plays the day like a film in her head, seeing it from every angle.

The face of the old nun, her eyes, the way her mouth moved when she said, "Your mother died, Jesse."

She died. Jesse flinches.

And the car park.

There *had* been a child, she *had* heard those desperate sobs, though neither Mack nor the man in the car park had.

Rory will offer explanations, if she ever tells him. She can hear him, hear what he'll say. Eva's death makes the child a symbol of her own loss, her own abandonment. Jung would have loved it too. But that *wasn't* what happened.

Jesse walks on. Ahead, the trees are less dense and the water rush is louder. It lulls her, softens the grip of anguish. A few steps more and she's standing on a riverbank. Close up, the roar of the water blocks anything else, even thought; it's almost a voice.

Jesse stares around. Dragonflies flit and dart, and a waterbird paddles among reeds in an inlet carved out of the bank. It's strange to find such a large, still pool beside a river in full spate. It's perfect somehow, the calm water and the trees, the sun glancing and bouncing off the surface of the pond.

What is it about this place?

It feels, it seems—what? *Like coming home.*

She walks to the edge of the pool and kneels. The breeze dies and the surface settles to a perfect reflection of the sky, but in the green depths, something moves. She leans closer.

The roar of water enters Jesse's head.

And in that chaos of sound, someone is calling her.

Jesse, here I am.

A woman's face is beneath the water. The eyes, pale green, pale blue, hold Jesse. *Are those jewels? Is this real?*

Hair floats and twines—an amber cloud moving like something alive.

The woman smiles. She's deeper, drifting deeper, holding up her hands.

Jesse's lying on the bank. She's reaching down, falling down, sliding into the green.

Arms enfold her tenderly, and she rests against the woman's shoulder as they float together through the green-glass world.

The bottom is a long way below, a long way, but Jesse can see it. And she can see what she has to do.

It's there among the weeds. She has to pick it up.

"Jesse!"

Her body rocked and buffeted, Jesse opens her mouth to protest.

The woman is gone.

No!

But Mack grasps her hand, an arm clamped around her chest. He churns up, up, as Jesse flails, silver bubbles streaming from her mouth.

Don't drop it, don't . . .

Urgency fades.

It's no longer important to struggle.

There's no point.

No point at all.

On the bank, Mack clicks to automatic.

No airway obstructions and *flip*.

Jesse's on her back.

Air.

Nostrils pinched, his breath in her mouth.

One, two, three, four.

Compress.

Hand heels against her sternum, full weight behind each push.

One, two, three, four.

Nothing.

Same again.

Air. Compress. Air. Compress. Air. Compress.

"Come *on*!" To himself, to Jesse.

Pale as old spaghetti, just as limp, Jesse opens her eyes. Her face is defenseless, newborn.

Mack sits panting. It's ridiculous and shocking but he's laughing, shaking his head as he reaches for her hand.

"Welcome back."

Jesse can nod, that's all.

His jacket lies on the grass, and he covers as much of her body as he can. "There's a rug in the car."

From somewhere, he finds the will to stand and then to run.

And return.

Kneeling beside Jesse, when she stares at him, it's as if Mack's never been *seen*, never been looked *at*, before this moment. And in her face such loss, such confusion, he wants to cry.

"Got two. Come on. That's it." Mack's babbling, helps her to sit up, pulls the picnic rug around her shoulders, and dumps the smelly, old dog-rug on top.

She says faintly, "Wet Labrador. Lovely."

Jesse's hair is all over her face. Mack drags it out of her eyes.

"Second time today, Mack. Careful." She can hardly speak for shaking.

"What?"

"You're holding me up again."

"I'll carry you."

"You'll do your back in." Not much of a joke.

"I don't think so. Good practice. Training starts soon." Mack's making conversation as he puts an arm under Jesse's knees and slings the other around her back.

The muscles remember when he scoops her up—all these years of rugby—and he starts the walk to the car; it's easier than he thought.

He hitches her higher, finds a rhythm, as Jesse leans into his shoulder.

The sound of the river recedes and all he hears is her breath. And his.

Jesse slowly closes her eyes. She's cold and she wants to curl up and never wake again. But something's digging into her chest and she remembers—and is glad. She still has it. It's wedged inside the sling. . . .

38

THE ESTATE office is a mess. Alicia knows it is, but she's not about to start tidying now—she'd be at it for days and days. *And*, she absolutely does not want to breathe in all those mold spores and dust. She's got enough problems.

It's impossible not to replay that moment. Rory's shock when she put her hands on his face. His expression. The gentle way he took her hands away and—

Stop!

Alicia will *not* let herself go there. She might feel sick, and she might feel like crying, but she cannot avoid what must be done right here, right now.

She slumps into a chair. Leather-bound account books stare at her—one for each month of the year, for every year—and they're all around the walls, neatly labeled in a number of different hands. From where she's sitting at her father's old desk, she can see the accounts from more than a hundred years.

Too much information! And the problem is, she knows it's all useless. She's been through this lot too many times.

But you might have missed something.

Alicia pulls the pile from the last five years closer.

Go on! She opens the ledger for the previous year. Flipping through the pages, her hand touches the word *December.* The month before her father died.

Here it is, all neatly written down.

The debits (too many), the credits (too few), the bottom line.

The bottom line. Disastrous.

Alicia sits back. She knows this story so well, all the mistakes her father made. Leasing the land and trying to keep up with repairs from the money that came in; not enough, never nearly enough.

She closes the ledger with a snap, gets up, goes looking.

That's where she put it. Alicia picks up a brochure and folds it out. She remembers why she hid it. She'd been so horrified she'd actually rung—actually had a conversation with the National Trust about gifting Hundredfield—that she'd put it "away" so she wouldn't have to see it again.

But there it is, wedged into one of the bookshelves between *Husbandry for the Practical Farmer* and the classic *Herbal Handbook for Farm and Stable.*

A car's crossing the bridge as she picks up the phone. It's Mack; Alicia knows the sound of the old MG. That must mean Jesse's coming back. Is that a good thing?

"Hello? . . . Thank you. Lady Alicia Donne here." She so rarely uses her title, but it's useful sometimes. "Yes, I'd like to speak to"—she peers at the brochure—"Dr. Elizabeth Humboldt, if I can? She might remember me. We spoke a few weeks ago and she sent me some information. . . . Yes, I'll wait."

Unseeing, Alicia stares out the window. It's a beautiful day now. The rain's held off at least.

"Dr. Humboldt, hello. . . . Yes, Alicia Donne. You do remember? . . . Excellent." Alicia sits down at the desk, spreads out the brochure. "Sorry not to have been in touch, things got busy. . . . Yes. You know how it is."

"What were you thinking?" Rory, furious, skewers Mack with a glance.

Mack's walking Jesse slowly into the great hall. Their clothes drip on the tiles. She's shivering. He says quietly, "This was all I had." He pulls the rug more tightly around Jesse. He's slung his jacket over her shoulders as well.

"Look at her. Jesus!" Rory hurries to a ground-floor bathroom.

"It's okay, Jesse. You'll be warm soon."

The girl sits gratefully with Mack's help. Unselfconsciously she leans into his shoulder and closes her eyes. She's so tired. Just wants to sleep.

Rory's back. He's got a bundle of towels, throws a couple to Mack. "I'll put these around you, Jesse, then we'll get you into a hot bath."

She nods, white-faced.

Rory strips off the jacket and the sodden rug. He hesitates. "What happened?"

Holding the girl, Mack just shakes his head. "Later."

"What do you mean, later?"

"Just what I said." Mack's tone is even.

Alicia's head appears around the estate-office door. Her eyes widen.

Rory takes control. "Can you run a bath for Jesse, please? A hot one?"

"Of course." Alicia hurries to the great staircase. "Bring her up." Her eyes are red. The others don't notice.

One on either side, the brothers help Jesse stand. Mack says gently, "Take your time. Absolutely no hurry at all."

Rory picks up on the tenderness. His expression changes. "That's right, Jesse. One foot after the other, that's all you need to do."

When they get Jesse upstairs, Mack can't help staring at Alicia. "What happened to you?"

Alicia ducks her head. "Bring Jesse into the bathroom, please. I'll take it from there."

"Are you sure? I can help."

"I'm certain, Mack." It takes real effort, but Alicia's back to cool as she shuts them outside.

Rory calls out, "Jesse should have some hot sweet tea. I'll bring it up."

The room has filled with steam when Alicia turns off the taps. "Let's get you in. Why don't I help with your clothes?"

Jesse's sitting on a stool beside the bath. Her expression is drained, her eyes blank. "I'm so sorry, Alicia. That's all I ever seem to say."

Alicia strips off the towels. "Top next. Left arm first."

Like a child, Jesse does as she's told as Alicia pulls the sleeve down and extracts her arm. "Sling side next."

Jesse's too tired to express an opinion. All of this feels like some complicated dream. Another one.

"Here we go." But the busy hands stop.

Jesse remembers what's next to her chest inside the sling.

Water spurts into the kettle from the tap. "What was Jesse like before the accident?" Rory takes it to the Aga. His face is drawn.

Mack says nothing. He's wearing a pair of Rory's jeans and a shirt. The shirt, in particular, strains across the chest and shoulders.

"Mack, we have to talk. I'm trying to find out if Jesse tried to kill herself."

Mack opens his mouth. And closes it again. "I don't know."

"You're lying."

Mack flares. "She was upset." Folding his arms, he leans back on the sink.

Rory get mugs from the cabinet. "After you went to Jedburgh?"

A reluctant nod.

"What caused that?"

"You should ask Jesse." Mack's mouth is clamped in a stubborn line.

The mugs bang down on the table. "Help me, Mack. Please." Rory's eyes are haunted. The tension amps down a bit. "Look, head injuries are tricky; maybe I've misjudged Jesse's situation." The kettle's starting to burble and spit. Rory takes it off the hob.

"Meaning?"

"Jesse may be more unstable, or fragile, than I thought." Rory makes the tea. His movements are jerky. *He* brought Jesse to Hundredfield. If the stress of confronting something she does not understand has primed her for a breakdown and a nearly successful suicide attempt, that's his responsibility. "Can you get a tray?" He takes milk from the fridge, pours it into a jug.

"You're slopping it." Mack swabs around Rory, pulls a tray from a cupboard near the sink. "You're asking me about Jesse's own very, very personal business. That's a conversation you should have with her."

Rory carries the mugs to the tray. Puts them down carefully. "She might try again. Would-be suicides often do." He's trying not to sensationalize.

That stops Mack.

There's a pause, and Rory says, "So, can you describe exactly what happened? Please, Mack. Try not to leave anything out."

Mack sits on a sharp response. "I was at the car—beside the road, where we'd parked—and when she didn't come back, I started to worry."

"Did you think it odd she wanted to go for a walk?"

"She might have needed to find a tree, and . . ."

"That aside, was there any other reason that—"

Mack prickles. "What do you mean '*that* aside'? It's a normal thing to do." He fields Rory's glance. "Okay. Yes, I was concerned about . . . about how Jesse was feeling."

"Why?"

Mack pauses. "She'd had a shock."

"At Jedburgh?"

A nod. "Jesse found out—ah—some aspects, shall we say, of her actual birth."

"And?"

"Not good." Mack shakes his head with feeling. "And then, when we left, well, she had hallucinations. Vivid, three-D, the full catastrophe: sound and fury and I don't know what else. And she spun right out. I persuaded her to get in the car because— honestly?—I thought she'd be better off at Hundredfield. Her suitcase is still in the trunk, by the way. When I picked her up this morning, she said she thought it was time to move on. Something about overstaying her welcome."

Rory absorbs that. "But you still thought she should talk to me?"

Mack hesitates. "Yes."

"Go on."

"I couldn't see her when I got to the river. And I just had a feel- ing, you know? So I looked over the bank into the pool, and there she was, under the water." Mack swallows. "You think people drown facedown, but Jesse was looking up. Her expression was really peaceful. Happy." Mack rubs his eyes vigorously. "I thought she was already dead. The rest you know. CPR, she revived, and I brought her back. I have no idea how long she'd really been under there."

Rory says absently, "She's a lucky girl."

"You said you don't believe in luck."

"Just a turn of phrase." Rory hands Mack the tray.

Propped on pillows, Jesse's sitting up in bed in a pair of Alicia's flannel pajamas. She's trying not to think. Not about her mother, not about the woman under the water, not about drowning.

Not about the missing child.

Just outside, she hears a murmured conversation. Alicia's talking to Rory. Jesse can hear Mack too. The voices rise and fall. Mack's not happy. She hears her name mentioned as Alicia brings the tray into the room and closes the door. Four teaspoons of sugar are dropped into the mug of tea and stirred. "Energy, Jess. You need it."

Jesse stares at the surface of the liquid as it settles. If she says anything, anything at all, Alicia will think she's nuts because she sure as hell does. Her gaze transfers to the towel-wrapped lump on her knees.

Alicia leans forward. "Just a sip." She guides the mug to the girl's mouth. "It's hot."

Jesse does as she's asked. She hesitates—as if tea were an unfamiliar thing. Another sip, and she gives the mug back.

"Rory thinks you should rest. He'd like to talk to you later, but only when you're ready."

Jesse unwraps the towel carefully. "Alicia, you saw this. Do you know what it is?" Jesse holds up an oval of blackened metal. Light catches the surface and it glints in her hands.

Alicia hesitates. "It's a face, isn't it?" She peers at the object. "Can I hold it?"

Jesse nods.

Alicia takes it carefully. She taps the discolored surface. "It might be silver." Her finger traces the shape of an empty eye socket. "Could it be a mask?"

"It was there, in the water, and . . ."

"You haven't finished your tea." Alicia offers the mug.

Obediently, Jesse takes another swallow. "How did it get into the river?"

Alicia's eyes widen. She stares at Jesse. "I'll be back."

Mack's in the passage outside Jesse's room. "Can I see how she is?"

Alicia hustles past. "Where's Rory? Ask him." She disappears down the passage to her room.

He watches her go. A beat. Then he knocks. "Only me."

"Come in."

"I hope you don't mind." Mack stops inside the door. "Rory won't be pleased, but . . ."

"I'm glad you're here." Jesse's face is all eyes and shadows.

It hurts Mack to see her looking so frail. He goes to the bed.

"I know I nearly drowned."

Mack sits. "Good thing you didn't." It's meant as a joke, but that thought, that Jesse might actually have died, that he might never have seen her again as a living woman, is overwhelming.

Jesse reaches out with her left hand.

He takes it.

"How do I say thank you for my life?" Barely a whisper.

He leans forward. Kisses her gently. "Consider that a down payment."

"I took this to my room last night and—" Alicia's returned.

"I'd better go, Mum'll be stressing." Mack gets up without haste. "See you soon."

"When?"

"Soon as . . ."

They're gazing so intensely at each other, Alicia feels like an intruder.

In the doorway, Mack points at Jesse and mimes calling on the phone. She nods. As the door closes, she slumps against the pillows.

"You need to see something." Alicia hesitates before she takes her grandfather's book to the bed. She leafs through the pages. "Here." She lifts the tissue paper that covers the illustration and turns it around for Jesse to see. "This once stood in the chapel."

Jesse stares. "Does she have a name?"

Alicia finds the text. " 'The Madonna of the River was a more-than-life-size statue of Christ's mother with Her infant son. She was also referred to as the Mother by local people, and the antiquity of this statue—it is said she was an object of pilgrimage before Norman settlement of the area—is attested by the fact that the image was carved from crystalline limestone, rather than oak. The Madonna was revered by mothers and childless women, and was also noteworthy for her *silver face and hands*.'" Alicia taps the page. The enigmatic disk lies between them on the bed.

"Is there more?"

Alicia continues, "'It was thought these objects may have been crafted in the early medieval period by the Master of the Hundredfield Rood, since the workmanship was similar. The eyes of the Madonna were inlaid with topaz and her hair was gilded copper wire. Over time, the gilding wore away to reveal the color of the metal beneath. This statue is considered one of the great lost treasures of Hundredfield. During the disturbances of the Border Wars, the Madonna disappeared and is believed to have been destroyed.'" Alicia looks up from the page. "Do you think . . ."

Jesse's face is flushed. "What color is topaz?"

"Greeny-blue? It can vary, I think."

"And she would have looked as if her hair were red?"

Alicia looks down at the page. "Could be."

Jesse gasps.

"What's wrong?" Alicia's seriously concerned by Jesse's expression.

"Can you find Rory?"

39

THE SONG was a cloud of sound I could almost see.

Outside the sanctuary, it ebbed to nothing. Closer to the altar, the music flowed again. The source was close, and, taking a lit candle from one of the stands, I began to walk the chapel walls.

I came to the Madonna's alcove. The hangings moved in and out, as if the stone behind were breathing. I pulled them apart. Inside, the doors of the screen stood open and the song grew louder, deep and slow.

From respect, I knelt before the Madonna, Mother of All. Our own mother's devotion to this image had been great; as a young wife, she had prayed here for children.

The candle flame wavered and I saw another light: a faint line of brilliance in the wall. It should not have been there.

I leaned forward. Panels of oak lined the Madonna's alcove to the height of my chest, and one was sprung slightly open, as if it were a door; from here, the light shone out.

But the gap was narrow and I used my knife to probe a way to make it wider. All the while, the song seeped through, now soft, now louder, moving like wind over water.

I found a post on which the panel could turn. It was simple enough but clever; no metal in the fittings—this was old work from skilled hands.

Crouching, I used my shoulder to push through, and wavering flame showed a tunnel sloping down to a glowing point. I could not tell how far away that light was, but I opened my arms to judge the space around me. The walls were two handsbreadth wider than my shoulders, with a roof close enough to brush against my head.

From somewhere distant the song came again, the thread that caught and drew me on. And there was something else—a rushing thunder; water, falling from a height.

I moved toward the glow and toward the singer. And as I came out from dark into a firelit space, it seemed a kind of second birth.

In sheer surprise I gaped.

Flames gilding her face, Margaretta sat on a broken plinth among a grove of tall, white pillars; she held the baby close against her chest.

It was the child who sang.

"How long have you been here?" I was not angry. I was awed.

"Since the night of the yule feast. And before that too. After her birth we hid here."

The baby ceased to sing. She stared at me as the air shivered with the last notes.

Light flared from the fire, and I saw two things. The first was Aviss; he was sleeping on a pile of skins at Margaretta's feet. The second was a stranger sight.

On all the walls of this cavern were red-handed prints pressed to the rock. Small hands, large hands. They seemed numberless.

"Each hand a woman's life, or her daughter's. So many, many lives."

"What is this place?" I struggled to take in the sight. I wanted to ask where they had come from, all these women.

Standing, Margaretta beckoned.

Deeper in was an opening in the rock. Around it, like the painted border of an arch, a trail of tiny handprints defined the shape. Holding the baby up, Margaretta helped the child stretch out her arm, and as she pressed the palm and fingers against the rock, I saw that both were red.

"These are her sisters. It is your turn now, Bayard." The baby was staring at me, and so was Margaretta.

"Why?"

"You will see." She gestured at water seeping through the rock beside a seam of ocher, dark as dried blood, and showed me how to wet my hand for the color.

It seemed some strange blasphemy, but I put my red hand beside the palmprint of Flore's daughter. In that flame-lit place it seemed to flicker as it dried.

Then I saw.

My handprint, a man's hand, was so much larger than those of the children, larger still than that of my niece. Fingers like sentinels, it stood as a warning and a protection beside hers. The promise I had made given form.

"I see no other hand like mine."

"No. You are the first. This is not a place for men." Carrying the baby, Margaretta bent low to lead me through the narrow way. "This is called the Red Door."

I followed, though my way through was harder than hers, and I entered a second cavern on my knees like a supplicant. But this was a place of wonder.

In the center of its floor was a dark pool, and a spring welled at its heart. The moving face of the water broke flame into jewels, and at the pool's farthest lip a stream fell away and disappeared.

"Where does the water go?"

"To the cistern in the stables. And when it floods, to the river through the old moat. It carries offerings from this place, when they are given."

I looked up and blinked. Above, ribs of stone fanned to form the roof. It seemed to me the structure must have been made by human hands.

Finally I understood. These caverns lay beneath the floor of the chapel, under the very foundations of the keep.

Margaretta beckoned. "Come closer, lord."

There was only the sound of falling water, the soft crack of distant fire. I hesitated. Was I afraid of the child?

Margaretta held the baby so the hand marked with ocher could touch my skin. I felt those small fingers explore my face as if my niece were blind.

"Why does she do this?"

Margaretta said, "She is learning."

"I do not understand."

The baby drew back into Margaretta's arms but did not cease to gaze at me.

"Flore brought me to this place before the child was born. And through her daughter, she has brought you here as well. It has always been a refuge in times of need."

The sense of the child's touch was still on my skin. "But you have no need to hide in caves, Margaretta. The keep will protect us and—"

"Hate is stronger than any wall." She bowed her head, and when she raised it, tears were in her eyes. "Flore's daughter must be given her name."

"The priest will not christen this baby."

Margaretta swallowed. "We do not need the priest. She is to be called Felice. Happiness. That is what her mother wanted."

She held out my niece.

Cradling the infant, I asked, "Why did you do that?"

"Hold her above the pool."

I hesitated, but did as I was asked.

And Margaretta said, "Mother, can you hear me?"

The baby was untroubled, smiling down at us both from my hands.

And, watching, the flow of the water seemed to ebb.

Margaretta clapped her hands. "We, your children, have returned."

The stream stopped flowing.

The girl gestured to me.

I saw what she wanted me to do and lowered the baby. Margaretta scooped water from the pool, and her voice grew in power. "Here is your daughter, and we are her guardians. Protect her, Mother. Her name is Felice."

Yes, it was a blasphemy. But I stood beside Margaretta for Godefroi. And for Flore.

And for Felice.

40

I RETURNED FROM the carpenter's workshop with small pieces of cast-off wood. My nephew was sitting on the floor in the kitchen beside his sleeping sister. He said nothing as he took the blocks I had found for him, and I watched as, with much absorption, he built them up into a tower and knocked them down, then happily started again. When he remembered, he peered at the baby, his face close to hers, as if to be sure she was breathing.

Felice, wrapped tight, looked like a wax effigy as she slept in a fleece-lined box away from the heat of the cooking fires.

"Lord, I must give Aviss his food." Margaretta lifted her son from the floor and took him to the trestle that served the kitchen as a workbench. The only stool was too high, and too dangerous, for the boy to sit on. She hesitated.

"I can hold him." My tone was gruff, but she handed me the boy without comment, and Aviss seemed not unhappy. I did not show it, but the child's trust pleased me.

As Margaretta went, I whispered, "Eat fast, little one." It was true. I must soon share the board with our men in the hall before we went back out to the walls, and as the kitchen women were already ladling barley and fish from the largest of the cauldrons into smaller vessels, I knew I had little time.

The child shifted and clapped his hands as his mother returned with a full bowl and a heel of bread. "He is hungry."

"That is the way with growing children, lord," she said with downcast eyes.

When the first spoonful went into my nephew's mouth, I leaned closer to his mother. "My brother believes Godefroi was bewitched. Have you bewitched me also?"

"Is that what you think?" Firelight caught the curve of Margaretta's cheek as she angled the spoon again.

"I do not know." I thought of the cavern beneath our feet and the pagan naming of Flore's daughter.

"No, Aviss. Let me do it." The boy had tried to grasp the spoon.

"He is old enough to feed himself."

"You know about babies, lord?" A pleasant enough remark but with a sting.

"Enough. He is a big boy now, aren't you, Aviss?"

Margaretta hesitated. "He will spill it. And he has so few clothes."

"There's a cloth." One of the cook women had left a rag on the table.

"If he flicks his food all over you, I shall not be blamed."

She sounded like any other harried mother, but there was a truce between us as I helped her tie the cloth around Godefroi's son.

The boy fed himself well enough as the cook women left with food for the men. "You see? Excellently done, Aviss."

"You should go. I can manage him, I always have."

I did not reply—what was there to say?—but the silence between us was comfortable as we watched the boy.

"Just one more mouthful." I was surprised by the pride I felt as Aviss steered the food approximately to his mouth. "There. Almost ready for your own knife. I shall give you one."

"You like him."

I looked up to see Margaretta staring at me. Her eyes had a silver sheen in the half-light. Tears.

"Yes. He is a fine child." I reached a hand to her face, and she turned her head away. "Look at me." When she did, the tears had spilled. With great care I wiped one away and then another. "Do not cry, Margaretta."

"There is much to cry about."

This was uncomfortable—the yearning I felt to hold this girl was a powerful surprise, though Aviss, big-eyed, was staring at us both and I would not frighten the boy.

She did not look at me as she said, "When Aviss was born, and our family was so shamed by what Godefroi had done, I was still blamed. That was very hard." Margaretta shook her head. "But yet I love my son."

"My brother was at fault, Margaretta, not you. Certainly not Aviss. Of course you love your little one."

She stared at me. "I do not understand why Godefroi did what he did to me, for my father told the truth that day. He *had* served Hundredfield with loyalty, we all had. How can your brother have been so cruel to us? So cruel to all his people?"

I shook my head. "Maugris and I are shamed by his actions, Margaretta. Shamed for all you have suffered."

The girl watched her son eat. "When your father said he would send Alois to the monks, he thought he was helping my brother. But Alois did not want to go, and my parents could do nothing to change the old lord's mind. Even I tried to plead for my brother. It was for this 'presumption' that I . . . that Godefroi"—Margaretta swallowed—"that your brother raped me. He said it was my fault; that by punishing me for disobedience, by making me an example, the people of Hundredfield would learn their duty better. And

Alois was still sent away. Then, I was set to wait on the Lady Flore. I thought it a final humiliation and yet it was not." She leaned down to wipe the child's face. "There. Have you had enough?"

The little boy nodded, though he was still staring at me.

I took the cloth from Margaretta's hand. "Help us with Alois, Margaretta. You are his sister. You know what kind of a man he is, what he might do."

She shook her head. "When he was sent away, Alois did not know I had tried to help him. He cursed us all." A bitter shrug. "I will do what I can. I do not want my brother to die. Or you."

One of the cook women had returned from the hall with an empty platter. She was staring at us.

I murmured, "There will come a time after this when we shall speak. And then . . ."

"Yes?"

I ran out of words. Perhaps there would be no "then." I heard noise growing in the hall as the food was distributed and stood to give Aviss into her hands. "Stay in Godefroi's chamber, Margaretta. You will be safe there. Lock yourself in; take food and water and do not come out unless it is Maugris or I that calls. And if Alois comes . . ."

I did not finish the thought. There was no *if*—Margaretta knew that. And we both understood what I had asked.

As I left the kitchen, I turned for one last look at that little trinity of souls. And it seemed to me that these three were all that truly bound me to the world.

"The girl is addled. Why hide from us?" Maugris was in the armory. "Where is she now?"

"In Godefroi's room, with the children. I've set a guard on the stairs for their safety."

"The baby?"

"She thrives."

"Where were they?"

I hesitated. "I was praying in the chapel, brother, and—"

"No more time for prayers, Bayard." Maugris yawned. And forgot his question.

"Margaretta will help us when they come. She will speak to her brother."

A snort. "If Alois does not kill her first."

"She tried to save her father from Godefroi, you saw that."

Staring out through the window, Maugris grunted. "The girl wants something—she hopes to profit by playing both sides."

I was exasperated. "She wants what all women want, Maugris. Food for her son and a safe place to sleep."

He shook his head, his face stubborn. "Nothing is as simple as that."

I would not fight with my brother now. We were both haggard ghosts. I said politely, "You have used time well."

In the armory, open coffers held newly sharp swords and axes, and bundles of arrows were stacked on the floor. "But to prepare for a siege—you think that the best way?"

"We cannot challenge Alois in the forest until we have more men."

"But there is still the virtue of surprise."

Maugris said sharply, "Surprise is not enough. No. I have set Robert to tallying stores and the cistern is full. Let them try to take this place. They will break against Hundredfield's walls, as so many have."

Discussion was useless. Hunched against the wind, men were climbing to the battlements below, and I lifted the latch to join them. "I must go."

"Wait!" Maugris nodded over the river. "Well?" It was rare for my brother to ask advice.

"Alois must come soon. He will surely know we have sent for aid. Our advantage grows with each day that passes."

"Then why does he wait?"

"What does anyone wait for? More men."

Maugris said confidently, "They will win us what time we need." He meant Hundredfield's household.

I did not reply. Since I had returned with Godefroi's corpse, fear had spread like a plague and our supporters decreased each day. Alois was a clever man.

Maugris hesitated. He closed the lid on a coffer and propped himself against it. "If the day does not go well when it comes, there is another way." He beckoned.

I followed him down to the hall.

The great room was empty and the fire had burned low. The ghost of the meal just eaten still floated in the air as Maugris strode to the high board. After a moment, he took Godefroi's seat and waved me to the stool at his right hand.

"What would you say to firing the keep?"

"When?"

Maugris actually grinned. "Not now, fool." The glance he gave was almost affectionate. "If we do not kill enough of them, we burn it down. After that, when we have won, we rebuild. Godefroi gave us the plans. We can improve Hundredfield's defenses." He looked almost happy.

It was good strategy to deny the enemy what he wants if all else fails, but it was a wrenching thought.

"We might get caught in our own snare. Denying them shelter, we deny ourselves."

Maugris got up and strode to the hearth. "Almost dead." He kicked the ashes, looking for coals.

I stood beside him.

"Look. Under your feet, Maugris."

"There's only the floor and the . . ."

The grin grew wider. "Old rushes. Well done, little brother. These will fire well. All that grease."

"And the trestles and the settles. They'll burn too." I would do it, if I had to. "Godefroi's new hangings are wool. They won't take flame easily. But there, above the screens. Do you see?" I pointed.

Years of our mother's labor had made the tapestries that hung above our heads. They were old and dusty, and the linen backing would burn. "If we start the blaze in the rushes around the hearth and in front of the screens, the hangings will catch and then the rafters." I did not think our mother would care—she would want us to live.

I hurried to the kitchens. Returning with coals in a leather bucket, I found Maugris piling furniture directly beneath the tapestries.

"There are things we must consider, brother."

Maugris raised a sweating, scarlet face. "What?"

I tipped the coals on the hearth and piled rushes to cover them. "The silver Christ and the Madonna. They must be hidden."

He passed a hand across his face. "Where?"

"I know a place."

"Then do it. Tonight. When there are none about to see."

41

OLLIE'S ON the end of Jesse's bed. He's put his head on her knees.

"You're sure you want to talk about it?" Rory's back is against the west-facing windows. His face is in shadow.

"No. But I think I should."

Rory takes note of those unhappy eyes. "You've had a very upsetting time, Jesse, and—"

"It's not what you're thinking."

Rory hesitates.

"I did not try to kill myself."

He says nothing.

"But . . ." A long exhale, and Jesse's expression changes. She's staring past Rory.

He resists the urge to turn around. "But?"

"Did Mack tell you about Sister Mary Joseph?"

"He tried not to."

Jesse finds some kind of a smile. "He's a good man, your brother."

"Yes." A brief admission.

"My mother's dead, Rory." Jesse huddles into herself as she

strokes Ollie's ears. "What a nice dog you are." Tears drop into the fur.

"Here." Rory's found tissues. He takes them to Jesse and sits quietly beside her.

Jesse blows her nose. "Did Mack tell you I didn't want to come back to Hundredfield?"

"He said your case was in his car."

"Alicia was very nice at dinner, and she invited me to stay on, but I just couldn't, Rory. I had to do it, had to move on." Her voice dies to a whisper. "But then, I saw something."

"What?"

Jesse gathers herself. "At the river. There was a woman under the water. And before you say anything . . ." She holds up a hand.

But Rory's silent.

Discomfited, Jesse shifts against the pillows. "*She* was there. It's her face I've drawn, Rory. It's her I see in the dreams, and when I was on the ventilator in the hospital." Jesse stops. As clearly as she can, she says, "She did not want me to die, she wanted to give me something. Maybe she knew Mack wouldn't let me drown."

Rory's staring at her.

Ollie barks, shattering the charged silence. He whines anxiously, scrabbling at Rory's knees.

"Smarter than anyone thinks you are." Rory scruffs the dog's ears. "What did she give you, Jesse?"

A Harrods bag is beside the bed. She hands it to him.

Rory unfolds the layers of towel warily. And stares at the eyeless face in his hands.

Jesse takes it back and holds it over her own face.

Rory pales. Living eyes stare out from that immobile, glinting countenance.

Jesse says, "Permit me to speak."

". . . so relaxed. More relaxed than you've ever been. Nod if you can hear me."

Jesse nods. She's lying on a couch in the library. Her hair, spread over the pillows, seems almost to glow as she holds the mask over her face.

Rory injects calm into his voice. He says soothingly, "That's good, very good. So, I will count down from five to one."

"There is no need." Older, deeper, the voice has a tone so different than Jesse's.

The spools turn and turn. Rory says, "May I ask questions?"

Jesse's head nods once. A graceful, courtly movement.

Rory swallows. "Who are you?"

Slowly, the mask over Jesse's face turns to look at him. "The messenger."

Rory cannot meet that glance.

"What I say is for the child to know."

He hesitates. "Yes."

"This is hard for you." The voice warms.

Rory looks up. "Yes. It is very hard." Conflict strangles his breathing.

"You are honest. She needs that honesty, having been lied to."

"I need to understand what you are saying."

"Accept."

"I am not used to . . . accepting. I am trained to question. That is what scientists do."

The voice is kind. "Be at peace. Let her hear this. The child must return the mother."

Rory's puzzled. "What do you mean? Jesse's mother is dead."

"Her family will tell her the meaning of what I say."

"Her family? But—"

"She will find the child who was lost."

As if a light has been flicked off, something changes. The mask is just a mask, not a face.

"Jesse?" Sweating, Rory lifts the mask away.

Jesse's asleep, deeply asleep.

42

ELIZABETH HUMBOLDT is a surprise. She's young—somewhere in her thirties—and charming. Optimistic, sunny, delightful: each word fits like a glove.

Opening the front door, Alicia is immediately wary. If she decides she wants to back away, that open face, those bright eyes, will make it harder. "Thanks very much for coming at such short notice." She holds out her hand.

Elizabeth takes it between both of her own. "This is an honor and a privilege for us, Lady Alicia. When you called me yesterday, I was so very glad." Elizabeth ignores the bandage; the two black eyes are more difficult.

"Alicia. Please." She extracts her hand from the oddly intimate grip of the other woman.

"Hundredfield is such a remarkable building—Alicia—a *collection* of remarkable buildings. And so important to the history of the country. This is a wonderful thing you're doing." Elizabeth leads Alicia a pace or two into the hall, as if she were the hostess. "But where are my manners?" A pretty laugh. "May I present my colleague? Dr. Brian Curlewis is a consultant expert to the trust for Norman-era buildings in the English border region."

Brian Curlewis coughs.

"Oh, *and* of course he's also acknowledged for his expertise in medieval architecture." Elizabeth beams at Alicia. Determined kindness spreads like a prewarmed blanket.

Alicia tries not to clench her teeth. "So, what is the actual . . ."

"Procedure?" An encouraging nod from Elizabeth.

"Thank you. Yes, that's what I meant. When we chatted— you'll have to forgive me—I just, that is . . ." Alicia is finding it hard to control her voice.

Elizabeth has large, soft eyes. They grow softer still. "Oh, this is all very, very preliminary, I do assure you. Today is only the first step. Think of it as a briefing on how we might approach the various options that could exist for Hundredfield within the work of the trust. If you're agreeable, Brian and I would welcome an opportunity to see more of the buildings. We can discuss any questions you might have as we go. Before we leave, we'll provide you with a pro forma contract—just to read through and discuss with your lawyers, of course."

Alicia murmurs, "Of course."

Ignoring the interruption, Elizabeth continues. "Brian and I will make a preliminary report to the regional office in the next few days. It will only be a very broad assessment, the first of a number if all goes well. And it goes on from there. Our lawyers come in later as the contract is refined to embrace Hundredfield's actual requirements and condition." She sounds apologetic. *Lawyers*. There it is again. That word always punctures the mood.

"I see." Alicia swallows. "There's rather a lot to see at Hundredfield in one day, but we could start with the New Range, since that's where we are. We have a number of state rooms in this building."

"What do you think, Elizabeth? I, for one, would be particularly keen to see the Tudor dining room. It's almost a legend, Lady Alicia, and so few people have ever actually seen it." Brian Curlewis looks quite excited.

Alicia takes a deep breath. "Perhaps we can remedy that in the future."

Unprompted, Elizabeth clutches one of Alicia's hands. "Oh, I hope so. I do so very much hope so."

"This way." Alicia extracts her hand with grace.

Small talk lasts just about the distance from the front door to the great staircase, and Alicia gets through by pinning a smile to her face. "There are so many eras represented in this part of the castle alone—as you would know. The Normans built the keep, of course, and the later medieval buildings—although quite a few are ruined, as you would have seen—were built anywhere from the twelfth century on." She steers them up the left-hand flight and throws the doors open to a long room; morning light fills the space with dazzled gold.

Brian stares around with bright, bright eyes. "And so much that is untouched. Original condition, I mean." He thinks he's being tactful.

Elizabeth stops with an intake of breath. "And these must be the famous Hundredfield nixies. The water spirits?" She's smitten.

A pair of double-height doors faces the little group. Framed by sinuous lines of apparently female figures carved deep into the reveals, there's a riot of forms to interpret.

"Yes. Though no one's ever been able to say with any certainty just what they represent. There's some sense that they're linked with our local legends."

"So very *mystical*, this part of the world." Elizabeth nods enthusiastically. "The Wild Hunt, for instance. I hear Hundredfield has its own?"

Her offside gently interrupts, "May I?" Brian Curlewis is punctilious. He absolutely will not inspect these tantalizing forms until given permission.

"Of course." Alicia stands to one side.

"They seem to have fins on their shoulders. That might support the nixie hypothesis." Brian makes room for Elizabeth.

"Exquisite. And such bold carving too. Unique."

Alicia clears her throat. "Not fins. Wings, I think you'll find—like dragonflies. And if you look, you'll see they don't really have faces, just eyes. Someone came up with the nixie idea, since that's as plausible as any of the other explanations, and it stuck. The palmprints are a puzzle, of course. No one knows what they mean." Alicia produces a long black key.

"They are indeed unusual." Brian leans in to inspect a ribbon of half-size human hands, forming a pattern around the central figures.

The wards in the lock click and the nixies spring apart as the doors open. "So, here it is."

A burnished surface as long as a short jetty stretches away into the room.

Elizabeth is startled. "This must be quite the largest oak table I've ever seen. Tudor, of course, as you'd expect." A quick smile for Alicia. "Brian?"

"Well, Tudor is not quite my era, but I'd have to agree." His eyes glint with the avarice of the scholar.

Touching the top, Alicia says, "It's hard to imagine this was ever a living tree."

Brian twinkles. "Do you think it knew, as it grew, that fate would turn it into a table?"

"If a tree actually ever thinks. Please, do sit." Alicia gestures to her guests. "The oak was cut on the estate. The family got wind of a visit from Queen Elizabeth one summer in the 1570s, and a frenzy of improvements began. This had been destined as a ship-builder's oak for Deptford, but it was sacrificed for her. And all for just two days and one night." Alicia drops into a tapestry-seated chair at one end of the table—a massive thing of black oak and gilded studwork. "*Sic transit gloria mundi*. 'So passes the glory of the world.'"

Elizabeth and Brian exchange a glance.

Brian says, "Did she actually come?"

Alicia stares at him. "No. She didn't. And it's fair to say that all those 'improvements' to Hundredfield for the visit that never happened began the process that, in the end, beggared my family." Her voice falters. "And here we are today, as you see. Poorer but not wiser. Definitely not that."

With some sympathy, Elizabeth says, "But this room will certainly bring visitors, Alicia, especially with all of the original furniture. You are so fortunate the collection has remained intact. So many are broken up for the money. And of course, the connection with Good Queen Bess is a guaranteed crowd-pleaser."

Alicia smiles politely.

"'Good'? I think you may find that's open for debate considering contemporary research." Brian doesn't quite sniff.

Elizabeth ignores him. "And just think, if she'd come, she might have sat in your actual chair, Alicia. It's certainly grand enough."

"And they'd have hung the monarch's cloth of estate from a canopy above, nothing surer." Brian gestures. "Do you know if it still exists? Restoration could still be possible."

"Possibly. We've never really gone through the attics or the cellars in a systematic way."

Elizabeth Humboldt clears her throat. "Alicia, perhaps now is as good a time as any to walk you through how surrendering this property to the trust could actually work; you should know our requirements and your potential undertakings and obligations. Brian?"

"Yes, indeed." Brian extracts a number of folders from his briefcase. He passes one to Alicia, another to Elizabeth. "All very straightforward and expressed in plain English. We find people appreciate that."

He smiles, Elizabeth smiles, and two pairs of bright eyes settle on Alicia's face as she opens the document.

Like crows, she thinks, *waiting for something to die.*

Jesse speaks up over the noise of the Saab's engine. "'She must return the mother'? What does that *mean*?"

Rory flicks Jesse a glance. "I don't know. The message was for you. You heard her." He's deeply, deeply uncomfortable talking about *her*.

"'Some people can believe ten impossible things before breakfast. I can't.' Alicia said that. You and she are so alike."

Rory shifts down rather than comment. But Jesse's right. A night's sleep and the questions begin; this whole situation could be career suicide if he pursues it. "What time did you make the appointment for?"

"I didn't."

Rory switches attention from the road. "He might not be able to see you. Mornings are rush hour in any doctor's surgery."

"How well do you know Alistair Nicholls?"

A signpost flashes past. Five miles to Newton Prior. "Very well. And I owe him a lot. When I went for the scholarship to Edinburgh, he was one of my referees."

"He was here when you grew up?"

Rory nods. "But he practiced in Edinburgh as a gynecologist before he came to Newton Prior. That's why I asked him."

"He's a GP now, though?"

"Being a specialist can be stressful."

Jesse murmurs, "'He said with feeling.'"

The sound of the engine fills up the silence.

A glance at Jesse's wan face and Rory says, "I'm still not happy about this."

"I'm not physically ill, Rory."

"I'm not talking about your body."

They're in the outskirts of the village; the square's not far.

"Where will I find you?"

"I'll meet you at the Hunt."

"When?"

Jesse snaps, "You are not my brother."

"No, I'm your doctor." Rory can be just as stubborn. He guides the Saab into a parking space. Turns the engine off. "Let me come with you, Jesse. It might be safer."

"Nothing's safe. Or certain. I'll find you when I've done what I have to do." Jesse gets out and walks away.

"I need to ask you a question."

The little Madonna in St, Michael's Church is smiling at Jesse. She's smiled for hundreds and hundreds of years.

"Is it you? Did she mean you?"

"I'm so glad you like her." Fred materializes from the side aisle of St. Michael's.

Jesse jumps. "You're just like a ghost. Has anyone ever said that?"

"It's the black clothes. I tend to blend in. May I join you?"

The murmur of prayer comes from near the main altar. "Who's on the bridge?"

A quiet chuckle. "My new curate, logging sky miles. Special morning service today—the Mothers Group." Fred sits beside Jesse and contemplates the Madonna and her son. "She might be homely, but so many, many people have found comfort in her presence."

Jesse stares at the Madonna's face. "She loves her baby. That makes her beautiful."

They sit in silence as the voice of a single child sings the twenty-fifth psalm, rising like birdsong into the rafters.

Fred murmurs, "We're very proud of our choir."

Jesse turns to him passionately. "There's so much that's glorious in the church. But"—she gestures at the mural behind the altar—"all that terror, all the suppression of feeling. And what they did to women? Look at that stuff!" Jesse glares at *The Harrowing* as if it's personal, the naked women being tormented by devils, the terrified girls being herded to hell.

"The church has always been frightened of women. You make life in your bodies. An echo of God, that."

"But nothing changes. Madonna or whore. Is that all there is? Depressing. Seriously." *Did they call you a whore, Mum?* Jesse shakes herself. "Sorry, Fred. I actually came to thank you. Your friend, Sister Mary Joseph. She's a wonderful person."

"Was it a useful meeting?"

Jesse struggles. "I know more now, but I'll never meet my mum."

His silence is kind.

"Sister Mary was there when I was born. She remembers that night. There was a young doctor, an honorary, on duty." Jesse stares at the little Madonna. "Do you know Dr. Nicholls?"

The priest smiles. "This is a village, Jesse."

"Is he a good man?"

"He's a very good doctor."

That's not quite the same thing. "I'm going to try to see him. Just to ask."

"If he was the doctor on duty?"

She ducks her head. "Yes."

Fred says gently, "Sometimes, wishing for something can distort reality." He gestures at the Madonna. "I am very fond of her, but in the end, she's just a statue. She can't grant wishes."

Jesse looks at him curiously. "But you're a priest. You believe reality-bending things every day."

"Maybe that's why I'm guaranteed to understand the worst that belief, and faith, can do."

"Is that a nice way of saying you think I'm wrong?"

"Alistair's not the only doctor in the borders." A faint smile.

"Of course. But he asked me to visit him if I needed help, so that's what I'm doing." There's the feeling of a fist clenching and unclenching in Jesse's stomach. Wrong or right, she's doing this. She stands quickly. "Even if she is just a statue, it's been helpful to talk to her. And to you. You both give me courage."

"Oh, I'd say you've got bags of that all by yourself. Come back when you need to. I'm always here."

"That's what Alicia said about Rahere."

"Oh?"

"Yes. A colleague of yours. In London. He helped me a lot."

"Pleased to know that. Pass on my regards, next time you see him."

"I might do that."

The Madonna's still smiling as Jesse leaves.

43

MUM?" RORY knocks at the closed door of his mother's office.

"It's not locked."

He swings around. Helen's in the corridor behind him. She's not defrosting in a hurry. "What do you want, Rory? I've got quite a lot of work to do." She opens the door and strides ahead of her son to her desk.

Helen's office is in what's left of the main priory building. It's a modern room inside an ancient shell, and oak beams, thicker than bridge supports, cross the ceiling and vein the walls, but the fourth wall is made entirely of glass, looking out into a cloistered garden. It should feel like a peaceful place.

"What I *want* is not to leave things as they are. Why does this happen, Mum? We're always pleased to see each other, but then . . ." Rory shrugs painfully as he sits opposite his mother.

Helen blinks. She hesitates. "When you were little, when it was just you and me, we looked after each other. We were close then."

He leans forward. "What changed?"

"I think," Helen says with some care, "you did. Boarding

school. You were different after that—all your posh friends. I thought you were ashamed of me."

"All my . . ." He stares at her. And shakes his head. "I didn't want to go, did you know that?"

She nods reluctantly. "But when Alicia's dad made the offer, I knew it would give you the start in life I couldn't. I thought you'd get over it."

It's an effort to speak. "I thought you'd stopped loving me. That"—Rory swallows—"you hated me and sent me away because of that."

Helen visibly deflates. "Why didn't you tell me?"

"I tried. You don't have the words when you're seven. And you'd met Charley. I didn't want to get in the way after so many years of struggle and unhappiness. But then, when I came home, there was no more Hundredfield. That broke my heart, Mum."

"That place!"

"It was our home."

"It was a trap! It's always been a trap for people like us. And the Donnes . . ." Helen doesn't finish the sentence. Jerkily, she puts carbon copy between two sheets of paper and winds them into the typewriter.

Rory says quietly, "They were good to us. They didn't have to be so kind. The house, paying for the school—"

Helen's face flushes. "Kind?" She starts to type, hitting the keys hard.

Rory grabs one of her hands. "Don't do this, Mum. Let it go."

She snatches her hand back. "They're with me every single day of my life, every time I look at you. Let it go? I still dream about Hundredfield, all those long, terrible years." Her agitation is painful.

Rory's shocked. He's never seen her like this. "I just want to make things better between us." He goes around the desk and, though it's awkward, puts his arms around her shoulders.

Helen cannot cry. "I was all alone. I had no one, except you.

He was wicked, that man. Wicked! He thought he could do anything he liked. And then he just ignored us—as if we didn't exist." Words force themselves out of her mouth as if they've been torn.

"You don't have to talk about Dad. I stopped thinking about him years ago."

She clutches his arm. "You don't understand. Your father, he . . ." She stops.

"If I don't understand, tell me why. I don't even know what he looks like. You must have kept something, Mum. A photograph. Surely you've got a photograph somewhere?"

"It's done." Helen clamps her lips tight as she goes back to the typewriter. She says with forced calm, "I need to get on."

"Do you know why I became a doctor, Mum? I wanted to help people. You can't do that unless you understand, unless you can get to the truth." Rory's not going away. He stands there with his hands on her shoulders, raising his voice over the peck of the keys. "That's what my work is, what all my research is about. There're always reasons why we are the way we are, there's always history. People cannot heal unless they come to terms with the past."

Helen's face is haggard. "That girl."

"Alicia?" He's puzzled.

"The other one. You talk about truth." Helen speaks in a rush. "Why bring her to Hundredfield, Rory? She talked you into it, didn't she?"

He shakes his head. "You know why. She's helping me with research. And Jesse's connected to the borders—not just because she was born at Jedburgh, either. More than that."

"Helping with your research? Girls like her." Helen starts typing again, rapid as gunshot. "She met you in the hospital, Rory. Think about that." She shakes her head.

"Girls like what, Mum?" Rory's calm is fraying.

Helen mutters, "She's wasting her time. And yours."

Rory perseveres. "No. She's not. Jesse's found out her mother died when she was born. She didn't know that before."

Helen rests her fingers on the keys. "So there's an end to it." She says with difficulty, "Poor girl." The sympathy seems real.

"Jesse believes Alistair Nicholls was there. She's going to talk to him."

Helen picks up a bottle of correcting fluid and minutely blanks out a single letter on the page. "You're distracting me, Rory." The keys clatter against the paper.

"Mum. Mum?"

Helen types faster. "I need to finish this."

Rory hesitates. His eyes are sad.

Helen nods. "Close the door, would you?" She's still typing as Rory leaves, and she keeps typing, but she's staring at the phone as the door clicks closed behind her son.

"Is Doctor Nicholls available, please?"

Jesse's standing at the counter in a crowded waiting room. She feels conspicuous.

"Do we have you on our books?" The woman on the far side of the counter—a barrier of sturdy Scots pine, which she rather resembles in plain defensiveness—purses her lips.

"No, I'm sorry. I'm not one of his patients, I'm a visitor, but he suggested—"

"Doctor has a very busy surgery this morning. If you leave your name and a number, I'm sure he'll try to call when he has a moment." With a *that's all I can possibly do* finality, the receptionist cranes her head around Jesse, holding out a clipboard. "Mrs. Pibroch? If you'd step up to the counter, I need you to fill out—"

"I'll see Miss Marley next, Mrs. Newby." A door has opened, and as Dr. Nicholls nods to Jesse, he ushers out the previous patient.

"But, Doctor." The receptionist half stands. The proprieties, and the proprietress of the waiting room, have jointly been outraged.

"This way." The doctor stands aside, allowing Jesse to precede him into the room.

As Alistair Nicholls shuts the door on the mutter of the waiting room, he says, "I'm delighted to see you again, Miss Marley. Please . . ." He waves to a chair with unattractive upholstery.

"Thank you." Jesse clears her throat.

"How may I help?" The doctor steeples his fingers and observes the girl sitting on the edge of the seat.

Jesse finds courage. "Doctor Nicholls, were you ever an honorary doctor—if that's the right term?"

"If you mean was I, or am I, a visiting physician on a pro bono basis? Yes. Not all can afford a specialist consultation if they must pay."

Jesse absorbs that information. "Mack took me to visit one of the sisters who had worked at Holly House in Jedburgh. That's where I was born. Sister Mary Joseph? She was the midwife in charge at that time."

Dr. Nicholls nods but says nothing.

"Sister Mary said there was a visiting doctor at Holly House on the night of my birth, but my mother died not long after." She swallows. "Her name was Eva Green. She had not been there very long and my father's identity was not known, then or now. I'm keen to pursue any leads at all. That was August first, and I'm twenty-four now."

"The year would be 1956?"

"Was it you? Were you the visiting doctor?" The words come out in a blurt.

"A Catholic institution would more likely retain physicians of the same faith, especially then. I am not Catholic. And it is a very long time ago."

He hasn't said no. "I'm sure you can understand how important this is to me, Dr. Nicholls." Jesse's trying not to plead.

"Certainly."

It's not that his eyes are cold, it's that their expression is far away.

"Please. If you know anything. Anything at all."

He hesitates. "I would have to check to be completely certain; however, I believe I may have attended your mother. Green is a common name, but Eva, of course, is unusual. Especially then."

Shock hits Jesse like a physical blow.

"Miss Marley?"

"You really were the doctor?" It's hard for her to breathe.

He nods.

"Sister Mary said it, my birth, was difficult."

He says gently, "Yes."

"Can you tell me how my mother died?"

"Are you certain, really sure, that you want to know?"

Jesse whispers, "I think of her all the time." She does not have other words to use.

Alistair Nicholls takes off his glasses and polishes them. Putting them back, he says, "It was blood loss. We could not stem the hemorrhage. Sometimes, no matter what is done for a patient, we do not succeed." He looks down at his hands. "Colleagues, other doctors, say they get used to it." He looks up. "But I never have. I never do." His eyes are defeated.

It occurs to Jesse that this man carries a burden of tragedy as if he were being punished for something.

"Do you know where she was buried?" Jesse gasps back tears. "If I could at least visit her grave . . ."

The doctor's face is troubled. "Did Sister Mary Joseph not tell you?"

"She seemed very tired and not especially well, so we left."

Dr. Nicholls searches for words. "One of the reasons I remember your birth was an event that occurred afterward. Miss Marley—Jesse—when the undertaker arrived at Holly House, your mother's body could not be found."

Jesse tries to absorb what he's saying. "I'm not sure what you mean."

"Her remains had disappeared. As far as I know, the case of that disappearance remains unsolved even now."

The phone on the desk rings, that noisy jangle jumping into the silence. "Excuse me. My receptionist only rings if it is an urgent matter." He half turns away. "Yes? . . . Very well, put her through." He lowers his voice. "Hello?"

Discretion is not required. Jesse's not listening.

In the fog of misery, Jesse doesn't see Dr. Nicholls turn back to look at her.

"Very well. Thank you for letting me know." He puts the phone back into its cradle, glances at his watch. "Miss Marley, I do apologize, but if I'm not to have an insurrection on my hands . . ." He stands. "I'm sure you understand I must cut our conversation short. I would have hoped to renew our acquaintance in happier circumstances."

Like a soap bubble, all hope in Jesse pops. For a moment she remains sitting. "Thank you speaking with me, Dr. Nicholls." *But you've just shut me down?* "I'm staying at Hundredfield, as you know."

A courteous nod, but he's opening the door.

Jesse gets up. "I'll leave a number with your receptionist. You might remember something more, or perhaps you'll know somebody else I should speak to. I'll talk with the police in the meantime . . ." She leaves the sentence unfinished.

He says politely, "I shall think on it, of course. Good morning, Miss Marley."

Among the confusion, something like defiance puts words into Jesse's mouth. "Rory speaks so highly of you, by the way. You're one of his heroes."

"Mrs. D'Acre's appointment was for eleven o'clock, Dr. Nicholls." The receptionist's reproach is addressed to Jesse.

The doctor beckons his next patient, an aggrieved fiftysomething woman, all twinset, pearls, and tweed, and Jesse is left unprotected to face Mrs. Newby.

"Doctor Nicholls asked me to leave my number." The lie is delivered unflinchingly. "I wonder if you have something I could write on?" Jesse waits, and from somewhere the gift of calm descends. After all, what can this woman do—deny the request?

Some huffing fuss is made before a pen and a pad are located and reluctantly offered.

"Again, thank you so much. For everything. I'll look forward to hearing from Dr. Nicholls." Jesse provides a charming smile backed by nothing at all. At least she's good at writing with her left hand now.

44

I S MACK about? Or Rory?"

Jesse's found her way to the kitchen of the Hunt. The pub's quiet ahead of the lunchtime rush.

"Mack's doing an inventory in the cellar. I can get him, if you like. Haven't seen Rory."

"I'll take over, Rachel." That cool voice.

Jesse turns. "Mrs. Brandon. Mack said he'd call me this morning, but I'm here instead." Jesse creates the brightest smile she can.

"Rachel, would you let Mack know that Miss Marley is here, please. Tell him we'll be in my office."

There seems no choice but to follow as Jesse is led out of the kitchen and through to the bar. She says, more loudly than she needs, "Thanks for your help, Rachel. Appreciated."

"No problem, Jesse. Anytime."

On the other side of the dining room, across a reception room, the door to the office is opened. "Here we are."

Jesse stops. "What a lovely room. You'd never know the cloister is here from the outside." Jesse hears herself flail. Cool people unnerve her.

"I like to be reminded that the present is built on the past.

Though in life, of course, you can only go forward." In perfect command, Helen sits behind her large desk. Black top, chrome legs, angular and formidable.

It occurs to Jesse that *angular* is a good word for this woman. There's little flesh covering the basic structure of muscle and bone, but the effect is not gaunt, it's strong.

Helen clears her throat. "I hear you've been given some news about your mother."

Jesse opens her mouth. And closes it. "Did Mack—"

"No. But I was sorry indeed when I was told. Very sad. I hope you're not too upset."

"It's . . . That is, I'd hoped . . ." Jesse's struggling.

"Since you know . . ." Helen hesitates. She puts both hands flat on the desk. "I should tell you that I did meet your mother—before you were born."

Jesse's more than bewildered. "But you—"

Helen cuts in carefully, "Your mother was a drifter, Miss Marley, a poor, troubled girl without family. No one knew where she came from. And when she died"—a pause, just a tiny fragment of time—"the authorities did not know whom to contact. I believe the parish took charge." She shakes her head. "As I said, very, very sad."

"That can't be right. Dr. Nicholls said her body"—a swallow of breath—"he told me it disappeared. That it's still missing and . . ."

Helen allows Jesse to flounder. "From time to time, we all make difficult decisions, Miss Marley. When you first began asking questions, I felt nothing useful could come from telling you what I knew; considering the facts as they are, the sadness this has caused you, I still think I was correct." Her eyes soften. "You should go home, Jesse. I'm sure your adoptive parents love you very much. That's where you belong: Australia, not here."

Something clicks in Jesse. "You know nothing about me, Mrs. Brandon. You have no right to speculate on where I might belong." Jesse gets up.

"If I can help you further, of course . . ." Helen's half risen. Her expression is uncomfortable.

"Thank you. I'll certainly be in touch." Jesse means it. If words are nails, no one's hammering this box closed.

"There you are." Mack hurries toward Jesse as she enters the dining room. Given the news that she's here, he's sprinted through the pub on his way to Helen's office. He stops. "What's wrong?"

Jesse's expression is dazed. "Your mother, she . . ."

Mack closes the gap between them. His arm's around her waist as if that's the natural thing to do. "Come with me."

An inglenook hidden by a settle is at the back of the empty bar. With great gentleness, Mack deposits Jesse against the cushions. "Do you want to talk?"

Jesse shakes her head. Her lips are blue-tinged, and that's almost the only color in her face.

"Right." Mack sprints to the bar, returns with a shot glass. "Drink."

"What is it?"

He puts the glass in her hand, guides it to her mouth. "All of it." He watches her swallow. And splutter.

"That's brandy!"

"Not much left. Keep going." His reward is the flush that changes her skin from white to faint pink. "You're having no fun at all right now, are you?" He sits beside her.

"Except there's you." Jesse almost topples as she leans against him. "Helen lied to me, Mack."

A nonplussed pause. "Why would you say that?"

"She knows what happened when I was born, but she pretended she didn't. She thinks I should go back to Australia." Jesse starts to shake. Sometimes, *sometimes*, it would be so comforting to talk to her mum in Sydney. Ask her advice. They used to be close when she was little. Tears leak and track down her face.

"Hey. Hey there." Mack thumbs the tears away. He murmurs, "There must be a reason she'd say what she did."

"She said she thought I'd be upset. She was lying."

"Mum's tough. Life's made her like that. But this is not about her, it's about you." He cups his hands around her face. "And me."

Jesse stares at him with huge, drowned eyes.

Mack lowers his head and kisses her. Soft. He murmurs, "Us."

She rests against him. And returns the kiss. His mouth is so sweet.

"When you're sad, I'm sad. Don't go back to Sydney, Jesse. Stay here. We'll work on being happy together." Mack was never a reckless man before today.

A movement catches Jesse's eye.

Rory's standing by the bar.

45

THE MOON was waning toward the last quarter, and I did not know if that was good or bad. Some commanders will not attack close to the dark of the moon and yet Maugris, a prudent man, had used that surprise to some effect. Was Alois a prudent man? I thought him clever, but that is not the same thing.

"Is all well?" I climbed to the battlements.

Rauf grinned when he saw me. "It will be."

We both knew how few we really were against the strength of Alois's band. Wrapping my cloak around my body, I began to walk the circuit of the walls. It was for me to be certain preparations were complete. Maugris would expect my report and blame me, rightly, if they were not; these were our natural roles: he the spearhead, I the shaft.

The walk was long and observant as the night grew colder. A half barrel of arrows stood midway between the posts of each two fighters, and braziers were set there also with billets of wood and pots of pitch ready to be melted in the fire. It was old-fashioned even then, but boiling pitch was rightly feared as a weapon of war.

Night deepened and the keep settled into the dark until, at last, only one light burned—in the armory. I returned to the battlements above the great gate.

"Rauf."

"Lord?"

I spoke quietly. "I need your help."

Another red dawn streaked the sky as I opened the armory door. "Brother?"

Maugris was gray with lack of sleep. "I am here." In one corner, propped against the wall, Sim, the best of our fletchers, snored noisily.

I stared around. The room was empty, the weapons gone. "All out on the walls?"

"Yes. The geese have no feathers left. We'll eat them when this is over. You?"

I nodded. "It is done."

Maugris held up a key to the annex off the armory. "Come with me."

Godefroi had been buried with his best sword, but the second-best, and three more, were laid up in the annex in locked chests. His personal bows were there too. Unstrung, five or six hung across pegs with their strings stored in waxed bags.

Maugris plucked the bows as if they were so much fruit as I followed him into the room. And stopped with a jolt.

Godefroi's armor stood behind the door, the metal ghost of our murdered brother.

"He was more your height than mine. Put it on." Maugris lifted the lid of a coffer and pulled out a hauberk of ring mail. "But aid me first."

After Maugris stripped off his mantle and most of the clothes beneath, I helped him lace a felt jerkin over his shirt and dropped the suit of mail over his body. The sideless surcoat he wore over the top was woven with our crest.

"You should carry this, brother." I lifted Godefroi's second sword from its resting place and offered it.

"Would he mind?"

"Too late to ask." I slid the sword into the scabbard hanging from Maugris's belt. "You are lord of Hundredfield now. One day soon, I shall dance at your wedding."

His face brightened. "But I shall not. I hate dancing."

"And yet, you can fight, Maugris. And you know what they say, 'Never trust a sword to—'"

"'—a man who cannot dance.' Yes. But *they* are wrong." The years, in that moment, dropped from his face. We laughed. Maugris was never graceful unless in a fight.

Voices. Shouts. The sound of running feet.

Maugris twisted to stare at the open window.

I went to see.

The morning was windless, benign and pretty—fair face, black heart—and on the far side of the river, men were massing.

"It has come."

"His armor. Put it on!" Maugris flung the words as he ran from the annex.

Alone, I buckled into the suit with some effort. And ran to join my brother on the walls.

"How many?" Rauf asked.

Maugris and I were crouched behind the battlements above the gate. Fulk had built well. It was possible to look out over the river below and not be seen. I did not answer. I was dismayed at the sight.

Maugris said carelessly, "Two hundred. No more. They shall be scythed like barley."

But of course there were more. Shaggy-haired, with wild, brown faces, the ground heaved as they gathered. They would be rabid dogs in this fight.

Maugris peered through an arrow slit. "I do not see Alois."

"Bayard!"

It was him. Little remained of the monk he had been, but choir training had taught him how to use his voice.

I went to stand.

Maugris pulled me down. "Not yet."

"Bayard de Dieudonné. Show yourself. Why hide? We are all friends here." Laughter swept the final words across the river.

I shook away my brother's grasp.

"See? I knew you could do it. Very brave."

From the height of the walls I saw him. The horse he rode was sturdy and small, and so hairy it looked like a goat.

I cupped my hands. "Nice mount you have there, Alois. By the way, what do you want? I am busy."

"Not so busy as you will be. Perhaps we should try a joust when our business is done. Oh, I forgot. You'll be dead."

"I do not ride against men on goats. It confuses my destrier." I was lucky. I stepped back as an arrow sliced the air beside my cheek and shattered against the battlement wall behind.

"My thumb slipped!" Laughter again.

"Stop sucking it." Another arrow, two more. I waited.

"We can go on like this all day. We have many, many arrows."

I sprang to the gap with Godefroi's best bow and fired. Two shots away and I heard a man scream. *One down.*

"What are they doing?" Maugris had bellied closer.

I dared to look. "Boiling like ants around the man I shot."

Alois called out again. "This glorious day is wasting, Bayard. Speak to me, for we are men of peace."

I caught Maugris's eye. He nodded. "But we are not." I fired again. Once more. A third time.

A growl like that of a great mastiff was lost in shouts and further screams. Maugris smiled as more arrows arrived to crash against the wall behind us. He picked up another of Godefroi's bows and stood beside me on the far side of the gap.

"I am losing patience, Bayard. You have a choice. Give us Hundredfield and perhaps we will allow you to depart in peace." Alois was not so cordial now.

Maugris shouted, "Terms already? A sign of weakness, Alois."

"You are both there? That is good. Brothers should die together."

I shouted, "What happened to 'depart in peace'?"

A roar, and arrows fell out of the shining sky.

We ducked and hugged the parapet close. Below we heard splash after splash in the river.

Rauf called out, "Skin boats."

Maugris yelled, "Ladders?"

"Yes. Held between two."

Maugris signaled to Rauf.

Rauf bellowed, "First rank!"

Our men stepped to their places.

A good archer, well supplied, fires best in a steady rhythm, and veterans of so many battles, our fighters went about their business as if shooting at the butts. The sun at their backs dazzled the men on the ground. It is always hard, firing into the sky.

"Arrows!" I yelled to Dikon and another lad, a turnspit from the kitchen. At a crouching run, they gathered what had been fired by those below as refills for us.

"Rauf!" Maugris signaled again.

He had seen what we had seen. Below, men were landing on our side of the river. Rauf bellowed, "Next rank!"

Two archers now stood at each gap in the battlements.

"Second fires down!" Rauf's order cut through.

The archers held. And fired. And fired. And men on both sides of the river fell.

I pointed. "There. Look!"

Maugris joined me. "Christ's eyes!" Ladders were going up against the battlements.

One of Rauf's men sprinted up from below. "The postern! They've breached the postern gate!"

Maugris held up two hands. "Hold the wall." And Rauf counted ten men down from the battlements.

On our bellies, we wriggled toward the entrance to the stairs that led down to the inner ward. Then the moment came to run the arrow storm.

I went first, and across that narrow space shafts broke and bounced off Godefroi's armor, and the doorway did the rest; I found myself inside the walls, a whole man, as others followed.

Maugris blocked the light and fell into the stairwell, panting. "Can't shoot to save themselves." He grinned.

46

I'T'S SO much easier having a conversation in your head. Saying the actual words, that's the really hard bit.

Jesse doesn't know where to begin. She doesn't know why she feels like that. And there's guilt. Of course.

Hang on. Mack kissed me!

However, from the time he'd walked into the bar and up to this moment, when they're more than halfway back to Hundredfield, Rory has said just five words. She's been counting.

"Hi" and "Seat belt" and "Nearly there."

"Rory?" *Wrong!* Too tentative.

He doesn't answer.

Jesse twists in her seat until she's staring at that profile. It's rigid. "I'd like to talk about Mack."

But she doesn't say that.

She says, "What's the time, please?"

"Twelve forty-seven." He taps the clock.

"Oh. Right." The dashboard clock. "Right time to talk, then." She plunges in. "About Mack. And me."

A muscle's twitching in Rory's jaw. "You're both grown-ups."

"Yes. But he is your brother."

"Half brother." It's said with no emphasis.

What does that mean? "I—we—that is, we didn't mean it to happen. Just that, sometimes . . ."

"Jesse, I did study psychology. You're vulnerable, and you see him as some kind of knight in shining armor. Completely understandable." The doctor voice. But the car's slowing down.

Maybe he does want to talk. "No, it's not that." *Is it?* "I'd just been talking to your mother, and, well, it was a pretty difficult conversation. I was upset. More than that, really."

That gets Rory's attention. "What do you mean?"

"She knew. Helen knew what happened when I was born. And she didn't tell me. Deliberately. She met Eva too. My mother. Helen said she was a drifter." Jesse's voice catches. *No! No more crying.* She sniffs hard.

"Tissues in the glove box." An automatic response.

"What, you *travel* with them?" Jesse sneaks a glance as she blows her nose. Maybe he's defrosting, maybe he isn't. Maybe she just doesn't care. In a stronger voice she says, "I don't know what it is with your mum, but—"

"Everyone has a shadow side."

"And thank you, Mr. Jung. I'm sure we're all grateful for that insight." A pause. "I think it's you two. She can't let you go."

"She's protective. Mothers are."

"Bit of layman's advice, Rory. Cut the apron strings."

This time, when he looks at her, she sees the truth. He's furious. But she meets his glance. She's pissed off too.

Abruptly, Rory pulls to the side of the road. Hauls on the hand brake. "None of this is easy, Jesse. It does not have to become personal, however."

She yells at him, "Personal? What your mother did to me today is way past personal. It's outrageous! So are you!" In that small space the noise is deafening.

Rory goes to start the car again. And doesn't. "But you did come back to Hundredfield."

"Yes!" Jesse's still shouting. She turns away. "Oh, bugger it." She thumps the dashboard. "Bugger, bugger, bugger!" Again. Harder.

Rory stares out through the windscreen. "Mum's always been very close to Mack. You need to know that." He starts the car, steers it back onto the road. They're almost in sight of the gates of the estate.

And isn't that good news. Jesse takes a breath. Controls herself. "And you. What about you?"

"What do you mean?" His voice is flat.

"A girl. Alicia, for instance?" She cringes. *So subtle.*

"Alicia?"

She sees him shift uncomfortably. "Well, what I mean is, she's very fond of you. You could be good together." Stop. Stop *now.*

"Friends is what we are." Rory shifts down as the car takes the corner into Hundredfield's drive. "Alicia's always just been family."

"But you want her to be happy."

Rory takes time to answer. The bridge is in sight. "I want everyone to be happy. Even Mack." He doesn't look at Jesse. "Here we are. Back home."

Another few minutes and the car stops at the front door.

Jesse gets out. *Whose home? Not yours, certainly not mine.* But she still walks through that door.

Alicia calls out, "Good to see you looking better."

Jesse closes the gate that leads to the kitchen garden. "Thanks." The last thing she feels, in any way, is better.

At the center of the radiating beds of fruits and vegetables is a roundel of bricks and a weathered bench. Alicia's sitting there. She gestures at the bucket of apricots overflowing at her feet. "The tomatoes are bad enough, but all this fruit!"

Jesse sits beside the other girl. "I could stew some for dinner if you like. Or make apricot crumble?"

They watch as dragonflies flit and hover above the surface of a small pond.

"It's so peaceful here. A green bower."

" 'Bower.' " Alicia shades her eyes against the light. She throws a stick into the pond, watches the ripples spread. "Sounds peaceful, but it's not like that here, not really."

"Define *peaceful*."

"Well, the opposite of *unquiet*. *That's* what Hundredfield is—unquiet. Like it's got a mind of its own suddenly." Another stick.

Jesse goes to say something. And doesn't.

"I've always liked the view from here." Alicia gestures to a gap in the wall around the garden. "That fell down when I was little, and Mummy stopped Daddy from having it repaired. She used to sit here on warm afternoons and I'd be at her feet; she'd tell me stories while we podded peas together." Alicia turns to Jesse in surprise. "I've just remembered. Mummy called this her 'bower' as well." She picks up an apricot. "Would you like one? Fruit grows well in a walled garden."

Jesse says semiseriously, "So what about fruit and veggies as a business? You'd be a sensation."

"Hey!" Alicia gets up. She shoos a blackbird away from some fallen apricots and bends to pick one up. "The trust people came today."

Jesse says cautiously, "How was that?"

"They seem interested." Alicia adds the apricot to the bucket. "But I change my mind every three minutes." She drops back onto the seat. "Maybe if the trust falls through, I'll take up your suggestion—get my hands dirty like a real farmer. What d'you reckon?" She laughs.

Jesse mutters, "I've seen stranger things." She pauses. "You said Hundredfield has a mind of its own now. What did you mean?"

Alicia bites into an apricot. "The past bleeds into the present. It won't let go. Damn!" Apricot juice has dribbled onto her T-shirt.

Jesse fishes Rory's tissues out of a pocket. "Have these. I don't need them."

Alicia mops the juice and licks her fingers. "Your drawings, that's what made me think of it. But there's more, there's always been more, and it's why leaving here, if I have to go, is agony." She's massaging her temples. "Unfinished business that started a thousand years ago."

Jesse takes a breath. "You're right about unfinished business. Before we went to Newton Prior this morning, Rory and I . . ."

"Don't upset yourself, Jesse. You must still be feeling so strange and—"

"This is not about what happened at the river. Did you know Rory's using hypnosis? As a tool."

"Go on." Alicia's staring at her curiously.

"He talks about my unconscious finding a voice. But it's not my voice on those tapes, not all the time. Today, well, when Rory played the tape back, I heard *her*. She said I must 'return the mother.'" Jesse swallows.

"What does that mean?" Alicia's expression is skeptical.

Jesse pauses. "I don't know. And this is going to sound very, very odd—I was wearing the mask on my face. I, or she, spoke through it. Rory heard her, I heard her. 'Return the mother' were the actual words she used." She stands restlessly. "'The past bleeds into the present.' Your words, Alicia. And at the river"—a deep, trembling breath—"she was there. She was in the water with me. She's not just a drawing, Alicia. She's not just someone in a dream. She's real. And she's connected to this place."

"I don't understand."

The background shrill of insects drills into Jesse's head as she watches Alicia's expression change. "What are you thinking?"

"Because she's linked to you, is this your way of saying you have a claim on Hundredfield?" The cool tone, the cool eyes.

"No. But I think she does."

47

IRE THE keep." Maugris took the stairs to the inner ward without haste. In crisis, my brother was calm. That is why men followed him. "Come to the postern when it is done."

Margaretta!

I ran for the tower.

If a man could fly upward, I took the stairs as if I had wings, and locked or not, I kicked the door of Godefroi's chamber open.

I had not warned them.

As I rushed through, there came a crack, a sound I heard but from somewhere far away, and then—I fell into night.

"Wake!" Pain. It came as I lay in a black and queasy bog. My eyes jangled open just as Margaretta poured water over my face again. Pushing her away, I tried to stand. And could not.

Aviss began to whimper.

I held out my hand as comfort, but the child screamed, and I saw that blood covered my whole arm.

Had I been injured and not known it? I touched my head. One side of my scalp ran red. The wound from Alois's camp had opened. "I was wrong to bring you here."

Margaretta said nothing. A heave, and she pulled me to my feet.

Aviss in my arms, the baby in hers, we stumbled down the stairs to the chapel.

I pulled the covering of the alcove aside. Margaretta gasped. The Madonna's plinth was empty.

I fumbled the panel open. "Go, but block the way."

She nodded. "Do not fear for us." She knew it was likely I would die. I saw it in her eyes.

Consecrated or not, I ripped coverings from the altar and pulled the Madonna's hangings down. "Block the tunnel against smoke. Do not come out." I pushed the material into her arms.

She knelt inside the opening with the children. "Bayard."

And I knelt also, my arms around all three.

She whispered, "Come back to us."

Between love and desire, I kissed her.

And pushed her inside. "Go." The door was pulled closed.

I forced myself to run from the chapel.

Upstairs, in the hall, I laid fire through the rushes and, as they burned, snatched some up and held them against my mother's tapestries until they bloomed a terrible rose.

Fire is an animal. It has a voice. As smoke began to drift, I heard it. A monster that grew in size and power as it leapt to eat the ancient rafters of the hall.

Blood in my eyes, I ran outside and counted the gates. One, beside the keep. Two, as the path turned to the pleasance. Three, at the garden itself, and—

"*À moi, à moi!*"

Maugris!

Deep in the melee at the postern gate, Hundredfield tunics were few, but my brother fought on with three men at his side.

I became the fourth.

Now three faced those who came from the river side, and we two, at their backs, took those who fought in the garden. Forward, slice, back, feint; practiced rhythm, well mastered, as the blades clashed and sang. We were armored and well trained. They were not.

A man went down before Maugris, screaming. His head was gone in a swoop. "Is it done?"

Another fighter tried for my eyes. I blocked his knife and took him through the guts. Blood sprayed from his mouth. Red rain. "It is done."

A crack and I looked up. The cap-house was burning as, around us, the pile of bodies grew.

"Close it." Maugris meant the postern gate.

I jumped forward with Tamas. Three to fight, two to build the rampart from still warm bones.

Under the swords as they wheeled and bit, we dragged dead men as if they were logs. Some we swung at those coming up. Some we built in a wall.

Maugris called out, "Back, fall back."

One of our fighters pitched on his face. An ax in his back.

Four of us now. Tamas and me to push, Maugris and one more to fight.

As I had pulled it open for Godefroi, now I began to close the postern gate—my shoulder like a bullock to the door as men howled and died in the narrowing gap.

The postern was heavy and thick, three layers of oak, studded and bound with iron. I felt the weight on the other side more and more, as the gate began to push against us.

Smoke was our savior. On that windless day it rolled from the top of the keep down to the river, an evil coverlet choking those on the path, while we in our mother's garden breathed clean air.

So we pushed back. And closed the gate. And dropped the lock bar down.

Maugris wheeled. "Now." He sprinted away. And we followed. Down to the inner ward.

48

As ALICIA and Jesse walk into the hall, the phone's ringing.

Jesse's closer. "Hundredfield, Jesse Marley speaking."

A gasp. "Is that you? Is it really you?"

Jesse doesn't know how to answer. She buckles slowly to a chair.

"Oh, talk to me. Please, say something."

Jesse's face works. "Hello, Mum."

There's silence. Then words spill out of the receiver. "We didn't know where you were, and I—I just so wanted to talk and, oh, I know you were angry, but—" The voice fractures.

Jesse hunches forward. It feels as if she's chewing concrete when she tries to speak. "Mum, look, I . . ." *I what?* "I wish none of this had happened, but it has." She draws a breath. "Where are you?"

"In Newcastle."

Jesse takes that in. "Australia?"

"No. England. Jesse. Are you still there?"

"Yes. How did you know how to find me?"

"I didn't, but . . ." There's a pause. "What's happened to you? Are you okay?"

How does she answer that? "Yes, Mum." Jesse closes her eyes.

"Oh, thank you, God. Your father and I were so worried. And when we heard nothing for weeks, we thought . . ." Another swallow. "We thought—oh, such dreadful, terrible things. In the end, I got on the plane in Sydney and flew to London. I didn't know where to start to look—it's been days of searching." The sob is stifled. "But last night, your father sent a telegram to the hotel. Your postcard arrived at home. So this morning I took the bus north."

This is too painful. Jesse interrupts, "Did you know she died? Her name was Eva Green, Mum. She was sixteen, and no one's named as my father." Jesse's throat closes over.

The response has a forlorn dignity. "I should have told you the truth years and years ago, but I thought I'd lose you, and . . ." The words crumble into gasps.

Jesse's shaking, vibrating, her jaw won't let her speak, and she's breathing so deeply, the world is a light-headed blur.

"Jesse?" Her mother's panicking. "Speak to me. Oh, please. Anything. Just talk to me."

Alicia puts a quiet hand on Jesse's shoulder.

Jesse grips the phone; she's curled herself around it. "A pen. Have you got a pen?"

There's a scrabble on the end of the line. "Yes."

"There's a pub called the Hunt in Newton Prior. English side of the border. Write that down. I'll meet you there. There'll be a room in your name."

"Yes. Oh, Jesse, I . . ." The line goes silent.

"Mum?" Jesse stares at the receiver. "Mum, are you there?"

She hears the disconnected-call sound.

Gently, Alicia takes the phone and puts it back in its cradle.

Jesse's face is dazed. "Her money ran out."

"Right." It seems the only thing to say. "Why did she ring you here?"

"I don't know. She sounded shocked when I answered." Jesse shakes her head. "The thing is"—she swallows—"Mum's here. In Newcastle."

"Oh. Okay." Alicia looks confused. "She's welcome to stay and—"

"No!" The response is instinctive. Jesse jerks back a little. "It's too close, having her here. It would be . . ." She can't frame the thought.

"It's not an imposition, if that's what you're thinking."

Jesse shakes her head. "There's so much to just . . . process. Too much *stuff*." She pauses. "She's taking the bus to Newtown Prior. I'll try to book her into the Hunt. Would you mind if I rang Mack?" *Just to talk to him. Just to hear his voice.*

"Of course not."

Jesse starts to dial with fingers the size and weight of hammers. *Let him be there, please, please, just let it be him. . . .*

"Yes, got that. Mrs. Janet Marley. Breakfast included, special deal for our friends." Mack's scribbling the name in the booking register that's kept on the front desk of the Hunt. "The Newcastle bus gets here midafternoon. We'll look after her like she's our own." He pauses. "Are you okay?"

"I don't know. Yes. No."

He speaks softly, "Wish I was there."

"Wish you were too." Jesse closes her eyes. "Oh, Mack, it's so good to talk. It feels like I've got nothing to hold on to anymore."

"Yes, you have. You've got me."

"Is that really true?"

"Try me. Anytime." He looks up. Helen's standing a pace or two away. Mack pivots, speaks more quietly. "So, we'll look forward to seeing her, and you, when she arrives. I'll let you know." He puts the receiver down. "Is there something you want, Mum?"

Helen strides over and turns the register around to read it. Her face changes but she says, "We're full, Mack. You shouldn't have taken the booking."

He stares at her. "No, we're not. We've got five rooms vacant."

Helen meets him head-on. "You'll have to ring the caller back and say you made a mistake."

For a moment Mack measures Helen's expression, then says gently, "What's the problem, Mum? You're upset."

"No. Listen to me. Ring whoever it was and do as I say."

Mack turns the phone around. "You ring. She's at Hundred-field. You know the number. Ask for Jesse Marley."

Helen hesitates. "Perhaps I put that badly."

He nods.

"But don't, just don't, talk to those people—any of them. Please. Just cancel the booking."

"Do you want to tell me why?"

She flares. "I don't want to *do* anything where they're concerned."

He says quietly, "Sorry, Mum. I took that booking in good faith. We have the room and I'm not going to cancel on a lie. Or a whim."

Helen's face works but Mack says nothing as he turns and walks steadily to the door.

Life, for his mother, has always been about control. But things are slipping. Mack can feel it.

49

ARE YOU really sure you want to go inside?"

"Yes." But Jesse's face is pale as she stares up at the keep.

Alicia hesitates. "Did I tell you it was repaired after the fire? The keep." Worried about Jesse, she's buying time.

"Fire?"

"Hundredfield was sacked in the early fourteenth century. The keep was torched but the structure pretty much survived. Thick walls. Very." Another pause. "Come on, then."

A flight of steps leads to the door in the wall. At the top, Alicia sorts out keys.

Jesse shades her eyes to peer at the summit of the keep. Like a soldier's dead body, these battered stones bear witness to casual, timeless violence.

Alicia calls over her shoulder, "It's quite safe. Been used as storage for years and years, and Rory's right. I don't really know what's in here."

In the ten minutes it's taken to walk to the keep, Alicia's become more and more tense. After the conversation in the kitchen garden, the last hour has tested them both.

"That one?" Jesse points to the largest of the keys—a monster with a shank half as long as a human forearm.

Alicia speaks loudly, as if silence might be a burden. "You'd think so, wouldn't you? But it unlocks a room under the cap-house at the top of the stair tower." She rattles the keys along the iron loop, selecting one. "This is it." Alicia inserts it in the lock. "I haven't been inside for such a long time. Only got as far as the outside with the trust before we ran out of time." A vigorous jiggle, and something gives within the ancient mechanism. She turns the key with both hands. "Watch where you put your feet, it'll be shitty inside. Bats."

"Bats?" Jesse steps back.

"Yes. They're mostly in the roof but we have to be careful." A push and the door groans open.

Jesse says, with feeling, "Yes."

"No, I mean we have to be careful of them—their welfare. All sorts of regulations about bats these days . . ." Alicia disappears inside trailing words like soap bubbles.

Jesse puts a foot on the stairs—and takes it off.

Alicia's head appears around the door. Her artificial manner wobbles at the sight of Jesse's face, but she pushes the door wider. "The chapel's in the base of the tower." A breeze scuttles past as if it knows where to go.

When she finally enters, Jesse's shadow is thrown across steps that twist up to an invisible roof. *You knew this place, didn't you? You heard the wind climbing the stairs.*

"So, we're going down, not up." Alicia flicks a flashlight into life. The stones of the staircase are massive pieces of granite, impressively cupped. "Just be careful, though. It's like the back stairs in the house, but trickier. Easy to slip over."

"I'm fine."

Together, they walk down into the dark.

"It's freezing in here." Jesse pulls her jacket across her chest.

"That's the spring. It's under the foundations. Got a mind of its own, that thing."

"You said that." But Jesse's not really listening.

"Did I?"

Light spills down the stairs into an anteroom and ahead to a pair of ancient doors, much scarred. "The chapel's through there, it's the oldest existing part of Hundredfield. Norman."

"You said that too." Jesse's quite spiky.

"Right. Of course." Alicia rattles the head of the key inside the lock. "Not having much luck today."

"Shall I try?"

Alicia steps back. "It's very stiff."

Jesse hesitates. She touches the key, warm from Alicia's fingers, and tries to turn it. Nothing.

Disappointment hits. She'd been sure, so sure, she could open this door.

"I'll get some oil."

Jesse tries again. "Wait!" As the key moves, the wards engage. With a click the lock gives.

Alicia eyes Jesse curiously. "Well done." Pushing the doors open, she sweeps the beam of the flashlight over the walls. Perhaps they were plastered once, but now the raw stone weeps, and moss and liverwort cluster in cracks where mortar's fallen out.

The light picks out piled-up lumber—old doors and windows, broken furniture, dark paintings in battered frames. And swings back to Jesse.

"Can I ask you something?"

Jesse holds her hand up to block the beam. "Sure."

"Do you feel anything?"

Jesse hesitates before she shakes her head.

"I suppose it's disappointing. The illustrations made the chapel look so opulent." Alicia flips the light across the floor as she wanders farther away. "This is where the altar stood. You can tell from the tiles." She holds the flashlight above, silvering her hair. "They were made in Winchester and brought all the way to Berwick by sea, then carried overland by pack mule to Hundredfield.

Cost one of my ancestors a bomb." Dark tiles inlaid with a lighter color glint as the light sweeps on.

"What're they?"

Alicia's jiggles the beam over a row of large, flat stones, laid directly into the floor. "Graves. There's speculation about who's buried here, but so many records were lost in the Border Wars. And the fire." She points the flashlight. "This one was important, though." She kneels, brushing dust from the stone to clear the inscription. "Do you see? *Domina*. The Latin word for 'lady.' And she was buried right in front the altar too—a place of honor."

"And this one?" Jesse stares at another of the stones; it's separated from the lady's grave by a slab with no markings at all.

"A total mystery. Very odd, though, that it's anonymous."

Jesse bends down over the third slab in the row. "Is that a cross?" The shape is faint in the eroded surface.

"No. It's a sword. It's the guard above the grip that makes it look like a cross. The grave of a fighting man, a knight most probably."

"Nothing to say who it might be?"

Alicia shakes her head. "It was thought to be Fulk, but the shape of the sword is too late to be Norman—so this grave's presumed to be a couple of hundred years later. Fourteenth century sometime. But the old reprobate must be buried here somewhere."

That name. "Fulk?"

"They called him the devil, or just the Frenchman. Time puts a gloss on murderers and thieves. The Normans were both."

Jesse sees something, a flash behind the eyes. "What happened to him?" *The river in raging spate, and a body—a man with terrible wounds—rolling over and over as the flood carries him away, open-eyed.*

"He was murdered at the end of a long, vicious, and profitable life; his son held Hundredfield, but he married a Saxon noblewoman, maybe that helped with the locals." Alicia flashes the beam up to the groined ceiling. "What you drew—the rood—

hung right here; if you look, you can see the marks where the screen on which it hung stood. And somewhere nearby"—Alicia trails her hand along the wall—"was the alcove that hid Our Lady of the River. My great-grandfather said it was close to the altar."

"I don't remember that."

Alicia looks puzzled. Light wanders across a pile of timber paneling stacked up against the wall. "Didn't I read that? Tell you what, why don't I go get the book?" Alicia hurries toward the doors.

"Hey! Leave the light."

Alicia puts the flashlight on a step. "Sorry. Back soon."

Jesse listens as the footsteps scatter away. She's used to the dark now, and faint daylight picks out the barrel of the flashlight, fading the living beam from silver to gray.

Unwillingly, she turns to stare at the wall near the altar.

"Hello. I came."

The whisper multiplies. The vaulted space has an echo.

Jesse has not been straight with Alicia; she felt, she feels, too much.

Slowly, she walks to the pile of paneling. And moves the first piece aside.

And starts to hum.

"Hi."

Alicia spins around. "Rory!" She's in Jesse's bedroom.

He steps back a pace. "Sorry."

"How did you find me?"

"I was looking for Jesse." He takes in the book in her hands. "Bit of light reading?"

Alicia manages a smile. "Not exactly."

"So, have you seen her?"

"Why?" Alicia tries to throw the word away. Fails.

"I'm her doctor. Why else?" He's uncomfortable too. This is not an easy conversation.

Alicia opens a drawer in a bedside table, takes out another flashlight. "She told me about the woman on the tape, by the way. The stuff about 'the mother.'" Alicia turns to face him, a stubborn set to her jaw. "Jesse said you were there. Is that true?"

"Yes."

"So? You heard what, exactly?"

"I've been asking myself that question since yesterday."

"And?"

A pause that neither breaks.

Alicia closes the drawer and strides to the door. "Jesse's at the keep. And before you ask, she convinced me to take her there. I'd better get back." They reach for the door handle at the same time, his hand over hers.

Alicia stumbles. If she could say even the smallest thing that's in her heart, she would. But she can't. She hesitates. "Why didn't you tell me about the tape?"

Rory can see how troubled she is. "Look, the last few weeks have severely rearranged my head."

"You're alone in that, of course." That flick of irony has an edge.

"No, I'm not, Alicia—you're right there too. So is Jesse." Rory looks through the open window. "The keep was the first thing she drew. Did I tell you that?"

Alicia mutters, "Oh, this is just ridiculous."

"You asked me what I thought. I still don't know. But somehow, we've booked these tickets. It's a waste if we don't go for the ride. To the end."

Alicia snaps, "What does that mean?"

"Ask yourself why Jesse's turned up just as you're trying to unload Hundredfield."

Alicia doesn't respond as she stamps past. Rory watches her go, but then, in a few strides, catches up.

"I could carry that." He means the book.

"I can manage."

They walk down the staircase and across the hall, past the suit of armor.

Rory tries to lift the ponderous silence. "Did you ever say who wore that?"

"No, I didn't. Just another nameless knight."

"Hope he was useful with that ax."

Alicia's ahead of him out the front door. "Never likely to know, are we?"

50

MAUGRIS YELLED, "Two ladders!" On the battlements the melee was fed by men climbing the walls, and the inner ward seethed with fighters from both sides.

An ax lay at my feet. I picked it up. In my other hand was Maugris's sword. "The horses?"

"Go!"

Death stepped to one side as I ran, but embers fell like red stars in the thatch of the stables, and smoke filled the barns as I bolted inside.

Helios was at the end of a line of panicked horses, all tied along a central pole.

"Stand!"

The stallion heard my voice. Quivering, he stood long enough for me to haul myself to his back. The ax did the rest. Barging along the line, I lopped the ropes and set the horses free. Snorting, plunging, they hurtled for the open doors and, crazed by fire and smoke and noise, broke like a storm on the inner ward.

I remember men's faces as they were run down. Some heard

us—and lived; some did not—and died under those hooves, for what I had set free would not be stopped.

On the battlements, Rauf and the archers still held. They cheered as they saw the horses run, and with the distraction, Maugris heaved a ladder back from the walls, men screaming as it fell.

But one ladder remained, and a man's head topped the battlements. It was him. Alois. His face was daubed with woad.

"Brother!"

Maugris turned. Too slow.

Alois jumped. Too fast. And his sword took my brother between shoulder and neck.

Rauf roared and closed the distance between them as I jumped from the stallion's back.

With ax and sword, I cleared a path to the stairs and up, and on the battlements I found them.

Maugris was alive, but twisting like a worm cut in two; Rauf and Alois swayed beside him, swords locked at the guard.

"Alois!" I screamed his name.

But it was Rauf who looked back. That was his death. Alois stabbed him in the neck.

I leapt as Rauf fell. Taller, stronger, I drove the monk back, back, and *down* to his knees; he should have died. But he was fast. Rolled away, and up.

"Bayard!"

Maugris, on one arm, slashed at Alois as the man's dagger nicked my throat. He caught him in the belly and the monk dropped, doubled over

I knelt beside my brother in a shining scarlet pool.

He lifted a hand to my face. He could not speak. Then the hand fell back.

"Maugris? Maugris!"

Fixed, without life, his eyes stared into eternity.

I closed them. And then rose up and kicked the ladder from the walls.

And turned with a roar. If Alois lived, I was his doom. But he had disappeared. And Rauf lay dead.

All those I loved, destroyed in that one moment. *Except Margaretta.*

"Look!" Tamas yelled, and pointed.

The fire in the keep, a tree burning from its crown, was dying. I ran.

The stairs of the tower was a throat and, roofless, breathed smoke into the sky. But the walls were stone, the steps, stone, and the stairs had no fuel to burn. Now, for lack of wood, the fire was dying, though the massive door of the keep still smoldered. I broke a way through with my ax, and the chapel itself was quiet. And dark. And I could breathe.

Panting, I sprinted to the alcove beside the altar, but I had no candle and could not find the door.

Help me!

Perhaps I called to the woman who had given me life, perhaps to Flore, but I was blind as I ran my hands along the panels.

I heard the voice of the child, faint and distant.

Then I found the unblocked door.

Who had opened it?

I did not care. The baby was singing me home.

51

OAK IS heavy, and Jesse's panting as she moves the last piece of carved wood aside. On her knees, she picks up the flashlight and shines it at the wall behind.

A hole opens like a mouth—it eats the light. Humming, she who could not sing, Jesse bends forward, and another voice joins her own—it's the same song. Jesse stops, turns off the flashlight to listen better. The song fades to nothing.

It wasn't a voice. Was it? Wind, maybe, or water falling—somewhere distant.

Jesse flicks on the flashlight, lets it play over the entrance, *because that's what it is.*

And hears it again. Faint, but someone singing. Yes, a voice.

Jesse enters the void on her knees. Ahead, there's a tunnel. If she stands, she can touch the wall on both sides; yes, it's narrow, but not so narrow she can't walk down the slope of the passage. Jesse splashes light as she goes. The air is sweet, and a breeze brings with it the smell of water and earth.

The song is louder. Without thought, she joins in and speeds up, flashlight bouncing and flaring. Ahead, there's . . . something.

⌒

The small woman in the cardigan dings the bell. She puts her case down. Modest and old-fashioned, it says she doesn't travel often. Waiting for service, she wanders from the reception desk. Not far.

"Mrs. Marley?"

She startles easily. "Oh. Yes, that's me." She hurries back.

"Welcome. We've been expecting you. Jesse called." A large young man with a streak of white hair smiles from behind the counter.

Janet Marley manages a nod.

"I'm Mack, by the way. The manager of the Hunt."

Another timid nod.

He clears his throat. "So, if you'd care to fill in a few details, I'll take you up to your room."

"Thank you. I'd like that."

It occurs to Mack that Jesse's mum must be tired. Australia's a long way away, and she's just endured a bus trip of some hours; no wonder her face is strained. "Can I get you a cup of tea?" He gives her a form to sign, and a pen.

"That would be lovely. You don't get real tea where I live." Two actual sentences.

Mack smiles encouragingly. "Sydney?"

"How did you know?" Janet's expression flicks to frightened.

"Jesse's a good friend. She mentioned she'd been brought up in Sydney."

"I talked to her earlier." Janet swallows. "I wasn't sure if all was well with her. You can tell with your child." She bites her lip.

Mack hesitates. "I'll get that tea. Five minutes, tops."

Janet watches him go. She looks down at the form. And drops the pen. Her hands are shaking.

"Hello, Janet."

Janet Marley wheels at the sound of that voice. She stands straighter. "Hello, Helen. I thought . . ."

"What did you think?"

Janet swallows. "That you might be at Hundredfield." She quivers like a rabbit in a snare. "Silly me." The twitch of that smile is ghastly.

Light bounces from step to step, but Rory and Alicia are still not talking.

Alicia calls from the doorway, "I've got the book." She stops. Flashlight shines on dripping walls.

Rory adds his voice: "We're both here."

Alicia's puzzled. "Jesse?"

"Maybe she's outside."

"We'd have seen her." Alicia hurries to the grave slabs in the floor. She jiggles the beam across the wasteland of family rubbish. Nothing seems different.

Rory's beside her. "Tell me the last thing you talked about."

"The graves. And the alcove, where the Madonna was supposed to be." She points the beam to the wall. "It's in the book."

"What else?"

"The stuff on the tape—the woman you heard. No, that was earlier—in the kitchen garden, before her mother rang."

"Her mother?" Rory grabs the flashlight, sprints to the stairs.

"Hey!" Alicia runs after him.

He flings over his shoulder, "We need to find her. She could be suicidal."

"No. Listen, Rory. Stop!" Alicia barks the word, and the sound rings through the chapel.

He pauses on the top step. Flashes the light on her face.

"You're wrong. Her mum said she'll tell Jesse the truth. No way she's going to kill herself. Not now." But Alicia's not sounding as certain as she was.

"Okay. So, where is she?"

She can hear water. The sound a stream makes falling from a height. The breeze is stronger on her face, but Jesse doesn't feel cold anymore. She strips her jacket off one-handed. She's silent. Listening.

The song is louder.

If Jesse half closes her eyes, it's almost as if she's seeing the light beside her bed, that comforting, welcoming, rosy glow; and she remembers when she saw sounds, in color, at the hospital.

She gropes forward, pushes out into space. And gasps. In the dark, there hangs a glimmering man, his body twisted on a great cross. Light flares on that contorted form; it finds the gemstones: the trails of scarlet that cross the metal torso, the wounds on the feet and on the hands.

Jesse's transfixed. She hurries closer. And trips. The flashlight rolls and bumps against something else, something tall and white, draped in rags.

Before the light blinks out, and the song stops, Jesse sees the bats, a squeaking black cloud. They bloom like a storm from the back of the cave. She screams. And screams. And is engulfed.

Mack's back with the tray. He nods to their guest. "I see you've met my mother." He puts the pot and cups on a small table. "Like a cup, Mum?"

"No tea for me, Mack. Welcome to the Hunt, Mrs. Marley." A nod and Helen strides away to her office. And closes the door.

"Sugar?" Mack's pouring. Looks up. And drops the pot as he darts to catch their guest. "I've got you." He lowers her carefully to a chair. "I'll get Mum to call the doctor."

"No. No!" Janet's breathing hard. Her voice cracks. "Where's Jesse? Please. I . . ." She's finding it hard to speak.

Mack's worried. The poor woman looks so ill. "She said to call when you arrived and she'd join you here. I was just about to do that and—"

"Oh, please. Can we just go to her?" Janet clutches his sleeve.

He sits beside her. "Um . . ." He's got a clear view into the dining room. The lunch service is finished, and Rachel and Jewel are setting the tables for dinner. "Just a minute."

Janet watches him sprint to the dining room and talk to the girl with the capable expression. They both look back at her. The girl hesitates. And nods.

Mack sprints back. "Right. All fixed."

Janet stares into the face of this giant with such kind eyes. "This means so much to me."

"This way. Car's in the square. Always happy to see Jesse."

Janet gets up. She leaves her suitcase without another glance.

From inside her office, Helen hears the *ding!* of the bell on the reception desk. It sounds again, and she half rises.

Voices murmur as Helen picks up the phone to dial.

A woman. A man. Another woman's voice.

Helen puts the phone back. Gets up. Goes to the door and opens it.

Behind the reception desk, Rachel is handing registration forms to the couple checking in.

"Where's Mack?"

"He asked me to cover for a couple of hours, Mrs. Brandon. It's no trouble." Rachel can read the signs. Helen's angry.

"Did he say where he was going?" But Helen knows; Janet Marley's suitcase is an orphan, dumped beside one of the chairs. Her eyes widen at the sight of the teapot on the carpet.

"Hundredfield, I think." Rachel points helpfully at the form. "Yes, your home phone number would be good, Mr. Dean. Just for our records."

Helen goes back to her office. In less than a minute she exits and strides to the front door, shrugging on a jacket.

"The teapot, Rachel." Helen points on her way past the desk.

"Certainly, Mrs. Brandon. I'll clean it up right away." Rachel watches her employer leave.

"Miss? The keys."

Rachel jumps. "Yes. Here you are, Mr. Dean. It's just to the right at the top of the first flight of stairs. Lovely view of the Beast Market. Enjoy your stay."

"For your trouble." Mr. Dean extends a pound coin.

"Oh, no need at all." Rachel refuses nicely. Americans, always so courteous; not like some.

The front doors of the Hunt are glass, and Rachel watches with interest as Helen throws open her car door, then backs from the space at speed.

Jewel hurries from the dining room. "That's done. Anything else?"

"Take the bags, would you? Room eight. Name of Dean."

Jewel's not happy. "Can't Mack take them up?"

"He's already gone."

"But my shift's about done."

"Just you and me here, now."

"Why?"

"Mrs. B's out too."

They both watch as Helen honks at a pedestrian who dares to get in her way.

"Good thing, from the mood she's in." Jewel looks nervous. Her normal response to almost anything.

Rachel sighs. "We can do it together. Come on."

It's a nightmare. A bat is trapped in Jesse's hair. Squeaking, scratching madness, animal and human, they're both frantic. On her knees in the dark, trying not to whimper, trying not to scream again. Nothing works.

"Shush." Alicia holds up a hand.

"What?"

"Shush!"

They both stop breathing.

"There!" Alicia hurries back down the stairs again. She's running through the chapel, flashlight bouncing, Rory clattering behind. In front of the back wall, panting, she stops. He joins her.

They both hear it this time. Muffled, but a scream. Definitely.

A woman's voice. Terror.

Rory's shoving boxes and chairs aside to get to the wall.

Alicia drops to her knees. "Look." The light shows the opening, close to the piled-up paneling.

She plunges through. And disappears.

Rory hesitates. He's never liked the dark.

52

I FELT MY way along the tunnel. Without light, the close smell of earth was all that was familiar, yet I could breathe—there was no smoke or taste of burning in my mouth. The song pulled me forward. I did not know if it was in my head or my heart.

I stumbled into the first cavern with the last notes as they died. Empty dark pressed my face like fingers as I walked forward, arms outstretched.

"Margaretta?" I called out, so that she would not be frightened. "Here I am."

Flint struck sparks like stars and a candle shone, fingers red around the shaft. A man stood there, waiting. I could not see his face.

I weighed the ax. "Show yourself."

A shuffle, and the flame shone higher.

"Swinson?" The damage to his face was stark. "How did you know?"

The man spoke over me. "Our history is your history, Bayard de Dieudonné. That is how I know."

"What do you mean?"

"A baby was born to our house too." By candlelight, his eyes were scarred holes as he limped toward me. "Out of pity, my great-grandfather covered the naked body of her mother with his cloak when he found her in the forest. And though the woman could not speak, they married." His voice grew stronger. "She was never seen again after the birth of her daughter. And though the child's father died fighting the Norman devil, that baby survived to breed. As a slave. The slave of your house, as we have been since."

"What do you want, old man?" I could not let him see I pitied him.

"My daughter and her son. I have nothing without them."

"You are wrong."

I turned. Alois bowed as he came through the red door, but not to me; blood had soaked his jerkin and his trews.

One hand gripped the ax, the other Godefroi's sword as I stepped forward.

"Not far, now." Mack's kept up a one-sided conversation for most of the drive.

"No."

"You know this part of the world?" A glance.

"Too well." The Scots accent had flattened over the years in Australia, but Janet's burr was coming back.

He shifts down. "Too well?"

Janet Marley doesn't answer. Eyes wide, she's staring at the gates of the estate as the car passes between them. In the distance, the river glimmers.

"Die!"

Swords clashed and sang. I parried, a pivot to the side.

A grunt. A slash. Both returned. Maugris had sliced Alois deep, but the man was good.

"The. Battle." Step, thrust, back, feint. "Is. Lost. Alois."

His blow went astray as I dodged the blade. "No!" Forward, forward, slash, pivot, and I slashed again.

Margaretta's voice. "Brother!"

"Get back!" My shout to her.

Alois dared me, "Look. Look at your whore."

But I did not. Sword hand, ax hand, sword hand, ax hand, I drove him to the wall, a dog with a wolf.

Margaretta sobbed and I flicked a glance. The dress had been sliced from her back with a whip and her face was a bloody mess.

I ran at Alois. He got a slash away—it clipped my sword hand. And sheared it off. I felt no pain as it fell to the floor, still holding the sword. Blood fountained as if it were not my own.

But I held the ax in my left hand. And threw it.

Alois dropped to his knees, the ax head in his chest. He wavered there, as if to pull it out. And toppled.

A wail. Swinson hobbled to his son and I staggered to where he stood. And put my good arm around the old man's shoulders. "Here it ends."

As I passed into the dark, I heard the child's voice calling. And saw Margaretta's face.

Alicia trips. Something's on the floor.

"Rory. Rory!" She crouches beside Jesse.

Rory bursts from the tunnel. "Jesse?" He pinches the skin on the back of her hand.

"What are you *doing*?" Alicia tries to pull him away.

"Reflexes." Another pinch. "Jesse!"

Jesse's fingers twitch. She frowns. And sighs.

Rory sits back. He stares, perplexed. A small bat chitters as it flits above their heads. "She's asleep."

"Asleep, but . . ."

"It's happened before. Look." He points. The light, held from above, shines down like a follow spot. Jesse's eyes are moving under her lids.

"That's . . . creepy."

"She's dreaming. Or . . ."

"Or what?"

He looks at Alicia. "Or she's somewhere else."

Alicia says politely, "Of course. She's what, on a cruise?"

He ignores the goad. "We should take her to the house."

Alicia drops the flashlight beside them and hurries back toward the entrance of the tunnel. "I'll get help."

"Wait." Rory stands. He points the beam. "Turn around."

Alicia stops.

Slowly, part by part, light reveals the great figure of the Christ.

Astonished, Alicia steps close, reaches up to touch the torn feet.

Rory joins her. "Is this in the book?" He turns her gently by the shoulders.

Alicia gasps.

The figure is so simple—so tall and slender, with little detail except that hands of blackened silver hold the child against the mother's chest. Rags of fabric hang around them both, and the stone they're made from glitters white.

"Jesse." Alicia hurries to kneel beside her friend. "Jesse. Wake up."

The girl's eyes snap open. "The bat. There was a—" She scrabbles to sit up.

Alicia breathes, "Look."

Rory plays the beam over the head of the standing figure. Light shows filaments of bronze streaming down like hair.

Jesse says wonderingly, "The Mother has no face."

53

WHERE IS she? You said she'd be here."

They're in the kitchens at Hundredfield. And Janet won't sit down.

"They can't be far away. Rory's car is outside." Mack wasn't sure where else to bring Jesse's mum; the front door was open, but Hundredfield seems empty.

"Rory?"

"My brother. He's staying too."

Janet pales. "Helen's little boy. He's here too." She's speaking to herself. Now she sits. Slowly.

"Yes. He's a doctor. Tell you what—why don't I go upstairs and see if Jesse's resting? She's recovering well, and he's looking after her."

"I knew it. I *knew* something was wrong." Janet stuffs a hand in her mouth.

There's the sound of feet on the staircase and the low murmur of voices. On any other day, the relief on Mack's face might have been comical.

Rory enters first. He stops, stares at the woman sitting in the chair.

She gets up. "Hello, Rory." Her voice shakes. "You won't remember me, but I remember you."

Behind, Alicia's helping Jesse through the door.

In the frozen pause that follows, Jesse looks from Alicia to Rory. And then at her mother's stricken face.

"Oh." Janet breaks. She stumbles to her daughter.

And Jesse opens her arms.

Rory strides back into the kitchen. "Before you ask, they're in Jesse's room. Janet's close to collapse."

"Yet you thought that was a good idea—to leave them alone?" Alicia's expression is grim.

Rory is stung. "Jesse asked me to help her. You heard her. She's an adult. It's her decision to talk to her mother. Not mine. Not yours."

A small, frigid silence. Then Alicia says, "You said you'd find a link between us all. But this?"

He shakes his head. "Jesse didn't know, Alicia. She didn't know any of it. You saw her face. She was stunned." He's trying to keep the discussion civil.

"Rubbish."

"Oh, so Janet was boasting, was she? So proud to tell her daughter, in front of us all, that she'd been a housemaid at Hundredfield with my mum? The woman's distraught at being back, we all saw that."

"Did we?" Alicia narrows her eyes. "I said this was a scam. Some kind of really, really elaborate plot to . . ." She runs out of words.

Rory's pacing. "Janet was shocked when she saw me. And you. Come on, Alicia, be reasonable."

Mack clears his throat. So far, he's been ignored. "I'm with Rory. I'd swear Jesse didn't know her mother worked here. She's genuine. Truly."

"Oh, certainly." Alicia's switched back to cool patrician.

Rory barks, "Stop it! Be grateful for what Jesse did today. She's changed your life with what she found."

Alicia pales. Then flushes.

"Hey, you two." Mack's more than uncomfortable. He's never heard his brother this emotional before.

A bell jangles on the wall.

Alicia, head held high, leaves the kitchen.

"Where's she going?"

"The front door, where do you think?" Rory flashes Mack an unfriendly glance.

"I'm an innocent bystander. None of this is *my* fault."

"I didn't say it was."

Mack grumbles, "Just trying to do the woman a favor. She said she wanted to see Jesse, so I dropped everything and—"

"You couldn't wait, could you? Just barged in, invited or not." Rory's tone is dangerous.

"What's that supposed to mean?" Mack stands fully upright. He's bigger and taller than his brother.

"Like a dog with your tongue hanging out." Rory uses his words like a whip.

Mack says slowly, "I get it. Envy. Because Jesse chose me, not you."

"Oh, grow up."

This uppercut is for real, and it drops Rory where he stands. Mack looms over his brother. "I did. You didn't notice." Shaking out his hand, he leaves Rory sprawled on the floor.

"Is Janet Marley here?" Helen's outside Hundredfield's great front door.

Standing in the open doorway, Alicia doesn't immediately answer. She's staring at Helen, an odd look on her face.

"If you don't mind, I'd like to know."

"Actually, I do. Mind, that is. You're not especially welcome here." That aristocratic drawl.

Helen opens her mouth. And closes it again.

As if she cares hardly at all, Alicia says, "I've a question for you, Helen. You've always been rude to me, or cold, even when I was little. Why is that?"

The other woman pales. "You Donnes. You think you can say what you like to anyone."

Alicia starts to close the door.

"Wait." Helen's face is different suddenly. Vulnerable.

Alicia waits.

Helen swallows. "You won't believe me."

"I shan't know that, shall I, until you tell me." Polite. Reasonable. Utterly implacable.

They stare at each other until Helen looks away. "I'd be grateful if you'd let me talk to Janet. Talk to them both. It's important, or I wouldn't ask." Helen doesn't know how to plead; this is as close as she comes.

Alicia says nothing, but she opens the door wider and stands to one side.

In the hall, the suit of armor waits. That eyeless helm watches as the women cross the hall together, Alicia leading the way toward the stairs.

Helen follows as if she were walking to her own execution.

"We couldn't take the risk." Janet's lying on Jesse's bed under a satin quilt. Rifle sights, her eyes are trained on her daughter's face.

"What risk? What do you mean?"

"I *couldn't* tell you. I just could not." Janet starts to cry without sound, tears slipping down her cheeks. "Dr. Nicholls told me I'd never have children."

"Dr. Nicholls." Jesse leans forward. "Mum?"

But Janet's deep in the past. "When you were born, and no one wanted you, it seemed . . . it seemed so like the answer to my prayers, all the longing I'd felt. Even your father agreed."

Jesse pales. *No one wanted you.* "I don't have a father. That's what it says on the birth certificate."

"You do. And he loves you. We both do. Maybe we never made that clear enough." Janet takes a trembling breath.

Jesse hands her tissues. "Go on."

"Alicia's mother. She arranged everything with the nuns, you see. The adoption was . . . it was unofficial."

"You mean it was illegal?"

Janet pleads, "These things happen all the time in families. It's for the sake of the child. In those days, there was such shame for the mother and for the little one, growing up illegitimate. It was always for the best."

"For the best." Jesse's incredulous.

"Adopting you solved so many problems. And the countess— Lady Elizabeth, that is—she helped us immigrate to Australia. As a family. They knew people, the Donnes. And in those days, no one thought to question someone like her." Janet shakes her head.

"Lady Elizabeth was Alicia's mother?" Jesse leans forward. "But why did she want to help? You were just a housemaid. And all the secrecy. What was that about?"

"She was such a tiny little thing, Eva." Janet's evasive. "Just like a child herself, really. A child with no one to turn to." Janet catches Jesse's glance. "It's true. She couldn't speak, you see, so no one knew what she was thinking. But then, that poor girl, when she died having you—" Janet gasps, blots her eyes, though more tears come. "Well, I couldn't let you just be taken away, could I? Not put in some orphanage and forgotten. Dr. Nicholls was on my side." She gulps, shaking. "I couldn't bear the thought of you crying and no one coming."

"Eva couldn't speak?"

"Well, maybe she could, but not English. Didn't worry the earl, mind. Not him. He made her understand what he wanted, right enough." Janet's expression hardens.

"The earl?"

Both hands over her face, Janet speaks through her fingers. "Lies compound, Jesse. Don't ever let anyone tell you they don't."

Behind her, the door to the bedroom opens.

54

TWO DAYS had passed, and the keep still smoldered, though we had cleared the inner ward of bodies; soon they would be buried, with Father Simeon to pray for them. And our fighters, those who remained, patrolled Hundredfield's damaged walls. We might have beaten Alois's men, but I was wary; their leader lay in his winding sheet, but another could arise. A reiver band is a monster: cut off one head, and another grows in its place. And so, when the drum of hooves was heard coming from the forest, I roared for horses.

Tamas, who commanded the battlements now, ran to me on the castle side of the great gate.

"Well?"

"We need you here. Let me take the men outside the gate." This was too polite.

I held up the stump of my right hand. It pained me very much, and blood seeped through the bindings. "I cannot fight and ride—is that what you mean?"

The boy—no, the seasoned fighter that he was—laughed.

I liked him for that.

"Yes. Outside these walls, you will be a burden in a fight."

This was too much truth. I said politely, "I control the horse with my knees. And I have an ax." I did. And had used it well with my left hand when Alois died. That surprised me still.

Margaretta was watching. For these two days, camping together in the roofless tower with her father and the children, she had nursed my body and I had nursed her spirit. But each morning she buckled me into Godefroi's armor. And that was what held me up.

Behind, Helios brayed a challenge as he was led into the yard. And he was answered. Horsemen were close.

Dikon held my stirrup as Tamas tried again. "We have too few men left. We cannot afford a sally that—"

"The walls are breached. We must go out to them. They will not expect that." Raising my only hand to the gate wards, I would have dropped it. But I did not.

We all heard the horn winding through the trees. Tamas ran, and I ran after him, to the battlements.

"Look!"

Look indeed. On the road across the river, a troop of horsemen came from the forest at half gallop.

I bellowed, "Archers!"

But Tamas had better eyes than I. "No!" He was pointing. "Hold!"

Anger flared in my heart at the challenge, but Tamas was right to do it, for on their shields was the blue lion of the Percys, rampant on a yellow ground.

I ran for the inner ward and up into the saddle as men massed behind me.

"Drop the gate!" This time, Tamas shouted the order, and he was obeyed.

As the gate came down over the gap, I spurred Helios and let him run, shouting, *"À Dieudonné, à moi, à moi!"*

I was lucky not to die.

The horsemen in our path were skilled. Some fired bows as they rode and cloth yards whined close, but I lay against the stallion's neck still bellowing, "*À Dieudonné!*"

"*Arrêtez!*" A shout. And no more arrows flew.

Halting the stallion, I called out, "Bèrnard!"

There, at the head of the troop in his Percy colors, was Maugris's friend from long ago. Bèrnard de Loutrelle had been a squire at Alnwick with my brother; and I, haunting their steps, had been cuffed for getting in their way.

"Bayard?" The man spurred his horse and we met in the middle of the river track. He saw the stump of my right arm and therefore clasped my left, as if I had truly been his brother. "I did not recognize you. Not with the blood, and the beard." He grinned amiably. "But Hundredfield still stands. All will be well when we shore up the walls. We have enough men." Between three and four hundred rode at his back.

"It is good that you came. We welcome you."

"Godefroi?"

"My brother is dead."

"And Maugris?"

I shook my head.

"Sergeant!" Bèrnard called over one of his men. "We shall escort the Lord Bayard." Fifteen were counted out from the troop. They would ride before us, an honor guard.

Bèrnard de Loutrelle and I entered Hundredfield together, the burned and shattered patrimony of the Dieudonné. As we clattered across the drawbridge and beneath the great gate, I called out, as he had, "All is well!"

Margaretta stood with the children in the inner ward. She was brave. She did not hide her battered face, her swollen, blackened eyes.

Bèrnard saluted. "Lady, you will be well guarded now."

She looked up into my face. "I thank you, sir. But there is no need."

My vision misted as I turned the stallion in a tight circle. "I shall return. And then . . ."

"Yes. There will be a then." Tears stood in her eyes.

Beside her knees, I saw Aviss, clinging to her skirt. "Give him to me."

Without hesitation, Margaretta held the boy up in her arms.

I took the child and sat him on the saddle before me. He stared at Bèrnard, big-eyed. "Aviss, stay here with your mother. You must lead the guard until I return. Do you understand?"

The boy gazed down at Margaretta. And nodded.

Returned to her arms, the expression on that solemn little face was transformed. He smiled at me, and I saw how like my mother her grandson was. And it seemed to me I was, at last, a happy man.

Holding the ax above my head, I called out, *"À Dieudonné, à moi, à moi!"*

"À Percy, à Percy" came the reply.

In memory, I feel her eyes on my back still as I wheeled the stallion and took him home, a destrier for the last time. My days of fighting were done.

55

ALICIA KNOCKS. "May we come in?"

Janet sees them first. Her terrified expression makes Jesse look around.

Jesse gets off the bed. "Actually, I was hoping my mother could rest."

Helen's standing in Alicia's shadow. "Perhaps we should all go downstairs and—"

"No." Forlorn, but definite. Janet sits higher against the pillows. "I need to show you something."

"Janet." Helen puts a lot of force into that one word.

"No, Helen. I have not come all this way to lie."

Three pairs of eyes are trained on Helen Brandon's face.

In a firm voice Janet says, "I want my handbag."

Jesse capitulates. She goes to a chair beside the window and picks up the bag—it's big and black and weighs more than she expected.

"Come in, Alicia. You too, Helen." Janet doesn't say *Let's get this over with*. But that's what she means.

The bag is clicked open and Janet takes out a large envelope;

she puts on reading glasses and looks at Helen. "Is there anything you want to say first?"

Helen Brandon's complexion is gray-white. She hesitates, then shakes her head.

Janet smoothes the flap of the envelope open, and the others watch as she takes out a sheaf of paper; it's folded in three and tied with faded pink ribbon. But the bow is knotted tight, and it's a silent minute before Janet can work it loose. She unfolds the stiff paper and there's a heading: "Deed of Confidentiality." Written in black-letter copperplate, the words pop off the paper as if they've been waiting to be seen again.

There's a moment of paralysis.

Alicia asks politely, "And that is what, exactly?"

"I signed this on August tenth, 1956." Janet leafs through to the back page. She points to her own signature—the letters round and careful. "We—both of us—agreed to all the terms offered by the earl. Your father." She's looking at Helen.

"Terms?" Alicia has her voice under control. She sounds only faintly curious.

Another name is written beside Janet's. The second signature is a scrawl, but Helen clears her throat. "Yes. Janet's right. We both signed."

"A little more information might be useful." Alicia sounds calm. But she hears the thump of her heart like a drum in her head.

Janet offers the document and Alicia takes it. "It's all in here." But her eyes are on her daughter.

In the corner of the room is a lady's writing desk, a piece of fussy Victoriana with a sloping lid. A pampered daughter might, long ago, have used it to write thank-you letters after a ball.

Alicia goes to the desk, and it seems natural she'll take the only chair. Jesse stands behind her shoulder as they begin to read.

Janet and Helen watch the girls. Janet is flushed, her hands gripped together on the counterpane. Helen's expression is impassive. After a time she sits in the window seat, staring at the empty sky.

Scanning the text in silence, Alicia pauses before she turns each page waiting for Jesse to nod. A clock with a delicate tick marks the seconds, and the minutes, as more than twenty pages are carefully read and turned. Finally, they reach the signature page, and Alicia turns the deed facedown. She stares from Janet to Helen. "How much of this is true?"

"All of it." Helen has her back to the room.

Janet nods.

Alicia gets up and instantly sits down again. She captures her hands between her knees to stop their shaking.

Jesse taps the document. "Alicia's father, the earl . . ."

Janet speaks in a rush. "Yes."

"It says that Rory, that you . . ." Alicia's staring at Jesse. Shock is taking over.

Helen talks so quietly, Jesse steps closer. "I did not want you to find out this way, Alicia, please believe me. When Janet arrived this afternoon, I tried to stop her from coming here. I knew what this would mean, and . . ." Finally, Helen turns.

Alicia holds up a hand. She says reasonably, "I think that's likely to be a self-serving lie, Helen. I believe you just wanted to cover your back, go on sitting on the truth as you've done for all these years. This situation has suited you well."

Helen half stands. "Your father rapes me, I get pregnant with Rory, I work here as a *servant*, and you call that doing well?" Her face is scarlet. She's trembling with distress. Or rage.

"Rape?" Alicia's face washes white.

Jesse puts a hand on Alicia's shoulder. "But this deed gives you the Hunt, Helen. I don't understand."

Alicia interrupts, "And whatever you say, whatever accusations you want to hurl at my father—who cannot defend himself—I'd call this document evidence of some kind of blackmail." Alicia's face is very cold. "Tell me the truth."

The other woman swallows. Faced with Alicia's glacial rage, she falters. "I had nothing. No one. I had to protect myself. And Rory."

Jesse says quietly, "This deed seems to say that we are all related. Is that right? Alicia and me and Rory? That we share a father? Alicia's father?"

Janet rushes in: "Yes. You're half siblings."

The silence is like a void opening in the floor. The words are said. They're all too frightened to move.

When Helen speaks, her voice grates in her throat. "Oh, he had form, your father. First me, because I was there and he thought it was his right." She takes a deep breath. "Just a kid, that's all I was, in service for the first time. And I didn't know how to stop him. Or who to tell. Who was going to believe me?" Her eyes brim, and her voice crumbles to nothing.

Alicia says calmly, "But in the deed, it sets out that the estate agrees to pay Rory's school fees. I would not describe that as abuse. I'd say it was a reward. Just what kind of services were you offering, Helen?" The cut is surgical and precise.

Helen says fiercely, "Your father wanted me to go to Holly House; he wanted Rory adopted. His own son. Your *brother*. Dr. Nicholls would have arranged it, like he did with her." She gestures at Jesse. "Oh, yes, they were all in it that time, him and the nuns and your dear mother, Alicia. The sainted Elizabeth." The name spits from her mouth.

Jesse is rigid. "That's cruel. And shocking."

Helen turns on her. "Shocking. Yes, it is. And it was. But it could have been us, my son and me. The nuns did that then—just took the baby from your arms straight after the birth; bound your breasts to suppress the milk. But her mother intervened. And Rory was born in the cottage we lived in. Oh, yes. He was born on Hundredfield, just like you, Alicia. Only you had all the privileges, all the comforts." Her face works. "And every day we had to look at each other. Every day. Rory was your father's *son*. We were dirt to him. *Dirt*." The words die on the air.

"Perhaps Lady Elizabeth wanted him to see what he'd done. Wanted him to face it." Janet's voice wobbles.

Helen is bitter. "Didn't stop him, though, did it? He did it again."

"But what happened with Eva? *Why* was I adopted out if Rory wasn't?"

"Rory wasn't what?" Rory's at the door. "Hello, Mum. Didn't know you were here." He looks from face to face, and his expression changes.

"You need to read this." Alicia hands him the document. Then she strides from the room.

56

A s she walks down the stairs, Alicia swallows, hard. She will not give in. She will not allow any of them to see how she feels.

But she stops with a gasp and clutches the banister as if the oak can stop the shakes. And the pain.

Above, on the walls, her ancestors look down, impassive.

Through tears, Alicia stares from a general to an admiral, to a colonel in the uniform he wore at Waterloo, all gold and scarlet. And there's her father—more scarlet and gold—a lieutenant in the Scots Guards, so handsome, so young. "Got anything to say, Dad?"

That painted face does not change. It never will.

Outrage. Fury. Love. Loss. How can she tell the difference?

Alicia looks down. The staircase seems steeper than the flank of a mountain. But she will walk those stairs, she has to go outside; she wants to know if the world looks different.

Rory puts the deed back on the desk. "So, are you going to tell me about this, Mum, or shall I ask Janet?" His eyes have no expression.

"I did what was best. Justice. For us both." She was angry only so few minutes before, but now Helen sounds crushed.

Rory folds the document into its accustomed creases. "So, it's true. That's why you didn't have photos of my dad. He was there all the time." A big man in a small chair, he gets up from the fragile desk and hands the deed to Janet. He can't look at Jesse. Not yet.

And she can't look at him. She clears her throat. Says nothing.

"How did you do it? Get him to acknowledge us both. Blackmail?" Now he flicks a glance at Jesse. His sister.

Janet clutches the deed to her chest. "Yes." Her face is flushed.

"Don't you dare, Janet Marley. I got you the child you wanted. And a new life. Without me she wouldn't be standing here today." Helen's voice is low, but Janet flinches. The tone is savage.

She. Even now, Helen won't say her name. But Jesse is not about to play this game. "So, what did you do, Helen?"

Helen Brandon's staring at her son. "I said, after Eva died, that I'd go to the papers. The *Mirror*, the *Sun*—I didn't care. I knew one of the scandal sheets would buy what I had to sell. An earl's illegitimate child, born from rape, is a scandal—though there was no way I could prove it, not after all that time." She looks away from Rory. "But *two* bastards, and a young girl dying at the birth of the second—supervised by a disgraced doctor—before her body *disappears*? That would have been a bomb going off at Hundredfield." This time Helen is defiant. "Lady Elizabeth had had enough. She made your father agree to what I asked."

"What do you mean 'disgraced'?" Jesse sits on the end of the bed, her face sheet-white.

"Why do you think he practices in Newton Prior? Dr. Nicholls had—what shall we call it?—a difficulty, in Edinburgh."

Rape. Child of rape. The words clamor in Rory's head but he shuts them away. "Alistair was disbarred." He flicks a glance at Jesse. "Negligence was proved against him when a young woman died during a difficult delivery in Edinburgh—he'd been drinking. Guilt made him a full-blown alcoholic, but he fought his way back and was reregistered. He's been an exemplary doctor all these years." Rory turns on Helen. "And he's your friend, Mum, he's been so good to us."

Helen closes her eyes. She cannot escape the severity in his voice. "He did what he did because Elizabeth asked him to. Eva died, he was her doctor; maybe that brought it all back. Perhaps he thought he could atone for what had happened before, but he agreed that a duplicate birth certificate would name Janet as the mother, and not Eva. He thought the child would have a better future in Australia."

"You can use my name anytime you like, Helen." But Jesse does not allow her voice to rise.

The interruption is ignored. "Janet was to register the birth when she got to Australia. You didn't need a passport for an infant in those days. No one checked. We were so trusting." Helen's eyes are bleak.

Janet's rocking on the edge of the bed. "I knew it was wrong. I always knew it. Sweet Jesus, dear God . . ." The plea is incoherent.

Rory asks, "But how did she get it—the duplicate?"

Helen shrugs. "There's two laws in this country, always have been. The rich always get what they want."

Jesse hesitates before she grips her mother's hand. "But don't you have to register a birth in person?"

"Who's going to question a nice young woman at a Registry Office with a baby in her arms?" Janet sounds wretched. "That's what I did. New migrant, new country, husband in tow. Many apologies for the slipup as we left Scotland . . ." She wipes her eyes and whispers, "They were very kind in Sydney. They said you were a lovely baby, that you looked just like me." She takes a deep breath. "They hoped we would all enjoy living in Australia."

Jesse says slowly, "And when I found the duplicate, and the British passport office questioned it because of the registration date . . ."

"The house of cards came down." Helen sounds beaten.

"I have to find Alicia." Rory gets up. He doesn't look at Jesse as he leaves the room.

The gate to the kitchen garden's open. Alicia's sitting on the bench by the pond.

"Hello."

Alicia looks up and they stare at each other. Brother and sister.

"I read it."

"Right." Absurdly, Alicia clasps her hands behind her back.

Rory says painfully, "Do you think it's true? That your dad, that I'm . . ."

Alicia hesitates. "I don't know." But she does.

"Rape." The word hangs in the air. Rory sits beside Alicia. "I used to envy you. Did you know that?"

She shakes her head.

"You had a father." Rory takes one of Alicia's hands. "Why did he never say anything?"

Her voice shakes. "You're asking me?"

The garden hums in the warmth. Bees working the flowers, birds dodging through the trees.

"If it's real, is that a good thing or a bad thing?"

"Perhaps we should let the lawyers decide." Pain snaps those words like twigs.

"Lawyers?" Rory's confused. "But isn't this about family?"

"That's when you need them most." She gets up, brushes past.

Rory watches as Alicia tracks back toward the house.

"Jesse," Mack calls out.

The solitary figure, made smaller by distance, wanders across the inner ward.

"Hey!" Mack shouts louder, waves his arms, even whistles.

The wind carries the sound and the girl looks back.

Alicia, hurrying along the terrace past the library, hears it too. Mack's covered a lot of ground by the time she sees him.

So's Jesse. She's running to Mack. He stops, arms wide, wide open. And folds her in. And holds her. Just holds her.

Unseen, Alicia watches. She's never felt more alone in her life.

57

WE STOOD together outside the chapel in the keep. Here was the least destruction, and since the sack we had all slept on the floor beside my mother's grave—Margaretta and me and the children, with their grandfather beside us.

"Will you promise yourself to me?" Ah, I remember speaking those words.

She gripped my fingers tight. "Yes. And will you?"

"Yes. Handfast. For the rest of our lives."

Ah, memory. Search the years . . .

There it is. The choking smell of tallow from the candle she held. I liked the smell from that day.

"Come with me."

"Wherever you wish, lady."

"You should not call me that. In the world's eyes I am still your servant." But she smiled at me so fondly.

I was enchanted. I had never before seen Margaretta happy. "We are promised now, and soon"—I waved to the altar—"Simeon will sing us a wedding mass and none shall say you are not the true lady of this keep."

She touched my face so lovingly. And stepped back to look in my eyes. "Bayard, you know what stands on the other side?" She meant the cavern.

I nodded. "Rauf and I carried the Madonna there together." Rauf. We had no wood for coffins when we buried him. But as Simeon intoned the final blessing and I went to cover Rauf's face with a napkin, a breeze lifted a lock of his hair—that streak of silver had always marked him as different. A strange moment, as if he waved to me from somewhere far away. I had yet to tell his wife at their farmstead by the river of his death. That would be a heavy burden for her, and my duty to care for her children.

"Is all well with you, my lord?" She must have seen the sadness in my eyes.

My lord. It had another meaning too. This is what a wife called her husband. "Yes. All is well with me."

"Shall we bring Her back to the chapel?" Margaretta gestured to the wall.

I hesitated. "There is something I must show you."

Perhaps Margaretta was puzzled, but when, later, we stood before the Madonna, I asked, "What do you see?"

"She has fine new clothes."

I nodded. Godefroi had commissioned a velvet mantle for the Virgin, a rich, deep blue. "And?"

"And Her face is clean."

"Yes." Since Fulk's time, soot from the lamps and incense and candles had made the faces and the hands of Christ and His Mother almost black. But now they shone, and the eyes gleamed clear blue. "Look closer."

Margaretta did as I asked. Then came the jolt. "Flore. This is her face. And the baby"—her hand shook hot tallow to the earth—"the Holy Infant, he, she . . ."

I took the candle from her. "Yes. Felice might have modeled for the child." Yet the Madonna and Her baby were old as old, older than the keep. "Matthias saw the Madonna's likeness to the Lady Flore when the face was first cleaned. That is what I think."

Margaretta spoke softly, "So *that* is why . . ."

"Yes. People try to destroy what frightens them."

Margaretta turned to me. "It was a miracle she came here. *She* was a miracle. And Felice is the sign to tell us that. This is not Christ's mother; *She* is our mother." Margaretta knelt before the statue, staring up into that silver face. "She should stay here, by Her pool." Light flickered on the handprints around the Red Gate.

Some—in the shadows—did they move?

I took the candle and stood beside the figure of the Christ. "Tell me what you see."

Margaretta's hand went to her mouth. "His face. And yours. They are the same."

It was true. Rauf had seen the likeness before I did, the night we brought the statues here.

"What does it mean, Bayard?"

"It means she has given Hundredfield to you and to me. My family did not deserve to hold this land, and long ago your family lost this place also." I knelt beside her. "But we shall hold it now, you and I. And our children. The old way, the old world has gone, and we begin the new one here. Today."

58

THEY WALK to the keep together, Jesse and Alicia, and this time the door is open. Alicia is angry and frightened, but she can feel it; a weight she's carried for so long is shifting. Yet, her whole body is tender, as if she has been beaten.

"You go first." Jesse pushes the door wider.

"Why?"

"Because you should."

Alicia summons the mask she usually wears. Calm, polite, clear about who she is; it's her armor. "We are going back to the chapel?"

"If that's okay?" Jesse's happy to ask permission. This is inevitable, they both know it, but if she can help Alicia, she will.

In the anteroom of the chapel, Alicia pauses. They both have flashlights. "Are you sure?"

Jesse's tone is helpless. "I don't think there's a choice." She steps forward and her light goes to the same place. The entrance.

"Did you know it was there?"

Jesse shakes her head. "But when you went back to get the

book"—she hesitates—"it was like being pulled by a rip tide, all the way out to sea."

"A rip tide?"

"A powerful current off a beach. You don't know it's there until it catches you up and drags you off your feet. Sometimes you drown."

"But you didn't drown."

"No. Not this time." The pair stand together, looking into the void of the tunnel. "This time it carried me home."

"Jesse." Alicia says her name like a breathed-out prayer.

"Come on." Jesse holds out her hand.

Alicia surrenders. She takes her sister's hand. They walk the tunnel together, the older leading the younger.

This second time, the cavern displays its secrets without urgency: the great silver Christ, his cross of olive wood canted against the wall, and the tall, white figure with the child in her arms.

Alicia is transfixed. Her flashlight plays over the trail of hands around the cleft in the rock. "So this is where they came from—the carvings on the door reveals." She stares, baffled. "There's so much I don't understand."

"Neither do I. But I was told I had to return the mother." Jesse's had the Harrods bag all this time. She takes out what is inside. "And that my family would help to find the child that was lost. I was lost. But you brought me here, Alicia. You began this—not Rory, you. I came to Hundredfield, and you brought me to the keep." Jesse steps forward and reaches up. The mask fits over the damaged stone of the head. "This is her face. We have given it back to her."

Tentatively Alicia smiles. "And what's through there?" She points to the opening in the rock.

"I don't know."

This time, there's no hesitation. The two bend under the archway of hands together.

Jesse's light plays over the water as it falls from the lip of the pool.

"It's red. What does that mean?"

"I don't know. Pollution?"

"Is that what you really think?"

Jesse bends forward, dips fingers into the water. "Might be."

"It's the same color as the garnets on the Christ figure."

Jesse nods. She's brought something else in the Harrods bag. A small bunch of flowers from Hundredfield's garden—borage and roses, Queen Anne's lace and sweet peas. And rosemary. She scatters them on the water and watches as the stream carries them away. Murmurs, "For remembrance."

Alicia asks curiously, "Why did you do that?"

"I don't know." Jesse turns to face her sister. "So, what do you want to do?"

Alicia stretches out her hand. "I think we should find Rory."

"That would be good." But Jesse's hesitant.

"None of this is his fault. Not this time." A trace of humor is in Alicia's voice as she scrambles over the lip of stone, back into the tunnel.

"He might not believe that." Jesse's following.

"Overdeveloped guilt complex, that man. Odd in a doctor."

Jesse scoffs, "Says you. You don't let him get away with anything."

Alicia stops. "I suppose you're right." She waits for Jesse to catch up. "Let's go home. Shall we? I hope he's there."

59

THE QUEEN. It's really the queen. Oh, doesn't she look lovely. And the duke! I can't believe it!"

Jesse and Janet have been on the pavement across the road from St. Paul's since early evening yesterday. Janet would have it no other way. They were both glad of their hastily purchased sleeping bags because the night was cold and quite dark. But everyone was friendly, sharing food and blankets, waving flags, singing "Rule, Britannia."

Almost zero sleep and an anxious, gray dawn, neighbor consulting neighbor on the footpath, offering memories of other rain-blighted royal weddings, but it had been a wonderful day so far.

"Can you really see through that thing, Mum?" Jesse's annoyed with herself. They should have bought two, but the periscopes were so expensive.

"It works a treat, even if they were bandits."

Janet shakes her head. London! The money! Everything's outrageous these days. But she manages to squeeze her daughter's hand as she wields the long, ungainly tube of cardboard above their heads. Crammed between so many others all equally desperate to see the groom arrive, it's not easy scanning the steps of the cathedral.

But Janet is so grateful, and so happy to see the future king of England on his wedding day that she dares the gray skies above St. Paul's to do their worst. Let it rain! Here she stands, free of the clouds of the past—free to stand beside her child sharing what Jesse had always planned. "There he is! There he is!"

"Where?" That mighty surge of sound is made of one word: "Charles!"

The small figure of a man, dwarfed by that immensity of stone, turns at the top of the steps and waves.

Janet gives a satisfied sigh. "Oh, isn't he handsome? The press are so unfair to that poor man. Charles! Charles!" Waving enthusiastically, Janet's got her face jammed against the viewing window. "Look! He's turning this way!" She waves again. One hand among so many.

Jesse waves too. The actual king of England-to-be. And then she remembers. Part of her blood family has a history as long as the Windsors'. Longer, maybe. But Eva? *Where did you come from? Who were you? How did you just disappear?*

Janet nudges Jesse. "You know, I heard a million people are here today. Doesn't surprise me a bit."

Jesse's jerked back to the present. "No. A million? Amazing." She stands protectively behind her mother, trying to make a bit of space for her. Janet's such a tiny woman. Anyone looking at them both would never think they're mother and daughter. *Big as a fridge, ridgy-didge.* But the taunt from school days doesn't hurt anymore. She likes being tall. Mack's taller.

"Rory's sister? *What?*"

That had been a moment. It was after Mack had found her in the inner ward.

"Yes. It's true. But do you want the best news?" *Poor man.* Stunned got nowhere near the right word.

"There's more?"

Jesse's heart had lifted, she had felt it physically. So the old saying was true. "Yes. There really is. You're not my brother, Mack. Not full, not half, not even a bit. We are not related. Period."

He had snorted. "I could have told you that."

"Oh, really?"

"We don't look a bit alike." That amiable grin.

Jesse feels that urgent hand on her sleeve again. "Yes, Mum?"

"You're not listening." Janet's jumping, yes, jumping up and down. "She's here. Look!"

There she was indeed, as the crowd surged and craned and roared. A girl in a fairy tale, getting out of a glass coach, on her way to meet her prince.

"Oh! The dress, look at the dress."

Jesse craned and angled with the rest of them. She wanted to see it. Something released in her heart. She was enjoying herself. Actually, really enjoying herself. Nothing would ever surprise her again, but fairy tales? What was all that about?

The small black-and-white TV brings the wedding into the kitchen at Hundredfield. Panning shots of the crowds in the cathedral, then a high point of view as the groom and his brothers walk into position at the high altar.

There's a tight shot as Andrew sneaks a look toward the West Door and nods to Charles just as the picture goes to snow.

"No!" Alicia hurries to the dresser, fiddles with the rabbit ears. The picture settles. She edges back to the table, eyes fixed on every flicker.

"Hello. I'd forgotten it was today."

Alicia startles. "Rory! How could you forget a thing like this?" He's standing just inside the back door. She didn't hear him come down the stairs.

Surprised, she's uncomfortable. So is he. "Come in. I can turn it off, if you like. I mean, what's another wedding? Seen one, seen—"

"—them all." He nods. "Yes. But why don't we watch it together? We can pass it on to the grandchildren."

Something complex passes across Alicia's face. "Yes. Yes, please stay. That would be nice."

With all the movement on the screen, all the noise, and Richard Burton's voice-over of the action, it's still curiously quiet in the kitchen at Hundredfield as Rory joins her at the table.

"Lovely girl, if a bit young." Rory's doing his best. He thinks Alicia doesn't notice as he keeps glancing at her face.

"I know just what we need." Alicia hurries out of the room. She calls out from the passage, "Where's Mack, by the way?"

Rory stares at the little screen as if there'll be questions about the dress. "With Mum. Been a rugged couple of days."

"Knew we had a couple left." Alicia's returned with a very, very large bottle of Bollinger. "Nineteen fifty-six. Not exactly cold, but not too bad."

Rory gets up. "Let me."

"I'm sorry about Helen. She's a proud woman. I suppose she did what she thought was best." It's a big admission, but for a moment, when she hands him the bottle, Alicia's expression wobbles. "Glasses!" She hurries to the cabinet. A collection of less-than-grand odds and ends of crystal is on a shelf.

"I, Charles Philip Arthur George, take thee . . ."

Rory times the pop of the cork to the moment when the archbishop says, "I now pronounce you man and wife."

"Can you hear that? They're all cheering! The whole of London!" Alicia turns to him with delight. "The whole world too. It's real, then. The fairy tale. Just like you said." She's trying to catch champagne as it foams from the neck of the bottle. "He looks a bit serious, though."

"Wouldn't you? Man's just got married in front of the world. Can't back out now."

"Hello, hello. Anyone home?" The door bangs open as Mack tows Hugh Windhover into the kitchen.

"I thought you were with Mum?"

"I was." Mack's not commenting.

Hugh clears his throat. "Lady Alicia. You're looking, ah"—it would be a lie to say she's looking better. The black eyes are a rich green-purple now—"brighter than when I saw you last."

"I am." Alicia hands their visitor a glass. She lowers her voice. "Sorry to waste your time, Hugh, but I don't think we'll be selling. Circumstances have changed in the family."

Rory, dispensing champagne, hears *family*. He smiles at his sister.

"I'm very pleased to hear it. Hundredfield should stay with the Donnes, Lady Alicia. That's my honest opinion." Hugh's suddenly aware that the others are watching them. "And you haven't wasted my time."

She looks at him, surprised. "No?"

He takes a sip of the champagne. Smiles appreciatively. "No."

"Oh, look. He's going to kiss her."

Standing behind the chair that Alicia's sitting in, Hugh murmurs, "Sensible man."

CODA

O LITTLE TOWN of Bethlehem,
How still we see thee lie.
Above thy deep and dreamless sleep . . .

The words of the carol float from the tinsel-decked radio as the old nun unfolds the sheet of paper.

Dear Sister . . .

She turns it over to see who's written to her. A bold signature, but it's readable. Jesse Marley. Sister Mary Joseph sighs. It's always so nice to get letters, but she doesn't know what more she can say to the girl.

I hope you don't mind me writing to you. It's a
few months now since we saw each other, and a great
deal has changed in my life. And since it's so close to
Christmas, I thought I'd just drop you this note to give
you some news.

"Cup of tea, Sister?" The sentence is delivered directly into an ear.

The old lady jumps. "Julie! I can hear you perfectly well."

"I know." The volume is barely different. "But I like to be sure. Christmas cake to go with a cuppa?" The lumpish girl in the Santa hat pours dark brown tea into indestructible china. "That's a treat. A letter."

Sister Mary Joseph takes the tea, shakes her head at the cake. Julie. Loud *and* nosy. *Yes, we all have our crosses to bear.*

"Julie, you forgot the sugar." Mrs. Valentine, Sister Mary Joseph's mah-jongg companion, claims the ward assistant's attention.

"We can't have that, can we? I'll just go and get it." Julie wields the tea trolley like a weapon on her way to the fake log fire. Numerous old ladies draw back as the wheels sweep past.

Once the trolley's nosed back through the door, Sister Mary reads again.

> *Where to start. First of all, you might like to know that I'm now engaged to Mack. He sends his very best regards. We're so happy, and planning to be married in spring next year when we can get all our family together in the one place; I think I said my parents live in Sydney?*

Sister Mary smiles. They suit each other, this handsome pair. And they'll have lovely children together; giants, but lovely all the same.

> *The other thing I wanted to let you know is that I'll be moving to Newton Prior next year. (I've been staying at Hundredfield for the last few months.) Mack has a house there, and we've been having great fun painting and pulling out walls ahead of moving in together.*

A tolerant chuckle from the old lady. After the wedding? Only perhaps.

> *However, and I hope I'm not being a nuisance if I ask you just once more, is there anything, anything at all, that you can remember after my birth mother died? Any detail will be helpful. Next year I'm planning to look for more information about the disappearance of her body, but I do need help.*

The nun closes her eyes. Polite but persistent, is Jesse. But what can she say to the girl? What should she say?

> *The police regard this as what is called "a cold case." That is, the file is not closed, but they have no plans to reopen it. But I don't feel I can rest until I know more about where she might be buried or, indeed, anything at all I can find out about her. My adopted mum can't tell me very much because, as you are aware, Eva couldn't speak, though she did tell me, and I know this sounds odd, that the earl arrived at Hundredfield with her one day. He'd been out riding in the forest and found her there.*
>
> *So, apart from the information you've been able to give me about my birth, there's very little else. But one day I may have children. And I'd like them to know who Eva Green was, and what happened to her. I'm sure you can understand.*
>
> *If you would like to write back to me, Hundredfield will find me until January, at least.*
>
> *I hope you have a very happy Christmas.*
>
> > *Warm best wishes,*
> > *Jesse Marley*

The old hands lie slack on the paper. *Christmas.* The word weaves like smoke through Sister Mary's mind as sleep beckons. Something about Christmas. What is it?

Her eyes fly open. She remembers now. She'd been invited to Hundredfield, an Advent children's party. Lady Elizabeth herself had sent the invitation, and that had caused a stir at Holly House. She'd met the countess, but only once or twice, and she wasn't sure why she'd been invited.

But snow, there'd been a great deal of snow that Christmas, hadn't there?

In the great hall at Hundredfield, a glass of sherry in her hand, Mary Joseph remembers staring out the window as that lacy veil began to fall. The countess had asked if she was enjoying herself, and if she was warm.

She'd said, "Thank you, Your Grace. I'm delighted to be here." And she was.

Then the countess had said an odd thing. "I just wanted to thank you for your help this year. Such a delicate matter."

Mary Joseph had been puzzled, and perhaps she'd shown it, for the countess said smoothly, "And here is my daughter, Alicia. Alicia, this is Sister Mary Joseph."

She'd shaken the little girl by the hand—so serious and, unfortunately, so plain, though wearing a pretty dress—but seeing a dark-haired boy all by himself, she'd said, "And who is this?"

The countess had turned. And paused. "That's Rory."

Just that. Nothing else. She'd not attempted to call the child over. In that awkward pause, the countess had swept her daughter on.

Sister Mary knows what happened next. Uncertain of what to do, she'd wandered around the hall, looking at paintings and a magnificent, if battered, suit of armor. An open door took her inside a library, and there, outside, where garden faded into shadowed forest, she'd seen her. Eva.

The girl was standing in a pool of light where there was no light. And Eva had smiled at *her*. A silver figure in the falling snow. And then she had turned and walked away into the trees. Into the dark.

Sister Mary Joseph closes her eyes. *Five months dead, but I saw her. And her white skin seemed silver in the light because she was naked.* How can she tell Jesse that?

Mrs. Valentine nudges her friend Miss Bester. "Should we wake her up? She'll miss dinner."

Miss Bester shakes her head. The letter has fallen to the floor but the old nun looks so peaceful. "Let her sleep, poor thing. She's earned it."

Mrs. Valentine nods wisely. "Done a lot of good in her life, Sister Mary Jo. Come along, then." The two old friends get up and leave the nun to her dreams.

They pass the Christmas tree and pause. "Looks lovely up there, doesn't she?"

Miss Bester nods. "Magical."

Among the tinsel and the lights, the silver fairy looks down from the top of the tree. Light from the windows gilds the white quilt covering the garden outside as fresh snow begins to fall, and the radio sings on to itself.

> *Silent night,*
> *Holy night . . .*

ACKNOWLEDGMENTS

Caerlaverock, Tantallon, Dunvegan, Cawdor, Eilean Donan, Alnwick, Bamburgh. The names roll like thunder out of the riven history of the wars between Scotland and England. Castles, each one of them—and so many more—went into the making of Hundredfield and the story I wove around that place. It grew slowly, this tale, and three times I went back to Scotland and the borders region to find the pieces that would bring my puzzle together.

First, twenty years ago, there was Dunvegan on the Isle of Skye, and the legend of the Fairy Flag. In some odd way that stayed with me—the story of the fairy woman who married a McLeod.

But it wasn't just the buildings that brought me back: It was the landscape and the light as well. And the people. I like Northerners. I like their toughness and I like their humor.

Then there's the work that the Landmark Trust does in rescuing smaller, but no less significant, structures than the great buildings preserved by the National Trust for Scotland. That needs a tribute here.

A year or so back, Andrew and I stayed in a fortified tower house in Dumfries and Galloway on the Scottish side of the borders. The Castle of Park is small as castles go, and it was just before the country shut down due to snow, so we wore a lot of clothes to keep warm. But it was there, in that frozen world, I found the bones of Fulk's great keep, with its staircase tower and twisting staircase leading up to the cap house. And in the mornings, I watched deer pick their way out of the trees, foraging for food. You don't see that where I live. . . .

And Rosslyn Castle, too. The home of the Sinclairs for hundreds of years, and close by the famous Rosslyn Chapel (of *The Da Vinci Code* fame). What a privilege it was to stay there as well. Each night I read ghost stories lying in the bath and drank red wine in front of the fire. It was Rosslyn Castle that gave me the bedrooms in Hundredfield's New Range, and the layers and layers of rooms and chambers stuck to the cliff and climbing into the sky. Half ruined now, what a vast place it must once have been.

Bamburgh, too, stays with me. That great hunched mass of buildings crowning a cliff by the wild North Sea gave me so much. There, in the courtyards behind the walls that men did indeed once patrol, was the very form and shape of Hundredfield.

Scotland. Cumbria. Northumberland. I never want to leave unless it's to go home.

But it's not just the country I'm grateful to here. There are a roll call of people I want to personally thank who, each in their own way, has made *Wild Wood* real.

First, last, and always, there are my publishers, Simon & Schuster worldwide, and most particularly Judith Curr, who has supported my books from the very beginning. And of course Sarah Branham—my dear New York–based editor who works with Judith in that great ziggurat on the Avenue of the Americas. Thank you both, so much. How awed and astonished I was to walk into that building for the first time in December 2000. And *then* to be handed a three-book deal, when I was already on my way back to Australia to roll production, finally, on the television series of *McLeod's Daughters* after waiting so many years. That was a day.

Lou Johnson, Simon & Schuster, in Sydney—thank you so much, Lou—and all her dedicated and hard-working team. Larissa Edwards and Anabel Pandiella are just two among so many who deserve my gratitude for all they have done to help my books on their way, past, present, and future.

And Nicola O'Shea, my Australian editor. Draft by draft, Nicola is the voice of reason when my own goes missing. Writing is tough sometimes. It's not a war zone, but it can feel like it if the writing day warps out of shape. Paranoia! Anguish!

Thank you, Nicola, again. One of us has to keep a clear mind, and I'm glad I've got access to yours.

My agent, Rick Raftos. Unflappable man! Thank you, Rick. Kind, decent, smart—that's you.

And thank you, too, to the friends I talk to during the writing process. Vicki Maddern. Yes, you. How compassionate you were when I was on the floor. Your calm helped me so much. It seems to me that writers, all over the world, must be a secret society. There are signs and signals by which we recognize another of our own kind. A light in the darkness, for instance. That's a pretty good sign. In your case, you held up a bloody big flaming torch, and I stumbled toward that beacon very gratefully. Thank God for you! And Prue Batten. How good it was to talk story and process with you. What courage you have, Prue, and that's an inspiration. Thank you.

Niki White, from Nikstar. I always thought that having a personal publicist was . . . well, remarkable. And I've discovered it is. Thank you as always, Niki, for the care and imagination you bring to helping me find ways to talk to the world from my ridgeline in Tasmania.

Of course, too, there's my family. I write for all of you, each adult, each child, and you're all in my head, all the time.

And finally, Andrew Blaxland. Dear husband, loving friend.

You built me an office this year out of a more-than-fragile shed. Now I can't believe my luck each time I open this door, because I'm surrounded by such beauty. And today as I sit here, in the place you've made for me with the long views over the hills and the water, my soul says thank you.

Posie
Huon Valley, Tasmania
March 2015